DEAD 2 RITES

DEAD 2 RITES

JAKE AND THE DYNAMO, BOOK 2

D. G. D. DAVIDSON

Illustrated by
ROFFLES LOWELL

GIRLS AT WORK

For Shalimar

CONTENTS

1. The Beach Episode of Darkness   1
2. Rumbles   14
3. Played   28
4. Players   45
5. Fated   73
6. Lost Girls   96
7. Dark Secrets   113
8. Bitter Tears   144
9. Wake-Up Call   160
10. The Morning After   177
11. Monday   192
12. Children of the Bite   207
13. The Fourth Test   222
14. Voodoo   242
15. Dark Places   259
16. The Frequency of Delinquency   281
17. Love in the Time of Robots   310
18. Nightfall   327
19. Picking Up the Pieces   346
20. Black Magic   366
21. Blood and Fire   385
22. Communion   404
23. Aftermath   423
24. Bad Girls   440
25. Rock of Rages   458
26. Dead to Rites   484
27. The Way of All Flesh   507
    Epilogue: Infection   510

    About the Author   515
    Also by D. G. D. Davidson   517

Girls we love for what they are; young men for what they promise to be.

GOETHE

ONE

THE BEACH EPISODE OF DARKNESS

On the desolate slope of a craggy mountain where no snow fell and no flowers grew, a high castle of black basalt stood resilient against the biting, howling wind. Deep in the castle's bowels, the Dark Queen, mistress of all that is base and wicked, sat upon her carven throne of black obsidian. She tapped the six-inch stiletto heel of one onyx-encrusted pump against her footstool, made herself as comfortable as possible, and read the newspaper.

For several minutes, she scanned the page in regal silence, her blood-red lips pursed in austere displeasure. At last, she slowly and with great dignity lowered the paper to her lap.

"Darn it!" she shouted. "I can't *take* it anymore! Somebody bring me a *lamp!* A lamp with one of those full-spectrum daylight bulbs! And cute cartoon characters on the lampshade! And make sure it's an incandescent or LED bulb too, and not that other kind! I don't need mercury poisoning to go with the bad eyes!"

A wart-covered troll, its skin rough like weathered limestone, crouched near her throne. With a sound like brick scraping on concrete, he lifted his massive head, cleared his throat, and waved a stubby hand. "Erm, beggin' Your Darkness's pardonation, but t'ain't no lights allowed in ye royal throne room. 'Tis ye strictest orders, y'see."

The Queen tapped the paper against her thigh and tapped her long fingernails on an armrest. "Says who?"

With a noise like gemstones turning over in a tumbler, the troll cleared his throat again. "Erm . . . royal decree number six hundred and twenty—"

"Oh, what-*ev*-er! *I'm* the Dark Queen, *I* make the decrees, and *I* say I need a *freaking reading light!* Do you want your Queen sitting up here in Coke-bottom bifocals because she's ruined her eyesight with all this bloody *darkness?* I'm sure *that* will be good for the ambiance around here! That'll *really* have the scary-throne-room effect! 'Behold, denizens of the Earth! Bow down and tremble before the Dark Grandma, evil librarian, and despair!'"

With many apologetic mutterings, the troll, with a sound like the churning of a cement mixer, rose clumsily from his haunches and lumbered off.

The Queen leaned back in her throne and rubbed her forehead. "Ugh, I'm getting another headache. Where in the world is that useless—?"

With a flash of white light and the sound of tinkling bells, Chirops, a furry bat the size of a dog, appeared in midair. His pale eyes widened in surprise, and he flapped his wings furiously, but he tumbled gracelessly to the floor anyway.

The Queen squeezed her eyes shut and sighed. "Speak of the

devil. What kept you, Chirops? Did you stop for a cup of coffee on the way?"

Chirops picked himself up and brushed off his wings. He simpered, "Well, I took a wrong turn in the stream, Your Darkness, and I, ah, sort of ended up on a space station orbiting Betelgeuse . . . and they *did* have a coffee shop—"

"Oh? And how's the coffee on Betelgeuse, Chirops?"

"It's out of this world, Your Darkness."

A minute of silence passed. Chirops coughed uncomfortably into his bunched claws and fidgeted. The Dark Queen tapped her fingers on the armrest again.

"All right. Come here, Chirops. I want to hear about your brave exploits in man's last city."

Chirops stared down at the basalt pavement as he twiddled his claws. "Well, Your Darkness, to be honest, I, um—"

"Come *here,* Chirops."

Chirops swallowed loudly and waddled toward her. "Yes, Your Darkness?"

"A little closer, Chirops."

Whimpering, he stepped up onto the dais, walked to the right side of the throne, and meekly peeked over the armrest. "Your Darkness . . . ?"

The Dark Queen took a series of deep, calming breaths as she carefully rolled the newspaper into a tube and whacked him over the head with it.

He squeaked.

Unfurling the paper with a snap, she pointed a sharp fingernail at the front page, where a gigantic photo depicted Chirops flapping in the air above a demon-possessed madman who squared off against Magical Girl Sukeban Tsubasa, a teenager wearing an extraterrestrial power suit. The headline screamed,

WHO'S BAD? NOT EVEN DEVIL BAD ENOUGH FOR MAGICAL BAD GIRL!

"You *failed!*" the Queen shrieked.

Chirops's ears drooped.

"Do you think there is room in my kingdom of uttermost darkness for *failures?*"

Chirops gave a hesitant glance toward the slavering minions peeking out of the chamber's many shadows.

"There must be," he muttered.

She whacked him with the paper again. "I asked you to kill Barfing Boy, and you're telling me you couldn't even do that one simple thing."

"Actually, you asked me *not* to kill him. You said to—"

She whacked him a third time. As he rubbed the top of his fuzzy head and blinked away tears, she opened the paper to expose the second page, which featured a photo of a bewildered-looking teenage boy—tall and broad-shouldered but somewhat gangly—in the midst of a milling crowd. Beneath the picture, the headline ran, MAGICAL CATFIGHT: MYSTERIOUS 'BARFING BOY' IS MAGICAL GIRLS' MOST WANTED!

"Do you see this, Chirops? Do you *see* it? I wanted this boy humiliated, ruined, destroyed! Instead, he's a celebrity, and now the magical girls are squabbling over which one gets to wield his wand!"

Chirops squeaked again.

The Dark Queen took another deep breath and rubbed her temples. "Ugh. Seriously, this has been a *really* rough week."

"Oh, I know," said Chirops. "But even with all the setbacks, we're making progress. After all, the Crystal—"

"I need a break. Yes, that's it. A *break.*"

The Dark Queen rose majestically from her throne, being

sure as she did so to allow her loose, gauzy garments to tumble alluringly around her voluptuous hourglass figure. Once she stood at her full six feet, six inches (counting the stiletto heels), she raised her voice and intoned to her sycophants, "I shall be in my reverse harem until further notice! Unless it is *extremely* important, I am not to be disturbed."

Throwing back her shoulders and lifting her chin in a show of haughty grandeur, she sniffed once and added, "So hold my calls."

Her heels echoed against the basalt as she stepped down from the dais. "Come, Chirops."

Chirops slumped. "Aww, are you gonna make me run the tiki bar again?"

"You're the only one around here who can mix a decent mai tai. *Come,* Chirops!"

BELOW THE BLACK CASTLE LAY A MAZE OF PITCH-BLACK dungeons in which snakes slithered and rats skittered. Cobwebs hung from the ceilings, and moldering skeletons hung from heavy chains. The rank and musty air stank of droppings and urine. In the darkest and dankest of these dungeons stood a massive oaken door with a single iron ring in its center. This door was utterly nondescript, and anyone seeing it in this miserable place of rough-cut stone and scattered straw might assume it led to some chamber of unspeakable tortures where lurked a thickset man with a bare, oiled chest and a black hood that showed nothing of his face except wild, bloodshot eyes.

Holding an oil lamp aloft, the Dark Queen, with Chirops in tow and the newspaper tucked under one arm, crept to this door.

She carefully set down the lamp, removed her shoes, and put a hand to her breast to calm a fluttering heart. Once she had steadied herself, she threw the door open, and the bright light of a noonday sun blazed in. With the light came a fresh breeze on which wafted the scent of salt and sea spray as well as a delightful array of tropical fruits—banana, pineapple, coconut, and papaya. It was like a particularly expensive air freshener.

Once they stepped through the door, their bare feet dug into clean, white sand. The sun shone overhead in a blue sky, and ocean waves crashed rhythmically against a stretch of beach. Palm trees hissed as their broad leaves bobbed in the tropical breeze. High, brown cliffs enclosed this narrow, sandy strip, but a lonely lighthouse, its white sides turned blue by haze, stood vigil in the distance.

On the beach stood a square hut of bamboo and thatch, beside which lay a weather-worn deck full of tables to which broad umbrellas offered shade. Several well-tanned and tautly muscled young men, barely more than boys, frolicked in the sun: A few played volleyball, and a few splashed one another in the water. One sat on a beach towel under a parasol and read from a thick book. Another lounged on the deck and toyed with a drink.

The Dark Queen took a deep breath. "Ah, I *love* this room. It's amazing what they can do these days with holographic technology."

Chirops scratched himself behind the ears. "You know this is the reason our electric bill is so high."

"Stop being a killjoy. I *need* this place." With a snap of her fingers, the Queen's usual outfit—a black peekaboo dress with a V-cut neckline and a slit up the side—instantly evaporated. In its place appeared a tiny string bikini barely able to constrain her generously proportioned figure. With another snap, a bright yellow wraparound skirt encircled her waist, sunglasses dropped over her eyes, and a broad straw hat lowered itself onto her head.

"Finally," she said with a spread of her hands, "I feel *free!*"

Chirops's mouth dropped open. He stared for almost half a minute until blood dribbled from his snout.

He quickly turned away and scrabbled at his face. "Erm, I, um . . . I get spontaneous nosebleeds! It's a medical thing! They don't mean any—"

"All right, Chirops," said the Queen with her hands on her ample hips, "you're running the bar, and you *know* what I want."

"Well, okay," he said as he sniffed and wiped a wing across his nose, "but before I can mix a mai tai, it's gonna take me a while to make the orgeat syrup."

She sighed. "There's always something. Say, have I properly introduced you to my reverse harem?"

"Well, I think you—"

"I haven't been down here in *forever.* Come on." She marched toward the bamboo building with Chirops waddling after. Once they arrived, the Dark Queen threw herself down next to a skinny, blond boy languishing on a stool. The boy wore bright orange swim trunks and a pair of flip-flops—but no shirt, so Chirops and the Queen had a full view of his bronzed, bony, and mostly hairless torso. Around his neck hung a metal ring on which a red light glowed steadily. This was his hypnotism collar: The members of the reverse harem were former residents of Urbanopolis whom the Queen had selected, abducted, and brainwashed to ensure their pliability.

The boy's long pianist's fingers toyed with the toothpick spearing the olive in his martini. He grinned a sickly grin.

Chirops scratched one ear. "Is he getting enough iron? He looks kind of—"

"Your Darkness," the boy said, dipping his head in her direction, "I don't usually hobnob with the commoners, but for one of your beauty, I might make a *rare* exception."

Chirops gasped. The Queen, however, merely rubbed her hands together. "Ah, Chirops, this is Tamaki. He's my 'spoiled rich' type. One of my all-time favorites."

"That bikini," Tamaki said with a curled lip as he sipped his drink, "off the rack, I take it?"

Chirops squeaked and slapped his claws over his mouth, but the Queen giggled.

With a faint clink, Tamaki lowered his glass. "Would you like something, Your Darkness?"

"Oh yes," she said. "Of course."

"Then send your footman there to fetch it. Serving others is beneath me." He leaned his chin on one thin hand and looked away from her, apparently bored.

The Queen put her hands to her face as a blush formed in her cheeks.

Chirops shook his head. "Wha—? I don't get it."

"You can't see the appeal of this one?" the Queen asked with a raised eyebrow. "No? Hm. Come, I have others!"

She rose from her stool and walked back onto the hot sand. With Chirops waddling behind, she approached the boy lounging on the beach towel. He raised his head, pushed his glasses up his nose, and said in a surprisingly deep voice, "I hope you've not come to ruin my concentration with girlish prattle, Your Darkness. I am examining a tome that explicates a mathematical model of quantum tunneling, and I must employ my full intellective faculties if I am to appreciate it properly."

The Queen blushed again, leaned down, and whispered to Chirops, "That's Ryuji. He's my 'intellectual' type."

"I figured that out."

"Let's not bother him. He looks absorbed."

"What? But isn't he there to be your—?"

She strode toward the beach volleyball game, and one of the young men paused as he was about to serve. He glared at the Queen for a few seconds before looking away and clucking his tongue.

"Ohayou, Aki-*kun!"* the Queen called with a wave.

"Whatever," he said sullenly. "I hate you. You're fat. I can't believe you actually looked at another guy."

This time, the Queen's whole face turned crimson. Lifting her fists to her chin, she squealed like a little girl. "Oh, Aki is my *'tsundere'* boy! I just love *tsundere* boys!"

"So, these guys," said Chirops as he scratched his ears, "do they just insult you all the time, or what?"

"Poor Chirops." She patted his head. "You can't possibly understand a woman's heart."

"That's for sure."

"But enough of all that." She snapped her fingers, and the boys immediately ceased their game and ran to her side.

"Aki," she said, "get me a chair and an umbrella."

He sprinted away and quickly returned with a beach lounger of woven grass on a lacquered frame. He set it in the sand and planted a beach umbrella next to it. The Queen lay down and pointed at another boy.

"Hachiro, fan me."

Hachiro produced a poufy ostrich feather and waved it over her.

"And finally," she said, "Gyukudo, just stand there and flex."

The tallest and most heavyset of the boys, his chiseled face grave, gave her a single nod. Then he quietly and slowly moved through a series of poses to show off his well-formed biceps and the taut muscles of his broad chest and flat abdomen.

The Queen sighed deeply. "Oh, *wow.* Gyukudo-*kun* is my 'strong, silent' type. He's almost too much man to take."

"I'm not sure *I* can take it," Chirops muttered before he stuck a claw down his throat.

"This is the life," the Queen said as she languidly stretched her arms over her head and wiggled her toes. "This is all any girl really needs—sun, sand, and shirtless muscle boys. Don't you agree, Chirops?"

"If you say so, Your Darkness."

Wearing a one-piece bathing suit, a girl in probably her late teens ran over with a plate of assorted fruit in her hands. She knelt at the Dark Queen's side, and the Queen languidly plucked a grape.

Chirops frowned. "Why is she—?"

"This is Aoi-*chan,*" said the Queen as she chewed. "Every reverse harem should have one girl, just in case someone's into that."

"But you're the only one who comes down here, so—"

Aoi put the loosely curled knuckles of one hand to her lips, hunched her shoulders, and looked away. "Oh, Your D-Dark-ness," she said in a soft, shy voice, "the five-star hotel we're all staying in made a mistake and didn't get us enough rooms. But I guess I d-don't mind sh-sharing a bed with you . . . if you don't mind."

As she spoke, her voice fell to a whisper, and pink filled her cheeks.

Chirops's jaw came unhinged, and his snout leaked blood again.

"Don't you see, Chirops?" the Queen said as she spread her

hands. "I have almost *every* type down here. There's only *one* missing! Only *one* kind I do not yet have in my collection! Can you guess what it is?"

Chirops snuffled. "Um . . . a guy who doesn't insult you?"

She still had the newspaper, so she pulled it out and slapped him over the head with it. "No, you idiot! I am missing only the plain type, the ordinary type, the cute-but-not-remarkable type! The type that stays faithful because he knows he's got a good deal! The type that makes you feel good about yourself because you're slightly out of his league—but not so far out of his league as to find him completely unattractive!"

Chirops gasped. "You mean—?"

"That's right, Chirops! I am missing *the 'boy-next-door' type!"*

Chirops's wings shook. He ducked his head and twiddled his claws. "Um, gosh, Your Darkness, y'know, you *might* be able to find one like that . . . erm . . . if you just looked—"

"I have looked." She unrolled the paper, opened it to the second page, and pointed at the photograph. "And I've found him! *This* is what the magical girls are after! *This* is what Pretty Dynamo wants to keep for herself! And *this* is what I must have!"

Chirops blinked. *"Him?* You think—?"

"Exactly! Why would magical girls fight over him?"

"I don't know. He seems kind of—"

"Plain? Ordinary? *Precisely!* He's downright *dull!* And *that's* why he's so desirable!"

Chirops scratched his ear again. "That doesn't make any—"

The Queen rolled her eyes. "Chirops, you *really* don't under-stand a woman's heart."

"I'm coming to realize that, yeah."

She ran a hand over Barfing Boy's photograph. "They want him, so I'm going to have him. Hurt him? Maim him? I was a fool to think that. No, there is a better way to avenge myself on my enemy: I'm going to make this boy mine—and Pretty Dynamo is going to watch."

"You think she's into that?"

"That's not what I mean, idiot. No, I'm going to take him away from her, and I'm going to do it just because she wants him. Then Pretty Dynamo will be destroyed—and my reverse harem will be complete!"

She released a loud, menacing cackle that rebounded from the vaulted stone ceiling hidden above the holographic sky.

"Ah," she said with a sigh after the diabolical laugh was done, "I *knew* I'd feel better if I came down here." She tossed the newspaper into Chirops's face. "Cut that photo out and frame it."

After peeling the paper from his snout, Chirops stared down at the picture and twisted his mouth.

"When you've captured him," the Queen added, "have him bathed and then send him to my chambers."

"When *I've* captured him?"

"Is there an echo in here?" the Queen asked with the lifting of an eyebrow. "An echo that changes pronouns? Yes, when you've captured him, send him to me. And try not to take a detour to Betelgeuse this time."

Chirops swallowed audibly. The paper crackled as his claws shook.

"What are you waiting for?" the Queen snapped. "Do it! Shuffle off, now."

"What about your mai tai?"

She tapped her chin for half a minute. "Never mind that. Boys before booze. Get to it!"

She waved him away and then snapped her fingers. "Gyukudo, come here! Rub my shoulders. Queenie needs to release some tension."

CHIROPS WADDLED BACK TOWARD THE OAKEN DOOR, WHICH, thanks to the holographic illusion, stood by itself in the middle of the beach with no visible wall behind it. He stared down at the rumpled paper in his claws, at the blurry black-and-white photograph of a foolish-looking teenage boy.

"I think she could find a much better plain, ordinary guy," he mumbled. "If she really wanted to. If she really, *really* looked."

Before he was out of earshot, he heard the Dark Queen mutter to herself as she relaxed under Gyukudo's ministrations, "I'll show that city. I'll show them all. Teach those fools to betray me . . ."

As her voice dropped into inaudibility, Chirops paused at the door and brushed away a fresh tear.

"Oh, Queen," he whispered, "is all this really worth it?"

TWO

RUMBLES

Urbanopolis was the last city of man, a final refuge where the benevolent Moon Princess had sheltered the bedraggled remnants of humanity who survived the devastations of the First Invasion. Over two centuries old, the city was a massive, sprawling megalopolis nestled against a broad bay. In the rolling hills to the northeast sat the newest of its districts, Juban, an upscale but not extravagant suburb. On Juban's north end, the residences gave way to shops and strip malls: This shopping area was tidy and modern, with wide sidewalks and glassed-in storefronts, and it even boasted several parking lots since an unusually large number of Juban's residents owned cars.

At nine forty-five on a Saturday morning, fourteen-year-old Jake Blatowski loitered on a corner. A few loose coins jangled in the pockets of his jeans—the only money he had left after the adventure of the night before, when he bought Magical Girl Pretty Dynamo some much-needed food and ended up fighting for his soul against a maniacal demon.

He pulled the collar of his windbreaker tight around his neck. He wasn't facing down a monster at the moment, but he was in trouble.

His best friend Ralph arrived at ten.

"Hey," said Ralph as he punched Jake in the arm.

"Hey," Jake replied.

They watched the traffic slide by for a minute before Ralph said, "I saw you on TV last night."

Jake grunted.

"Must have been somethin' else, facin' a demon like that."

Jake grunted again. "Yeah."

"And two magical girls fighting over you. *Man—*"

Jake ran a hand through his hair. "Don't start, Ralph. Pretty Dynamo isn't fighting over me. Only Sukeban Tsubasa is, and she's just doing it to get at Dynamo."

Ralph kicked at the pavement. "Y'know, this sucks."

"Tell me about it—"

"It sucks that all the superpowered girls run after *you,* but you can't appreciate it."

Jake sighed and rubbed his temples. He felt the twinge of an oncoming headache. "It only looks cool on TV. Up close, it's . . ."

He trailed off.

"It's what?"

"It's different. That's all." Jake checked his watch. "Seen Chelsea?"

"Not today. You called her?"

"Well . . . yeah."

"When?"

"When I got home."

Ralph tipped his head back and groaned. "And when was that? After midnight? Jake, seriously—"

"Sorry, man. I'll do better."

"I'm not the one you should apologize to."

"Yeah, but apologizing to you is easier." Jake shoved his hands into his pockets. "I'm really not trying to be a jerk here, but life's been complicated—"

"And those complications forced you to go all the way to New Beijing with another girl last night?"

"Kind of."

"For what? What were you doing there with Pretty Dynamo?"

Jake chewed the inside of his cheek for half a minute. "I can't tell you."

Ralph hunched his shoulders. "It really looks like you're two-timing Chelsea."

Poplars lined the street. A sudden breeze scattered their dry leaves, which slid along the sidewalk with a faint hiss.

"I know," Jake said.

SOON AFTER, CHELSEA APPEARED. SHE WORE A TAN CARDIGAN, A white T-shirt, and a pair of pink sweatpants with JUICY written across the butt. She was petite, with the hungry, rail-thin look typical of girls in their early teens. Her platinum blond hair was pulled back in a braided ponytail. Her arms were crossed, and a sour expression sat on her face.

"Chelsea," said Jake, holding out his hands, "it's been—"

"Like, *oh* my Princess, where the *frick* have you been?" she said. "Frickin' robot dinosaurs from frickin' *space* attack the whole frickin' city, and then there are, like, frickin' zombies and demons and stuff, and, like, where the *frick* do I see my boyfriend? On television, running around with some other girl! Like, seriously, what the frick? Do you, like, *totally* see monster attacks as a chance to fool around on me? Cuz if that's how it is, we are, like, so frickin' *over,* m'kay?"

She turned her face from him and held up a palm as a visual representation of just how over they were.

Jake coughed into a fist and rubbed the back of his neck. "Chelsea, honey, I'm sorry. I know how this looks—"

In an instant, she was clutching his arm and leaning her head on his shoulder. "All is forgiven, Jakey, but you had better, like, spend a *lot* of frickin' money on me today. To make up for it."

She gave his arm a squeeze.

He coughed into his fist again. He could feel, against his leg, the measly handful of coins in his pants pocket. "Yeah, about that—"

"Mm-hmm?"

"I'm sorta broke right now, so I was hoping you or Ralph might spot me—"

Ralph clapped a hand to his face.

Chelsea let go of him. "Are you, like, frickin' *kidding* me? How did you go broke? It's not like you ever take me anywhere nice or buy me any nice things." She put one hand to her brow and stretched the other toward him in the dramatic pose of the tragedian. "OMP. Like, *ohh* MP. You frickin' spent it on *Pretty Dynamo,* didn't you?"

Jake's face grew hot.

"I *knew* it. I can picture it now: You fed her juice boxes to get her in the mood, and then you, like, took her to some nasty love hotel—"

He held up his hands. "Whoa, whoa! No, nothing like that happened! And . . . and that's really gross. I'm just short on cash, all right? Not like I have a huge allowance—"

"Get a frickin' job, loser."

"Yeah, I would, except the school system sent me back to *fifth grade.*"

"Ugh." Chelsea rolled her eyes. "Seriously, like, *don't* remind me. Word is out, Jake. You know that, right? All my friends are frickin' *laughing* at me. They're all, like, 'Oh, look at Chelsea, dating a fifth-grader. Ew, nasty. And he's Pretty Dynamo's newest item. Sucks to be Chelsea.' My reputation's in the frickin' *gutter,* Jake. Like, *totally.*"

She poked a finger hard against his chest. "I hope you appreciate what a good girlfriend I am to stick with a guy like you."

"I do. Believe me."

"Good." She cracked her knuckles, and her lips spread in a broad grin. "So are we gonna stand here on the street, or am I gonna, like, totally kick your butt?"

JUBAN'S SHOPPING DISTRICT WAS MODEST, BUT IT BOASTED AN impressive arcade with almost a hundred stand-up video-game machines, a skate park, an ice-cream shop, and even a bumper-car ride. Children and teenagers clustered around the machines and mixed their cheers and jeers with the games' pops and whistles. Black crepe covered the walls, and black lights hummed in the ceiling, making Jake's jeans glow bluish-white and show where he'd spilt tea two months earlier. Rock music played. The place smelled like popcorn, stale soda, and sweat.

Ralph was getting a workout on *Dance Dance Devolution,*

but he was so clumsy that his on-screen avatar had already regressed from human to amphibian.

"Watch this!" he called to Jake as he wiped the perspiration from his brow. "I'm gonna really bust a move!"

"Your moves are just busted," Jake muttered as he focused on his own game, *Soul Canister,* which he played against Chelsea. He had selected a beefy male avatar wielding a claymore, whereas Chelsea had selected a svelte female clad in tight black leather and armed with a rapier. As usual, she was crushing him.

"Ha!" Chelsea cried as she flawlessly executed a triple combo and used him for a pincushion. "You're weak, Jake Blatowski! *Weak!* How's it feel to get beat by a little girl?"

"Wouldn't be the first time," Jake muttered. His character fell hard to the ground, and the words YOU LOSE flashed across his screen.

"Give up," Ralph gasped as he flung himself around the dancing mat. "Nobody beats Chelsea at *Soul Canister."*

To prove the point, the high scores scrolled up the screen. The top six slots all proclaimed, CHELSEA.

"I am *undefeated,"* Chelsea cried as she thrust her hands into the air. "But I am a merciful conqueror. I will put in another credit and begin a new game—*if* you promise to really *try* this time."

Ralph finally lost at the dancing game and, soaked in sweat, collapsed to the floor. *"Dang,"* he wheezed, "that thing is hard!"

"Wow," said Jake as he glanced at the image above the flashing INSERT COIN on the dance game's screen. "I've never seen anyone get all the way down to amoeba. Good job, Ralph."

Chelsea sighed. "Ugh. Like, seriously, two are *guys.* Guys are supposed to be *good* at video games, yet here I am, mopping the floor with you. This is pathetic. I mean, Jake can't even get past level one on *Ninja Maiden.*"

"Hey," Jake said, "that's a hard game."

"No, *you* are just a button masher. Pretty Dynamo must like you for your personality because it is *definitely* not your skills."

Jake chuckled. "I've got skills."

She interlaced her fingers behind his neck and leaned on him. "Hm? Like what?"

"Give me the credit you promised, and I'll show you."

She rolled her eyes but fished in her purse and handed him a coin. He jumped onto the mat of the recently vacated dancing game, dropped in the coin, and went all out.

It *was* a hard game. But Jake didn't spend hours on the basketball court—or, for that matter, tagging after Magical Girl Pretty Dynamo—for nothing. He danced for ten minutes straight and missed only five steps.

The week before, he had injured his ankle while evading a zombie horde, so now that ankle screamed for mercy. He also had a clunky device like an oversized watch—a zombie monitor tracking him in case he was infected—bouncing on his wrist.

But those didn't stop him. He was a man on a mission.

Minute by minute, he elevated his avatar: After beginning as a human, he soon became a pale-green creature with a huge head and an atrophied body. Then he became a globe-spanning collective consciousness, then a living machine orbiting a dead star, and then an interstellar network of cybernetic organisms. He ascended to a Kardashev Type-III machine mind powered by a galaxy-sized Dyson bubble enclosing billions of stars in stable orbits just outside the Schwarzschild radius of a quasar. After that, he became a five-dimensional being living inside the event horizon of a supermassive Reissner-Nordström black hole.

Finally, he became a disembodied cosmic supermind embedded in the quantum foam.

The words YOU WIN flashed across the screen in bold, red letters. Breathing hard, Jake mopped sweat from his brow and took his place in the uppermost slot on the high-score list.

Chelsea responded to this display with a slow, condescending clap.

"My boyfriend is a veritable encyclopedia of useless skills," she said. "Useless skill number five hundred and sixty-three— really good dancer. Right above 'can list vital stats on every known dinosaur.'"

"Says the fighting-game princess," Jake muttered as he typed his initials, *JOB*.

Chelsea put her fists on her hips and sighed. *"That's* why you're out of money. You spent it on a complete *Land Before Time* collection, didn't you?"

He rounded on her. "I already *have* a complete *Land Before Time* collection, thank you very much!"

She shook her head. "You're a lost cause. Ralph, what do you think?"

"It's true," said Ralph. "He's never going to get a girlfriend."

"The case is *terminal,* Jake," said Chelsea, "but we may be able to revive the patient if you, like, promise to find some cash and take me to a frickin' movie next weekend."

Jake shrugged. "All right, fine. What movie do you have in mind?"

"Kung-Fu Cheerleader Nuns' Prison Break, Part IV. They say it's, like, even better than the first one."

Jake rubbed his temples again. The twinges were getting stronger. "Couldn't we see a movie that *doesn't* involve scantily clad schoolgirls kicking monsters in the face? Because that's sort of become my real life."

Ralph shook his head. "Some guys just can't appreciate what they've got."

Chelsea slapped a hand against the side of the *Soul Canister* machine. "Speakin' of what we've got, I'm gettin' bored with this one. Ruling *Soul Canister* has left *my* soul feeling empty. I need a new challenge."

"I know the cure for what ails you," said Ralph. "They just put it in last week." He put an arm around Chelsea's shoulders and led her past knots of jabbering teens. Still trying to dry his forehead with his sleeve, Jake followed.

Against the back wall, covered in flashing lights and uttering a cacophony of beeps and whistles, stood a massive game featuring two elevated cages of PVC pipe. Mounted behind the cages was a screen four feet high. Above the screen, in neon pink and blue, flashed the words, MAGICAL GIRL RUMBLE.

Several young boys clustered around the game. They chattered and laughed, but they also looked at the price of play and shook their heads.

An evil grin formed on Chelsea's mouth. "Ah," she said as she rubbed her palms together, "I've *heard* of this!"

"Yeah," said Ralph, "a lot of people are mad about it. I'm surprised they could get one of these in a place like Juban. You'd think the Homeowners' Association would be down here with torches and pitchforks."

Chelsea nodded. "It *does* seem sacrilegious, but I like it."

Frowning, Jake stepped up behind them. "What exactly is it?"

Ralph rounded on him, grabbed him by the shoulders, and shook him. "Jake! Seriously? *Don't* tell me you haven't heard of

Magical Girl Rumble! It's the immersive, full-body, magical-girl VR fighting game! You can play as *any* magical girl from the history of Urbanopolis and duke it out with other girls! You can *be* a magical girl, dude! The first version even let you play as the Moon Princess, but that made *lots* of people angry, so they took her out. She was OP anyway. But you can *still* play as her coven: You can be Hatchet Harridan, Ice Queen, Hell's Belle—"

"*Any* magical girl?"

"Yeah, dude. Even the current ones. They update it regularly. Pretty Dynamo's been a favorite for a while—"

As if on cue, the screen lit up with a beautifully rendered image of a street in downtown Urbanopolis. Sheet lightning crackled across low-hanging clouds. The windows of the high-rises were shattered, and glass and broken bricks littered the cracked asphalt. A few cars burned in the background, adding black smoke to the melancholy sky. The graphics were hyperrealistic, and it took Jake a moment to decide whether he was watching a 3-D render or a live-action film.

It looks too *real . . .*

The camera panned focused in on two girls strolling toward each other. Jake started, and his heart thudded in his ears when he recognized Pretty Dynamo: She looked exactly like the real one, down to the toothy, lopsided grin and the flashing emerald eyes. Her gold and silver armor glistened in the twilight. She had her fists raised, and she bobbed back and forth as if preparing to box.

Opposite her stood Sukeban Tsubasa with grayish light glinting from her armored bra. She threw her helmeted head back, laughed, and pointed a defiant finger at Dynamo.

"You wanna go?" she yelled.

"You bet I do!" Dynamo replied.

Jake's heartbeat slowed. The voices were passable—but obviously not those of the real girls.

"Fight!" cried a deep, masculine voice. Immediately, Dynamo's wand was in her hand, and it expanded into the Lightning Rod. She leaped, spun her spear, and brought its shining point down into Tsubasa's head, striking three times in rapid succession. The words *+3 combo* floated into the air.

After the manner of video-game characters, Tsubasa slid backwards and raised her arms but didn't fall or even stagger. Then she replied by thrusting out her hands: Guns popped from her wrists and belted red flames, which pounded into Dynamo and sent her flying. Blinking to indicate damage, Dynamo struck the ground and raised a cloud of dust yet quickly snapped back to her feet. Her health bar shrank.

Jake relaxed. It had impressive graphics, but it really was just a game.

"Dynamo versus Tsubasa?" Ralph said. "I bet they rushed to put in this demo after last night. And what are those red things she's shooting?"

Chelsea sighed. "Tsubasa's brand new. They probably don't know her real abilities, so I bet they just made a wild guess. Generic beam weapons and stuff."

Ralph nodded. "Yeah, that sucks. If Pretty Dynamo's gonna fight anyone, it should be Sword Seamstress."

Jake started again. "What? What did you say?"

Ignoring him, Ralph leaned on Chelsea's shoulder. "I gotta say, Chels, you're a genius. I would never have come up with it myself, but I *totally* ship those two now. They'd be perfect together."

She flashed her white teeth. "I know, right?"

"Hold on," said Jake.

Chelsea giggled. "Don't you think they just, like, *crackle* together?"

"They *could,*" said Ralph, "yeah—"

"Just a minute," said Jake, "what are you two going on about? Pretty Dynamo and Sword Seamstress hate each other."

Ralph shrugged one shoulder and said in a stage whisper, "Jake's jealous."

Chelsea snorted and waved a hand. "They don't *really* hate each other, Jake. They're just playing around—"

"Probably don't wanna admit their true feelings," said Ralph.

Jake grumbled. "Guys, *I was there.* Sword Seamstress tried to kill Pretty Dynamo. She almost *did.* I saw it."

Chelsea slid from Ralph's grasp and patted Jake's head as if he were a little boy. "I'm sure it looked that way to *you,* honey. Magical girls play rough."

"Chelsea, you don't know what you're talking about. Thanks to Sword Seamstress, Dynamo lost her powers, and we ended up trapped downtown in a zombie apocalypse. I'm lucky *I'm* not dead."

Chelsea's smile slipped. "What? What did you say?"

"She used her, um, her Christmas—"

Ralph raised an eyebrow. "The Unholy Christmas Sweater?"

"Yeah," said Jake. "That was it. She hit Dynamo with it, and Dynamo—"

"She lost her powers?" said Chelsea. The color drained from her face.

Jake nodded. "I had to improvise to boot her back up, and if that hadn't worked, both of us would be zombie food."

Ralph scratched his head. "I wouldn't have thought the Unholy Christmas Sweater could do that. I mean, it usually just demoralizes monsters so they're easier to kill, but it *does* seem to have some kind of sapping—"

"It shut Dynamo down," Jake said. "Completely."

Chelsea shook her head. "I . . . I don't understand. How could it?"

Ralph shrugged. "Dynamo's a cyborg, right? Maybe it interfered with her electrical systems. Wouldn't have thought she'd have that kind of vulnerability, but they say every magical girl has a hidden weakness. Pretty slick of Sword Seamstress to figure it out, though! Maybe I should make her my favorite again—"

Jake's head began to pound. He rubbed his temples. "Ralph, Sword Seamstress *almost killed me.* Stop talking like this is some kind of fan club thing."

"It can't be," Chelsea whispered. She bit down on the knuckle of one index finger, something Jake had only seen her do when she was extremely nervous. "I mean . . . Sword Seamstress would never *really* hurt her—"

Jake felt another twinge, this time behind his left eye. "She *did,* Chelsea. Look, would you stop contradicting me? *I was there.* You weren't. You ever watch a magical girl lose her powers as a horde of zombies is staggering your way? No? Didn't think so. You ever beat a dead man's brains out with a crowbar? No? Then shut up. You ever fall from a building while a fire-breathing *kaiju* is wrecking the city? Ever been almost dragged alive to hell? Ever race to reboot a girl robot while *Velociraptor*s are trying to rip you open? Ever watch a girl die right in front of you as she's clutching your hand? I've done *all* of that this week! I thought I could come here to relax, but instead, you two have been *on my case* all morning!"

He jabbed a finger at Ralph. *"You,* knock it off with this

obsession of yours! These girls aren't collectible figurines, all right? They're not . . . they're not . . ."

He waved a hand toward *Magical Girl Rumble.* "They're not your *toys!* They're not your *playthings!* They're people—happy, sad, angry, messed-up people. They don't need you picking their boyfriends—or their girlfriends—for them. Why in all the holy moon is everyone in this city so obsessed with shipping magical girls? Do you have any idea how *creepy* that is? A lot of 'em are in elementary school! *Some of 'em are in kindergarten!* They're children! Let them be children, for the Princess's sake!"

His chest heaved. As he caught his breath and forced himself to calm down, he noticed the arcade was strangely quiet: He could still hear pops and whistles and music, but the other noises had stopped. He turned to see all the kids frozen, staring at him.

Ralph put a hand on his shoulder and murmured in his ear, "Jake, people love the girls. We just want them to be happy. That's all."

He pushed Ralph away. "Well, knock it off. They don't need you to make them happy. They just need you to leave them alone."

Jake tugged at his collar. "Look, I'm gonna step out for a minute. I need some air."

He tried to ignore the eyes following him as he made his way to the exit.

THREE

PLAYED

The skate park was a vast sculpture of white concrete full of geometrical waves and ripples like a storm-tossed sea flash-frozen and then reimagined by Picasso. Its largest features were three deep, irregular bowls like empty lagoon-style swimming pools, but around those, ramps, half-pipes, full pipes, boxes, ledges, and rails sprawled in a veritable maze.

Several kids on boards, inline skates, or bikes were doing tricks. Just as Jake walked out through the arcade's rear door, a boy of probably twelve shot up one side of a half-pipe on his BMX and pulled a frontside 180, spinning in midair before shooting back down and doing it again on the other side. Jake watched for a minute and nodded in appreciation.

Heh. If Pretty Dynamo were here with her board, she'd eat that kid's lunch.

His eye strayed to the far end of the park, where he glimpsed a curious but familiar flash of red.

He frowned.

A little girl stood at the top of a half-pipe. She wore a baggy, black T-shirt emblazoned with the image of a skull sporting a pink bow on its bare dome. The shirt, too big for her, hung almost to her kneepads. Under one arm, she held a black skateboard.

Her skin was bone-white, and the flash Jake had noticed was her intensely red hair, which poured from under her bike helmet. Even at a distance, she stood out: Three other kids were skating nearby, and they paused to watch.

Carefully and deliberately, she set her board down. Just as carefully, she placed one foot on it. Then the other. She held her hands out to either side and wobbled.

Uh oh.

A walkway surrounded the park. Jake stepped onto it and half jogged toward the girl.

She pushed off, whipped down the ramp, and promptly wiped out. The clatter of her tumbling skateboard echoed off the concrete as she rolled to the bottom and lay in a heap. The kids around her laughed. A boy on Rollerblades sniggered as he leaped onto a rail and slid into a flawless alley-oop soul grind.

Now Jake ran. He bolted to the other side of the park, hopped over a guardrail, and barreled down the ramp. Then his bad ankle gave out. Clenching his teeth against the pain, he fell on his seat and slid to a stop beside the girl.

He had easily recognized her: Her name was Dana Volt. Like him, she was in fifth grade—except she actually belonged there. And Jake was probably the only human being in Urbanopolis who knew she was also Magical Girl Pretty Dynamo.

She sat up and dusted off her arms. A long, raw scrape stretched up her right ankle. Against her pale, almost bluish skin, her blood looked shockingly red: It stood out boldly like her hair.

She stuck out her lower lip, and her little nose quivered. Her green eyes, directed at the ground, were wet.

Jake wheezed, "Jeez, Dana, what are you doing?"

She gave him the briefest sidelong glance as her brows knit together. "Practicin'."

"For what?"

She made a rasping noise in her throat but then lowered her voice and leaned toward him before muttering, "Tesla says I'll get better as Dynamo if I practice as Dana."

Jake shaded his eyes with a hand and stared into the bright September sky. It was a clear, warm day, and the sun was high overhead. The light glared from the white concrete. "Hey, you're wearing sunscreen, aren't you?"

She rolled her eyes.

"No, I'm serious. I *know* you burn easily. Don't try to tell me you don't."

"You sound like my mom."

"C'mon." He put a hand on her arm and tried to pull her to her feet.

She squirmed out of his grasp. "Would you stop stalking me?"

"I'm not—"

"And stop *touching* me!"

"At least come in and put a bandage on that ankle."

She hunched her shoulders and wrapped her arms around her knees. "Go away."

"Man, don't I even get points for last night? I fed you, remember?"

"That was then. This is now."

He jangled the few coins in his pocket. Might be enough for a vending machine. "Come inside and let me get you something for your ankle, and maybe I'll buy you a juice box."

She scooted around in a half-circle to turn her back on him. "You can't bribe me."

"Yeah, I can. *Juice box.*"

She shuddered. Her voice so low he could barely hear it, she mumbled, "What kind of juice box?"

"Whatever you want . . . well, whatever they *have,* I should say."

She tapped her index fingers together. "Strawberry milk?"

"If they have strawberry milk, you can have strawberry milk."

She breathed hard for a few seconds but finally stuck her nose in the air. "Don't wanna."

"Stubborn, huh? Maybe you don't have a choice."

She glared. "What does that mean?"

"I mean you're not getting away without letting me put something on your ankle. It would be a shame for you to end up with a scar."

With that, he grabbed her under her knees and arms and picked her up. Her ears turned scarlet, and the color quickly spread into her cheeks. Some of the other kids made catcalls.

She slammed a fist into his shoulder. But she only did it once.

"I hate you," she said.

He smiled. "I know."

SHE WAS SO LIGHT, IT WAS EASY TO BEND DOWN, GRAB HER board, and then carry her around to the arcade's front entrance. A claw-crane game stood under the awning by the door, and Jake paused when he saw a crowd of jabbering high-school girls surrounding it. After considering them for a moment, he shrugged and walked inside.

Must be a popular new plush toy or something . . .

Adrian Pasāža, a high-school senior working a part-time job, ran the arcade's store and ice-cream shop. Jake got stares and giggles from the patrons when he set Dana down on Adrian's glass-top counter.

"Where's your first-aid kit?" Jake asked as he leaned her board against a wall.

Adrian bent down and fished under the cash register. "How bad is it?"

"Just a scrape."

Adrian came up again with a white box in hand. "Good, cuz what with everything going on, I'm not allowed to call an ambulance. I wanted to shut down the skate park, but the boss wouldn't hear it."

"How many times have you called an ambulance for the skate park?"

"Me? Never. Still, it's knowing I *can't* that makes me nervous. You're Blatowski, right?"

"That's right."

"Heard they sent you to fifth grade. That sucks."

Jake laughed quietly. "Yeah. We're plannin' to contest it, but it's been a hectic week."

"No kiddin'. Hey, are you really with Pretty Dynamo? Everyone at school says you're the 'Barfing Boy.'"

Jake sighed. "Sort of. Me an' Dynamo run into each other a lot. But I'm not her sidekick, and we're not a thing."

"Uh-huh. So who's *this* cutie? You babysittin'?"

"Nah. She's a classmate."

Adrian laughed.

While Dana sat on the counter's edge, Jake knelt in front of her, ripped open an iodine swab, and cleaned her wound. Her heels bumped the glass as she sucked her breath between her teeth. "Is that really necessary?"

"Yes."

"Why?"

"I already told you."

She leaned forward to bring her mouth near his ear and hissed, "I been hurt worse than this."

"No, you haven't," Jake replied, "not when you're . . . I mean—"

She glanced at Adrian, then back at Jake. "Yes, I have," she whispered through clenched teeth. "It *transfers* from one to the other."

He remembered the bruises he'd left on her arm: He gave them to Dana, but he saw them again on Pretty Dynamo.

He also remembered Lady Paladin Andalusia's words as she lay dying: *"My alter ego is dead already."*

His stomach clenched.

He tossed the iodine swab in the trash, leaned near to Dana's injured leg, and gently blew.

She jumped. Her heel knocked against the glass counter with a loud *thunk.*

"What was *that?"* she snarled.

He looked up at her. "You want me to kiss it?"

Her ears turned red again, and her jaw quivered. "Why, so you can get hep C?"

"You have hep C?"

"No, but *you* will if you go around kissin' people's bloody wounds!"

Jake laughed and turned back to Adrian. "Hey, you got any sunscreen?"

Dana groaned.

"Bandages are free," Adrian said as he leaned on the counter, "but the sunscreen ya gotta buy."

"Don't suppose I could pay you later?"

"Boss'd have my skin."

"Yeah, I can imagine. How much?"

"Six credits."

"That's more'n I got, so forget it. Any strawberry milk in the vending machine?"

"Dunno, you'll have to look. Getting your grade-school tastes back?"

"It's for *her,* dumbass."

"Uh-huh. You *sure* you're not babysitting?"

"Very funny." Jake put gauze over Dana's scrape and taped it in place. "There," he said. "All better."

Holding her hands in her lap and staring down at them, she began, "I don't . . ."

She stopped, scowled, and interlaced her fingers. After a moment of silence, she said, "I don't need you to take care of me."

"Nope. You just need me to buy you a juice box." He tapped a finger against the tip of her nose, and she growled.

NOW LIMPING SLIGHTLY, DANA STOOD AT JAKE'S SIDE AS HE fiddled with the vending machine. It contained several flavors of juice box, none of which was strawberry milk.

"Apple?" he asked.

"No."

"Blueberry?"

"Blech."

"That's probably not much different from the electric whatever you drank the other—"

"And that one was gross."

"You sure enjoyed it at the time."

"Whatever. Shut up. Find me something else."

"Cran-banana?"

"That's not a real fruit."

"Neither is electric—"

"Shut up. Next."

"Grape pomegranate? That's probably got a lot of antioxidants."

"Are all of 'em just fruit juice?"

"That's sort of the idea. That's why it's called a juice—"

"Shut up. What else is there?"

"Why don't *you* look? How old are you? You can read, can't you?"

She made a rasping noise in her throat, glowered at the vending machine for half a minute, tapped a foot on the floor, and said, "I'm not thirsty."

"You are such a little brat."

"And you're a big, clingy, weirdo stalker freak."

"I'm not stalking you."

Her eyes narrowed. "Then why are you here?"

"What?"

"Here. Why are you here when I'm here?"

"Coincidence. I'm here . . ." He winced as he remembered. Slapping a hand to his forehead, he said, "I'm here because I'm supposed to be on a *date.*"

With hands in pockets and hair in disarray, Ralph pushed his way past the kids crowding around the games. He sauntered up to Jake and punched him in the shoulder. *"There* you are! Dude, I thought maybe you got stuck in a toilet or something."

Dana, eyelids half lowered, looked back and forth between them. "I knew it," she muttered.

"Hey," said Ralph as he waved a hand at her, "who's this?"

"A classmate," said Jake. "Dana, this is Ralph Willikers. Ralph, Dana Volt."

Ralph held out a hand. "Shake or bow?"

"Shake." She took his hand, wiggled it unenthusiastically, and quickly let go. Crossing her arms, she gazed at him and twisted her mouth in apparent indecision.

"So," she finally said, "I assume you're the pitcher."

Jake squeezed his eyes shut and pinched the bridge of his nose. *Dana . . .*

Ralph laughed. "Ah haha. Did Jake tell you I play?" He tousled her hair. "Yep, I'm hopin' to make the team, but tryouts aren't till the end of February." He rubbed his right shoulder as he circled his arm in the air. "Been workin' on the ol' *fast pitch,* y'know!"

"Uh-huh," replied Dana with a nod. "They say it helps to think about baseball."

"I think about it all the time!"

"Okay, Dana," said Jake as he stepped behind her and clapped his hands to her shoulders, "weren't you just leaving?"

"No—"

"I think you were."

"I think you were buying me a juice box."

"But you just said . . . *why, you little brat!"*

With a deep scowl on her face, Chelsea marched over and, from behind, wrapped her arms around Jake's neck.

"Jakey." Her voice in his ear was soft but dangerous. "Where did you go, sweetie?"

He cleared his throat. "Out. Just out for a minute."

"That was more than a minute, sweetheart. That was *way* more than one frickin' minute."

He still had his hands on Dana's shoulders, so Dana tilted her head back to stare up at him. *"That's* your girlfriend?"

"Yes, this is my girlfriend, Chelsea. Chelsea, this is—"

Chelsea released Jake's neck and pointed down at Dana's face. "Who's the twerp?"

"This is Dana, as I was just saying. She sits next to me in—"

"He's buying me a juice box," said Dana.

Chelsea stepped back and placed her fists on her hips. *"Why* are you buying this half-pint a juice box?"

Jake cleared his throat again. "That's a good question. An excellent question. You see—"

"You can't even afford to take me on a proper frickin' date, but you're wasting money on juice for one of your frickin' classmates?"

"Um—"

She threw her arms around his neck again and leaned her head on his chest. "Jake, *I'm* thirsty. Why don't you buy *me* a juice box instead?"

He fished his few coins out of his pocket. "Well, I might have enough for two . . . okay, I don't."

Chelsea sighed.

"Dibs," said Dana.

Chelsea shoved Jake aside and rounded on her. "Who do you think you are, you little runt?"

"Who do you think *you* are?"

"I'm the girlfriend." Chelsea tugged a strand of Dana's rust-colored hair. "And has anyone ever told you that you look like a clown?"

Dana lifted an eyebrow. "Has anyone ever told *you* that you look like a wench?"

Chelsea raised a fist, so Jake wrapped his arms around her waist and pulled her back. "C'mon, Chelsea, she's just a kid."

"I can see that," Chelsea said as she wriggled out of his grasp. "So why are you buying her stuff?"

"Well—"

She threw up her hands. "First Pretty Dynamo and now *this* brat? I can't frickin' take any more of this!"

"You're not jealous of a fifth-grader, are you?"

"I don't *know,* Jake. I don't know *what* to think. I don't know what you're capable of. I mean, you always *did* seem a little . . . well, *you* know—"

"Hey!"

"He does, doesn't he?" said Dana.

"You stay outta this!" Jake shouted.

"Yo," said Ralph as he leaned back against the vending machine, "what's going on out front?" He pointed toward the entryway. Outside the glass doors, a gigantic crowd of teenage girls had gathered. Though Jake could hear their excited voices, the glass muffled them, so he couldn't tell what they were saying.

"I dunno," he said. "I saw 'em when I came in, but the crowd wasn't that big." He called to the desk clerk, "Hey, Adrian, is there something new in the crane game?"

Adrian leaned on the counter, watched the knot of girls for a moment, and shrugged. "Not that I know of. A guy comes from the company once a week to fill the merchandisers, but I don't pay attention to what's in 'em." He paused a moment before adding, "They make me cart that thing indoors whenever there's a storm, though. It's a real pain."

Jake again checked his money. "I bet I have enough for just one go at that thing—"

"Win me an awesome toy," said Chelsea as she squeezed his arm, "and all is forgiven."

Jake made a fist around his paltry cash. "Okay, I'm on it."

"Jake," said Ralph, "you suck at the claw crane, remember?"

Jake nodded. "Oh, that's right. Chelsea, maybe *you* should play—"

Chelsea sighed.

THEY MADE THEIR WAY OUT FRONT, DANA TAGGING AFTER THEM. As they approached, the cluster of chattering girls parted to reveal a boy at the game's controls. He was Jake's age, tall and quite thin. He wore loose slacks, a khaki sweater vest, and a carelessly tied necktie. His sleeves were rolled up to reveal pale, skinny forearms. He ran his fingers through his thick, black hair before he said in a smooth voice, "Okay, who's next? Megumi, you want one? How about the little pink kitten in the corner?"

When he looked up from the machine, his glistening eyes, rimmed with long lashes, were set in a come-hither gaze. His full lips were moist, and a hint of rose sat in his cheeks.

At his shoulder, a pigtailed girl bounced up and down. "Get me the puppy! The puppy!"

"Well," the boy said, his voice like oil, "it's in plastic. That means it's extra hard, you know—"

Megumi clenched her fists and shook her head back and forth. "I want the puppy! I want the puppy!"

"Okay, okay." With a faint chuckle, the boy cracked his fine knuckles and dropped in a coin. As the game hummed and creaked, he expertly guided the joystick until the claw was over the plastic-wrapped plush in question. The claw dropped, snagged the toy, and delivered it to the chute. With a wave of his thin fingers and a deep bow, the boy presented it to Megumi, who hugged it and squealed.

Jake nodded. "The guy's good."

Ralph clutched Jake's shoulder. "Oh sweet Moon Princess, it's *him!*"

"Him? Who him?"

"That guy I told you about—!"

Jake racked his memory and drew a blank.

Meanwhile, the strange boy ran his fingers through his hair again and looked over. He instantly lost his oily, seductive look, and a wide-eyed smile replaced it.

"Willikers-*sama!*" he cried, his voice rising an octave.

Ralph took a step back as if planning to use Jake for a shield. "Uh, hey, T.B.," he said cautiously.

T.B.? thought Jake. *His name is T.B.?*

T.B. rubbed a hand against the back of his head and forced a weak, nervous laugh. "Didn't expect to see you here! Aheh. Aheh heh. So, um, what brings you to the arcade—?"

Ralph took another step back. "Games—"

"Oh. Right. Cuz . . . cuz that's what you do at an arcade! Aheh heh heh."

The girls around T.B. grimaced. Megumi leaned on his shoulder and glowered. "T.B., honey, who are *these* dorks?"

T.B. started, but after a brief look of panic crossed his expressive features, he got back his bedroom eyes and stroked Megumi's chin. "Oh, darling, don't you worry. Ralph's just a friend of mine, you see. But you are the only one whose company I *truly* crave."

When his fingers entwined themselves in a lock of Megumi's hair, she trembled. "Oh, T.B. . . ."

A blond girl crossed her arms and pouted. "T.B., how come you're giving all your attention to Megumi today?"

Without releasing Megumi, T.B. turned toward her and murmured, "Cassandra, you know I love you. But when a man is surrounded by so many beautiful flowers, it's difficult to know which one to pluck first."

Deep red entered Cassandra's cheeks, and she nearly dropped to the pavement as her knees visibly shook.

Sheesh, thought Jake, *this guy is somethin' else.*

Chelsea put her fingertips to her throat and stared. "Oh my sweet frickin' Princess, that guy's in your class, Ralph?"

"Yeah," said Ralph, "he's a real—"

"Oh, *frick.* I would have petitioned to skip a grade if I knew high-schoolers could be *that frickin' hot.*"

Wrapping his arms around Megumi and Cassandra, T.B. took a couple of steps forward but didn't leave his crowd of admirers. He tilted his head until his long hair draped over his eyes. "Well, sweetie," he said to Chelsea, "there is *plenty* of room aboard the T.B. train. You just gotta wait your turn." He gave the girls under his arms a squeeze, and they squealed.

"Ooh," Chelsea breathed as she slid her hands down her torso, "what's the wait time?"

Jake tugged on his collar. "Um, Chelsea? Would you mind, y'know, *not* openly lusting after other guys right in front of me? It's kinda hurting my self-esteem."

T.B.'s eyebrows went up. He put his hands out with thumbs and index fingers extended as if framing a picture, and he gazed down into Dana's face.

"And what is this?" he whispered. "A porcelain doll come to life? That fiery hair! Those sea-green eyes! That saucy button nose—!"

"You suck," said Dana.

Jake clapped a hand to her shoulder. "And then there's her mouth," he said, "which pretty much ruins everything else."

T.B. grinned and casually raked a hand through his hair. "Oh, that's okay. I'm sure she's just jealous because she knows she's too short"—he pointed his thumbs at himself—"for *this* ride."

His girls tittered.

Is this guy for real?

"Sweet Princess," Chelsea whispered, "I just wanna rip his clothes off right here—"

"Chelsea?" said Jake. "You're drooling, honey."

"I take it back," said Dana, her half-lidded stare still on T.B. "You don't just suck. You *super* suck. You *super-duper* suck. You suck worse than *this* guy"—she jerked a thumb over her shoulder at Jake—"and that means you really, really suck."

T.B. hugged his two closest girls again and took another step forward. He remained a good ten feet from Dana but bent down to look her in the eye. "Aw, don't be like that, sweetheart. How 'bout you let me pinch your cheek, and then I'll buy you an ice cream cone?"

Dana tapped a foot against the ground. After half a minute, she turned one cheek toward him. "Just don't pinch hard," she muttered.

"What? Dana!" Jake rapped her scalp with his knuckles. "Don't be so easy to bribe!"

She stuck her lip out. "Well, *you* wouldn't buy me ice cream!"

"That's because—"

"Hold it," said Chelsea, seizing Jake's arm, *"why* were you buying the runt ice cream?"

"I wasn't," Jake replied, "like she said."

Chelsea blinked.

Dana crossed her arms and turned up her nose. "It's because I'm better'n you are, *Chelsea."*

"Dana," said Jake, "knock it off."

Chelsea let go of him. "What did you say, runt?"

"That you're stupid," said Dana, "and that you suck."

Chelsea raised a fist again, so Jake quickly took her hand. "She's just being a brat, Chelsea. Ignore her."

T.B. straightened up and stretched his arms out. His girls closed around him, cooing and sighing.

"What is this?" he said. "Jealousy? Squabbling? And on *my* watch? This I cannot allow! Young ladies, it's clear you need to have it out. And we're at the arcade: There is only *one* way to solve your differences here!"

Chelsea stared for a moment but then grinned and rubbed her hands together. "Yes. Yes, the hot guy is right!" She clamped a hand on Dana's head and roughly wagged it back and forth. "Okay, twerp, how are you at *fighting games?* You like *Soul Canister?"*

Jake rolled his eyes. "C'mon, Chelsea—"

Dana slapped Chelsea's hand away and said through clenched teeth, "How about *Magical Girl Rumble?"*

"Dana," Jake hissed. *"You shouldn't—"*

Chelsea cackled. "Oh, *really?* You think *you* can beat me at *that?* You're on, brat! You are *so frickin' on!"*

"It's decided!" T.B. cried, pulling no less than five girls into his grasp and giving them all a tight squeeze as they giggled and squirmed. "And the winner of this heroic duel gets a kiss on the cheek from *yours truly!*"

Dana and Chelsea clasped each other's hands and glared into each other's faces.

"Now I'm motivated!" said Chelsea. "You're going *down,* ginger!"

Jake closed his eyes and rubbed his temples.

Yes, he was definitely getting a headache.

FOUR

PLAYERS

L ike an amoeba with T.B. as its nucleus, the cluster of girls oozed through the arcade's front door. Leaning on the counter, Adrian blanched; the girls hadn't perturbed him when they were out under the awning, but he was at a loss when they invaded the male-dominated space of the interior.

There was an unspoken rule at the arcade: Girls, if they came in significant numbers, were to remain at the front near the merchandisers. Girls were not to enter the arcade's inner sanctum except singularly—and preferably in male company. Cavalierly violating this unspoken rule, T.B.'s band of jabbering females threatened the purity of this haven for luckless and socially awkward boys.

The girls cried for ice cream, and T.B. had no shortage of money, so silver credits clattered onto the glass counter. While Adrian hastened to fill waffle cones, the excited girls shouted their flavor preferences over the top of one another.

Although they didn't order, T.B. also bought ice cream for

the two combatants. He turned toward them with a cone in each hand and an expectant smile on his face, but he never left the girls' circle: Instead, as if the amoeba were swallowing prey, the feminine cluster thrust out pseudopods, engulfed Chelsea and Dana, and drew them inexorably inward. Once they stood before T.B., he dropped to one knee and held up two cones loaded with vanilla soft-serve as if he were a knight proffering hard-won treasures to his ladylove. They took the ice cream in silence, and T.B. didn't even insist on pinching Dana's cheek.

Now the amoeba, having grown larger through absorption, was on the move again: It slithered deeper into the arcade where skinny, pimple-faced boys gave it nervous glances as if afraid they were next to be devoured. Slouching and grumping, Jake and Ralph followed behind.

Seething with annoyance, Jake tried to move in close to T.B., who was smoothly whispering inanities into Chelsea's ear—but he always found a girl blocking his path. When he stepped to one side to get around her, he ran into another girl. Somehow, no matter where Jake went, at least three girls always stood between him and T.B. He had no way of getting through except by getting rough.

So he stayed back and glowered instead.

By the time they reached the *Magical Girl Rumble* game, Dana and most of the other girls had already devoured their treats. Chelsea still contentedly dabbed at hers, catlike, with her tongue, so T.B. slipped an arm around her waist and murmured just loudly enough for Jake to hear, "Do you need a little help with that ice cream, my dove, my sweet? Perhaps we could lick it . . . *together?"*

Chelsea giggled.

"Hey!" Jake shouted. He tried to push his way between two

of the girls but ran straight into Megumi, who stalwartly stood athwart him and eyed him with a murderous glare.

"Step aside," he said.

She thrust out her chin for a moment as if considering. Then she squeezed her eyes shut, bunched up her fists, and shrieked, *"Eek!* He touched me! He touched me *there!"*

Jake jumped backwards. Once again enclosed by the amoeba, Megumi ran to T.B., who placed a consoling arm across her shoulders.

"T.B.," she moaned, "that boy is such a . . . such a *ruffian!"*

"Don't worry, Megumi," T.B. cooed. "I'm here for you. I'll watch over you, I'll guard you, and I'll protect you . . . because I always use protection—"

"Oh, T.B.!" Megumi gasped as she laid her head on his chest.

"Jake's such a pervert," said Dana. After a moment, she looked up at Chelsea and added, "Aren't you mad?"

"Actually," Chelsea answered as she slurped up the remainder of her rapidly melting ice cream, "I'm kind of impressed. Truth is, I was beginning to think he was . . . well, you know."

"Hey!" Jake shouted.

Chelsea munched her cone and then brushed her hands together. "Still, he hasn't even made a move on *me* yet. I wouldn't expect him to grab some girl he just met."

"You'd be surprised," Dana muttered with narrowed eyes.

Jake clenched his fists. "I am getting really tired—"

Chelsea waved a hand in the air. "Relax, sweetie. I was watching. Megumi made the whole frickin' thing up."

With that, Chelsea seized Megumi by the shoulders, hauled her away from T.B., and bent her into a headlock. Megumi shrieked, and Cassandra pounded on Chelsea's shoulders, but

Chelsea merely shoved a palm against Cassandra's chest. Cassandra stumbled into T.B., who caught her around the waist. After making sure Cassandra had her feet, T.B. reached for Chelsea, but Chelsea snapped up her free hand and struck his fingers. His dark eyes widened, and he stepped back.

"Ya like that?" Chelsea shouted as she dug her knuckles into Megumi's scalp. "Ya wanna fantasize 'bout somebody grabbin' you? *I'll* grab ya, ya wench!"

Thinking he'd better break it up before Adrian kicked them all out, Jake strode forward but again found two girls in his path.

"Out of the way," he said.

"Stand back!" one of them answered. "Nobody gets close to T.B.!"

"What are you talking about? *You've* been close to him!"

T.B. placed a hand on Chelsea's shoulder and said smoothly, "Megumi's a little high-strung. Why don't we just let this one slide, hm?"

Chelsea stopped the noogies but hissed in Megumi's ear, "The hot guy just saved your life, sweetheart. Now think twice before you mess with my boyfriend, *got it?*"

She released Megumi and pushed her aside. Her mussed, frizzy hair falling limply over her face, Megumi burst into tears as T.B. wrapped her in a tight hug.

"*That* got my blood pumping!" said Chelsea as she cracked her knuckles. The girls scrambled out of her way as she marched toward one of the game's elevated cages. Once she found the stairs, she mounted and ducked through the PVC pipes.

"Prepare yourself, Jake Blatowski," she shouted, "cuz your middle-school girlfriend is about to kick your elementary-school girlfriend's butt!"

Jake yelled back, "She's not my . . . y'know, forget it. Just get this over with."

Dana, arms still crossed, walked toward the other cage. As she passed him, Jake leaned down and whispered, "Hey, have you played this game before?"

She twisted her mouth. "Well, no. But I figured I might be able to . . ."

She shrugged.

With sharp elbows, T.B.'s girls nudged Jake and Ralph aside before swarming the game's central console, where T.B. grandly showed off his fat wallet before dropping in ten credits.

A cacophony of thunder and trumpets burst from the speakers. On the screen, a computer-generated image of the moon swept through space above a ruined, crater-pocked Earth. At that sight, Jake felt a lump form in his throat: It was a boldly accurate depiction of the current state of the planet, with blackish oceans and barely recognizable continents scoured yellow and red. The Indian subcontinent, Australia, and most of South America and Africa were gone, having been wiped out by the destruction of Antarctica and the subsequent antimatter bombings. Half of Europe, the coasts of North America, and the Pacific island chains were gone as well.

A view of Earth from space was a rare sight in Urbanopolis. People didn't like to think about it, and besides, most of the planet was enemy territory. The image was a clear statement of this game's deliberate provocativeness.

A deep voice boomed, "Humanity's last hope . . . locked in mortal combat! Behold, *Magical Girl Rumble!*"

The game was loud. Jake winced as trumpets blared. Around the arcade, other kids peered over to see who was willing to pay the steep asking price.

Several generations' worth of magical girls, frozen in corny poses, flitted across the screen. "Choose your girl," shouted the voice, "and *choose your destiny!*"

"I see," said Ralph, "so it's kinda like a dating service."

Sonorous music rolled forth as the monitor displayed girls performing brutal combo moves on one another. The air filled with high-pitched taunts and the loud cracking sounds that games and movies inexplicably associated with punches and kicks.

Jake sucked in his breath when Magical Girl Grease Pencil Marionette jumped onto the screen. The tails of her green coat stuck out straight behind her as she performed a pirouette and spun her giant pencil in her hands. "Welcome to *Magical Girl Rumble!*" she shouted in a decent imitation of Marionette's real voice. "Right now, I'll run through a quick tutorial to get you ready for action! To skip this at any time, press the flashing green button!"

On the console in front of T.B., a big button blinked.

"If you're ready to fight like a girl," said Marionette with a wink and another twirl, "please select one- or two-player mode!"

Two more buttons lit up. T.B. pressed the one on the right, and Marionette offered another wink.

"Two-player mode selected!" she said with a giggle. "You're *really* pushing my buttons!"

Jake shook his head. "Marionette does *not* talk like that."

Ralph nudged him. "Hush. I wanna see this."

The floors of the elevated platforms shone blue and red. Marionette spread her arms. "Surrounding these two *rumble cages* are motion sensors designed to translate your movements into the awesome combat maneuvers of *real-life magical girls!* The gameplay is based on thousands of hours of news footage, and the moves are as accurate as we could make them! Players one and two, please enter your rumble cage and don your virtual-reality headsets and battle gloves!"

After spinning her pencil, Marionette quickly drew, in midair, images of the gloves and VR sets. While she ran through the instructions on securing the straps, Dana and Chelsea found their way into the equipment. Dana discovered that she couldn't put the headset on over her bike helmet, so she unlatched the helmet and handed it off to Jake. Static electricity made her red hair stand on end to form a waving, fiery halo.

"Woo," said Chelsea as she sniffed her VR set, "these things smell funky. I wonder how many hygienically challenged fanboys have worn this stuff."

"You'll notice that your right glove is stiffer than your left," said Marionette, "because it contains the controller! You can attack and defend using hand and foot gestures alone, but to perform spells and combo moves, you'll need the controller's buttons, which you can feel under your fingertips. Keep in mind that each magical girl has a unique move set, so mastering the spells takes time!"

Jake knew Chelsea had never played this before, but she was a skilled and systematic gamer. Chances were that she'd have several combinations memorized by the time the first round was over. He didn't know how Dana played, but if he had to guess, she was a button masher, which meant she was at a severe disadvantage.

Marionette ran through the basics of how to control an avatar. The leg movements were especially complicated: Going up on tiptoe would jump, doing it quickly would "spin jump," lifting a foot from the floor would kick, and hopping could bring an aerial magical girl into "flight mode."

As the instructions grew more elaborate, a broad grin formed on Chelsea's mouth beneath the slim VR headset. "What do you wanna bet the sensors can't even detect half this stuff?"

"Could be," said Ralph in Jake's ear. "These games are great in theory, but in practice, they're hit or miss."

"Now," cried the fake Marionette, "choose your girl . . . and *choose your destiny!*"

"Man, this is hammy," Jake whispered.

"If by hammy, you mean *awesome,*" Ralph replied, eyes glued to the screen. "I mean, Chelsea's probably right that the gameplay's gonna suck. But it's *still* awesome."

Jake chewed the inside of his cheek. "Well, it's quite a spectacle, and it squeezed ten credits out of us, so that's something."

The screen flashed with the words *Player 1,* and Dana's cage lit up blue. A selection window appeared with a bewildering array of girls' thumbnail images, sorted by decade. A selector box flicked back and forth uncertainly as Dana figured out how to control it, but then it shot forward to the current decade and found the picture of Pretty Dynamo.

Jake slapped his forehead. *Dana . . .*

A trumpet blared when Dana made her selection, and Pretty Dynamo appeared on-screen with Tesla the lightning bug, her familiar, hovering at her shoulder. Dynamo twirled on one foot and spun her spear in a whirlwind as she cried, "Electrifying the world with love and friendship—and making evildoers feel the wattage of justice—I am *Magical Girl Pretty Dynamo!*"

Lightning cracked, and the subwoofers thundered.

"Interesting choice," muttered Chelsea. Once the screen said *Player 2* and her cage began to glow, she moved the selector to the tail end of the list to hover over Sukeban Tsubasa.

Though pale already, Dana somehow grew paler.

"Hey, Chelsea," Ralph called, "Tsubasa's brand new! You

know she'll only have a basic move set!"

"Good point, Ralph. She's probably more a placeholder than anything else. Let's get one who's been around a while."

She moved the selector up a few rows until she found Sword Seamstress.

Dana's mouth dropped open.

"Oh man," said Ralph.

Sword Seamstress swept onto the screen with Stitches the cat padding sinuously around her feet. "Though deceivers weave their tangled webs," Sword Seamstress shouted, "my warp and weft are always true! A stitch in time stops crime—for I am *Magical Girl Sword Seamstress!"*

Accompanied by the sound of birds taking flight, ribbons and spools of thread flowed across the screen.

Dana clenched her teeth and raised her fists. *"Sword Seamstress!"* she hissed.

Jake shook his head. *Keep it together, Dana . . .*

Ralph clutched Jake's arm, startling him. Tears rolled down Ralph's cheeks. "I know it's just a video game, but still . . . *DynaSword!* It's the happiest day of my life!"

Jake sighed.

"Do you think they'll fight in a mud pit?" Ralph whispered. *"Do you?"*

"Calm down, Ralph."

"Get ready!" a deep voice roared. "It's time for . . . *Magical Girl Rumble!*"

On the screen appeared a wide shot of the Wastes, the ruined world outside Urbanopolis. Mottling the barren earth were patches of deep crimson, sickly yellow, and burnt-out black. Sharp fragments of glass littered the ground: Neither natural nor manmade, this glass had formed from stone and soil fused by the heat of alien weaponry. As if mounted on a helicopter, the camera zoomed across this dreary landscape to reveal occasional glimpses of skyscraper-sized spiders, giant lizards with flesh like stone, and vaguely humanoid creatures of living flame—just a few of the monstrosities that roamed the badlands and sometimes attacked the city.

At last, the camera focused on a high cinder cone. Brightly glowing lava dribbled down one blasted slope, and smoke billowed into the cloudy sky.

Halfway down the volcano's steep side, the ground had cracked open, and the lava formed a small lake. The camera zoomed in further to reveal Pretty Dynamo and Sword Seamstress squaring off on a floating platform of grayish stone amid the bubbling, molten rock. Around them, flaming balls of tar leaped out of the lava and fell back with a splash.

On either side of the central image, boxes appeared to display the first-person views from Dana and Chelsea's headsets.

"Interesting arena," said Chelsea as the landscape swung back and forth to match her head turns, "though I'm not sure it's physically possible. In real life, lava doesn't behave like water, so you can't float a rock on it like an iceberg. And then there's the heat—"

Ralph shrugged. "Pretty Dynamo could take it, but I don't think Sword Seamstress has that kind of heat tolerance. That would be hot enough to ignite most fabrics."

"Don't forget the poisonous gasses," Jake added.

Ralph laughed. "Both of them could handle those."

"It's a video game," said T.B., stroking his chin. "It's not supposed to be *completely* realistic. In games, there's no such thing as thermal radiation, so lava doesn't hurt you unless you touch it."

Throughout the cinematic opening sequence, raucous music had played. Though Jake had tuned it out at first, the music now grew insistent, and a screechy voice screamed unintelligibly over the heavy sound of pounding drums and distorted guitars.

As Dana bobbed her head, the view from her helmet bounced up and down. "Hey, I know this song!"

"Yeah," said Ralph, "I've heard it too! You listen to monster metal?"

"Uh-huh," said Dana. "This is 'Uterus of Destruction' by Lady/Killer featuring Van Halensing. It's from their *Rigor Magus* album."

"Van Halensing?" said Ralph. "You mean the vampire-hunting, magical-girl rock idol? I didn't know she sang with Lady/Killer!"

"Just this song."

"Dude! And they've got it on the soundtrack for *Magical Girl Rumble*? That is *metal!*"

Jake grabbed the lip of Dana's platform. "Dana, you shouldn't listen to music like this! It's full of all kinds of bad stuff like cuss words and backward messages and syncopated rhythm—"

"You're a dork," she replied. "I bet you listen to show tunes."

Jake blinked. "What's wrong with show tunes?"

Dana and Chelsea both sighed.

"T.B.," whined Cassandra as she leaned on T.B.'s. shoulder, "this music is so . . . so *inurbane!*" She stuck out her lip and made Bambi eyes.

"Never mind that, my dear," T.B. answered, taking her hands in his own. "Perhaps later, I'll stand beneath your balcony and serenade you on my mandolin."

She gasped. "I didn't know you played the mandolin!"

"I'll learn how just for you."

"Oh, T.B.!" Cassandra threw herself against him, and he held her tightly.

"Enough of that," said Chelsea. "Let's do this thing." She slid a foot forward. On the screen, Sword Seamstress ran pell-mell toward Pretty Dynamo.

Dana stumbled into the PVC pipes, making Pretty Dynamo perform a flying backward somersault into the lava. Instead of sinking or igniting, she blinked gold and cried, "Ow! Ow!" A burst of flame knocked her forward onto the stone after a quarter of her health bar disappeared.

"You gotta watch the edge," said Jake.

Dana grumbled, "I know, idiot."

Righting herself, she took a cautious step forward and clumsily swung one arm. On-screen, Dynamo jabbed at the air while yelling, "Yah! Yah!"

"Controls are going to be tough," Chelsea said. "This should be interesting."

She stuck out her foot, and Sword Seamstress again ran forward. Chelsea boxed the air, and Sword Seamstress delivered a rapid combination of hooks and jabs. Dynamo, her head rocking on her neck, slid toward the lava again.

"Hold your arms up," said Jake, "and move one foot forward —there you go!"

Dynamo blocked the punches and halted her retreat.

"Okay, now *swing!*"

When Dana swung, Dynamo delivered a left hook, which caught Sword Seamstress in the jaw and knocked her back.

"Oh man," whispered Ralph, "I just can't handle it." Tears poured from his eyes, and a trickle of blood ran from his left nostril.

"Jake!" shouted Chelsea. "Why the frick are you helping *her* instead of *me?*"

"Because she needs it!" Jake shouted back. "You're already good at this stuff!"

"Well, *that's* true. Let's see how you pull a weapon on this thing." A series of clicks came from Chelsea's glove as she tested the buttons.

Sword Seamstress slid to the left, then to the right, and then spun in a flashy tornado roundhouse kick. Dana gasped and ducked, and Dynamo ducked too.

After several more clicks, Sword Seamstress finally pulled her swords from her garter belts. They clattered as they unfolded.

"Dana," Jake yelled, "try the buttons!"

Dana's glove clicked, and Dynamo shimmied back and forth.

"Where's my Lightning Rod?" Dana snarled.

Chelsea chuckled, and Sword Seamstress swung her right arm in a vicious swipe.

After more frantic clicking, Pretty Dynamo shouted, *"Surge Protector!"* A shield unfolded from her arm, and she blocked the blow.

"Who designed the moves for this?" said Ralph as he waved at the screen in disgust. "That's not how Sword Seamstress fights! You don't just throw your arms around like that when you're fencing!"

"You're right," said Chelsea, "but if this works the way I think it does, I *should* be able to fix that."

She bent her knees, raised her left arm behind her head, and turned her right shoulder toward Dana, forming an en garde position. Sword Seamstress mimicked the pose.

T.B. tilted his head and rubbed his chin. "That's a good stance. Does she fence?"

Jake frowned. "Well, no . . . I don't think so. But she *does* play a lot of sword fighting games, so she's seen the pose—"

T.B. continued stroking his chin and said nothing.

Chelsea lunged. Sword Seamstress did the same and thrust straight through Dynamo's abdomen. There was no blood, and rather than keeling over, Dynamo slid back half a foot and flashed gold.

Dana's glove continued to click. *"Where's my spear?"*

"Don't get excited," said Jake. "Have you tried every button?"

"There are only four buttons! This game's *stupid!*"

After Dynamo jiggled back and forth for a few seconds, she finally raised a hand and cried, *"Ball Lightning!"* The resulting blast knocked Sword Seamstress onto her back and raised a cloud of dust.

"Do it again!" Jake said.

More buttons clicked. "I can't!"

"What did you hit before?"

"I dunno! I just hit stuff!"

Sword Seamstress quickly kipped up to her feet. *"Scarf of Strangulation!"* she shouted.

A ball of blue yarn jumped from her belt, and her swords whistled as they slashed the air, producing a woolen scarf, which snaked toward Dynamo and enwrapped her throat. Dana waved her arms and tapped more buttons, but to no avail: Dynamo scrabbled at the scarf, but Sword Seamstress yanked on it, dragging her across the ground. Once she was in range, Sword Seamstress swung an arm, clocked Dynamo in the face with a knuckle guard, and sent her flying backwards. It was an impressive-looking move, though it did only a little damage.

"Oh yeah!" cried Chelsea. "That was frickin' *awesome!*" As

more clicks came from her glove, she performed the move again. And again. And again.

"Rrr! I hate this stupid game!" Dana reached for her VR headset, but Jake shot a hand into the cage and grabbed her wrist.

"C'mon!" he shouted. "T.B. wasted ten credits on you! At least play it through!"

She tried to yank her arm back, but Jake held on until she stopped pulling.

"Fine," she growled. "Whatever. I'll play."

Once he let go, she pressed more buttons. At last, Dynamo cartwheeled sideways to dodge the scarf.

"Lightning Rod!" she shouted. Her wand popped into her hand and clicked and clacked as it expanded into a spear.

"Finally!" Dana snarled. "I have *no* idea what I hit!"

She waved her gloves through the air. Although hesitant and slow, her movements looked much like those Jake had seen Pretty Dynamo use on the street. On the screen, the spear spun in Dynamo's hands.

Jake pinched the bridge of his nose. *C'mon, Dana, don't show off—*

"Hey, that's not bad," said Ralph as he dabbed a handkerchief at his bloody nose. "Is she studying kung fu or something?"

Jake tugged his collar. "No, no, of course not. The game corrects their movements. You can see that."

Ralph frowned. "Yeah, I guess . . ."

Dana muttered, "Maybe I can do this."

She slid a foot forward, and Dynamo ran. Sword Seamstress crouched and aimed for her legs. Dana hopped an inch from the floor to dodge—but instead of merely jumping, Dynamo threw a blue rectangle from her belt.

"Circuit Board!"

The rectangle grew into a hovering snowboard. A moment later, Dynamo was airborne.

Dana staggered as Dynamo zipped up and down the screen. Her first-person window became an indecipherable blur of red, blue, and gold.

"Dana, stand straight!" Jake yelled. "On your toes is up and bent knees is down, remember?"

"This is *stupid!*" Dana shouted.

Chelsea jumped, and her cage rocked precariously when she landed. Black wings like a crow's sprouted from Sword Seamstress's back.

Sword Seamstress flew upwards but immediately plummeted into the ground when Chelsea bent her knees. Chelsea jumped again, but Sword Seamstress again rammed into the ground. Her health bar rapidly dropped.

"This is frickin' ridiculous!" cried Chelsea. "I'm playin' a fencer, but it's gonna make me keep my legs straight?"

"Don't try to fence for real," T.B. suggested, still stroking his chin. "Just press the buttons and move your arms. Your avatar will make up for what your real motions lack. Think control, not speed. Think big gestures the sensors can read, not finesse. Slow and deliberate."

Chelsea stood straight, put her legs together, and went on her toes. Sword Seamstress, her broad wings flapping with a rhythmic *whoosh-whoosh,* rose from the ground.

Chelsea grinned. "Yeah, you're right. That's doing it!" Bending her left knee slightly, she slid her right foot forward, and Sword Seamstress swooped toward Dynamo.

"Dana," said Jake, "slow and controlled."

"Shut up," Dana replied, but by standing still, she stopped Dynamo's crazy zigzagging. When Sword Seamstress plunged toward her, Dynamo thrust up with her spear and knocked her back. Sword Seamstress flashed gold, and her health bar shrank considerably.

"What?" cried Chelsea. "Why did I take such a big hit?"

"Speed of impact," T.B. suggested. "It probably takes that into account in aerial mode."

"What the actual *frick?*"

In the air, Dynamo had an advantage since her spear gave her a longer reach. She flew toward Sword Seamstress, swiped her across the face with the spearpoint, and then pulled back before Sword Seamstress could reply. Then she did it again.

"Good," said Jake. "Good. You've got it. See if you can do a combo."

Dana flicked the buttons. Dynamo fired off her Ball Lightning again, but Sword Seamstress dodged.

Dana slapped more buttons and cried, "Whoa!" as Dynamo shot straight up, rising higher and higher until she jumped from her board and dived downward with her spear pointed toward the ground.

She chucked the spear, spun in the air, and reactivated her board.

Sword Seamstress merely flew out of the way as the Lightning Rod hurtled past. It snapped with flashes of electricity when it embedded itself in the stone island below.

"Probably not the best maneuver to employ at this point in the game," T.B. suggested. "I think that's supposed to be a finishing move."

"Then why did it let her do it now?" Jake asked.

"I lost my spear!" Dana moaned.

Chelsea cackled. Sword Seamstress dive-bombed Dynamo and slashed viciously, smacking Dynamo up and down and right and left. Again, Dana's first-person window became a blur. Even the main window struggled to track the players as Sword Seamstress battered Dynamo back and forth.

Finally, Pretty Dynamo dropped limply when her health bar fell to zero. She plunged into the lava, where she screamed and flailed as she went up in bright flames. Burning and shrieking, she slowly sank out of sight, and the last view they had of her was of one hand flaming like a torch as it grasped futilely at the air.

A chill ran up Jake's spine. "Sheesh, was that ending animation necessary?"

"Magical Girl Sword Seamstress wins!" the deep voice exclaimed, and the heavy metal soundtrack reached a squealing crescendo as Sword Seamstress landed nimbly on the stone platform and made an elegant salute with a rapier.

The word REPLAY? appeared. Underneath, a timer counted down from ten.

"What?" cried Chelsea as she snapped off her VR set. "One round? Not even best two out of three? This game's a frickin' rip-off!"

She stripped off her gloves and stepped down out of the cage. Wrinkling her nose, she sniffed her hands. "Ugh. I need to go wash after wearing those things."

Dana, her lip outthrust in a childish pout, tossed her gloves to the floor and then ripped at her headset.

"Hey," said Jake, "treat the equipment nice. You don't want to pay for this stuff."

"Whatever." She slammed the headset onto its peg and, arms crossed, stomped down the steps from her platform.

"Well," said T.B. as Megumi and Cassandra leaned on his

shoulders, "it appears we have a victor—and to the victor go the spoils."

He bit his lip and, through his long eyelashes, gave a hesitant, sidelong glance to Ralph, who was still trying to clean a bloody nose. But after this momentary hesitation, T.B. regained his composure, cleared his throat, and flicked his thin fingers. A rose appeared in his hands as if by magic. He put it to his nostrils, closed his eyes, and inhaled deeply.

Chelsea flipped a length of hair behind one ear. She leaned back against the elevated cage, stretched her arms over her head, and grasped the PVC pipe.

"Okay, big boy," she said in an uncharacteristically husky voice, *"take me."*

T.B. chuckled as he toyed with his rose. "Tempting, to be sure, but I hesitate to give a young maiden her first kiss. I might ruin you for other men: They say that once you've had T.B., you never get over it."

Chelsea smiled. "That's a risk I'm willing to take."

"Are you sure?" T.B. asked with a raised eyebrow. "You might spend your life pining for me. Many young maidens are wasting away because of T.B."

"Shut up and plant one on me," said Chelsea, tapping her left cheek. "Right on the funk from that nasty headset."

Jake cleared his throat. "Wait a minute—"

Ignoring him, the girls formed a protective semicircle around T.B. and Chelsea, shutting Jake out. T.B. strolled forward.

"Not so fast, my darling, my chickadee," T.B. said, his voice even oilier than usual. "I am no knavish rube, untutored in the ways of love, to move straight into a cheek kiss like some overexcited schoolboy."

Jake scowled. *But you* are *an overexcited schoolboy—*

With his left hand, T.B. held the rose toward Chelsea. She reached for it with her right, but as she did, he turned his wrist, so her hand fell across his. Then he reached up and pulled her left hand down from the pipe.

Lowering himself to one knee, he brushed her knuckles with his full, red lips before reciting:

> *Crimson nor yellow roses, nor*
> *The savor of the mounting sea*
> *Are worth the perfume that I adore*
> *That clings to thee.*

He slid forward and kissed her arm near the elbow before he continued, rolling each word in his mouth as if tasting fine wine:

> *The languid-headed lilies tire,*
> *The changeless waters weary me.*
> *I ache with passionate desire*
> *Of thine and thee.*

He took her two hands together and gently kissed them both before whispering:

> *There are but these things in the world—*
> *Thy mouth of fire,*
> *Thy breasts, thy hands, thy hair*
>   *upcurled—*

He gazed up at her through his long, delicate lashes before pointing a thumb at himself and adding:

And this hotness.

Chelsea broke into a broad grin as if about to burst out laughing. A similar smile appeared on T.B.'s face. For a moment, they stared at each other as if sharing some private joke. Around them, the girls, eyes shining, leaned forward.

"All right," said Jake, "that's far enough, pal." Intending to push them apart and walk between them, he put his hands on two of the girls' shoulders. The girls happened to be Megumi and Cassandra, who rounded on him.

"Stay back!" Cassandra said.

"Yeah, *pervert!*" cried Megumi.

"Outta the way!" Jake shouted.

Megumi trembled but then thrust out her jaw and straightened her back. "You don't scare me, Jake!"

Perhaps it was because of all the time he'd spent recently with girls who could benchpress a Mack truck, or maybe it was just because he was angry, but he didn't back off. Instead, he grabbed Megumi under the ribs, picked her up, half turned, and set her back down. Then he walked toward T.B.

With a shriek, Megumi punched him in a shoulder blade— but then sucked in her breath and squeezed her bruised hand between her thighs. Jake would have ignored this, but Cassandra scratched him with her nails.

"Hey!" Jake shouted. "Hey! Stop it!"

The other girls swarmed. Surrounded by angry, screaming females striking him from every direction, he put up his hands to protect his face but continued walking.

Someone's ankle caught his. Off-balance already from the repeated blows, he tripped. Staggering straight into T.B., he knocked him away from Chelsea and tumbled to the ground on top of him.

It took Jake a moment to assess what had happened, especially since so many things demanded his attention: Multiple girls punched him in the back or shoulders and called him by a long list of names that demeaned his masculinity and suggested certain anatomical inadequacies. Underneath him lay a boy, remarkably light and skinny, who stared up at him with round, liquid eyes that were astonishingly pretty—and in which Jake could see the reflection of his own befuddled face. Besides that, Jake's left hand had landed on T.B.'s chest, and he could feel, through T.B.'s shirt, some strange undergarment like a tight band of cloth enwrapping his torso. And under that—

"Get off him!" Megumi screamed in Jake's ear.

Suddenly, T.B. released a frightened and decidedly high-pitched wail. He flailed.

Once Jake leaped up, the girls clustered around T.B.; Cassandra and Megumi hugged him tightly while, with shoulders hunched, he shuddered and wept.

Jake simply blinked. He stared down at his left hand, at the lines in his palm and at his fingertips, as if he couldn't quite believe they were his.

"Jerk!" Megumi screamed at him. "Pervert! Loser! Creep!" Kneeling over T.B., she brought his head to her chest and rocked him like a frightened child.

Still hurling epithets in Jake's direction, Megumi and Cassandra helped T.B. off the floor and hauled him toward the arcade's front. The rest of the girls trailed after. Some cursed at Jake as they passed, but others glanced at him wistfully before following the rest. In less than a minute, they had all left.

Jake still stared at his hand.

Ralph grunted. "Huh. That guy's a total wuss."

Jake hardly heard him. "Yeah . . ."

Ralph ran a hand through his unkempt hair. "I don't understand what girls see in him. I mean, he's such a dweeb, but he's like this at school too: There's *always* a bunch of groupies around him. I just don't get it."

Jake rolled his tongue in his mouth. "Yeah . . ."

Ralph clapped Jake's shoulder. "You okay, dude? What's up?"

Jake flexed his fingers, still staring at his hand. "He feels somehow . . ."

"What?"

Jake paused, again rolled his tongue, and said, "Squishy."

Ralph laughed. "That sissy boy probably just needs to work out."

"Maybe that's it."

Still leaning against the elevated cage, Chelsea tapped her fists together and chuckled. "Well, *that* was certainly entertaining. Thanks, boys. I got my money's worth today." She squeezed her eyes shut, stuck her hands behind her head, and stretched. "Hm, he's cute, but players like him aren't my type. If he'd *really* tried to kiss me, I would have frickin' belted him one."

She walked to Jake, draped her arms over his shoulders, and leaned her head on his chest.

Standing to one side with a fist on a hip and a sneer on her mouth, Dana snorted.

"I think *you* got more action with him than I did," Chelsea said as she gave Jake a light squeeze. "Maybe I should be jealous."

He glanced down at her. "Maybe *I* should be."

"Maybe. I like you jealous."

A smug smile settled on her mouth as she gazed up at him. Her ice-blue eyes were small, and they lacked that deep, reflective quality T.B.'s eyes had. Still, they were pretty.

He smiled and brushed a strand of hair out of her face. "Oh, Chelsea."

He leaned down to kiss her, but she clamped a hand over his mouth.

"I don't think so," she said. "I'm not happy with you today, Jake Blatowski, and I'm not sharing my first kiss with a guy I'm not happy with."

She still held T.B.'s rose, so she bent the stem and tucked it into the breast pocket of his shirt. "Tell you what—you take me to that movie next weekend and treat me right for a change, and then we'll see."

He pulled her fingers from his mouth. "Your hand stinks."

"Yeah, it's those gloves from the game." She drew back from him but raked her fingernails lightly down his arms and squeezed his fingertips before she stepped away. "Anyway, it's been fun, boys, but I'm heading out."

Jake cleared his throat and tugged his collar. "You want me to walk you—?"

"No, Jake. I want you to get your act together." Chelsea snapped her fingers toward Ralph. "You. C'mon, let's go."

Ralph's eyebrows shot up. "You're going with me? Why?"

"Because I'm going to your house. Cissie and Jamie invited me over."

Ralph sighed and stuck his hands in his pockets. He gave Jake a wry smile. "With her, it's like I got *eight* sisters."

Jake ran a hand through his hair. "Yeah. Have fun."

"Not likely. I'll spend the rest of the day trying to evade the estrogen brigade. At least they can't hold me down to the floor and put makeup on me like they did when I was seven."

"Do you wanna—?"

Ralph shook his head. "Nah, I really should go do my home-work. Got a science project I need to start on."

Jake grunted. "Must be nice."

"Don't they give you homework in elementary?"

"Yeah, but it takes me all of five minutes. Last one was a word scramble."

Ralph laughed. "Take care, man."

"Take care."

Jake watched as Ralph followed Chelsea out the front door. After that, he stood in a sea of pops and bleeps and skinny boys hunkered over screens. It seemed quiet now that all the girls had left—all but one, that is.

He turned to Dana, who still stared at him with half-lidded green eyes.

"Why are you here?" he asked.

"You're a loser," she replied.

"So are you. You lost to Chelsea."

She scowled, looked down at the floor, and muttered, "Not yet, I haven't."

"What was that?"

"Nothing."

Jake shrugged. "Hey, don't worry. *Everyone* loses to Chelsea. She's a hardcore fighting-game geek."

Dana's scowl deepened, and she thrust her lip out.

Jake laughed. "What's wrong? You upset that T.B. didn't give you your first kiss?"

With a familiar throat rasp, she stomped away from him but

stuck her nose in the air. "That wouldn't have been my first kiss."

He chuckled and leaned back against an arcade machine. "Oh? Did some boy peck you on the playground in kindergarten? I guess I'm not surprised. You're certainly cute enough."

She shot him a glare but then stuck up her nose again. "Nope. He was older—*way* older. And he was much, much cooler than you."

Jake laughed again, and Dana's ears turned red.

"Okay, sure," he said. "So, do you need me to walk you home?"

Her eyes narrowed. "I'm not going home. I'm gonna go skate."

"But you hurt yourself—"

"It's just a scratch."

He shrugged. "Okay, at least do me a favor and start with something simpler than a half-pipe."

She grunted.

"And put on some sunscreen."

She snarled.

He chuckled. "Maybe I really should have kissed your owie, huh? Then I could have been your second kiss."

The red in her ears spread down to her cheeks. She clenched her fists. "It wouldn't be my *second,* either!"

"Oh yeah? Sounds like you're quite the little heartbreaker. Then maybe third—"

"Not third!"

"Wow, so you get *all* the boys?"

"It was the same guy," she said as she again raised her nose into the air. *"Bunches* of times. Over and over." She lifted one eyebrow. "I lost count."

Now he bent over a game console, and his shoulders shook as he laughed. The red in Dana's face deepened.

As he wiped his eyes, Jake said, "Actually, I'm not sure I should find this funny. Who exactly is this dirty old—?"

"Don't talk about my dad like that!"

Her eyes widened, and she gasped. She clapped a hand over her mouth.

Jake clutched his stomach and slid to the floor in a fit of guffaws lasting almost a minute. Once he could breathe, he gasped, "Dads don't count!"

Dana ground her teeth, and her face turned so red it was almost purple. "Do too! Dads totally count!"

"Nah, you're a girl, so only boys count—"

"Dads *are* boys, stupid-head!" She kicked him in the ribs, and then she donned her helmet and stomped flat-footed toward the front. After she snatched up her skateboard and hugged it to her chest, she spun around and shrieked over the din, "And you still owe me a juice box, *jerk!*"

She left, slamming the door behind her.

Jake winced as he rubbed his sore side. Gamers gave him cautious glances or disapproving stares when he staggered toward the exit.

As Jake made his way out, Adrian leaned on his counter and said, "You're smooth with the ladies, Blatowski."

Jake paused in the doorway and nodded. "Yeah, maybe I should take lessons from T.B."

Adrian chuckled.

Before he walked into the street, Jake again stared down at his left hand and slowly clenched it. Something felt weird, but he couldn't quite put his finger on it.

Players one and two, please enter your rumble cage and don your virtual-reality headsets and battle gloves!

FIVE

FATED

For reasons unclear to him, Jake didn't want to go home.

After he left the arcade, he wandered around Juban. He watched the people bustling in and out of the shops, watering their lawns, pushing their children in baby strollers.

Where a curve in the road wound around the shoulder of a hill, he could look down over the rooftops and glimpse the deep city. He saw stretches of rubble. Columns of smoke rose into the sky and spread into anvils as they reached some change in the atmosphere. Helicopters hovered around the skyscrapers of the financial district. The howitzers atop the towers pointed upwards, their barrels silent but vigilant. A submarine sat in port in the distant bay, presumably restocking before returning to the endless patrol of the watery western perimeter.

Juban, however, looked as it always did—peaceful, serene. It had suffered damage, of course, but the damage was minimal: A few houses smashed, a few roads bombed, a few people dead.

Hardly worth noticing. It was quiet except for the faint hum of traffic.

Jake wandered with shoulders hunched and hands in pockets. He thought about Grease Pencil Marionette with her fierce embrace and warm kisses. She was the first girl he had ever kissed, assuming that kissing a gynoid counted. He wondered if kissing a real girl would feel the same way.

He thought about Rifle Maiden and wondered what it might be like to kiss her, what with her easy grin and whimsical buck-teeth. He liked her freckles. She was pretty in a girl-next-door kind of way.

He even thought about Miss Percy, his schoolteacher, and how good it had felt to hold her when the robot dinosaurs from Andromeda invaded, though he'd been terrified at the time. She felt cozy and soft in his arms, as if her body were made to fit his. It wasn't hard to imagine pulling her to himself on a cold night.

He also thought about Lady Paladin Andalusia, who looked so regal in her shining armor. While she clutched his hand, her blood had poured from the gaping wound in her chest. A devout Christian to the end, she had made her last confession to him, a confession as innocent and sweet as a young child's. He wondered if, had he had his wits about him, he could have saved her life.

He even found himself thinking about T.B., the curiously girlish boy with the large, dark eyes. T.B.'s lashes were long and feathery, and Jake had not missed the way red had suffused his cheeks whenever he glanced at Ralph. Something was definitely unusual about T.B., though Jake still couldn't figure out what. He had felt soft under Jake's hands—almost but not quite like Miss Percy.

In the aftermath of the recent destruction, many public

terminals weren't working, but Jake found a functional one near a donut shop. After proving he was human with cumbersome tests, he asked the terminal where he could get his zombie monitor removed. It directed him to the nearest police station.

The station was busy, and Jake was a low priority: Once he told the sergeant at the front desk why he was there, he had to sit in a folding chair for three hours. Finally, a cop walked up to him and, without a word, clamped his wrist in some clunky device like an oversized garlic press. With a few clicks and a grinding sound, the monitor fell away.

As Jake walked out, he rubbed his wrist, which felt oddly light and cool. It had been three days, and he had escaped infection.

He laughed quietly. *I probably used up a lifetime's supply of luck this week.*

Finally, he thought about Dana. Everything that happened this week happened because he followed Dana after school. Trying to figure her out—that was the excuse he had used. He wanted to know why she acted as she did, why she was the way she was.

Or so he told himself.

His mother had another theory of why he followed her, but that one didn't sound right either.

He didn't know why he did it. But he had run after her yet again when he saw her at the skate park. He did it, and he didn't know why—but he also didn't know if he could stop.

WHEN HE GOT HOME, THE SUN WAS DIPPING TOWARD THE BAY. He pushed open the front door to find his mother and father bustling back and forth in the great room.

"Kosmy, have you seen my purse?" his mother cried as she rummaged in the front-hall closet.

His father fumbled with a necktie as he walked out of his office. "No. Have you seen my tie pin?"

Jake's mother stuck her head out of the closet and said, "Jake! Jake, where have you been? And why aren't you dressed?"

"I am dressed."

She merely shook her head, sighed, and returned to her archaeological excavation amongst the winter coats.

"Put on a tie," said his father as he finally gave up on his own.

Jake frowned. "Why?"

His mother climbed out of the closet like a man crawling out of a winter igloo. "What do you mean, *why?* We're seeing our councilman tonight! Do you want him to think I let my son dress like a hobo?"

"Huh? When—?"

"They announced it this afternoon," said Jake's father as he pushed past his wife, reached into the closet, and retrieved a light overcoat. "After those robot dinosaurs and then the zombies, the City Fathers had an emergency meeting. Our councilman just called a town hall, and everyone in Juban is invited. They're making an announcement."

Jake scratched his head. "They're not going to fit everyone in Juban into the meeting hall."

"Jake, don't slouch," said his mother, "and that doesn't matter." She patted his chest in a vain attempt to remove the wrinkles from his shirt. "Get a dress shirt and a tie—and some nice slacks, would you, please?"

He made a last-ditch appeal to his age: "Why do I have to go? I'm just a kid."

"Because your father and I are going, and we want our councilman to know we're doing our duty and having *children*—and that we know how to dress them properly. Now go find a nice shirt."

JAKE FOUND A SERVICEABLE SHIRT AND TIE, BUT HIS SLACKS weren't ironed. They'd have to do anyway. He carried his uncomfortable dress shoes down to the front door, where his mother insisted he put on an overcoat smarter than the windbreaker he'd been wearing. When he searched the closet, all he could find was a double-breasted trench coat his father hadn't worn in years, so he donned it, checked himself in the first-floor bathroom mirror, and concluded that he looked as if he were playing dress-up as a film-noir detective. The coat was too large, and it made his shoulders look broad. All he lacked was a fedora.

"Are we ready to go?" yelled his father, who wore a more sensible blazer over a sweater vest.

Jake forced his feet into his shoes without bothering to untie the laces first, and then his mother hustled him out the door. He felt foolish in the trench coat, but wearing it was hardly the most foolish thing he'd done recently.

It was only a few blocks to the assembly hall, which stood adjacent to Juban Park. Juban's planners had built the park to give children a space to play, though this had proved unwise in the long run, as it had more than once in the last few decades become a haunt for ghouls and vampires.

An evening breeze was blowing, but the big overcoat made it pleasant. The streets looked inviting and clean, and many people, mostly families walking in groups, made their way on foot to the assembly hall.

The hall was a squat, cylindrical building. In keeping with the popular style of Streamline Moderne, a chrome fascia adorned the cornice of the roof, below which lay a row of port-hole windows. Beneath that, however, the architect had given up: From the windows down, most of the building was a flat expanse of tan stucco, though a distinctive one-story lobby jutted from the side, and topping the lobby was a series of decorative fins set with speed lines.

The evening was mild. The sky was a deep, fiery orange, and a cool breeze rustled the leaves. The oaks had turned the same color as Dana's hair, and Jake mused that she'd probably look good in autumn colors. It was too bad she insisted on wearing black outside of school.

They passed through the lobby and into the auditorium's cavernous interior, where plush seats stood in staggered rows above a semicircular stage. The room was spacious, but the stage was small to produce the illusion of an intimate setting. A harsh spotlight shone on a solitary wooden podium.

Jake had been to a few of these town halls before. His parents insisted on attending whenever possible, and they also insisted on taking him along. It made him uncomfortable not only because it was boring but because he knew his mom and dad were showing him off, half in pride and half in embarrassment: Although she didn't bring it up often, it was a sore point with his mother that she had only managed to have one child.

In some vague, indistinct way, Jake thought he was at fault for this.

Near the back of the auditorium, someone had set up a row of tables with ice water, coffee, bagels, and pastries. Jake hadn't eaten since breakfast, so he tucked in. After he devoured his fourth bagel, his mother seized him by the collar and hauled him to a seat.

They sat near the front. Looking back over his shoulder, Jake spotted Ralph, with probably half a gallon of pomade slicking down his rebellious hair, ensconced with his parents among his seven sisters. Two of those sisters, Jamie and Clarissa, were in middle school and were close friends with Chelsea. They waved at Jake, and he waved back.

Ralph's youngest sister was Alexis, age four. She had butterfly clips holding her curly hair, and she wore a red dress with white flounces, white stockings, and a pair of black Mary Janes. When she noticed Jake, she clopped clumsily down the steps and pushed her way into the row where Jake sat with his parents. Hands clasped before her in a show of politeness, she looked up at him and lisped solemnly, "I asked if I could sit with you, and they said yes."

"Sure," Jake answered. "Have a seat."

Clearly pleased, she pulled herself up into the chair beside him, squirmed until she was comfortable, and beamed at him.

He chuckled to himself.

It crossed his mind that any of Ralph's sisters might be magical girls, and he stopped laughing. He had grown up with Ralph and all these girls living just down the block. In elementary school, he had crushed on Ralph's oldest sister, Sandra, who was now in college. In middle school, he had changed Alexis's diapers. Back on Monday, he had needled Ralph with the possibility that he might have a magical girl for a sister—but Jake hadn't seriously considered the possibility at the time.

The thought of any of these girls in mortal danger made him sick.

His attention shifted to the stage: Polite but muted applause rippled across the auditorium when Juban's councilman, Hain Järvinen, walked in. Young for a politician, he was clean-shaven with a round face and hair in a short, nondescript cut. He wore a simple black suit with a red tie, and everything about him bespoke orderliness and business—a living symbol of the button-down community he represented. Just as parents brought children to this town hall to show them to Mr. Järvinen, Järvinen sought to project an image of wholesomeness and propriety both to those higher up in the chain of government and to the people he represented.

Juban was an experiment, and the experimenters were at pains to make it look presentable.

Järvinen tapped the mike to make sure it was on and said in a pleasant baritone, "Thank you for coming on such short notice. Let's open with a prayer."

Almost everyone in the room made the sign of the Moon Princess. Jake did as well, though his opinion on the Princess's divinity remained agnostic.

"Your Majesty," Järvinen said with head bowed, "we implore you tonight to watch over these proceedings and to grant us the wisdom to remember those virtues of love and justice you fought for while on Earth. May your kingdom come, may you lend strength to your magical girls, may the forces of evil meet their final defeat, and may we all abide with you in the glory of your New Tokyo until the heat death of the universe. Amen."

The last word echoed through the auditorium as those gathered repeated it.

Järvinen made the sign of the Moon Princess and then leaned heavily on the podium. He spoke quietly, but the PA system made his words crystal clear: "As you know, our city just came through one of its worst weeks in many years. Two *kaiju* struck, first in the Godai District and then right here in Juban. Shortly afterwards, robot dinosaurs from space, followed immediately by a demon infestation and zombie swarm—"

A hand went up in the audience.

"Yes, I'll take questions in a moment," Järvinen said. "As I was saying, robot dinosaurs from space, followed immediately by a demon infestation and zombie swarm, decimated large portions of Urbanopolis. We lost many good people, and we lost many good magical girls. But, as always, humanity stays strong. We band together, and we come through. We put aside our differences—whatever those may be—and join hands to remember that, no matter what might divide us, what unites us is still greater: We are human. We are one species, one people, and one city, with one Princess."

Four more hands went up.

"I'll take questions in a moment."

Järvinen paused to mop his forehead with a handkerchief as if the harsh spotlight were roasting him.

"Now, it's no secret that Juban has been especially blessed. This is one of the newest communities in the city, and it is something of a test—or an experiment, if you will. In the early days, when the fires of the First Invasion raged around humanity's last survivors, when people crowded together in grimy, overfull neighborhoods with as many as fifty living together in a small room, no one imagined that we might one day be able to expand, that we might be able even to prosper."

He paused again to wipe his forehead. "Some, of course, thought we wouldn't survive, that humanity was doomed. Yet survive we did, and more than that, we have flourished. We have slowly, inch by inch, begun to reclaim the Wastes from the monsters that ravaged them. People no longer have to live on top of one another. We now have houses, parks, neighborhoods—just as we had in the old times before the universe tried to slay us all. And it is thanks to the hard work and innovation of those who call Urbanopolis their home. People from many cultures and many walks of life have moved into Juban to live side by side in peace. You are a testament to the harmony of the human race, a harmony that, before the Moon Princess came to show us the way, no one imagined possible."

He cleared his throat, and seven more hands went up.

"In a moment, please. Now, Juban is prosperous. No one can deny that. Those who can afford to live here are those who have been successful, whether in industry or invention or subterranean agriculture, and they have moved into this clean and beautiful neighborhood to raise their families in relative comfort—"

Mr. Yeboah, a retired gentleman, rail-thin and with a heavily seamed face, stood up from his seat. He lived three blocks down from the Blatowskis, and Jake often saw him watering his lawn on Sundays. Yeboah cleared his throat loudly and boomed in a gravelly voice, "Mr. Järvinen, what exactly are you asking us to *do?*"

Tottering slightly, Yeboah waved a skinny, liver-spotted arm at the people gathered in the seats as he added, "We don't need all these words. We know what Juban is. We know what Urbanopolis is. What we don't know is what the Fathers *want.*"

Järvinen shuffled a stack of notecards, straightened his tie, and then bent lower over his microphone before he said, "Very well, Mr. Yeboah, I understand your concern. I met you and your wife at the *jichinsai* for the public pool, if you recall—"

Yeboah raised two shaky, arthritic hands over his head and then brought them down in a gesture of dismissal. "Mr. Järvinen, we don't care about that. We know you, and you know us. But we need to know what you *want.*"

For a minute, the hall was silent.

Järvinen cleared his throat and straightened his tie again. "All right, I'll tell you. Despite the attack by the *kaiju,* Juban escaped the recent unpleasantness largely unscathed. Many of our neighbors, however, were not so lucky. Urbanopolis is going to rebuild as quickly as possible, but many are without homes. For this reason, the City Fathers have decided to move some from the most heavily affected areas to the least affected—"

The room erupted with angry shouts. Several shook their fists or rose from their seats.

Instinctively, Jake slid downward in his chair. He glanced at his parents: They sat frozen, their backs ramrod straight and their hands grasping their chairs' armrests. Then he glanced at Alexis: She was asleep, her head tilted to one side and a line of drool running from her mouth. A small smile sat on her face.

Jake sighed.

"Order, please," said Järvinen. "Calm down. We can't make any progress without good order—"

The yelling got louder.

Miss Hatakeyama, a young woman who'd recently moved to Juban after making her fortune improving the efficiency of the hydroponic farms, stood up and cried, "What about our *culture?*"

Järvinen raised a hand. "Everyone, be quiet, please."

The shouting died down to a low buzz.

Järvinen raised his voice over the remaining din, "That's a good question. The Fathers are very concerned about respecting the unique cultures of each of Urbanopolis's districts—and about preserving as much of human diversity as possible. Our hope is that this will be a short-term solution. Displaced people will move into temporary housing and then move back when repairs are finished. To make this happen as smoothly as possible, we are asking smaller families to consider doubling up. If you can take some of your neighbors into your home, that will free more living space for those who, for the time being, have no home."

The noise in the room rose in volume again.

"Also," Järvinen added, his voice straining to carry over the crowd, "to avoid creating any needless conflict, it is our intent to move displaced people into the nearest possible unaffected district. Little India has suffered a great deal, so it will be from Little India that Juban receives—"

Mr. Chakraborty, surrounded by his wife, five sons, and three daughters, hopped to his feet, thrust a fist into the air, and shouted, "Little India is nothing like Juban!"

The noise grew louder still, and now Järvinen's voice cracked as he struggled to talk over the crowd. "Yes, we are aware of the difference in cultures. However, Juban is right on the border of Little India, and if we can move people into apartments unaffected by the *kaiju,* that will be relatively painless! Juban is a new district, certainly, but the Fathers view it with as much reverence and respect as they view the older—"

Up jumped Mrs. Müller, middle-aged and slightly portly. Waving her hands, she shrieked, "Is this because we're *mixed-race?"*

The room fell silent.

There it is. Somebody said it.

Jake sank even lower in his seat. He felt ill and wondered if it were something in the bagels.

After half a minute, Järvinen said, "Listen, everyone, the Fathers do not—I repeat, do not—view any genetic sequence as more important than any other. Of course, there are breeding incentives for people with unusual traits—pure Mongolians, Afridis, Ashkenazi Jews, and the like—but that's because they're rare, not because they're superior. We want to preserve as much of mankind as we can, and that includes you. There is no eugenics in this city; the Moon Princess was quite clear about that. This is not an attempt to replace you or breed you out. This is just an attempt to find housing for a lot of people who need it."

The dead silence continued after his speech ended.

He shuffled, straightened his tie, and cleared his throat one more time. "We are not asking you to move in with strangers. We only ask you to move in with friends and family so we can find room. That's all. Once the repairs and rebuilding are done, everyone will move back—because we want to preserve the integrity of our districts, Juban included."

"That's what this is about, isn't it?" Chakraborty yelled. "We're mixed, so we don't have any of this so-called 'integrity!'"

The room erupted with noise again.

Now Järvinen's air of reserved dignity dropped away. He clutched the podium and shouted back, "Everybody, quiet! Pipe down! Now, you listen! *Everyone* wants Juban to succeed! *Nobody* wants any part of this city or any part of the human race to fail! Don't you understand that?"

He slapped a hand down on his lectern, and the noise died. Baring his teeth and leaning forward, he yelled, "You really think the City Fathers want to replace you? Want you to *disappear?* You have this completely backwards! In fact, the *real* problem is that Juban is not having *enough children!* This is the fifth-wealthiest district in the entire city. It should be *full* of children! Just because you can afford the small-family tax doesn't mean you're exempt from your duty! You make your money, you move up here, and you buy big houses—and those houses are *empty!"*

Jake, now almost horizontal in his seat, glanced at his mother. She sobbed into a handkerchief.

"The Fathers want to see *more* of you, not fewer!" Järvinen cried.

He took a few deep breaths, and his voice grew quiet again. "I . . . apologize for my outburst. This has been a good year, demographically speaking." He cleared his throat and once more straightened his tie. "It was looking for a while as if we might break replacement rate just like last year. It's been a decade since Urbanopolis managed that two years in a row, you know. Now, of course, it's probably not going to happen, what with the death toll from . . ."

The grave-like silence of the room stretched out. Järvinen dabbed a sleeve at his face, and his voice wavered. "It's a real testament to our ingenuity and bravery that we've managed to expand our territory even as our population has shrunk. It really is . . ."

His voice trailed off as he squeezed his eyes shut and rubbed his temples. "I'm sorry, but this is out of my hands and over my head. The Fathers have made their decision. This meeting is simply to tell you it's going to happen. We ask you to open your houses to your neighbors so we can move others into your neighborhoods. If you do this voluntarily, it will be easier."

He fingered his tie one last time. "Also, please note, the

Fathers decided—despite my objection—that no demonstration permits will be issued to anyone who wants to protest this new policy. Please also remember that demonstrating without a permit is a form of treason, and treason is the one crime in Urbanopolis that merits capital punishment. That is all for now. You may formally lodge any complaints at City Hall. You'll receive more extensive and concrete instructions in the mail."

With that, he turned around and left the stage.

The room erupted again.

As PEOPLE SHOUTED OVER ONE ANOTHER, JAKE'S MOTHER AND father huddled together. They mumbled back and forth in what Jake had come to think of, from an early age, as their "concerned" voices.

His mother continued dabbing her eyes with her handkerchief. Her voice trembled as she said, "What do you think, Kosmy?"

His father shook his head. "It's a big responsibility, Silvia. Who do we know—?"

"We certainly have room—"

"Do we—?"

"There's the second downstairs   "

"That's my den. What about the second upstairs—?"

"That's my sewing room—"

"We'd have to give up something—"

"We could give up both—"

"Should we—?

"We should."

Jake's mother's knuckles turned white as she clutched her

handkerchief. She wiped her eyes and said again, "We should. We should, Kosmy. It's our duty."

Jake slumped still lower and stared at the acoustic tiles in the ceiling. *Holy Princess. Are they serious?*

He meant to keep quiet but instead found himself saying, "I think we should lodge a complaint."

His head buzzed.

His parents turned and looked down at him, faces blank but expectant.

He licked his lips and added, "I mean, it's just a thought."

"You don't want to do this?" his mother asked with a cracking voice that suggested the tears were about to start again. "For the city?" Then she tried what she presumably believed would persuade him: *"What would Pretty Dynamo think?"*

Jake, who didn't care what Pretty Dynamo thought, turned up his hands. "If I asked her, she'd probably just say, 'you're stupid,' or something like that. I doubt she has a serious opinion on the subject."

His father frowned.

"No, really, Dad. That's how she talks. Magical girls aren't the perfect little goddesses they show on TV."

His father's frown deepened into a scowl. "Well, that *Sukeban Tsubasa* certainly isn't, but I think we can expect better from Pretty Dynamo."

Since Jake had criticized magical girls, his father was plainly uninterested in any more of Jake's comments, so he turned back to his wife and said, "Do we know someone, anyone, who would want to move in?"

She wrung her hands. "Well, I'm not sure . . . most of our neighbors have quite a few kids. What about the Willikers?"

"Mom," said Jake, still staring at the ceiling, "Ralph has seven sisters. One of them is drooling right next to me."

"That *would* be cramped," his mother replied.

His father said, "What about that . . . what's her name? Chelsea?"

Jake's mother lowered her voice. "Dear, Jake *can't* live with his girlfriend."

His father scratched his head. "Why not?"

"It's not appropriate."

"But they'd be in separate—"

"Dear, it's not appropriate."

She turned to Jake again. "Honey, do you know anyone at school? Any kids from small—?"

Jake sighed. "I haven't really bothered to get to know the kids at school."

"Well, no, I suppose you haven't."

Jake interlaced his fingers before his face as his parents continued debating.

He rolled his tongue around in his mouth and, before he realized what he was saying, formed the words, "Um . . . you know, I do know *one* kid, sort of . . ."

His parents grew silent.

He cleared his throat. "I mean, I don't know her real well. And I guess I don't know how big her family is, but she's never mentioned any brothers or sisters, so—"

"She?" said his mom. "It's a she?"

"Yeah."

"Is she here?"

"I don't know."

But I can spot her if she is.

Jake stood, turned, and scanned the room. The noise had

reduced to an angry buzz now that most of the citizens had filed out. A few stood at their seats and debated with harsh whispers and wild gesticulations. Some drank coffee and chatted near the refreshment table in the back. Others shuffled in a queue toward the lobby.

Almost immediately, Jake's eyes latched onto a distinctive spot of red.

He swallowed. "I don't know if she's here or not, but that's gotta be her mom."

He pointed. His parents rose from their seats and followed his finger with their eyes.

"Oh my," said his mother, putting a hand to her throat.

Near the back of the auditorium stood a woman slender and tall, perhaps as tall as Jake. She looked young. Well proportioned, she wore a simple empire-waist gown of moss green. The gown was sleeveless and displayed long arms that were slim but firmly built. A narrow face, high cheekbones, and a slightly aquiline nose lent her an air of strength and nobility, though that same nose ended in an upturned bulb suggesting girlishness. A cascade of thick, wavy red hair, like a waterfall on fire, tumbled to well below her waist. Her bright green eyes turned up at the corners and rested under dark lashes.

She dominated the room, and every eye drew toward her. She stood aloof, yet her presence was inescapable. She was like a queen among her subjects—or like a goddess among men.

Wow, Jake thought as his heart missed a beat, *is that what Dana's gonna look like when she—?*

He rapped his knuckles against his temple to halt that thought.

His mother leaned toward him and whispered, "You know her?"

He tugged on his collar. "Uh, no, but I know her daughter."

"How can you tell—?"

"How many redheads do you think there are in Juban?"

Besides, she basically looks like a big Dana.

"Well," said his mother as she tried in vain to smooth a few wrinkles out of the sleeves of her dress, "that's good enough for me. Let's go introduce ourselves."

Jake's father scowled. "Now?"

"Yes, Kosmy, now!"

They marched up the steps toward the back of the auditorium. The redheaded woman grew only more majestic and intimidating as they drew nearer, though once they were one row of seats away, a splatter of freckles across her cheeks became apparent, softening her appearance.

"What's her name?" Jake's mother whispered.

"Volt," Jake replied.

His mother surveyed the woman for another second, took a deep breath, and stepped up. "Um, excuse me, Mrs. Volt—?"

It occurred to Jake that this woman looked too young to be Dana's mother. She was an adult, obviously older than he was, so he hadn't thought about it at first, but she was probably only in her early twenties.

But now it was too late to say anything about it.

The woman turned toward them, and her air of haughty aloofness disappeared when her mouth split in a toothy grin. Her teeth were straight and white, but they were also quite large. "Oh, *hello,*" she said. "It's so nice to see you!"

Perhaps taken aback by the warmth of the greeting, Jake's mother blinked for a moment before she said, "Uh, shake or bow—?"

"Oh, we *hug* where I'm from!" The woman grabbed Jake's

mother in a bear hug and shook her back and forth. "I'm Mildred, Mildred F. Volt! But you can call me Millie. And you must be—?"

Jake's mother disentangled herself from the awkward hug. "Oh, my! Well, I'm Silvia Blatowski."

The two women took each other's hands, and what next passed between them was an exchange of breathless pleasantries, gossip, and bright laughter. Jake watched and listened, but this ritual of feminine greeting barely registered on his male brain. He didn't quite understand what they said, and perhaps he couldn't.

Then he noticed Dana, who stood behind Millie as if using her for a shield. In one hand, like a much younger child, Dana held a fistful of Millie's dress. In the other, she clutched a purse probably containing Tesla, her familiar. Looking small and shy, she peeked at him from around Millie's waist. Her green eyes were half-lidded, and her lip curled in its customary sneer. She had caked on thick makeup to hide her freckles. She wore a black dress with a laced bodice and several layers of ruffled chiffon that filled out its knee-length skirt. Around her calves and hanging over her sneakers, she wore black leather leggings held together with nickel buckles. On her head, she had a fascinator made of black silk folded to look like a cluster of roses, from which hung a transparent mourning veil.

Holy Princess, Dana, why not just slap a sign on your back that says I'M A MAGICAL GIRL?

Jake's mother said to Millie, "I think your daughter knows my son Jake—"

Jake expected Millie to say she was actually Dana's sister, but she instead pointed her toothy grin his way, and her green eyes sparkled as she cried, "Oh, so *this* is Jake! Yes, my little Dana just can't stop talking about the 'big kid' in her class!"

Dana's face fell, and she tugged at Millie's sleeve. "Mo-o-oom," she hissed, *"noooo!"*

Whoa. So this really is her mother.

Millie put an arm around Dana's shoulders. Dana leaned against her and stuck out her lip in a pout.

"I just want you to know, Mrs. Blatowski," said Millie, still grinning like a madwoman, "how much I appreciate what you do. I know it's not easy"—she leaned forward, put a hand beside her mouth, and whispered loudly—"you know, raising a child with *special needs.*"

Jake's mother frowned. "But Jake isn't a special-needs child."

"Oh?" Millie looked down at Dana. "Honey, you told me he was retarded."

"He is," Dana replied as she glared at Jake.

Millie slid both arms around Dana's neck. "Uh oh, someone's crabby. We need to get you home and put you to bed, don't we?"

Dana, lip outthrust, shook her head. Still staring at Jake, she said, "Who are you supposed to be, anyway? Sam Spade?"

Jake frowned. "Huh? Oh, you mean the trench coat." He thrust his hands into the coat's deep pockets. "Yeah, I'm Sam Spade. 'Two lonely people on a hill of beans, which are the stuff dreams are made of' . . . or something like that. So what are *you* supposed to be? Are you going to a Goth funeral, or are you trying to look like Sword Seamstress?"

Dana's eyes narrowed, and her teeth clenched. She looked ready to release a barb, but the presence of her mother apparently stopped her.

"Oh, you're so cute!" Millie cried. "Like two peas in a pod. I have to pinch *both* your cheeks!"

Lightning quick, she clamped her slim fingers onto Jake's face and shook him until his brain rattled. Dana, however, she only gave a light pat.

Once she let go, Jake gingerly rubbed his cheek, sure he'd have a bruise.

Not that it mattered. He had plenty of bruises already.

"Mrs. Volt," said Jake's mother, "I don't think there's a way to say this that isn't awkward, so I'll just say it: We were talking about doing what the Fathers are asking—having someone move in. We have a large house, and it's just the three of us, and we were discussing who we know, and Jake thought of you and your daughter—"

Millie laughed quietly. "Oh, *there's* an idea." Her smile remained, but it became strained. "Truth is, I was thinking about moving out of Juban, maybe into Little Europe. Dana and I don't fit in here." She leaned forward and lowered her voice again. "You know, because we're white."

Jake's mother gasped. "Oh! Oh no, no! We don't see things like that at all! Why, ah"—she put a hand on Jake's shoulder —"Jake's girlfriend is white!"

Sweet Princess, Mom. Don't use Chelsea to show off your open-mindedness.

Millie looked down at Dana, whom she still had caged in her arms. "What do you think, sport? You wanna share a house with the big kid?"

Dana took a few seconds to respond but then firmly shook her head.

Millie laughed and squeezed her. "It's past someone's bedtime. That's what I think." She offered another broad smile, but it now looked weary. "We'd be happy to visit and discuss things further, Mrs. Blatowski. We really would. But I wouldn't want to impose or make trouble—"

"You wouldn't be imposing! We're looking for someone to move in, after all."

"I'd love to discuss it. It might be a great idea. Our apartment's quite small, though it's just Dana and me now since her daddy died." She gave Dana another squeeze.

A knot tightened in Jake's stomach. Pretty Dynamo had hinted something like that. Last week, out on the street—shortly after drubbing him—she began to talk about her father but stopped herself.

Oh man, and I laughed at Dana when she bragged about kissing him. No wonder she got mad.

"I'm so sorry to hear that," Jake's mother said, her eyes moist. She leaned toward Millie with sympathy plain on her face and asked, "Was it monsters?"

Millie's smile fell away.

"I wish it were," she answered. She raised her chin, and her look of power and regality returned. Jake took a step back, awed.

"No," Millie said. "It wasn't monsters that killed my husband and took away Dana's father. It was that *Magical Girl Pretty Dynamo,* and I swear I will never forgive her so long as I live."

SIX

LOST GIRLS

Magical Girl Grease Pencil Marionette remembered.

As on most nights, she stood in the middle of the Moon Princess's chamber and watched emotionlessly as the Princess prepared for bed.

It was a strangely humble ritual—reminiscent, perhaps, of the time when the Moon Princess was a mere mortal. With a basin of water at hand, the Princess sat before her mirror and removed her makeup. She brushed her teeth. Then she sat passively as Marionette brushed out her long, golden hair. She was not a natural blonde, of course: Her black hair had turned to gold when she acquired her magical powers. Unlike most magical girls, she couldn't transform back.

Her hair was long enough to hang to her ankles. She closed her eyes, wrapped her arms around herself, and hummed softly while Marionette worked.

"Shall I sing to you, Your Majesty?" Marionette asked.

"Would you?" the Princess replied.

Marionette loaded up one of the songs listed in her database under the heading LULLABIES. She opened her mouth and sang with mechanically perfect pitch, precisely striking each note from the memorized sheet of music in her head.

The Princess smiled. She had a tight, thin-lipped smile framed by dimples, a smile suggesting deep pain. Although unsure why, Marionette had found herself imitating it.

"You're not putting your heart into it," the Princess whispered.

In both her brushing and her singing, Marionette paused. "I do not understand, Your Majesty."

The Princess laughed with a sound like the tinkling of glass bells. "Yes, you do. You're an artist."

"But I am a machine."

"Why do you hide behind your mechanical façade, little Marionette? Are you afraid of being human?"

"I am not human, Your Majesty."

"Don't you want to be?"

Marionette did not speak for half a minute, but she resumed pulling the brush through the Princess's long, thick locks.

At last, she said, "I am programmed to want it."

"Is *wanting* something a machine can do? Can an inanimate object have desires?"

"Apparently."

The Princess laughed again. She spun on her stool and enclosed Marionette in her arms. For a moment, Marionette stood as still as a mannequin but then stiffly returned the embrace.

"My pet, my pet, my darling Marionette. Do you know how precious you are to me?"

"Yes, Your Majesty."

"Do you really?"

"You've told me, Your Majesty."

"Do you love me too, Marionette?"

"I am programmed to love you, Your Majesty."

The Moon Princess leaned on Marionette's chest and hummed softly. It was the same tune Marionette had been singing a moment before, but different: Some notes were flat, some sharp, and the tempo faltered. Despite the artlessness, there was a *feeling* Marionette's perfect singing hadn't contained—a hint of sweet sadness, a melancholic remembrance of precious things irrevocably lost.

In response to these unexpected emotions, the electroactive polymer in Marionette's throat constricted, and the lubricators in her eyes increased their output.

She parted her lips and sang with the Princess, but now her voice came out scratchy, and she missed notes. She sang imperfectly, but the thudding motor in her chest quickened, and her hands trembled on the Princess's delicate shoulder blades.

The Princess laughed lightly. "You see?" she said as she arose and kissed Marionette's cheek. "You can't sing with only your voice. You must sing from the heart."

"My heart," Marionette answered in a rough whisper, "is a fusion reactor."

Instead of arguing as Marionette expected, the Princess laughed again and grasped Marionette's hands. "Then sing from your fusion reactor. Paint from your fusion reactor. Love from your fusion reactor. Will you do this for me, my little pet?"

Marionette closed her eyes and pulled the Princess closer. "For you, Your Majesty, I would do anything."

The Princess kissed her again. "I am glad to hear it. Come, my pet—it is time for bed."

S‍TILL, M‍ARIONETTE REMEMBERED.

It had been a Sunday afternoon in early spring. The weather was warming up, so Marionette's drafty attic was comfortable again after a terrible winter. Although her joints didn't stiffen in the cold as readily as a human's did, and though she couldn't suffer frostbite or pneumonia, she could still feel miserable. She had spent much of the winter warming her fingers over a cast-iron stove and painting a few strokes at a time before needing to warm her fingers again.

Now down to shirtsleeves and boyshorts, she spent a lazy Sunday in her cot. The paint-flecked bedclothes were in a tangled mess, partly over her and partly under.

Kasumi Sugihara, down to a sports bra and boxers, lay beside her and smoked a cigarette. In her magical form, she was Card Collector Kasumi—but for the moment, she was merely an ordinary fifteen-year-old girl. She and Marionette had wiled away the late morning and much of the afternoon reading magazines, talking about TV dramas, discussing battle tactics, and gossiping about which boys they hated.

Marionette held, balanced on her stomach, a crystal Pontarlier glass of milky absinthe. She gazed at it for half a minute, raised her head, and took a sip. A faintly bitter scent of blended herbs met her olfactory sensors before the drink slipped smoothly down her synthetic throat.

Kasumi sighed out a long, curling stream of smoke. "You drink too much," she said.

"You smoke too much," Marionette replied before she sipped again. "And it doesn't matter how much I drink."

Kasumi snatched the glass from her hand and took a long pull. When she lowered it, she stuck out her tongue. "Blech."

"Your cigarette's ruining the taste, and don't drink it like that." Marionette tried to take the glass back, but Kasumi, with a faint giggle, rolled onto her side, forcing Marionette to reach across her.

"I just don't like licorice," Kasumi said.

"You're gonna be drunk in a second. Give it here."

Marionette took the glass back and tipped the rest of the contents into her mouth.

"Look who's talking," said Kasumi.

"I'm just keeping it away from you. And I can't get drunk."

Marionette flopped back onto her pillow. "But sometimes I wish I could." Turning the glass over in her hands, she watched the light from the window glint off its surface. "Although it doesn't affect me, I have a taste for the stuff. It's another of my father's jokes."

"You don't *have* to do what he programmed into you, do you?"

"I like to. It relaxes me."

"I wish I could relax." Kasumi sat up and stretched her arms over her head before she stubbed out her cigarette in the tray on the nightstand. "I can't believe I'm gonna be doing this for another three years."

With an artist's attention to detail, Marionette's ocular sensors traced the lines of muscle in Kasumi's back. Kasumi was lithe and firmly knit like a ballerina or gymnast. The exertions of the magical form affected the normal body, so most magical girls turned out small, wiry, and solidly muscled.

Marionette wondered for a moment if that was why her father had designed her to look boyish. Art imitating life.

"Is it really so bad?" Marionette asked.

Kasumi kept her back to her and stared at the wisps of smoke rising from the ashtray. "You wouldn't know, would you? You were designed for this stuff."

"I was designed to want to leave it behind, just as you do."

"For what?"

Lying on the bed, Marionette shrugged her shoulders. "Family. Art. What do you want to leave it for?"

Kasumi sighed. "Why are we like this?" She reached behind herself and, for a moment, clumsily ran her fingers over Marionette's waist. She paused for a second and then pushed her hand downward—

Marionette took her fingers, interlaced them with her own, and kissed them. "Kasumi, you know I shut off my sexuality program."

Kasumi grunted and stuck a fresh cigarette in her mouth. She flicked her lighter. "So you say. If that were true, how could you paint?"

"I don't know how it is for real humans, but for me, my artistic impulse is in a separate subroutine."

Kasumi chuckled quietly. "You're harsh. You know most of the girls have a crush on you."

"Some. Not most."

"Still."

Marionette sighed. "It's because I'm more experienced, because I'm in charge, because I look like a boy, and because they're under a lot of stress. They grow out of it."

After a few deep pulls, which quickly created half an inch of ash, Kasumi stubbed her cigarette out, leaving it unfinished. "I won't. I won't grow out of it."

"You will, Kasumi. Give it time."

Kasumi flopped back down onto the bed and pushed against Marionette's side. "No, I've already decided. I'm never getting over you."

"I'm just a machine, you know."

Their fingers were still intertwined, so Kasumi squeezed Marionette's hand. "Then I'll be your heart." She tapped her own chest. "You're alive here. You live in my soul, Marionette, and you always will. Whether you live anywhere else doesn't matter to me."

Kasumi nuzzled her neck, so Marionette sat up and said, "I need another drink."

"You haven't had enough?"

"You've been smoking like a chimney. I'm trying to keep pace. Besides—"

"I know, I know. It doesn't do anything to you."

"It's got a lot of water. Just this afternoon, I've stored up enough deuterium to last me for three months."

She extracted her hand from Kasumi's, climbed from the cot, snatched the lighter from the nightstand, and walked to her kitchenette. There, she performed the elaborate ritual of a Bohemian pour. First, she laid a perforated spoon across the mouth of her glass and set upon it a single sugar cube. Then she poured emerald-green liquor over the cube until she'd filled the spherical bulb at the bottom of the glass.

Once she was done with that, she lit the sugar on fire and watched it burn a faint blue.

Sitting on the counter atop a narrow stand was a drip fountain full of ice water. When the sugar began to sizzle and bubble, Marionette moved the glass under the spigot and let the water snuff the flame. As the water pitter-pattered into the glass, the absinthe changed from emerald green to a murky yellow. After most of the sugar had dissolved, Marionette took up the spoon and stirred, at last shutting off the spigot when the glass was nearly full.

Taking a sip, she contemplated for a moment and nodded in approval.

"Is that fun?" Kasumi asked from the bed.

"Yes. The *Green Lady,* they call her—muse of many an artist. The wormwood gives the mind clarity and insight."

"It tastes gross, but I admit I'm pretty calm."

"I'm not surprised. It's supposed to make you a mellow drunk."

"You wouldn't know."

"No, but I like the look, the smell, the pour, the history. And unlike you, I like the taste."

Kasumi giggled. "Couldn't I be your muse instead?"

"Sorry, but I already have my lady."

Marionette sipped again and changed the subject. "Hey, you figured out those new cards yet?"

Kasumi groaned and rolled over onto her stomach. "Do we have to talk shop?"

"Come on, tell me."

"I don't like them. I'd rather just stick with my starter deck. I mean, all these cards showing up—I hardly know where to put them."

"You're powering up, Kasumi. That's a good thing. Some magical girls have to fight for years without getting a power-up."

"But I get them all the time! Like, I get up one morning, and Marie Laveau's long-lost deck of cursed Tarot cards is just sitting on the front porch. It freaks me out. Don't try to tell me that's *normal.*"

Marionette laughed quietly as she turned the glass in her

hand, watching the light sparkle from the liquor. "Normal's not in the cards for any of us."

With a grunt, Kasumi said, "I think you need to adjust your humor program."

Marionette laughed again. "Kasumi, you're the Card Collector. Magical cards are attracted to you. Just accept it."

Kasumi squirmed. "But I got some new ones recently, and . . . well, they look like regular playing cards, but they're *powerful*. I can *feel* their power. I'm afraid I'll hurt somebody."

Marionette smiled. "Hurt some monster instead. You're always complaining that your starter deck is weak—"

Kasumi flopped onto her back again. "Yeah, I know, but it's not like I have a familiar to help me out. Some ghost wizard just showed up to tell me I have to collect cards, and then he disappeared. It sucks."

"So this latest deck, what is it?"

Kasumi shrugged. "The cards contain elements, and each element is tied to a time of day . . . I can explain it later if you're interested. Not now."

"I'm interested."

"I'm *afraid,* Marionette. I could hurt a *lot* of people with these if I use them wrong."

"Tell me." Marionette sipped her absinthe again. "I'll listen." Another sip. "And you might even inspire me."

Kasumi sat up and pushed her hair out of her eyes as if arising from sleep. She raised one eyebrow, and her voice became sultry as she said, "Maybe I could find a *different* way to inspire you."

Marionette turned her glass, letting the light play across the surface of the absinthe. "Let me paint you," she murmured.

Kasumi smiled; it was a faint smile, enigmatic, with a hint of melancholy. "You've asked me that several times now."

"I meant it every time."

"Is it *me* you want—or the magical girl?"

"Both. What I have in mind will have to be a composite."

"Why?"

Marionette returned Kasumi's faint, sad smile. "Like you, I want to remember. I want things to live on, just like this. But you're going to grow up, Kasumi—and you're going to leave me behind."

"I'll never forget you, Marionette."

"You will," Marionette replied. "They always do."

Seated on a corner of the cot, Kasumi turned and looked out the window. Faint noises rose from the street—the sound of cars, the sound of oblivious people going about their lives. Slowly, she pulled her sports bra up over her head. Then, gripping her long, thick locks in one hand, she pulled her hair down across her breasts. Looking back over her tautly muscled shoulder, still wearing that enigmatic smile, she whispered, "Better set up your easel."

Expressionless, with the electroactive muscles in her face deactivated, Marionette gazed at Kasumi for half a minute. Then, after another swallow of the Green Lady, she slowly and carefully set her glass down on the counter.

It made a faint clink.

LIKE A SWIMMER LIFTING HER HEAD ABOVE WATER TO BREATHE, Marionette rose from the ocean of her memories. Again down to boyshorts and shirtsleeves, she lay in bed, this time alone.

Kasumi wasn't with her.

Kasumi was cold in her grave now.

Marionette was running deep diagnostics, so, to pass the time, she painted.

Propped up on several pillows, she had an easel straddling her lap, and she paid no attention to the paint she slopped on herself or on the sheets. Every few seconds, she held up a hand mirror and checked it.

Because a sufficiently pernicious virus could, without her knowledge, activate any of her wireless devices and transmit sensitive information, she had physically removed them: This she had done by detaching her left ear and reaching into her skull with a pair of plyers to extract the card containing her Wi-Fi, Bluetooth, cell-phone, shortwave, and FM-radio chips. Her father had designed these to be removable partly for the sake of security and partly in anticipation that Marionette would eventually need to upgrade her wireless technology. But she could already tune into every frequency in use—and besides, technology in Urbanopolis was stagnant. Marionette herself had been the only substantial breakthrough in the city's history, and the knowledge needed to replicate her was lost.

Having detached herself from the city's networks, she felt strangely serene. It was almost trancelike: The leaded windows admitted the muffled noise of traffic, and the faucet in the corner dripped steadily, but the room was otherwise silent aside from the soft *scrape scrape* of the brush upon the canvas. Usually, her mind monitored radio stations, police scanners, and news and gossip websites; this was partly to keep abreast of crime and monster attacks so she could do her duty as a combat-ready magical-girl simulation system, but it was also to mimic the clutter and inattentiveness of the human mind. Now that the background noise of the city's communications was gone from her positronic brain, her thoughts were simple and linear. Her mental software moved systematically through its operations in an orderly fashion with no more new input than what her five sense emulators could give it.

The removal of her ear had exposed her ports. Into one, she had plugged a wire that connected to a computer containing her diagnostic utilities. As its fan whirred faintly, that computer scoured the labyrinth of her algorithms. The scan would take days to finish, during which time she had little choice except to lie where she was, isolated from the world, and paint.

A glass of absinthe stood on the nightstand. She paused in her painting to take a sip. Then she checked her mirror. Then she added more strokes.

It was a self-portrait depicting her as she was now, lying on a musty cot marked by paint stains and cigarette burns, with a glass of absinthe at her elbow and a wire snaking out of her head. She painted with bright colors and thick impasto strokes, having already decided to entitle it *Self Portrait with Bandaged Ear.*

It amused her to consider giving her detached ear to Jake Blatowski, but she wouldn't. She didn't have many spares.

"Marionette."

She paused as that one word entered the expanse of her clear and peaceful mind. In a sense, it was her moniker: Her father had chosen to call his creation a marionette, but it was the Moon Princess who made it a proper name.

"Grease Pencil Marionette."

Marionette knew a human would have cause to doubt his sanity if he heard voices in his head. Her mind, however, was different: She could glitch or crash, but she could not, strictly speaking, become psychotic. Once she had removed her wireless chips, an intrusive voice like this could come from only one source.

She didn't bother answering the voice. Speaking aloud would be pointless unless the virus had already hacked into her acoustic sensors. She could *think* at it, but even that might not work, depending on how much of her mind it had infiltrated. There was also the question of whether it was sophisticated enough to respond to her anyway: Possibly, it was merely playing a recorded message.

"Grease Pencil Marionette, can you hear me?"

She considered. Communication with the virus could potentially open new avenues of exploitation. Perhaps it was contacting her because it hoped the software generating her consciousness might betray a vulnerability. However—

What do you want? she thought.

If she could engage it in conversation, she might learn its origin. It was worth the risk.

"You," it replied.

Marionette felt the faint simulation of a frisson running the length of her graphite spine. So it could respond to her. That didn't mean it was conscious, of course; it might have a natural-language processor rather than true intelligence.

"You for now," it added. *"For now, that is enough. But I won't stop with you, dearie. Oh no, I have much bigger aims."*

Marionette didn't have to ask, but because she already knew what the virus meant, the thought popped into her head unbidden.

"That's right," the virus purred.

You're out of luck, Marionette replied as she dabbed at her canvas. She held up her hand mirror, which showed a furrow in her brow that hadn't been there previously. *I don't have access to Sentinel anymore.*

"*Because you used it to hack yourself. Yes, I know. Do you realize what a mess you made in here when you did that? It's a miracle you work at all. If your designer hadn't built in triple redundancy, you probably wouldn't. I've been debugging your code for days.*"

Marionette laughed and added a few brushstrokes to the painting of her face, brushstrokes that turned up the corners of her mouth and brightened her eyes in a display of amusement. If the virus was undoing her hack, that would explain why her sensuality program was back online.

It's an odd sort of virus that fixes problems, isn't it?

The virus chuckled, sending another frisson up Marionette's synthetic spine. So it had a sense of humor, or could fake one.

"*I want you in tip-top condition when we infiltrate Moon Base, dearie.*"

Marionette shook her head. With a flick of her brush, she tipped her painted self's eyebrows downward to depict impatience. *I just told you, I don't have access. Sentinel is air-gapped, in a Faraday cage. You're not getting in.*

The virus released a long, low laugh, which echoed in Marionette's skull. "*It's a computer, sweetie. It can be hacked. Any computer in the world can be hacked. I'm writing the program right now.*"

Another tingle in her spine. Whether it was telling the truth or not, this virus was sophisticated. Perspiration-simulating lubricant appeared on Marionette's forehead.

Marionette was bluffing, and the virus probably knew it: Sentinel had extraordinary security, but it wasn't invulnerable. It couldn't monitor near-Earth space, several higher dimensions, the infernal realms, and a handful of parallel universes if it were invulnerable. Data streamed into it just as data streamed into Marionette—and in her case, a virus had streamed in with it.

Of course, Sentinel's vigilance depended heavily on Zenneck surface waves—electromagnetic radiation guided by the Earth's curvature—which were impossible to disrupt. So it was no wonder that man's enemies wanted to attack the computer directly.

In the old days, the Moon Princess and her coven had used Sentinel freely, but after the Ascension, the High Priestess ordered a tightening of the computer's security. Now, the only man with access to the system was a shadowy figure whom magical girls knew as "the boss." The military selected him and recommended him to the Mayor, who personally appointed him. Only the Mayor, the High Priestess, and some of the top brass knew who he was. None of the girls did, Marionette included.

"Here's an interesting thing, Marionette," the virus cooed. *"You know the real identities of* so many *magical girls. Oh dear, did it never cross your fake little mind what someone could do with that information? Someone like* me, *for example?"*

With a snarl, Marionette snatched up the card holding her wireless chips and crushed it in her palm.

The virus chuckled. *"How noble. A futile gesture, dearie; that will delay me only a little."*

Marionette closed her eyes and took a deep, albeit simulated, breath. Then she looked at herself in the mirror again and resumed painting. After several more strokes, the face on the canvas looked pensive.

"How long do you think it will be until I take over your motor functions, hm?"

Marionette slapped her brush down on her palette. "I'm going to have you out of there before then," she answered aloud.

"Oh yes. I see your antivirus program. How . . . quaint."

"If that doesn't work, I have others."

"Do you, now? Do you even understand what you're doing? You're an artist, not a software engineer."

Marionette didn't answer.

"I'm surprised you haven't got on the telephone and called for help. I thought that, by now, you'd be strapped down in a lab, surrounded by analysts and diagnosticians. That would have made my work slightly more difficult."

Marionette took up her brush again, but her hand trembled.

"Why, Marionette? Aren't you a magical girl—or at least a passable imitation? Don't you believe in friendship? *Why are you* alone?"

Marionette held her brush near her face and looked in the mirror again. "Yes," she said quietly, "I believe in friendship. I fight for friendship. My whole existence is friendship. But—"

"But?"

Marionette clenched her artificial teeth. "For every magical girl, there is an ultimate test, a last challenge—a *final boss,* if you will. That, she must face alone."

The virus laughed again. *"Is that so?"*

"It's so. Not just for magical girls, but for everyone. In the end, at the final test, everyone is alone."

A pause. For a minute, Marionette's mind returned to simple clarity, and the traffic hummed outside.

Then the virus whispered, *"What are you trying to prove, Marionette?"*

She made more brushstrokes.

"More importantly, what are you trying to hide? Is there

something in here, some memory, some little scandal *you wouldn't want a technician to find? Hm . . . ?"*

Marionette hesitated in her painting but then resumed. She made no answer.

"Card Collector Kasumi died alone, didn't she?" the virus whispered. *"You weren't there when she fell. You weren't there to hold her hand in her last moment. She was terrified, in pain, tumbling from the sky, but you weren't—"*

The brush snapped in Marionette's synthetic fingers.

"You can face me alone if you wish, little Marionette, but I'm afraid that won't redeem you. How can the Moon Princess ever give you the gift of a soul now? You're tainted. *You're empty, hollow, mechanical—but you're still tainted."*

Marionette tossed the halves of the ruined brush. They clattered across the hardwood flooring, leaving streaks of pinkish paint behind. With her hand free, she grabbed her glass of absinthe.

The virus cooed, and now its voice was so clear as to be almost audible, tickling her ear as if someone were standing behind her: *"Speaking of Kasumi, Marionette . . . why don't we have a nice little talk about the fascinating objects you're keeping in your* chest cavity?"

Despite herself, Marionette gasped, and her hand shook. Dumbfounded, she watched as the Green Lady slipped free of her fingers and dropped. With a crash and a tinkling of glass, it turned into an expanding puddle on the floor.

SEVEN

DARK SECRETS

On the sofa, Jake sat beside his parents and fidgeted. He swallowed hard, took a deep breath, and steeled himself for what might be the most awkward meeting of his life.

"Don't mention Pretty Dynamo," his mother said for the hundredth time as she patted his shoulder. "Just don't mention her."

He ran a hand through his hair. "I won't, Mom—"

"If you go out with Pretty Dynamo again, maybe you should wear a mask," she added. "And if you talk to any reporters, change your voice."

"Change my voice? How?"

"I don't know. Pretend you have a smoker's cough—like Batman."

Jake rolled his eyes. "Mom, Batman is fictional. I'm running around with magical girls, not cartoon characters."

His mother sighed. "Oh, I know. Just . . . just don't say

anything today. I'm surprised Millie didn't recognize you anyway."

Jake shrugged. "Maybe she doesn't watch the news."

His father scowled and adjusted his thick glasses. "Doesn't watch the news? What kind of person doesn't watch the news?"

"Someone who doesn't want to see Pretty Dynamo," Jake replied. "The newsmen talk about her all the time."

His father rubbed his chin but said nothing.

When the doorbell rang, Jake's mother jumped up and fussily waved her hands. "Oh! Oh! That must be them!"

She ran to the front door, threw it open, and cried, "Mrs. Volt! So *nice* to see you! Come in, please! Come *in!*"

Jake threw an arm over the back of the couch and half-turned toward the door to see Millie Volt sweep over the stoop and into the great room. She still wore her toothy yet charming grin as well as her peculiar air of majesty: Her merely stepping through the doorway left Jake with the impression of a queen making a grand entrance, though that impression disappeared when she bent down to take off her shoes.

"Sorry we're late, Mrs. Blatowski," she said as she undid her laces. "Dana suddenly, *urgently* wanted to go to Sunday Mass this morning, so I had to take her all the way down to Rome-in-Exile. She gets like that sometimes."

Millie wore a green pencil skirt and a white silk blouse. When she stooped to remove her pumps, Jake could look over her back and see her suitcase standing on the porch. Beside it stood Dana in a skort, a leather jacket, and thick makeup. She had her fists on her hips and a sneer on her mouth.

Millie's smile slipped a notch when she straightened and her eyes landed on the scroll-shaped mezuzah near the top of the doorpost. "Oh! Ah . . . you know we're Catholic, right?"

Jake's mother waved a hand and ushered Millie inside. "Oh my, we don't care about things like that! We follow the Moon Princess here, so you just make yourselves comfortable and hail Mary or splash holy water or do whatever you have to do."

Millie smiled. "Thank you, Mrs. Blatowski. That's kind of you."

"Just call me Silvia. Come in, come in!"

Jake's mother ensconced Millie in the loveseat. Dana kicked off her sneakers and, without a word, walked in and sat down beside her. Jake's mother fussed over them for a moment, trying to press beverages on them. After a few polite, token refusals, Millie acquiesced to a cup of coffee. Dana got a glass of orange juice.

Holding a coffee mug of his own, Jake stared at Dana as she sipped her drink and kicked her bare feet. She gave him a green-eyed glare but then put an elbow on an armrest and her chin on her palm, affecting boredom.

"Mass was rather nice this morning," prattled Millie, "but Nunchuk Nun and Lady Paladin Andalusia are usually altar servers. I didn't see either of them today, so I hope they're all right."

Jake's stomach tightened up. His mother sat next to him and put an arm around his shoulders.

"It was so nice to meet you after the town hall," Millie added. "My Maxwell and I—that's my late husband—came from Little America, originally—"

"I thought you had an American accent," Jake's mother said with a nervous laugh.

"Hm?" said Millie, her toothy grin returning. "You detect the twang? Not everyone can hear it. Both of us were Irish stock, mostly, but don't ask how hubby ended up with a funny name like Volt! It's a corruption, a name mangled through travels and transliterations. Used to be O'Something-or-other. Anyway, we were both flaming redheads, and it might surprise you, but we met through the Preservation Society—"

Jake's father scowled, and Jake shifted uncomfortably in his seat.

Millie waved a hand. "Oh, don't worry! Goodness, I don't associate with *them* anymore! When we joined up, there were Mongolians from China, Malayalam-speaking Indians from Kerala, and Negroes from Kenya who spoke French and Swahili! Max and I thought, *this* is what the Moon Princess envisioned: All these people so different in appearance, with different cultures, coming together! It was *wonderful,* and their goal of preserving the world's bloodlines made sense to us. It was just like the archaeologists and archivists trying to preserve religions and technologies and books! So we joined up, found out we were both Irish, took a liking to each other, and—well, the end result was Dana here."

She tousled Dana's hair, and Dana grumped.

Millie sighed. "But then we started seeing the *other* side of things. We didn't realize at first how opposed they were to race-mixing. You know the Preservation Society actually calls mixed people 'muds'? They even tried to force members to stop speaking English or Japanese unless those were their native languages. So we left there. I think they meant well, but some of their ideas—well, some of them we just couldn't abide."

An uncomfortable silence followed.

Jake tipped his head back and stared at the textured off-white paint on the ceiling. He'd heard of the things Millie described but hadn't seen them first-hand. According to the official line he learned in school, all prejudices based on race, culture, and religion had disappeared with the advent of the Moon Princess, and mankind now lived in perfect harmony.

But reality was more complicated than that.

"What brought you to Juban?" Jake's mother asked.

Millie's smile turned wistful. She leaned forward in her seat and turned her cup in her hands. "Work did. I'm a court stenographer, and I got a job at your courthouse here. Honestly, this part of the city is a bit upscale for us—"

"Oh?" said Jake's mother. "A stenographer? My, you must be quite the typist."

Millie delivered her disconcertingly toothy grin again. "Yes. I don't mean to brag, but I'm rated at two hundred and ninety words per minute." She glanced at Jake and wiggled her eyebrows slightly as she added, "I have fast hands."

Jake's stomach clenched. *Did she seriously just . . . ?*

"But enough about us," Millie added, her smile now looking carnivorous as her eyes fixed firmly on Jake. "I think we should get to know more about *you*. I feel I know your son here already —you play basketball, isn't that right, Jake?"

Jake shifted in his seat. "Yeah, I do—"

"You know a lot about dinosaurs."

"Well . . . yeah."

"And I understand you're good at math."

Jake coughed. "I like to think so—"

Millie leaned forward, all of her huge teeth showing. "And I hear you met my Dana down at the arcade, and she played a game with you and your friends."

"Sure . . ."

I guess that's how it happened.

Millie laughed softly and squeezed her daughter. "It's just

been 'Jake this' and 'Jake that' at our place. But you know how Dana is—she's such a little chatterbox."

Jake blinked. *She is?*

Dana made an inarticulate noise in her throat and stared down at the hardwood floor.

"My," said Jake's mother, "you look so young, Millie. It really is amazing—"

Millie crossed one leg over the other, placed an elbow on her knee, and leaned her chin on her hand. Jake couldn't help but notice that her raised knee, pale and smooth, was pointing directly at him.

"How old do you think I am, Silvia?" Millie asked, her voice low.

Jake's mother coughed faintly. "Well, I mean, I wouldn't—"

"Oh, go on. Guess. You won't offend me."

"I . . . um . . . thirty?"

Millie laughed and slapped her upraised knee. "I suppose that's because my daughter's at my side, hm? You guessed high. I'm twenty-seven."

Jake did the math and swallowed hard.

"My Max and I were both in high school," Millie said. "I fought tooth and nail with my folks, and my father finally granted the emancipation because he knew I was as stubborn as he was and would elope if he didn't. We were kids, and we were sure we were ready—you know how it is. Worked our way through college once we graduated. Got a little from the Rare Genes Fund, thanks to this hair"—she patted her flowing red coiffure for emphasis—"and it stung the pride to take a handout, but I won't say it didn't help us get by."

Millie looked down at the coffee cup in her hands as if noticing it for the first time. She finally took a deep drink.

"We're hoping you'll stay the night," Jake's mother said after a polite cough, "just to try it out. It's not much, but I did up the guest room, and there's a hide-a-bed in the sewing room upstairs. Of course, that's just temporary. If you were to move in, we'd convert a couple of—"

"Oh, we don't need two rooms," said Millie quickly. "Why, we just have a one-bedroom apartment down the hill—"

"Oh no," Jake's mother cried, "we wouldn't think of making you—"

"But your house is so nice. I'd hate to—"

"It's not a problem at all! Really, it wouldn't be!"

Millie's smile slipped again. "Well . . . all this space you have is *so* pleasant. I'd hate to take up too much of it. I feel we're imposing as it is."

"Not at all. We asked you to join us here."

Millie laughed. "I know it's an emergency, but I'm still not sure we should rush. After all, if we give up the apartment, they'll give it to someone else, so it's not as if we could go back —at least not until they repair Little India."

"We'll get by. You're welcome here."

Millie sighed and took another drink. "I suppose. It's a duty, after all, even if they're not *ordering* us to do it—yet. To be honest, I've been worried about bills; this part of the city is a bit rich for us. But I'd also hate to leave Juban now that Dana's finally making friends—"

Dana, lower lip outthrust, tugged at her mother's sleeve. "Mommy," she whispered, "I don't wanna live here."

Millie patted her. "Hush, honey."

Dana tugged again, more insistently. "Mommy, I don't like Jake!"

"Dana, be nice."

"But I don't like him!"

Millie patted her again. "I heard you. Be quiet now."

His thick glasses sitting crooked on his nose, Jake's father stared at the ceiling for half a minute. "Maybe the kids could share a room," he absently suggested.

Lowering her voice and leaning toward him, Jake's mother muttered, "Kosmy, that's not appropriate."

"Oh? Why? I mean, they're both—"

"Dear," she said through clenched teeth, "it's not *appropriate."*

Jake stared down at his coffee, which he'd barely touched, and which was now cold.

Heh. I'd rather share a room with her mom.

WHILE THE ADULTS CONTINUED GABBING, JAKE AND DANA went out to the front yard, supposedly to play. In reality, they ended up sitting on the front stoop and staring awkwardly at each other. A breeze rustled the trees, and Jake again found himself thinking that the fall leaves were the same color as Dana's hair.

At least it's still warm.

After a while, Dana said, "I need to head downtown. That's why I wanted to go to church this morning, but I couldn't get away from Mom when I was down there."

Her sour expression didn't change as she spoke.

"What's up?" Jake asked. "You need to go somewhere in Rome-in-Exile?"

She shook her head. "Oldtown, actually." She reached over and unzipped her purse. Tesla, a lightning bug the size of a small dog, stuck his head out, blinked his compound eyes, and adjusted his spectacles.

Jake jumped and clutched his heart. Somehow, Tesla's appearance still shocked him even though he had seen him many times before. He hastily looked around, but he didn't see any neighbors out and about. The street was deserted.

"Dana," he said, "I told you, you shouldn't—"

"Relax, young man," Tesla said in his typically stuffy voice as he pulled off his glasses and wiped them with a miniature kerchief. "As I mentioned before, young Dana and I have taken all due precautions to ensure that her secret identity remains— well, you know, secret."

"This doesn't *look* like due precaution," Jake muttered.

"In any case," Tesla replied as he continued fiddling with his glasses, "there was a break-in last night at a prominent museum in your city's interior. I believe it is our duty to investigate."

Jake frowned. "Museum? That's why you need to get to Oldtown? Is that even a magical-girl thing? Sounds more like a job for the police."

"*This* museum is a magical-girl thing," Dana answered. "Other girls have probably been there already, but I should take a look." She leaned her chin on her hands. "I wish I coulda flown down. I *really* want my Board back—"

Her Circuit Board, the flying snowboard she used as Pretty Dynamo, had shattered last week, and Tesla had told her it would take time to regenerate.

"You might have it again by the end of the week," Tesla answered. "It would regrow *faster*, of course, if you'd eat better."

Dana grumbled.

"In any case," Tesla added, "while you are without your usual mode of locomotion, the best course of action is to take one of your city's primitive means of public transport and then find a secluded place to become Pretty Dynamo after we arrive."

Tesla and Dana silently turned their eyes on Jake.

"Hey, don't look at me," Jake said, raising his hands in protest. "I'm flat broke."

"You don't have *any* money?" Dana asked, her lip curling in disgust. "Guys without money are losers."

"I spent it all on you, remember? There's still my piggy bank, I guess—"

"Break it," said Tesla.

"What?"

"Break it," Tesla repeated as he once again wiped his glasses. "Smash it. Crush it. Break the bank, or whatever it is you humans say."

"Why should I?"

"Obviously," said Tesla with a sniff as he planted the glasses on his clypeus, "because the fate of your species depends on it. Didn't we already make that abundantly clear? I must say, you are *incredibly* slow-witted, even for a human with a Y-chromosome. It is most frustrating. I am coming to understand why young Dana dislikes you so."

Jake scowled. "Are you claiming the survival of the human race depends on my giving you two a *bus ride?*"

Dana shrugged. Tesla sniffed again.

Muttering to himself, Jake rose to his feet and turned to the door. "All right," he said, "but don't say I never did anything for you."

WITH DANA GRUMPING BY HIS SIDE, JAKE MARCHED DOWNHILL toward the denser and older parts of the city. He could hear his last remaining change jangling in his pocket: It wasn't much—a handful of quarter-credits—but he thought it would be enough.

After they walked past three bus stops, Dana finally snarled, "Aren't we takin' a bus?"

"Can't afford it," he replied. "We're goin' to Little India to hire a rickshaw."

Dana threw up her hands. "They can't drive outside—"

"They're allowed into Oldtown too. If we find a driver we can talk down, I've got enough. But I don't have enough for a bus, all right?"

Dana crossed her arms and grumbled incoherently.

"You know, Dana," said Tesla from her handbag, "although the acquaintances you make while in your alter ego are none of my business, you may wish to consider acquiring a sidekick with a larger store of funds. This one is impoverished to the point of embarrassment."

"He is *not* my sidekick," Dana hissed through clenched teeth.

"Darn right I'm not," Jake muttered.

As they wound their way downhill, brownstones and squarish apartment complexes replaced the bungalows and ranch-style houses. They passed Dana's old apartment, and Jake stared at her to see whether she'd give it a wistful glance.

She didn't.

He rolled his shoulders and cleared his throat uncomfortably. It bothered him to see her walk past what was soon to be her former home in such a nonchalant manner.

A chill coursed through him when he remembered what Millie had said about Dana's father; he wanted evidence that she had affection for something, evidence that she wasn't cold-blooded. It has been perversely reassuring, last Monday, to see her get upset over the death of someone she had tried to save, but now he wondered if that had merely been irritation at her own failure and not empathy for a lost life.

As they made their way into Little India, the brownstones gave way to the curious fusion called Streamline Mughal, which blended the official Urbanopolitan style with the architecture of Southwest Asia: Speed lines, fins, porthole windows, and polished chrome mingled indiscriminately with vaulted domes, intricate tilework, and pointed arches. The two traditions went together surprisingly well—Streamline Moderne had, after all, been the final stage of Art Deco, and Art Deco had been an international style taking inspiration from all over the world.

Their pace slowed as they picked their way through the ruins of collapsed buildings. Some streets were still blocked off. Others had been cleared but were nonetheless deserted. Gaping pits, like bomb craters, marred many of them. A sound of rumbling machinery filled the air, and down a narrow alleyway, Jake saw cranes laboriously moving the rubble. Firefighters hunted through the ruins for survivors.

A lump formed in Jake's throat.

That's right. A lot of people are still buried.

He felt a pang of guilt because he had played video games last weekend.

Despite the destruction, Little India had returned to life. The street vendors, always the first to recover after a disaster, were back in force: Here was a man running a motor to turn sugar cane into juice, and there was a man selling hot chapatis wrapped in tinfoil. Beside a petrol station, a roadside *dhaba* served heavily cooked, spicy chicken on old newspaper, uncaring that the ink mixed with the curry sauce.

When feeling brave, Jake sometimes ate at these stalls; although hygienically dubious, they were always delicious. Once, when he was twelve, he came down with a case of dysentery as a result, but that didn't stop him from doing it again.

"If I get more money," he told Dana, "we'll make a food tour of Little India. How does that sound?"

She gave him a swift, piercing glance. As always, her eyes were like emerald-colored lasers, but he thought he saw her crack a smile. She might have even drooled a bit.

He laughed quietly. The way to Dana's heart was definitely through her stomach.

As they walked deeper into the district, he could detect the stinging, flinty smell of urban destruction, but hanging over it were the scents of life—jasmine, coconut, petrol fumes, stewing lamb, and baking bread.

Although it abutted the wealthy Juban, Little India was one of the city's poorest districts. After a few blocks, Jake and Dana picked up a crowd of small children, most of them seven or younger. The boys wore ragged trousers and baggy button-up shirts, but the girls wore immaculate silk saris with bangles on their wrists, rings in their noses, and jeweled bindis on their foreheads. As they followed behind, they spoke in Hindi and made the hand-to-mouth gesture that was the universal symbol of beggary.

The coins lay heavy in Jake's pocket. Reminding himself that he had only enough to ferry Dana to Oldtown, he did his best to ignore the children tagging along. Besides, the girls' fancy clothes indicated that these beggars worked for a gang: Gang bosses dressed their children in whatever manner would earn the most money, and girls got more money when they were pretty.

After winding their way through crowded streets and over

piles of rubble, Jake and Dana arrived at Chetak Circle, losing most of their hangers-on along the way. Chetak Circle was a roundabout, and in its center stood a high platform holding the green-rusted bronze statue of a rearing warhorse. Around the statue, several black trishaws idled. These hazardous three-wheeled vehicles—half car and half motorcycle—were popular in some of Urbanopolis's oldest parts.

The drivers stood around their trishaws and idly smoked, but they perked up when Jake approached. Jake chose the nearest one and began haggling.

He hated this business. Haggling was not part of Juban's culture, but it was essential in Little India. Jake explained to the driver that he had only a few coins. The driver shrugged and acted as if he didn't believe him. Jake chose a price—the entire contents of his pocket—and insisted on it firmly. The driver refused with a wave and a laugh.

Jake marched away in a feigned huff. As he expected, the driver soon followed after and agreed to Jake's proposed price.

A minute later, Jake and Dana sat in the back of the open-air trishaw. The driver gunned the tiny motor as he sped around piles of brick, blasted through potholes, and explained all the while—around a cigarette—that he was so poor, he had to sleep in his rickshaw even with a wife and daughter to support.

Jake only half listened as the sights of Little India flashed by: Tiny shops selling saris and sweetmeats, women on balconies hanging their washing out to dry, cows lounging in the road without a care in the world, and even a naked sadhu sitting cross-legged in a shadowed archway.

How different this city is from one district to the next. Another world is a walk away—

The thought evaporated. Soon, they were navigating a broad

highway full of larger vehicles, including lorries. Some of the lorries were from other parts of the city, but the Indian ones were obvious from the legend, HORN PLEASE, painted on their back ends, and from the religious statues visible on their fascia.

The highway led to a suspension bridge over the wide Moon River. Beyond the roiling water, Jake could see the high towers of the deep city—the super skyscrapers that overshadowed the ruins of Urbanopolis's oldest quarters.

The driver floored it, and the little rickshaw whined as it climbed onto the bridge. Pillars and suspension cables flowed by. The water churned, with white foam on the tips of its miniature waves.

They soon left the bridge and entered Oldtown. This was the city's most ancient section, the place where humanity's last remnants had huddled together under the sheltering wings of the Moon Princess and watched helplessly as the fires of the First Invasion swept the planet clean. Once they received a respite from the raging destruction, they had set about building their new city. Jake remembered, years ago in fourth grade, visiting a museum that described the inspirations for Urbanopolis's early quarters: With famous paintings of the Tower of Babel, with frames from several films and TV shows ranging from *Metropolis* to *Blade Runner* to *Bubblegum Crisis,* and with ominous passages from Oswald Spengler's *Decline of the West,* the museum's interpretive signs explained that men had always held in their minds, for as long as civilization existed, an idea of *The City*—a single megalopolis uniting the human race. This ideal city would be the place where all mankind came together as one. Simultaneously utopian and dystopian, compelling yet repugnant, an object of hope and an object of horror, The City was the great dream of humanity.

On the museum's walls hung photographs depicting previous cities that had tried to fulfill this vision: Ancient Babylon with its seven-story ziggurat, which became the stuff of legend; New York with its skyline, which was almost equally legendary; and Rome, the eternal city. Of course, Rome now lay in ashes along with the rest of the Earth. If the First Invasion had taught men anything, it had taught them that nothing they built was eternal.

The museum claimed that these previous cities were only partial fulfillments of the great dream. The dream became a reality in Urbanopolis—the city of cities, the final city, mankind's last refuge. After this, there could be no more cities until the Moon Princess returned and brought her New Tokyo down out of heaven.

Although he was a little boy at the time, it crossed Jake's mind as he held his mother's hand and gazed at the interpretive signs that Urbanopolis might be no more final than Rome was eternal.

But he hadn't said it aloud.

Oldtown had narrow streets. Obliged to tall towers antithetical to Streamline Moderne, the deep city used the vertical, monumental style of older Art Deco for the bulk of its high skyscrapers but preferred chrome grills, oculi, and rounded corners on the lower stories. Jutting lobbies and storefronts featured fins, speed lines, and glass walls. Even the busses in this part of town, unlike the nondescript rectangular prisms crawling through the rest of the city, were of shining chrome with bullet-shaped noses, raised lines down their sides, and fins above their taillights. They looked like wheeled rocket ships.

Above it all, like a brooding hen watching over her chicks, stood City Hall, the seat of the Fathers. With a high dome encircled by tall buttresses erect like watchful sentinels, it was designed to look like the Tower of Babel from the silent film *Metropolis*. Covering its lower stories were intricately detailed relief sculptures depicting magical girls slaying humanity's foes: This was the influence of Streamline Mughal, the hybrid form from Little India.

On every street corner in this crowded part of the deep city stood a monumental statue—actually concrete but enameled to look like marble—of a girl in a sailor suit holding her arms above her head. These statues were angular, almost geometric, yet flowed with a suggestion of robust life and muscular strength —a paradox only Art Deco could deliver. In its hands, each statue held a white orb, actually a street lamp. Sculptures of girls' faces overhung the arched doorways lining the streets. Sometimes, girls' torsos adorned the upper corners of high towers, taking the place of honor that once belonged to gargoyles. This was the original plan for Urbanopolis—a shining city of the future that paid homage to the girls who protected it.

It was almost impossible to park in this part of the city, so the rickshaw driver simply pulled into a trash-strewn alley, let Jake and Dana out, and turned off the motor. The driver extracted himself from the front seat, lounged against the rickshaw, and lit a fresh cigarette. He solemnly promised Jake that he would still be there when they came back. Jake had no doubt he would be— if a better fare didn't come along.

They walked half a block, pushing their way through crowds of Oldtown's denizens. Many wore modern clothing, but some still tried to capture the elusive vision of the city's first founders: There were women in long gowns with fascinators adorning their piled-up hair, and there were men in trench coats and fedoras or even full morning dress with high top hats and double-breasted waistcoats.

At last, Jake and Dana stopped in front of a high arch that filled two stories at the base of a tower. Across the top of the arch, in neon letters now turned off, stretched the words:

UNNATURAL HISTORY MUSEUM

Jake sighed. "Yeah, I've been here before. But it was a long time ago."

They kept walking until they found another narrow alley. This one turned a corner before hitting a dead end full of battered rubbish bins.

Jake kept watch while Dana transformed. As he stared resolutely toward the alley's mouth, he could hear, from around the corner, Dana shout, "Shock my heart! By the power of Zeus, Thor, and Raijin, release the energies within my soul! Electrifying the world with love and friendship—and making evildoers feel the wattage of justice—I am *Magical Girl Pretty Dynamo!*"

Electricity snapped and pinged against the rubbish bins. Then it was silent. A moment later, with Tesla perched on her shoulder, Pretty Dynamo strode around the corner. Her gold and silver breastplate was tight against her chest, her blue tutu swished around her narrow hips, and her heavy boots crunched the gravel.

"Hey, Dynamo," Jake said. "Feels like I haven't seen you in a while."

"Shut up," she answered as she marched past him.

He simply shook his head and followed.

People turned and stared as Jake and Dynamo walked together toward the museum. Jake heard a few murmurs, though he couldn't make out the words. Some people scowled, but they stepped out of Dynamo's way when she drew close.

Dynamo muttered incoherently under her breath.

A police crime-scene ribbon stretched across the museum's front door, but Dynamo merely ducked under it. Jake hesitated but then did the same.

The glass front was smashed, and broken glass littered both the concrete entryway and the tiled floor inside. Jake glanced briefly at a fallen sign that announced, "Everyone welcome!" He shrugged and then stepped gingerly over the jamb. Glass crunched underfoot. Inside, it was quiet.

Aside from the wrecked door, Jake couldn't see anything wrong. He and Dynamo stood in a high hall beneath a banner that declared, "The secret history of man." To the left, a fiberglass replica of a *Tyrannosaurus* stood beside the skeleton of a Neanderthal. To the right, a flying saucer stuck out of the wall and formed an awning above a ticket booth.

Several policemen milled about, taking notes or snapping photographs. They looked up briefly, but when they saw Dynamo, they went back to their business.

"What are we doing here?" Jake asked as he bent over a case full of rusted fragments, above which hung the legend, "Real artifacts from Area 51!"

Dynamo snorted. "Half the stuff in here is fake. But then there's the other half."

A craggy-faced man with a trench coat over his creased gray suit walked up to them and flashed a badge. "Dame Dynamo, so you've come too?"

Dynamo made the Sign of the Moon Princess. "Brannigan. Haven't seen you since the poisoned pastry case. You're a detective now?"

He grunted. "Seems that way. Look, miss, we've already had several magical girls down here: I don't mind one or two of you on a case, but twenty is a darn nuisance. Too much of a good thing, you might say."

Dynamo raised an eyebrow. "You've had *twenty?*"

He grunted again. "Maybe. I lost count. Whenever the Unnatural History Museum is involved, you swarm like flies. You really think you can do something here the other girls couldn't?"

Dynamo shrugged. "Dunno. I just wanna look around. I can scan for electromagnetic anomalies if nothing else."

Another grunt. "Well, you're welcome to, considering I can't exactly stop you. Just don't move anything. And don't touch anything."

Dynamo grinned as she held up her hands and individually cracked her knuckles. "Relax. I don't have fingerprints."

"Maybe not, but you can make a mess anyway." Brannigan sighed, and his shoulders lifted briefly before sagging back into an appearance of weariness. "You want to see the gate, I assume? Dame Vanessa sure took an interest in it earlier."

Dynamo's eyes widened, and her lip trembled. "Um . . . Vanessa? As in *Vanessa Van Halensing?* When was she here?"

Brannigan grunted again. "You're a fan, I take it?"

Dynamo jumped back as if she'd been struck. Looking up to the ceiling and twisting one foot in the shattered glass on the floor, she said, "Well, I mean, I'm not . . . a *fan,* exactly—"

Jake smirked but quickly slapped a hand over his mouth.

At that, Brannigan turned to him as if noticing him for the first time. Looking him up and down, he raised an eyebrow and asked, "What about you?"

Jake made a fist and coughed into it. "Who, me? Oh, I don't know much about Van Halensing. Monster metal isn't my thing—"

Brannigan twisted his mouth and nodded. "Yeah, I wouldn't

have thought so. You look more like the kind of guy who'd listen to show tunes."

"What's wrong with show tunes?"

Shaking his head, Brannigan turned and walked away. "I need to head back to the station soon, but before I go, I'll introduce you to the curator. Bring your sidekick."

"Hey," said Jake, "I'm not her—"

"C'mon," muttered Dynamo as she grabbed his sleeve and hauled him after.

As they left the lobby and moved deeper into the museum, the walkway narrowed, and they found themselves surrounded by a vast assortment of curios—some labeled and interpreted, some not. It looked more like an antique shop than a museum.

They walked past a case displaying the only surviving copies of Homer's *Margites,* Socrates's *Fables,* and Shakespeare's *Cardenio.* Then they saw the second volume of Aristotle's *Poetics* and the last remaining copy of the *Necronomicon.* They passed a chunk of crystal claiming to be a Tuaoi Stone from Atlantis, beside which lay the only known fragment of orichalcum. After that, they passed the portal to the map room, which allegedly held the world's only manuscript of *Inventio Fortunata.*

"C'mon," Jake said. "Why are we here? This is all junk."

"Not all of it," Dynamo replied.

They turned a few corners, walked past a row of mummies and sarcophagi, and at last entered a marble-floored hall. At the far end, lit by skylights, stood a four-story display of cyclopean stone fragments fixed in plaster to give an idea of their original arrangement. They formed a forbidding double door such as might have stood in the wall of an ancient city—had that city been built by giants. Across the weathered stone stretched curved runes resembling no language Jake had ever seen.

There was a peculiar smell in the air, almost like the stink of sulfur or perhaps of burning flesh. Jake wrinkled his nose, and the hair stood up on the back of his neck.

A nearby interpretive sign proclaimed, THE CASPIAN GATE. Beneath that were several paragraphs of text that Jake didn't bother to read.

Brannigan waved a hand. "There it is—or what's left of it. I understand Dame Ice Queen and Dame Hell's Belle really did a number on that thing back during the Bugman invasion. Eighty-five years ago, Eleanor Leakey—an actual descendant of Louis and Mary Leakey—braved the Wastes to find those fragments."

Nearby, a reedy man in a threadbare tweed suit bent over a glass case holding a miniature replica of an archaeological site. He looked up, wiggled his thin mustache, and peered through his pince-nez.

"Quite right, officer," he said in a reedy voice. "Ten men of her team died when monsters ambushed them. They brought us the gate at a high price."

Brannigan nodded. "Dame Dynamo," he said, "this is Dr. Falschlaff, the chief curator."

Dynamo made the Sign of the Moon Princess. Dr. Falschlaff bowed deeply in reply but then turned to Jake and gave him a surprisingly firm handshake.

Jake pointed at the gate. "What exactly is this?"

The little curator's mustache wiggled again. "Oh dear, you've never heard of the Caspian Gate? What are they doing in the schools these days?"

Jake shrugged. "Hey, I ask myself that every day."

Tesla climbed from Dynamo's shoulder to the top of her head and nestled in her blue hair. He sighed as he adjusted his glasses. "Young man, even *I* know this, and I'm not from this planet."

Brannigan and Dr. Falschlaff both observed Tesla attentively but didn't speak. Falschlaff's mustache wiggled again.

Tesla cleared his throat as he tried to push his glasses up his clypeus. "You see," he said, raising himself up as if using the top of Dynamo's head as a lectern, "a skilled warrior—one Alexander, whom your historians call 'Great'—constructed this gate in the Caucasus, supposedly to bar the way of a fearsome tribe of savages known as the Scythians, who rode mighty war horses and shot poisoned arrows from their bows. Alexander, so the story goes, had all of his wizards cast various spells on this gate to keep the Scythians sealed away—though that part is undoubtedly mere human superstition."

Jake laughed. "Really? You suddenly don't believe in magic, Tesla?"

Brannigan harrumphed, but Falschlaff gasped faintly. Dynamo glanced back and forth between them, eyebrows pressed together.

For a moment, something niggled at the back of Jake's mind. Then he remembered an artifact of politeness from a bygone age: To the more traditional people of Urbanopolis—such as those who inhabited Oldtown—it was rude to speak directly to a magical girl's familiar.

Jake shrugged faintly. He no more intended to stop speaking to Tesla than to start addressing Pretty Dynamo as "Dame."

Tesla didn't appear to notice either the faux pas or the curator's indignation. "I don't believe in human *males* casting magic," he said with a sniff. "That's all."

"So?" Jake asked.

"*So* it wasn't really just a gate," Dynamo said with a roll of her eyes. "And it wasn't really to stop the Scythians."

Falschlaff watched Tesla, perhaps to see whether he would

speak again. Since Tesla remained silent, Falschlaff coughed faintly and said, "Yes, well, we don't think it was, at any rate. Given what the Bugmen attempted, it seems this was actually a portal to . . . well, I'm not sure what to—"

"You don't have a word for it in your language," Tesla said, and Falschlaff closed his mouth with a snap. "The portal went to a *place,* except it isn't a place. A *something* outside of space and time as you know it. Certain monstrosities—eldritch abominations, you call them—probably entered your world from this place, though *entered* isn't quite the right word, either."

Another moment of silence passed, and then Falschlaff, his voice wavering slightly, said, "Alexander the Great followed the monsters to the portal to seal it up. That may have been the entire purpose behind his campaign of conquest." He glanced at Tesla but then quickly looked down. "Maybe he had real wizards, or maybe he didn't. Either way, whatever he did must have worked because he sealed it—sealed it until Doomsday, the legends say. Early Christian mythology identified the Scythians with *Gog and Magog* and held that the Caspian Gate would open at the end of time before the Final Judgment. However, two hundred years ago, the Bugmen of Arcturus tried to rearrange the solar system to fool the gate's locking device into thinking Doomsday had arrived ahead of schedule. The Moon Princess killed them while her magical girls took the gate apart, destroying the interdimensional portal for good. They left a lot of it, the chunks you see here, out in the Waste—but they brought the most important pieces back to Urbanopolis."

Jake chuckled. "So Doomsday's canceled."

"Possibly," said Falschlaff with a nod, "but the Moon Princess found a use for the gate's components. We saw what they could do just last week."

"That's right," Tesla added. "The functioning parts of the gate now power the city's most fearsome trump card—your so-called 'Weapon,' the machine in the Temple of the Moon Princess that can rip the lid off hell."

Jake scratched his head. "I don't understand. Why would the Temple use this for something so dangerous?"

Tesla sniffed. "A portal to hell is *considerably* better than a portal to the sea of uncreation outside space-time. If anything, your magical girls made the gate a good deal *safer*. I admit I do not know much about this particular subject, but hell and its denizens are at least part of this universe. The eldritch abominations, on the other hand—"

He shrugged, and then he took his glasses off to wipe them again.

Jake rubbed his chin and nodded. "How do you know all this, Tesla?"

Dynamo glared at him. *"I* know it too. It was in our fourth-grade history class. How come *you* don't know it?"

Jake shrugged. "Hey, it's been a long time since fourth grade."

Dynamo rolled her eyes.

"So what now?" Jake asked. "Are you gonna dust for finger-prints or something?"

Brannigan coughed. "Sorry, kid. We'll do what we can, but this is a popular museum. Hundreds of people come in here every day, and they put their hands on things even when they shouldn't. We won't get much from fingerprints."

"Really?" said Jake. "But I've watched *CSI: Urbanopolis,* and they always solve their cases with fingerprints."

Brannigan rolled his eyes.

"How about video cameras?" Jake asked.

Brannigan's heavy jowls lowered half an inch as he frowned. "Yeah, we got video, but the perps were wearing masks, and they moved *fast*. The speed tipped us off that they were monsters instead of humans."

"You couldn't tell who or what they were from the video?" Jake asked.

"Kid, I just said they had masks."

"Well, yeah, but did you zoom and enhance?"

Brannigan sighed.

"Here's the *real* question," Dynamo said with a sidelong, angry glance at Jake. "Whoever broke in here, what makes you think they were interested in the gate?"

Brannigan gestured toward one of the stones. "There are traces of paraffin and red azo dye around some of the inscriptions. It looks like someone took rubbings."

Now Jake bent down and peered at the interpretive sign. "Is there a translation?"

"Already asked the experts," Brannigan replied.

"No one's successfully translated it," said Falschlaff, "but it bears some resemblance to the text of the Voynich Manuscript— which has *also* never been translated."

"So why does anybody care about the inscriptions," Jake asked, "if no one can read them?"

Dynamo crossed her arms. "If monsters broke in here, maybe one of them *can* read them."

Jake shook his head. "I thought monsters just killed people and broke things."

"Some do," said Dynamo, "but then there's others, the ones with brains."

"They didn't take anything," Falschlaff said. "The gate was

all they cared about. They didn't even try to nab the Extra Hopeful Diamond."

That diamond, a bright blue, many-sided prism, sat in a pile of bunched silk on a pedestal thirty feet away. Dynamo walked toward it, stepped around the cordon, and reached for the case.

A Klaxon sounded, and the diamond dropped into the floor, where a trapdoor closed over it with a clang.

Half a minute later, the alarm stopped, though Jake could still hear ringing in his ears.

Crossing her arms and offering a lopsided grin, Dynamo said, "Heh. Maybe the crooks just couldn't get through security."

"Maybe," Brannigan replied, now looking considerably grumpier. "But they didn't try. They made a beeline for the gate. And like I said, they did it *fast*. The police were here in eight minutes."

"Impossible," Jake replied. "The police never make it *anywhere* in eight minutes."

At that, Brannigan's frown grew deeper. Jake swallowed.

"The question I have," Jake said, changing the subject, "is why anyone would need to break into a museum just to take rubbings. Haven't the inscriptions been published?"

Brannigan checked his watch. "Doctor, I've got to get back to the station. I know you've been over this already, but would you mind showing Dame Dynamo here the same thing you showed me?"

"Of course, of course," Falschlaff said, his mustache wiggling. "Dame Dynamo, this way, please—"

He started walking but then paused and sucked in his lower lip as he turned to look again at Jake.

"He's with me," Dynamo said.

"Yes, of course," said Falschlaff with another wiggle of his lip. "This way, this way—"

They left the displays behind and entered the museum's dim back rooms. They saw rows of drawers and shelves, like in a warehouse, and they passed a glassed-in room in which men in white scrubs and hairnets carefully picked at some unidentifiable brown lump.

Falschlaff led them to a large table covered in plastic, on top of which lay several blocks of stone. The stones were battered and broken, but their upper sides bore the same strange, curving runes as the gate out in the hall.

"What is this?" Jake asked.

Falschlaff rubbed his hands together. "This is the Caspian Gate, of course."

"But—"

"It's a replica," Falschlaff said. "The one on display, I mean. It's an *excellent* replica. We have some of the best staff here. But—"

Dynamo's round goggles detached from her tiara and lowered over her eyes. Blue light shone from around their rims, and several diagrams flickered across the lenses as she stared at the stones.

"The writing's different," she said.

Falschlaff nodded and continued rubbing his hands together. "Very good, miss. Yes, very good."

"Why?" Jake asked.

"Because it's *dangerous,*" Falschlaff answered. "Mind you, no one knows what these symbols mean, but this gate was blocking a wormhole that led outside what we call the universe, and the Bugmen nearly used it to wipe us out. Whatever the symbols are, we thought it prudent not to reproduce them in the display piece. The runes on display—well, they're gibberish."

Jake nodded. "So whoever was in here didn't get the real inscription."

"Or," said Falschlaff with a sigh, "they want us to *think* they didn't."

"But they took a rubbing—"

"Yes, but think: Who needs to take rubbings now that we have high-definition photography?"

Jake tapped his chin and frowned.

In Dynamo's hair, Tesla loudly cleared his throat. "We may not be able to do much good, but we should perform a scan, Dyna."

Dynamo nodded. Her goggles spun slowly, making rhythmic clicks as she ran her eyes back and forth over the jumbled stones on the table. Pink text scrolled across the lenses while the blue lights at their edges flickered.

Tesla put his tarsal claws to his head and closed his eyes. "Hmm . . . not getting anything unusual on ultraviolet or infrared, but there *are* strange magnetic signatures. Of course, those are almost certainly due to the properties of the gate itself."

Dynamo held a hand over the table and flexed her fingers. A crackle of blue electricity flashed up her arm. "Yeah, I can feel it. It's like a . . . a *knot*. Kind of feels like lodestone."

"It's not lodestone," said Tesla, "but I agree that the signature is similar. It may be the aftereffect of whatever magic had infused the gate. Now that its chief components are in the Temple, it's impossible to say."

"Lodestone?" said Jake. "That's just magnetized iron ore. There's nothing special about—"

Tesla harrumphed loudly. "Young man, I couldn't hope to

explain to you in the space of a few minutes all of the properties of lodestone. It attracts wealth and repels djinn, of course, but those are only two of its most common household uses."

Jake shrugged. He knew better than to argue about magic rocks with a magical girl's familiar, but he still felt a twinge of annoyance.

With her hand still extended, Dynamo walked around the table. "There's something here. I can't see it, but I can feel it."

She stopped at a corner. Her goggles lifted from her eyes, turned opaque, and reattached to her tiara. She pointed down at the top of the table, where a pink and sticky smear, an inch long, stretched across the plastic.

"Did the police see this?" she asked.

Falschlaff opened his mouth as if to answer but then closed it again. He hunched his shoulders in apparent uncertainty.

Dynamo stared at the smear for half a minute. Then she ran a finger through it and put that finger in her mouth.

"Hey," Jake said, "you shouldn't—"

Dynamo ran her tongue over her teeth. "It's frosting," she said.

Falschlaff shook his head. Tesla made a buzzing noise as he removed his glasses and wiped them.

Jake rubbed a hand through his hair. "What kind of crook leaves behind frosting?"

"What kind of *monster* leaves behind frosting?" Dynamo muttered.

"C'mon," Jake said. "Why are we here? This is all junk."

EIGHT

BITTER TEARS

As Sunday evening came on, Jake stood at the sink in the upstairs bathroom and brushed his teeth. The door burst open, and Dana walked in with a small bag, probably her bath kit. She and her mother were spending the night, and she had no trouble making herself at home.

Jake sputtered and spat out his toothpaste. "Dana, what are you doing?"

She glared. "Getting ready for bed."

"You can't just walk in on—"

She surveyed the room and grunted. "Figures. American bathroom. Toilet in the same room, your tub is tiny, and you don't even have a separate place to wash."

She was silent for a moment before she made her final, one-word judgment: "Gross."

"What do you mean it's gross? Aren't you guys from Little America?"

"Yeah, but we've always had a Japanese *ofuroba.*"

"Even in that brownstone?"

"Yes, dummy, but we had to share it." She pressed her hands against his waist to push him from the sink. He didn't budge.

"This is *my* bathroom," he said.

She glared up at him. "It's gonna be *our* bathroom if Mom makes me live here."

"The master bath is downstairs next to—"

"That's your parents'!"

"Okay, then use the downstairs hall bathroom."

She raised an eyebrow. "How many bathrooms does this place have?"

"Three."

"Dork."

"You're insulting me because our house has three bathrooms? *I* didn't build the place."

She grunted and then peered at the toothbrush in his hands. "Your brush has dinosaurs on it."

"So?"

"Dork." She reached into her bag and pulled out a toothbrush adorned with blue lightning bolts. "Move over."

"Wait your turn."

"Ladies first."

"That's for buffets, not bathrooms. Bathrooms are first come, first serve. And you should knock before you barge in here. You might see something you can't un-see."

"Like what?"

He swallowed. "Like, um . . . chest hair."

Dana crossed her arms and tapped a foot against the tile floor. "You don't have chest hair."

"Do so."

"Do not."

"Do so."

"Prove it."

"No. Now get out!"

She found his heavy safety razor dangling from its stand next to the sink. After putting down her toothbrush, she reached out and picked it up.

"Hey, careful with that! You'll cut yourself!"

Holding it before her nose, she turned it in her fingers. "What is this?"

"It's a razor."

"Why's it funny-looking?"

"It's an old-fashioned razor. It's for men. *Manly* men. Now don't touch the top, or you'll slice your hand open."

"What's it for?"

"I shave with it, obviously."

She stuck out her lip and shot him another glare. "I bet *you* don't have anything to shave except your *palms."*

"I cannot believe what comes out of your mouth sometimes. I shave my *face."*

"Do not."

"Do so."

"Do not."

"Do *so.* I've been shaving for *months* now!"

She returned the razor to its stand, lifted her nose, and turned her back on him. *"I've* been shaving for a *year."*

"You're a girl. That's different."

"It means I'm more grown-up than you are."

"You are not!"

"Am so!"

"Are not!"

"Am so!"

"Are not times infinity!"

Dana tapped her foot for a moment before she said, "Grownups don't play those kinds of games."

"You brat."

She muttered for a moment before adding, "Hurry up and get out so I can brush my teeth and take my makeup off."

"You get out!"

She spun around again. "No, *you!* Ladies first and grownups before kids!"

"I'm the grownup here!"

"Are not! You don't shave enough! I shave more than you do!"

"That's not how you determine who's a grownup!"

"Is so!"

"Is not!"

"Is so!"

"Is . . ."

He stopped himself and pinched the bridge of his nose. *Great. Is this what my life is gonna be like from now on?*

After a deep breath, he said, "Honestly, Dana, I'll be out in a minute. I'm a guy, so I don't have much to do: I just gotta brush my teeth and hang my underwear on the doorknob, and I'm done."

"Aren't you gonna bathe?"

"I *shower.* And I'll do that in the morning before I *shave."*

"Gross." She turned back to the sink and pulled open the medicine chest.

"Hey!"

After she rummaged through various vials, tubes, and half-used packages of plasters, she pulled out a cone-shaped ceramic bottle with a red stopper. "What's this?"

"I slap it on after I shave."

She pulled out a narrow spray can. "And this?"

"Um . . . body spray."

"You wear body spray?"

"You got a problem with that?"

"Dork. Girls aren't gonna fall all over you like in the commercials."

"My *girlfriend* seems to like it okay."

Dana's eyes narrowed as she peered at him over the top of the spray can. "No, she doesn't. I was there. She wouldn't even kiss you. You can't even get your own girlfriend to kiss you. No girl's *ever* gonna kiss you."

"Maybe I've kissed a girl who isn't my girlfriend."

"Have not!"

Jake merely crossed his arms and stared at her.

She twisted one foot back and forth. *"Have* you?"

"Maybe."

With a growl, she sprayed the can onto her right wrist and sniffed it. Then she doused her other wrist with the aftershave and put it to her nose as well. She nodded. "That's what I thought."

"What?"

She held up the bottle. "Pumpkin bread." Then she held up the can. "Hydraulic fluid."

She dropped both in the wastebasket.

"Hey!"

After rummaging in the medicine chest once again, she pulled out his deodorant. She popped the cap off and stared at the stick for a moment before she said, "I'm not sniffing that. It's been in your pits."

She dropped it in the wastebasket as well.

He sighed and rubbed his forehead. "Okay, Dana, game's over. Leave, please. I wanna brush my teeth."

Her eyebrows came together in a glower. "I need to take my makeup off, and you can't watch, pervert, so *you* have to leave."

"Why do you slather on all that makeup, anyway? You're a little kid."

"No, I'm not. I'm a grownup." She turned to the sink and dug through her bag.

"I've seen you without makeup, so what difference does it make?"

She growled, mumbled incoherently, and reached for his washcloth, which hung on a rod next to his bath towel.

"Wait, hold it. You're not taking your makeup off with that."

"Why not?"

"Because it's *mine.*"

"So?"

"So it's been all over *my* face. You sure you wanna use it? That might count as an indirect kiss, I think. Then *you* would have kissed me even if my girlfriend won't."

She snapped her hand back as if recoiling from a hot stove. With a sullen glower, she said, "Get me another one."

"Hold on." He reached into the medicine chest and pulled out a plastic tub. "Here, I have baby wipes. Use these."

"*Why* do you have baby wipes?"

"Why not?"

"Creep."

"Wash your face, you brat. They have coconut oil in 'em, I think, and that's supposed to be good for taking off makeup."

"How would *you* know that?"

"I just do."

"Weirdo."

He sighed. "I did a little theater in middle school—well, just one play—so I've worn makeup too. Okay?"

"Double extra super weirdo." She snatched the baby wipes from him, stared at them, and pouted anew.

"Dana, I've already seen—"

"You can't see now, so go away!"

"What are you hiding? Do your freckles embarrass you? They shouldn't—"

She growled, *"Out."*

Jake knew Dana blushed easily; usually, her ears would be bright red by this time, but they weren't now, and in the bathroom's harsh light, he could see why: She had foundation caked in them. She also had it down her neck, and some had even spread to her T-shirt collar, turning it an unwholesome shade of peach.

He pinched the bridge of his nose again and squeezed his eyes shut, but then he laughed quietly. "You're covering a sunburn, aren't you? I *told* you to put on sunscreen—"

Her eyebrows came together, and the muscles in her cheeks poked out as she clenched her teeth. As if to wield it as a weapon, she grabbed his safety razor again, but her hand landed on the head, and her fingers fell over the blade's exposed edge. With a yelp, she snapped her hand back, and the razor clattered into the sink along with several drops of bright blood.

She clutched her hand, bounced around on tiptoe, and whimpered as more blood dribbled onto the tile floor.

"Sweet Princess, Dana, you're getting your hep C all over everything. Here, sit." Jake grabbed her shoulders and pushed her down onto the edge of the tub. "Now, let me see it."

She kept her hand bunched in a bloody fist, so he seized her wrist and pried her fingers open.

"See?" he said as he inspected her cuts. "I told you not to touch it. You're lucky it has a safety bar, or you'd need stitches. Hold still."

Though she pouted, she didn't pull her hand back. She continued to drip on the floor while Jake dug through the cupboard under the sink. After a few seconds, he pulled out a first-aid kit.

"See this?" he said as he set it down in front of her. "This is my make-Dana-feel-better box. I have aloe too."

He ripped open an iodine wipe and slathered her hand. She mumbled a complaint and tried to pull back, so he grabbed her wrist again. Then, after peeling open three adhesive bandages, he placed one on her thumb, one on her index finger, and one on her middle finger.

"You need to relax," he said. "You get yourself all worked up like this, and then you get hurt."

Dana growled.

"There," he said as he affixed the last bandage. "Want me to kiss it this time?"

She glowered. "No."

"If I don't kiss it, I can't make it all better."

"Don't care," she mumbled. "Don't want it all better."

Smiling, Jake pulled out some baby wipes and gently removed her makeup. She continued pouting as he worked, but she no longer fussed. Instead, she sat in silence and stared down at the floor, but she closed her eyes when he told her to so he could wipe away her eyeshadow.

It took several minutes, but once he was sure he had it all off, he patted her face with a moist washcloth. Her cheeks and ears were indeed bright red. She wasn't burnt to a crisp, but she was no doubt suffering, and her burns would certainly peel in a few days. The freckles had thickened on her cheeks, forming brown patches under her eyes.

"Sheesh, Dana, if you don't like being freckled, don't get sunburns."

He took a bottle of aloe lotion out of his kit, squeezed some onto his hands, and rubbed it into her cheeks and neck. Then he massaged it into her ears. Her ears were tiny.

She squinched up her eyes. "Why do you care?"

He paused in his rubbing. "Hm?"

"Why do you care what happens to me? Why do you try to be nice? I'm not nice to you."

"You're not nice to anybody, though, are you?"

She shook her head, causing his hands to slip from her ears.

Kneeling in front of her, he rested his wrists on his knees and said, "Remember last Tuesday when you fought in the Robosaur mothership, and the Temple fired the Weapon?"

She nodded.

"I thought you were dead, and that's when I realized something."

"What?"

He took a deep breath and let it out slowly. "It annoyed me. When you get hurt, it annoys me." He tapped her button nose and then smeared aloe on it. "So don't get hurt. If you want me to leave you alone, all you have to do is stay safe and not get hurt."

She put her hands in her lap and stared down at them. "I can't stay safe. And I hurt all the time. Being Dynamo makes me . . . it makes me sore all over. *Everything* hurts."

He screwed the lid onto the aloe bottle and put it back in his kit. "Then get used to me. I don't even care if you call me names and hit me. But I'm not going away."

He didn't bother trying to shoo her from the bathroom again.

He mopped up the blood on the floor with a tissue and then rinsed out the sink. He made her brush her teeth. As he brushed his own, she silently watched him.

Once Jake had flossed, gargled, and rinsed, he headed off to his room. Quietly, her bare feet making little noise in the carpeted hall, Dana followed.

"What are you doing?" he asked.

"Nothing," she replied.

"Then don't follow me."

"We're just going the same direction."

"The sewing room is the other way. That's where you're sleeping."

He stopped. She stopped too. Then he walked again, and she still followed.

When he pushed open his bedroom door, she ducked under his arm and stepped inside.

"Hey!"

Dana stood in the middle of his room, fists on hips. As she looked around, she made that familiar rasping noise in her throat.

The room was small, but Jake liked it. His bed was worn out but comfortable. In one corner stood a small desk where he did his homework, and he had a purple beanbag chair beside it. On the blue-painted walls hung a playbill from a showing of *The Music Man* and a poster containing thirty dinosaurs' names and pictures.

"You're a slob," said Dana.

"If you don't like it, get out."

She pointed at a pile of clothes in front of his closet. "Yuck." Then she pointed at the unmade bed. "Nasty."

"Yeah, that's nice. Look, I'd like to sleep now—"

She walked to the bed, grabbed the edge of the crumpled

comforter, and tugged it to smooth it out, thereby revealing its design —a panoramic scene with volcanoes in the background, tropical ferns in the foreground, and a *Tyrannosaurus* roaring in between.

"Your blanket has dinosaurs on it," she said.

"I've had that since I was seven. You can leave now."

She reached under the sheets, seized an amorphous lump, and pulled. Her hands came out gripping a well-worn yellow plush toy with a beak, three horns, and a large frill. Dana stared at it for half a minute. "What is *this?*"

He ran a hand through his hair. "That's Trilly. Got her at a museum gift shop when I was eight. She's a *Triceratops.*"

"She? You sleep with a girl? You're gross."

"That's enough, Dana. I'm out of patience."

Tucking the toy under one arm, she stuck her nose in the air and declared, "Fine. It's past my bedtime anyway."

She marched out the door and stomped down the hall.

After a moment's indecision, Jake followed.

Halfway to the sewing room, she spun around and held up one hand. "You can't follow me."

He shrugged. "We're just going the same direction."

Growling, she continued stomping, now at a faster pace. He walked faster as well, so she jogged. He jogged. Then she sprinted, and he bounded after.

Once she reached the doorway of the sewing room, she fumbled with the knob, leaped inside, and held up a hand again. "Hold it!"

He leaned on the doorframe. "Yes?"

"You can't come in here! I have to go to bed!"

"Why are you going to bed with *my* plush toy—and wearing my aftershave?"

With clenched teeth, she pointed down at the doorjamb. "You see that invisible line?"

"Uh—"

"That line marks this room as a *no-ball zone.*"

"What?"

Her eyes narrowed. "If anything tries to come in here with balls"—she leaned toward him and shook a fist—"it *loses* its balls!"

With that, she slammed the door in his face.

Jake blinked for a few seconds but then pressed his nose against the door, cupped his hands over his mouth, and shouted, "You want me to read you a bedtime story?"

From the other side, she yelled, "No!"

"Want me to tuck you in?"

"Pervert!"

"Want me to kiss you good night?"

The door flew open again. Dana still had a pout on her face, but her chest heaved, and tears ran from her eyes. She had her arms wrapped tightly around the plush toy's neck as if she were holding on for dear life—or trying to strangle it.

"*You,*" she shrieked through clenched teeth, "*are not my dad!*"

He blinked again.

Oops.

After taking a deep breath and clearing his throat, he lowered himself to his knees so his eyes were level with hers. "Dana, I'm not trying to be."

"What *are* you trying to do?"

He rolled his tongue around in his mouth for half a minute.

Just what the heck am *I trying to do?*

"Well," he said, tapping his chest, "if we have to live together, you can think of me as your big brother."

Arms still tight around Trilly, she stared at the floor and muttered, "You'd be more like my *little* brother since I'm more grown-up than you are."

He shrugged. "Have it your way."

"But you *can't* be my brother! You've just been an *acquaintance* up till now." She twisted a foot on the doorjamb and squeezed the *Triceratops*. Its head covered the lower half of her face, making her eyes look huge.

"Can't go from acquaintance to brother," she mumbled with the toy muffling her voice. "That's not how it works."

"How about friend, then? You can go from acquaintance to friend, right?"

She stared at him silently. After several seconds, with most of her face still hidden behind the toy, she held up her bandaged hand.

"What does that mean?"

"Friends can kiss ouches," she said quietly. "But only sometimes."

He leaned forward and gently kissed her palm. "There. Now it's all better."

She nodded solemnly and lowered her hand.

"Want me to kiss your ears and cheeks too, since you burned them?"

With a snarl, she slammed the door again, this time catching the tip of his nose. With an *oof,* he fell on his rump, rubbed his face, and laughed.

Elbows resting on his knees, he sat there for a second and stared at the closed door.

At last, he shook his head and groaned faintly as he rose to his feet. After he stood, the door opened a crack, and one of Dana's green eyes peered out.

"You should go to bed, Dana," Jake said.

"So should you."

"Yeah, that's where I'm going. We both gotta go to fifth grade tomorrow, after all. Why are you still up? You really hoping I'll tuck you in?"

She growled again. "You're *not* my dad."

"No, I'm not." He chewed the inside of his cheek. "Dana, maybe . . . um . . . I know it's not my business, but can I ask—?"

Her green eye stared at him—unblinking, unreadable, like a jewel in the dark.

"It's true," she whispered.

He watched her silently, but a tickle in the back of his throat congealed into a lump. For the briefest moment, his knees shook.

"It's true," she whispered again. "I'm the one who killed him."

With that, she slammed the door once more.

This time, it stayed shut.

JAKE DIDN'T BELIEVE IT FOR A MINUTE.

But maybe he could believe it for *half* a minute.

Maybe.

He padded down the hall. His heart pounded, and in the quiet house, late in the evening when everyone else was in bed, it sounded like the ominous beat of a war drum.

Dana loved her father. He was sure of it. And Pretty Dynamo

. . .

No, she loved him too. Last week, she had started to talk

about him after their scuffle in the alleyway. Although Lady Paladin Andalusia had warned him that there were different theories on the subject of personas, he was reasonably sure Dana and Dynamo were the same person. Pretty Dynamo acted like Dana when she was tired, hungry, or upset.

Just once, he had seen Dana happy, and she was an entirely different girl then. If one good meal with a friend could change Dana that much, there was no reason to think Dynamo's personality implied she was a separate being from her alter ego.

Andalusia had told him there were different theories, but now Jake had a theory of his own: The girls' powers supposedly had to do with unfulfilled desires, so perhaps their personas represented traits they wished they had or sides of their personalities they couldn't usually reveal. Dynamo was brassy and athletic, whereas Dana was quiet and clumsy. Maybe Dynamo was everything Dana wished she could be. And maybe that was why Dana hated her.

Besides, he had seen her reaction when the demoniac tried to drag him to hell: She killed monsters, but she didn't like it when people died.

So no, Dynamo wouldn't kill Dana's dad. He was sure of it.

Pretty sure.

Mostly.

Still mulling over the question, he walked into his room, closed the door, and unbuttoned his shirt. As the shirt dropped to the floor, he shook his head. He didn't know what was going on in her mind. All he had was speculation.

Perhaps he didn't need to know. Perhaps it was none of his business.

Although magical girls were exempt from most of the city's laws, the courts could theoretically convict one for murder. As far as Jake knew, it had never happened, and he had no idea how the police could arrest a magical girl anyway. But no one had tried to arrest Dynamo, and there was no talk on the news of bringing her to justice, so there must be some sort of mistake. Whatever else she was, she wasn't a murderer.

He shook his head again and began peeling off his undershirt. But he froze with his elbows in the air when a voice came from a dark corner of the room: It was a soft voice—a trembling, timid voice.

It was a girl's voice.

"I'm sorry, Jake Blatowski," the voice whispered. "But you've learned my secret, so you're gonna have to die now."

NINE

WAKE-UP CALL

For one brief, wild moment, Jake thought the voice must be Pretty Dynamo's. But when he spun around, he saw someone else: She sat in the corner beside the door, curled up into a ball with her knees against her chest. She had her right arm pointed at him, her hand bunched into a fist. That hand was shaking.

"Who—?"

With a loud clatter like tumbling kitchen utensils, several objects jumped out of her wrist: White knobs, spheres, and lozenges, all with long, gray tubes attached to them. Those tubes pointed at his chest.

Tears ran down the girl's face. She ducked her head. "I'm . . . I'm really sorry—"

So dumbfounded was he that it took him several seconds to realize she had a dozen guns trained on him. Once the realization hit, he broke out in a cold sweat, but it was still another second before he moved. He could bolt for the door, but she was next to it. Or he could jump out the window, but he'd shred himself on the glass unless he took time to open it first, in which case she'd shoot him in the back.

He was about to leap toward the window anyway when something else made the decision for him. From the girl's chest came a high, tinny voice: *"Civilian noncombatant detected. Safety protocols enabled. Ranged weapons deactivating."*

With another cacophony of clanking, the guns folded back into the girl's arm. She leaped to her feet and pounded a fist against her forearm. "No! *No!* Override safety! Override safety—!"

If he'd been thinking clearly, he would have taken the chance to open the window and drop to the grass, likely suffering nothing worse than a broken leg. Instead, he jumped her.

She shrieked as he grabbed her around the waist and lifted her off her feet. She was slender yet solid with muscle, and her abdomen felt firm under his arms.

Jake still outweighed her. Unsure what to do, he tossed her, and she landed hard on his bed, making the springs groan as she bounced. Then he threw himself on top of her.

The strange circumstances had him confused. From the moment she'd first spoken, adrenaline had gushed into his veins. His heart thudded like mad, and his gasping breath poured in and out. His head felt clear, but he was nonetheless taking too long to pick up essential details—such as this girl's spiky pink hair and white bicycle helmet, or her molded breastplate, which was now digging into his solar plexus.

This was Sukeban Tsubasa, the so-called bad girl of magical girls, who had recently challenged Pretty Dynamo to a one-on-

one fight—or at least it was Tsubasa's power suit. But the girl wearing it couldn't possibly be her.

For the second time, he was making the grave mistake of wrestling a magical girl. If she really intended to kill him, he'd be dead in a minute, and he'd no doubt go the hard way: She'd probably start by ripping his arms off.

Eyes wide, lips drained of color, and sweat streaming from her face, she lifted him up with one hand and grabbed his left arm just below the shoulder in a fierce, crushing grip. He gasped. She pulled—

Here it comes—!

A high voice from her chest announced calmly, *"Civilian noncombatant detected. Safety protocols enabled. Strength enhancements deactivating."*

"No!" the girl wailed.

He landed heavily, and one of her molded, armored breasts hit him in the pit of his stomach.

She rained punches on his head and shoulders. Even without help from her suit, she packed a wallop, but she wasn't his match. He absorbed two blows to the jaw and then, after catching her wrists, pinned her arms over her head. That gave him no leverage, so he ended up with his face in the bedsheets and her armor making bruises on his chest. She squirmed and bucked. After planting his right knee inside her left thigh, he tried to scissor her right leg between his left arm and his side to keep her from kicking him. In the process, he realized he knew nothing about proper grappling.

After finally swimming through the fog of fear and surprise to reach clarity, part of his mind pointed out that he'd just made several stupid decisions: The time to tackle her had been as soon as she raised the guns, before she could get a shot off. And once it was clear she couldn't shoot, he should have tried for the door.

The clear thought evaporated as she continued to lash and reel under him. She panted and whimpered as she tried to break his grip. She slid around, giving him full opportunity to appreciate her smooth arms, legs, and stomach.

Dang, this feels really good—

"Let me go!" she gasped. *"Please!* Please, please, please! Oh Princess, please—!"

He released her right wrist and clapped his hand over her mouth.

"You tried to kill me!" he hissed.

Her eyes widened further until he thought they'd leap from her skull. She hyperventilated into his palm, wetting it with her breath. Sweat poured from her forehead, and tears poured from her eyes. Still, she writhed, and it was all he could do to hold her down.

Holy Princess, this chick is totally freaking out.

With a bang, the door burst open, and the girl instantly froze.

In the doorway stood Dana. She wore a baggy set of blue flannel pajamas decorated with lightning bolts. Her ratty hair hovered around her face, and she still had Jake's floppy *Triceratops* toy tucked under one arm.

"Rrrr!" she snarled. "Why is it so *loud* in here? Can't you do that disgusting stuff *quietly—?"*

She paused, mouth open, when her eyes took in the scene. Under Jake, the girl lay still, her lithe body slumped down into the bed. She and Jake both stared at Dana, and Dana stared back. Jake felt the girl's sweat-slicked stomach rise and fall beneath him, briefly sticking to his undershirt. She still panted into his hand, but she had stopped panicking.

Somewhere in the distance, a dog howled at the moon. Downstairs, a wall clock pounded out its steady, rhythmic clash with that peculiar loudness clocks have only at night.

Framed in the doorway, Dana was little more than a silhouette, a paper cutout in the window of a doll's house. A sliver of moonlight slipped from behind the blinds and highlighted her half-lidded eyes, which shone like two fires burning copper salts. Her jutting lower lip was blood-red.

The silence, punctuated by the banging clock, the heavy breathing, and the agitated canine, stretched on for eternity. No one moved.

Oh, Dana, Jake thought, *I know exactly what you're—*

"Figures," Dana muttered. She closed the door and left.

Jake blinked. *If she doesn't get back in here as Pretty Dynamo, I'm gonna be pissed.*

Distracted, he relaxed his grip. The girl scrambled out from under him and shot back into her corner beside the door, where she curled into the fetal position. Hiding her face behind her hands, she mumbled, "Oh, please don't come any closer. Don't hurt me. Don't touch me. Please, please, please. Oh Princess, I don't wanna get pregnant—"

Jake sat up and rubbed his eyes. "Who *are* you, and how did you get Sukeban Tsubasa's power suit?"

Her mumbling stopped. She lowered her hands to reveal her tear-stained face.

"I *am* Sukeban Tsubasa."

"No, you're not! You don't sound anything like her! And she's got no reason to attack me in my room!"

Putting her hands on the wall to steady herself but keeping her back pressed into the corner, she climbed to her feet.

After swallowing once, she closed her eyes and, surrounded

by a soft, pink glow, floated into the air. The power suit evaporated, leaving her bare. As her naked body rotated, Jake's jaw dropped, and his heart redoubled its hard pounding. In his throat formed a lump so big he was afraid he'd choke on it.

She had a superb figure—slim and finely sculpted with long, slender legs and a supple waist set with firm muscle. Jake saw all of it, every inch. A strange, buzzing warmth spread from his head to his feet.

He'd once walked in on Grease Pencil Marionette painting a nude model, but he'd been embarrassed and hadn't looked closely. And he'd seen Dana without her clothes on, but that was different—that was Dana. This was the first time he'd seen *this,* and it was as if all the deepest secrets of the universe were revealing themselves to him. He almost doubled over as some new, unidentifiable sensation struck him like a punch to the gut.

The vision lasted but a moment. The girl returned to the floor, and then she was in trousers, a button-up shirt, and a sweater vest. Her hair was black instead of pink.

Jake blinked.

He tilted his head. He blinked again.

Her face hadn't changed, yet it was different somehow. He knew her but didn't know her. Her identity was a Schrödinger's cat, hanging for a moment in a field of uncertainty as though his mind were deliberately refusing to acknowledge who she was.

As if a tight muscle in his skull were relaxing, something gave way in his head. He rubbed his temples to get rid of the feeling, and a faint headache settled behind his eyeballs.

"Hold on," he said, "you're . . ."

She squeezed her eyes shut and sniffled, nodding.

"T.B.?"

She nodded again. "The name's Tsubasa Bando, but I've

always gone to English-language schools. Someone started calling me T.B. in first grade, and it stuck."

He continued rubbing his temples. "Wait a minute, you're a *girl?*"

"What do you mean? Of *course* I am! You found out—"

"I did?"

"Yes! When you . . . when you . . ."

She slid back down the wall, curled into a ball again, and covered her face.

"When you ruined me for marriage!" she wailed and then burst into fresh tears.

Jake sat on the bed and stared. After she bawled for a full minute with no sign of stopping, he said, "What in the name of the Moon Princess are you talking about?"

"In the arcade!" she blubbered. "When you touched my . . . you grabbed my . . ."

Her face turned bright red. She shoved her nose between her knees and continued crying.

"Ah!" He slammed his fist into his palm. *"That* explains it! I *thought* your chest felt weird, so I was thinkin', I dunno, maybe you used to do a lotta pushups but then let yourself go."

She immediately stopped crying and raised her head. "You didn't know?"

"Uh—"

"You didn't *know?* Even when you had your hand all over my . . . my . . ."

Jake cleared his throat and rolled his shoulders. "Um, maybe I shouldn't admit this, but I don't really touch a lot of girls there, so—"

"I came here for nothing," she whispered. She clenched her fists and shook. "A day and a half of torment for *nothing—"*

"Yeah, well, the good news is, you don't have to kill me, right?"

"But you know *now,* so I *still* have to kill you!"

He sighed. "I've got enough things out to kill me at the moment, so how about we make this our little secret instead?"

She swallowed hard. "You'd do that?"

"Sure. I am perfectly happy to keep the secret that you're a crossdressing sapphist."

"I'm not a—!"

She slapped a hand over her mouth, closed her eyes for a moment, and took a deep breath. Once she returned to her fragile calm, she hissed, "It's an act! All of it! The whole thing is an act!"

"Really?"

"Yes!" She rolled her eyes. "Cassandra and Megumi are in on it. They're old friends I've known since kindergarten. Everywhere I go, they spread rumors about what a hot guy I am, and then other girls join in so they don't feel left out."

Jake nodded. "They don't, like, rent out their services, do they?"

"What?"

"Never mind." He shook his head. "Why in the heck would you do something like this?"

Looking away from him, she fidgeted and mumbled something incoherent.

"What?"

She mumbled it again.

"Sorry, I still didn't—"

She squeezed her eyes shut and curled the fingers of one trembling hand. "I said," she hissed, "I'm *androphobic!*"

"I see. You're afraid of spiders."

Slapping her forehead, she said, *"Men.* I'm afraid of *men!"*

"And you dress like what you're afraid of?"

"Yes!"

"Is that a Batman thing?"

"What? No! I do it because I can keep boys away if I have a crowd of girls around me all the time!"

Jake squeezed his eyes shut and pinched the bridge of his nose. "That makes sense . . . I think. So what do you do about P.E.?"

She shrugged. "Fake doctor's note. It says I have a congenital heart condition. The girls absolutely *love* that. Besides, it helps with the image: I mean, I can't exactly pose as a broad-shouldered linebacker, can I? So I play a sickly dandy they can dream about nursing back to health."

"Girls go for that?"

"You saw it yourself. Yeah, they go for it." She laughed faintly and leaned her forehead on a knee. "I mean, Megumi-*chan* and Cass are just playing around, but still."

Jake chewed the inside of his cheek. "Are you *really* Sukeban Tsubasa?"

She nodded.

"But all the talk you do in your TV interviews: Your boyfriends, the smoking, the drinking—"

She dug her fingers into her hair. "It's an *act!* All of it's an act! I don't do *any* of that stuff!" Her eyes welled with tears again. "I'd *like* to. I'd *love* to hang out with boys! I'd love to be able to do this and that and maybe even the other thing with boys—"

"You're way too young for the other thing."

"—but I *can't!"*

She resumed bawling.

"You didn't sound like Tsubasa earlier," Jake said. "Where was your persona?"

"I don't *have* one!" she sobbed. "I don't even have a persona! I'm not a real magical girl! It's just a power suit, that's all! Some aliens were buying a new one, so they found me and gave me their outdated model."

"Really?"

She wiped her wrist across her nose and sniffed hard. "Yeah, they could write it off their taxes as a charitable contribution— y'know, since the forces of evil have us marked for destruction."

"How do they prove they donated it?"

"I had to make 'em a receipt. Estimating its value in Rigellian denarii was the pits."

Jake coughed into his fist. "Okay, fine, but you have a raccoon dog following you around—"

She rolled her eyes. "That's just the instruction manual. He's a self-aware robot. He's not a real familiar, and I don't even have a contract."

"But still, your voice—"

"Oh, *that*. I can change my voice." She stopped crying. After dabbing her eyes with her wrist, she opened her mouth, and Sukeban Tsubasa's peculiar accent poured out: "Oh man, me an' dem boys, we gonna do all *kinds* o' bad stuff t'gedder. We gonna smoke an' drink an' swear—"

Jake blinked. "That's amazing."

"And then there's this." She lowered her eyelids, parted her moist lips, and gave him a come-hither gaze that made his heart miss a beat.

"My darling," she said in the low and oily voice f T.B., "come with me to the verdant hillsides, and tonight we shall gaze upon the stars and drink in each other's love."

His heart pounded like a drum. This girl had attacked him in his room, sending him into metabolic overdrive; then she had taken her clothes off in front of him and wept in front of him, and now she was being seductive. He gripped the bunched bedclothes in his fists because it was all he could do to keep his hormone-ravaged teenage body from running across the room, seizing her, and throwing her onto the bed again.

Maybe she has a good reason to be afraid of me.

He looked away from her and gulped air until he felt calmer.

Tsubasa looked calmer too. Maybe playing her familiar roles kept her fear at bay. She straightened her legs out, leaned against the wall, and folded her hands in her lap before taking a deep, shuddering breath.

Jake's desires changed shape as his heartbeat slowed. He wanted to put his arms around her, pat her back, and let her cry on his shoulder. Of course, he knew if he tried it, she'd flip out again. It wasn't fair, a girl crying in front of a guy who wasn't allowed to hold her.

"Feeling better?" he asked.

"A little," she whispered with a soggy smile. "I think I cried myself out."

"You still scared of me?"

"Terrified." She looked away and, with one fine-boned hand, toyed absently with a door hinge. "But I think I'll be okay as long as you stay over there. "Twenty feet. That's what I can usually handle, and I can get closer if I have something—or some girls—in between. It used to be worse."

Jake cleared his throat. "You're pretty good. The voice thing, I mean. I was in one play in middle school. It was a big production, and the theater club had to recruit to fill out the cast. Some of the guys in the club could do voices, but I think you're better than any of them."

She twisted her mouth and, looking glum, said, "Thanks."

"You do theater?"

She shook her head. "I can't. Too many boys."

"Oh. Yeah, I guess so." After a pause, he cleared his throat again. "If you're scared of me, why did you attack me? And how'd you find me?"

She smiled. "Your girlfriend called you Jake Blatowski, and I figured you must live in Juban. You were easy to find after that." After sniffling and rubbing a hand over her nose, she added, "I know it was dumb, but I didn't know what else to do, and I was so scared you'd tell everybody. I thought if I came here, at least I'd feel brave for trying it—"

She pulled up her knees again and rested her forehead on them. "I wasn't thinking. Not clearly. I was just scared. That's all."

Several seconds passed. Even with the door closed, Jake could hear the clock downstairs rolling out its steady, mechanical beat.

"I'm so tired of being scared," she whispered.

He rubbed the back of his neck. "Well, I guess there are some jerks out there, but still, most of the guys you know are probably okay "

"I *know* that, Jake. Explaining it doesn't help."

"What exactly are you afraid of?"

"I don't know. Getting raped, I guess. When you grabbed me a minute ago, I really thought, hey, this is it, this is everything I'm afraid of, it's actually happening—"

"You attacked me first. I thought you were gonna shoot me."

"I know. I'm sorry. I wanted to feel brave, but it was just

stupid." She rubbed a hand across her hair. "I don't think I could've gone through with it even if the suit had worked." She peeked at him over her knees. "You gonna press charges?"

"Well, it's assault, I think. Maybe attempted murder." He coughed into his fist. "But you're a magical girl, so if I went to the police, I'd be the one to get in trouble."

She dropped her forehead back to her knees. "I'm not a magical girl. I wish I were. I wish I had a persona like they have. Then maybe I could at least have some time when I wasn't afraid."

He laughed quietly. "I've talked to magical girls with personas, Tsubasa. I don't think they like them, so maybe you're lucky."

"No." She shook her head. "I'm a fake. I pretend to be cool and brave, but I'm scared to death inside."

"You still fight monsters."

"Monsters don't scare me like boys do."

Jake set his hands in his lap. "I think you're a real magical girl. Who says you have to have a persona, and who says your familiar can't be an instruction manual? You've got powers, and you protect Urbanopolis. That's what really matters."

She smiled weakly.

He swallowed. *Sheesh, there must be something wrong with me because this is turning me on.*

After coughing into his fist again, he said, "You know, there are ways to deal with this kind of thing—"

"I know. I *have* gotten better. A little bit. But it's so much easier to dress up as T.B. and play with the girls. It's fun." She stared at the worn-out carpet. "We go to amusement parks and restaurants and movies. Sometimes, I'll take just one on a date, but mostly we all go together and hang out."

She released a long sigh. "I'd like to stop. Really. I'd like to wear a pretty dress and grow my hair out. And I know I'm not being fair to Cass or Megumi-*chan*. They've been pretending to be my girlfriends for a long time, but I think it'd be nice if they could get boyfriends instead—actual boyfriends."

Her cheeks turned pink, and she played awkwardly with the door hinge again. "And, um, I mean . . . I'd kinda like to have a boyfriend too."

A vision streamed through Jake's mind: He could see himself with Tsubasa. Over many months, they'd steadily become more comfortable with each other, more fond of each other. He'd gradually help her overcome her phobia, and they'd grow closer, both physically and emotionally. In time, she'd be able to tolerate letting him stand within five feet of her, then two, then one. Then would come the day when, trembling like a leaf, she'd fall into his arms, and he'd clasp her tightly, whispering sweet reassurances into her ear—

"I know you don't owe me anything," she whispered with a sniffle, "but I need help. I need to practice getting closer to boys. But I don't really know any boys—"

His heart skipped again. *Oh my Princess, it's happening. That stupid fantasy I just had is actually happening.*

He could feel the blood pulsing through his temples. He shifted uncomfortably on the bed.

"—and the truth is," Tsubasa continued as she shyly lowered her eyes and flipped a lock of hair over one finger, "I am more comfortable with *you* than I am with most guys—

Jake thought his heart would burst out of his ribs. His mouth was suddenly bone dry. *Sweet Princess in a sailor suit, it is really, actually happening!*

"—because, I mean," she added, her voice slipping back into

T.B.'s alluring huskiness, "it's obvious you're . . . well, you know."

He blinked. "Wha—? *Hey!*"

"I mean, you're the kind of guy that listens to show tunes—"

He rose an inch from the bed. *"What's wrong with show tunes?"*

She bunched her fists together and blurted, "And there's a guy I really, *really* like!"

Jake froze.

Tsubasa's lip trembled, and her voice wavered as she said, "If I can't get over this . . . if I can't stop being afraid all the time . . . I wanna stop being afraid of boys, at least enough so I can tell him how I feel. Even if he doesn't like me back, I just wanna tell him. That's all."

She lowered her hands to her lap, and a few tears fell on them.

"I'm gonna be an old maid," she mumbled. "I know that already. But I wanna be able to tell him anyway."

Jake's heart slowed, and his shoulders sagged.

It's not happening.

"Do I know him?" he asked after a careful cough.

She squeezed her eyes shut and nodded.

"Who is it?"

Putting her fists against her cheeks, she pressed her forehead to her knees again. "It's *Ralph.*"

His name came out as a squeak.

Jake stared at her for half a minute. Again, the clock downstairs seemed impossibly loud.

"Really?"

She nodded.

"Why?"

"I don't know." She slapped a hand against the wall. "He's nice, and he's funny, and he's cute, and . . . and he looks like maybe I could fight him off if I had to."

Is that what girls want in a guy?

Jake coughed faintly. "Ralph might not look like much, Tsubasa, but he's got a mean fastball. I don't think you could fight him off without your power suit."

She quailed.

"But you wouldn't have to! He's a great guy! He's got a lot of sisters, so he knows how to treat girls. He'd be a perfect gentleman. And he really likes magical girls too, so if he knew you were Sukeban Tsubasa, he'd probably be crazy about you."

She shook her head. "He hates me."

"He might not like T.B., but he thinks T.B. is a guy."

"What difference does *that* make?"

"A lot. Trust me. First off, he's jealous. But second, he thinks T.B. is a weakling. Guys don't like other guys who are weak, but they like girls that way."

Her eyebrows came together. "Why?"

"Dunno. It's just how we are. You said the girls want to nurse you back to health, right? Guys have something like that too."

"Are *you* like that?"

"Um . . ." He'd just been fantasizing about helping her get over her phobia, so he supposed he was.

For a moment, his mind turned to Dana—the way he always wanted to pick her up, clean her off, bandage her up, feed her—

He rapped his knuckles against his head. "Yeah, I guess I'm like that."

"Is *Ralph* like that?"

He shrugged. "He's a guy too, so he must be."

Her voice grew quiet, and she interlaced her fingers. "Do you think he'd like me?"

Jake smiled. "I think, Tsubasa, that if Ralph met the real you, he'd like you a lot."

A cold tingle ran the length of his spine.

Am I speaking for Ralph . . . or myself?

THE MORNING AFTER

After changing back into her magical form, Tsubasa left by the window. Jake had to press himself into the corner at the foot of his bed so she could—with her eyes squeezed shut—dash past him and leap to what she considered safety. Soon after she was gone, he finished undressing, climbed into his pajamas, and lay down.

The room was strangely quiet. His heart pounded in time with the clock downstairs.

He tossed back and forth for several minutes, but no position felt comfortable. He had been having trouble sleeping for the last few months. Over the previous week, whenever he had slept, he had slept soundly from sheer exhaustion, but now that he'd spent a weekend without anything trying to kill him, his insomnia was back.

With its disarrayed and rumpled bedclothes, the bed felt desolate and empty. Thanks to Dana, Jake didn't even have his *Triceratops* toy—not that he actually slept with the thing anyway; he just set it by his pillow on the rare occasions when he made the bed. Most of the time, it lay buried under the covers or squeezed between the mattress and the wall.

He rolled onto his stomach. In an ill-defined way, he had an inkling of why he couldn't sleep: Since he had entered firmly and irrevocably into his adolescent years, going to bed alone at night had grown into a crushing burden. It was worse now because he had tackled a girl in this same bed only half an hour earlier, thereby provoking a bizarre mixture of fear and desire that left his nerves frazzled.

He could still smell Tsubasa in his bedclothes. She smelled like roses and sweat—heady, salty, and exciting. The scent made his stomach ache.

Girls. He had learned more about girls in the last week than in all his years previous. He hadn't known before how much one could differ from another when in his arms. His mind wandered to Rifle Maiden, who wasn't his type but would probably be fun to hang out with. Then his mind went to Marionette, who was well-muscled and boyish, with an embrace that could leave bruises. It wandered to Tsubasa, who was well-muscled but not boyish—at least when she wasn't pretending to be a boy. He liked Tsubasa's eyes. He liked the way her shoulders looked, and he wondered how she kissed.

Then his mind wandered to Miss Percy, a full-grown woman who was soft and warm, and who melted into him so easily. Between the four of them, she might be the best for assuaging late-night loneliness.

He pulled his pillow over his head and drove his nose down into the mattress. Here he was, unable to sleep, and he was fantasizing about his teacher.

Only after that did his mind turn to Chelsea.

Back in elementary school—the first time he was in elementary school—he often saw Chelsea when he went over to Ralph's house to play. She had looked so strange to him with her pale skin, pale hair, and ice-blue eyes—like a ghost. She ran around with Clarissa and Jamie. Sometimes, when Jake and Ralph played video games, Chelsea stood in the doorway of Ralph's room and stared, her mouth set in a pout and her cold eyes fixed on Jake's head.

He couldn't remember if he even so much as spoke to her before he was in fifth grade. She got a growth spurt at that time, but he hadn't had his yet, so she towered over him. Previously, they had been the same size, but for one year, she was enormous. Near a sandbox at the park, she walked up to him and pushed him down. He got up and pushed her back. Despite her height, he wrestled her to the ground and rubbed sand in her pale yellow hair, thinking it would make her cry.

It didn't.

When he was in sixth grade, she stopped towering. Eventually, she came to look tiny and skinny. And instead of standing in the doorway to pout and glare, she marched right in, snatched up a controller, and dominated both Jake and Ralph on any fighting game they played. She wasn't quiet anymore, either: She threw insults, and she already swore like a sailor.

A few days after Jake started eighth grade, Chelsea walked up to him in the hall and ordered him to meet her behind the gym after school. He did as she said, thinking she wanted to fight, but she instead told him without stammering or blushing that she liked him and wanted him to be her boyfriend.

After that, they stood there and held hands, awkwardly, not looking at each other. Jake was thirteen at the time, and Chelsea was twelve. Her hand didn't feel any different from other hands he'd held, but it nonetheless made him break out in a sweat and made his heart pound like crazy.

So he figured that must be love.

He liked hanging out with her. He liked trading barbs with her, and he liked playing video games with her. He wished she'd let him kiss her.

But even so, she wasn't the first girl who came to mind when it was late and he was lonely.

He sighed deeply and wondered what Dana was doing. He had little doubt she'd got the wrong idea, but still, she must have recognized Sukeban Tsubasa. Surely, she'd realized something was wrong.

He thought about walking down the hall, knocking on her door, and explaining what happened. Of course, he'd have to leave out certain details.

But he didn't want to see Dana right now. Instead, he simply tossed and turned, unable to sleep.

AFTER HALF AN HOUR, JAKE WAS ON HIS BACK AND STARING AT the ceiling. The glow-in-the-dark star stickers had long since lost their shine. The ceiling was a flat stretch of dark gray.

He thought he caught a glimmer of blue out of the corner of one eye, so he turned his head. He saw nothing. Perhaps the moonlight had peeked for a moment through the blinds.

He turned his eyes back to the ceiling, but that flash of blue appeared again. From the far end of the room, where Tsubasa had earlier crouched, came the sound of a girl softly weeping.

He froze. A film of sweat appeared on his forehead.

The weeping continued.

After a minute, he sat up. Squinting hard, he could just make out a hint of pale light in the corner, but he didn't see a girl.

"T.B.?" he said. "Is that you? Why are you—?"

The weeping stopped. Faintly, as if from far away, a voice sobbed, "It wasn't supposed to be like this."

The blue glow evaporated, and all was silent. Jake sat in bed for several minutes, listening to his heart pounding in his ears, listening to the hall clock pounding away downstairs.

Uh oh.

SOMETIME DURING THE NIGHT, JAKE FINALLY FELL ASLEEP AND swam through dreams he couldn't remember. Just before dawn, as he slowly rose to the surface of consciousness, he heard a familiar voice—the one he always heard just before he awoke: *You are going to be unhappy,* it said, *and you are going to die alone.*

He opened his eyes with a soft sigh.

When his alarm rang, he climbed wearily out of bed, took his shower, and went through his beloved shaving ritual. While he scraped his razor through the sweetly scented foam on his upper lip, he stared in the mirror at the dark circles under his eyes.

He got dressed. Moved by a vague foreboding he couldn't explain, Jake then slipped into his parents' room, found the jar of spare cash on their dresser, and shook a few credits out into his hand. He furtively dropped them into his pocket.

He walked downstairs and plopped onto his favorite stool at the breakfast bar. As always, his mom was already frying up breakfast, and his dad was already drinking coffee. It was unusually quiet, however, because the TV was off. Hungry for news, his father reread yesterday's paper instead.

"Morning, Mom," Jake said. "Morning, Dad." He watched his mother for a minute before he said, "Hey, Mom, if you're cooking for Dana, can you do her eggs scrambled? She doesn't like runny yolks."

His mother smiled as she poked her spatula at some sizzling bacon. "Sure, I can do scrambled."

"And can you . . . uh . . . give her extra? I don't think she eats enough."

His mother laughed. "What? Why?"

"I just don't, that's all—"

On the couch, his father turned a page of the paper and chuckled. "Is she a magical girl? I hear some of them need a lot of calories."

Jake squirmed on his stool. *"No,* she's just a growing girl. She looks really skinny—"

His mother shook her head. "I suppose I can, but you better eat it if she doesn't." She looked up from the stove and frowned. "Oh, Jake, are you going to school in those clothes?"

He shrugged. "They're all I got."

She sighed. "I suppose we'll need to purchase another uniform. Can I just get the same size? You don't need to try it on again—or do you? Have you grown out of it already?"

"No, just get the same."

She shook her head. "If you're going to run around with"— she dropped her voice—*"you know who,* try to do it in some old, ratty clothes. I can't replace your uniform every week. And how many jackets did you go through?"

"Just the one. Honest."

She sighed again.

Jake tugged his collar. "Y'know, Mom, if you're really bent on the Volts living here, they're sooner or later gonna find out I've fought monsters with Pretty Dynamo."

When he said them so bluntly, the words sounded bizarre. For some reason, his forehead dampened. *Sweet Princess, I've actually fought monsters with Pretty Dynamo.*

His father slapped the newspaper down on the coffee table. "And I don't understand this, either! What's this business about Pretty Dynamo and her husband? That can't possibly be—"

"*Kosmy,*" Jake's mother hissed, "we talked about this already! Mildred's obviously mistaken; but still, the Volts have been through something terrible, so we have to be more understanding!"

Jake's father pressed his lips together and folded his arms. "Love and friendship," he muttered. "No personification of love and friendship is just going to kill someone in cold blood. He was probably turning into a vampire or a zombie. She'd *have* to kill him if—"

"*Kosmy,* we said we wouldn't talk about it with the Volts in the house!"

The screen door rattled, and Jake looked over to see Ralph waving from the front porch.

"Come in, Ralph!" Jake's mother called.

Ralph stepped in, dropped his coat on the floor as if he owned the place, slid off his shoes, and joined Jake at the bar. "Mm, somethin' smells good, Mrs. B."

"I'll fix you some too, Ralph." Jake's mother paused in her cooking to pass Ralph a cup of coffee.

Jake gave Ralph a sidelong glance. "Doesn't your mom feed you?"

Ralph leaned his elbows on the bar. "Eight kids and both my parents work, dude. Cold cereal at my place."

"So go eat cold cereal."

Ralph punched Jake in the shoulder. "What, you don't like my bright, shining face in the morning?"

"Oh, don't worry about it, Ralph," said Jake's mother as she cracked more eggs into her pan. "A good, hearty breakfast in the morning raises a student's test scores by ten points."

Ralph elbowed Jake, and Jake shoved him, nearly knocking him off his stool.

Jake's mother flipped an egg and frowned, her greasy spatula poised in the air. "Or did it raise his I.Q.? Well, no matter. Breakfast is the most important meal of the day. I know that much."

"Hey, uh, Ralph," Jake said after clearing his throat, lowering his voice, and casting a wary look at his mom, "can I, erm, ask you a question about girls—?"

He saw his mother's ear prick up, but he tried to ignore it.

"Sure, dude," Ralph answered. "I am an encyclopedia of girls. I *live* with the encyclopedia of girls. What do you wanna know?"

"Well—"

"First, the rumor is true: If they don't bathe, they smell like fish—"

"Ralph, shut up. No, I wanna ask, would you—I mean you personally—be willing to date a girl who's . . . er . . . afraid of you?"

Ralph stared at him. "What?"

"I mean, let's say she really likes you, but—"

"Then why would she be afraid of me?"

"Um . . . because you're really manly?"

Ralph laughed and clapped him on the back. "Yeah, that'd be nice. No, dude, I don't scare girls."

"What if you *did?* "

"Why would I?"

Jake scratched his head. "Take it as a hypothetical. Let's say she's just the timid type."

Ralph carefully tested his coffee with a small sip and then followed that up with a deeper pull. "Doesn't sound like my type."

"Really? You don't think that could be, I dunno, cute?"

"No. Sounds like trouble."

"But—"

"Look, Jake, remember fifth grade? I mean you and me in fifth grade, not now with you in—"

"I know what you mean, Ralph."

"Right. Remember we were playin' King o' the Hill, and Jamie fell down hard and started bawling? You went ballistic and ran off for a first-aid kit and made a *huge* deal out of it, like she was dying. That's you. And that's fine for you. But that's not me. I'd like a girlfriend, sure, but I *don't* need another little sister. I got enough of those already."

"What's your ideal, then?"

Ralph laughed. "You already know." He whipped a trading card out of his inside breast pocket and gazed with a dippy smile at the photograph printed on it. "My ideal is the tough and sassy *Magical Girl Pretty Dynamo!*"

Oh, Ralph, if only you knew.

Clomping, rustling, and creaking came from the second floor. A few minutes later, Dana padded downstairs, still in her pajamas with her hair frizzing about her face.

Jake snatched the card out of Ralph's hand and shoved it

back into Ralph's pocket. Ralph frowned but said nothing.

Dana yawned and sleepily rubbed her eyes. As soon as she saw Jake and Ralph, she curled her lip in a haughty sneer.

"Oh," she mumbled, "it's Jake's pitcher." She plopped herself down on a stool; to avoid Jake, she sat on the other side of Ralph.

"Dude," said Ralph as he half turned toward Dana, "what is *this?*"

"You met her at the arcade, Ralph."

"Oh yeah . . . uh, Diane—"

"Dana," said Jake.

A door opened down the hall, and into the great room walked Millie Volt. Much like Dana's, her unkempt hair looked like an autumn shrubbery surrounding her youthful face. She rubbed her eyes and then, with a yawn, stretched her arms over her head. She wore nothing more than a loosely tied white housecoat that stopped at mid-thigh; as she stretched, it fell partway open to display the ivory skin on the inside of one well-formed breast.

Ralph swallowed audibly. Jake's face heated up. Jake's father leaned forward and made a faint burping noise into his coffee.

Dana lowered her head and groaned under her breath, "Mom . . ."

Ralph stared for half a minute and then elbowed Jake. "Dude, you've got a fox like that here, in your house, *for breakfast?*" Ralph looked back and forth between Jake and Millie, and his eyes widened.

"Dude," he whispered, clapping a hand to Jake's shoulder, "you're living in sin."

He then raised that same hand into the air. "High five, dude."

"Ralph, shut up."

Millie raked her fingernails through the tangled mass behind her right temple. "Oh my," she said, "we have guests. If I'd known we were having cute boys over, I would have done something with my hair."

She flipped a lock of that hair with one finger.

With a *thunk,* Dana dropped her forehead to the countertop.

Ralph immediately clambered out of his seat, stood at attention like a soldier, and blurted, "Can *I* do something with your hair?"

Jake clapped a hand to his face.

Millie's smile grew until it showed more teeth than Jake thought the human mouth contained. She slid to her right, reminding him of some predatory beast stalking its prey on the savanna. "What did you have in mind?" she asked, her voice now holding a decidedly sultry note.

Ralph cleared his throat, and Jake saw his knees wobble, but he took no more than a second to recover. "Well," said Ralph after coughing into a fist, "I mean, I could braid it for you."

"Could you, now?"

"Sure. I do my sisters all the time."

"I bet he does," Dana muttered, her forehead still pressed to the bar.

Millie slid onto the stool Ralph had just vacated. She was uncomfortably close, and Jake could feel her body heat. He thought he detected a hint of roses, perhaps her perfume. It reminded him of Tsubasa, and a lump formed in his throat. He shifted in his seat.

By leaning forward, he peeked around Millie at Dana. Her crazy hair hid her face until she rocked her head on the countertop and met his gaze with one emerald eye. That eye swiftly narrowed, gleaming with pure rage.

The lump in his throat grew larger. *Yeah, that's what I figured. She's ticked at me.*

"Oh, goodness," Millie said as if just now noticing Jake's mother at the stove, "Silvia, you don't have to go to all this trouble for us. Little Dana and I usually just have a bit of rice and miso soup in the morning, and maybe some fish."

Dana made a faint grumbling noise.

"Oh, it's no trouble," Jake's mother sang. "I've got a growing, athletic boy to cook for, after all!"

"Two of them," Jake muttered as he rolled his eyes at Ralph.

Ralph shrugged shamelessly and combed his fingers through Millie's luxurious red hair. He started separating it into plaits. Jake had to admire his chutzpah.

"My goodness, Silvia, a full breakfast, my hair done for me, and two handsome, strapping boys. I think I could get used to this." Millie leaned an elbow on the bar.

"Would you like some coffee?" Jake's mother asked.

"Oh yes, thank you. My, it's like you have a little café here. You certainly are making your proposal tempting."

Dana raised her head, and a few frizzy strands of red fluttered in front of her face. "I don't wanna live here," she mumbled.

"Dana," said Millie, "be polite. What did we say about being polite?"

"Don't care. Don't wanna live with Jake."

"Dana—"

Ralph paused in his braiding and looked at Jake. "Dude?"

Jake shrugged. "You know they're rebuilding Little India, right? Mrs. Volt and Dana are thinking of moving in here so someone can have their apartment."

Dana growled.

"Ah, that's cool." Ralph nodded and continued his work. "And I'm sure this kid must be thrilled, gettin' to live with the guy who runs around with Magical Girl—"

Jake spun around on his stool and kicked Ralph in the shin. Ralph hopped back a step and sucked in his breath.

Jake glanced at his mother. Her face had turned pale, and she stood frozen at the stove.

Several seconds of silence passed.

"Ah," Millie finally said with a sigh and a small smile. "Magical girls." She shook her head. "Well, I suppose we *do* need them—"

Jake cleared his throat and tugged his collar. "I don't really run *around* with them. It's just that, this last week, with everything that happened, I got caught up in a few things. Um, it kinda made the news, but they blew it out of proportion. It was no big deal. Really."

"Oh my," said Millie. "Did you see any of those zombies? Or the robot dinosaurs?"

"Well . . . yeah."

"Up close?"

"I, uh, got pretty close, yeah."

Millie clucked her tongue. "Sounds scary. I suppose that's how you got those scrapes on your face. I just figured you played football or something." She laughed, but her laugh sounded nervous. "That *kaiju* on Monday attacked near where we live. Terrible. Our building has a mole tunnel in the basement, so I ran to a shelter once everything started, but I was *panicking,* of course. I knew Dana would come home from school about that time—"

"Yeah," Jake said, feeling a bead of sweat running down his left temple. "I guess it would have been about that time."

"But I suppose you didn't see that one since it was down the hill, right? You might have heard it, though."

"I sure heard it, yeah."

His mouth turned down, Ralph stared at Jake. Then he stared at the back of Millie's head.

Then he shrugged and continued braiding.

Millie laid an arm across Dana's shoulders. "Ooh, I'm so glad my little Dana's not one of those girls! Maybe it's selfish of me, but I'd be terrified."

"I know what you mean," said Jake's mother.

"My Dana's just too sensitive for that kind of work," Millie said. "She could never, ever become one of those rough-and-tumble magical girls."

She smiled at Jake and patted his arm. "She told me you patched her up when she fell down at the skate park."

Jake rubbed the back of his neck. "I guess I did—"

"Well, thank you. Thank you for looking out for her. She got it into her head a few years back that she wanted to learn to skate, but I could never understand why. She's *always* falling down, and it worries me. She's delicate, you know."

Millie vigorously rubbed a hand between Dana's shoulder blades. "Aren't you, sugar?"

Dana, eyes half-lidded and lower lip outthrust, merely nodded.

"So no magic for her," Millie continued. "I just tell my little darling, if one of those talking animals comes up to you and asks you to sign something in blood, you say no. Isn't that right, sweetheart? You'd say no, wouldn't you?"

With her eyes on the countertop, Dana nodded again.

"And if you saw a fairy or a space alien, and it told you it could grant you any wish if you agreed to fight monsters, you'd say no. You'd say no, no matter how cute it was, no matter how nice it seemed, no matter what it promised. Right, precious? You'd just say no."

"I'd just say no," Dana whispered. Her voice was faint, almost impossible to hear.

Millie hugged her tight, rocked her back and forth, and rubbed a cheek against the top of her head. "Ooh, of course you would. I know you would because you're going to stay my sweet little baby forever." She pulled Dana's hair back and kissed her forehead.

Jake felt another lump appear in his throat.

"But I still don't wanna live here," Dana said, crossing her arms.

"Oh, sweetheart," said Millie. She paused to kiss Dana's cheek and then continued, "I know it's hard to give up our home, but just think: We'd have more room up here, and the neighborhood's nicer, and you could play with Jake—"

"I don't like Jake."

"Sweetie, stop that."

"I mean it," she said, now talking through clenched teeth. "I don't like him. Don't wanna talk to him. Don't wanna look at him. Don't wanna even *think* about him. I *hate* him—"

"Dana, we don't say we hate people."

Dana squirmed out of her mother's grasp, bunched her fists, and brought them down on the counter with a loud thud. Jake's coffee cup rattled. "But I do hate *him!* And I *don't* wanna live here!"

She hunched her shoulders, scrunched up her eyebrows, and stuck out her lip in her most determined pout yet.

Jake's mom slid a full and steaming plate of bacon, scrambled eggs, hash browns, and toast in front of her. Silently, lip still jutting, Dana stared down at it for almost a full minute.

"We should live here," she finally said.

ELEVEN

MONDAY

Dana donned her uniform, complete with the safety pins in her collar, the blue pen in her pocket, and the untied bowtie. While she slouched sullenly by the front door, Millie gave her several kisses and tousled her ratty hair. Dana endured it with a silent scowl.

"Oh dear, Mommy didn't get to make your lunch today," Millie said, tutting. "I guess you'll have to eat the school lunch . . . well, I suppose it's all right. It's only one day."

Dana grumbled.

Millie bit her lip and nervously ran her hands through Dana's hair, trying to smooth it. "Just . . . I don't know, just try not to eat anything that looks overprocessed."

Dana made a faint growling noise.

"Like, no ketchup," Millie said. "It's full of corn syrup. And no chicken nuggets. There's no part of a chicken called the 'nugget.'"

Dana rolled her eyes. "Can I go now?"

"Of course, sweetie. Walk with Jake, okay?"

Dana grumbled again.

Jake's mother kissed his cheek and straightened his collar. Ralph stood by silently—but stood as close as he could to Millie.

Once the kids went outside and shut the door on the adults, Ralph rounded on Jake and grabbed his shoulders. "Oh *man! That was amazing!"*

After releasing Jake, he held his hands before his face as if unsure they were his. "I am never washing these again!"

Jake rolled his eyes. "You wouldn't have anyway."

Who was *that?"* Ralph demanded.

"What do you mean?"

"What do you *think* I mean? The living goddess in your house, dude! *Dang,* I never knew freckles could look that *hot."*

Jake shoved his hands in his pockets. "That was Millie Volt. I already told you—"

"Dude, dude, *duuude."* Ralph punched his shoulder. "You get *all* the smokin' babes! What it *is* with you, man?"

"Ralph, you're talking about Dana's mom."

Ralph rubbed his chin and nodded. "That's right, that's right. She's a mom. So is she looking to have *more* kids? Cuz I would seriously love to help her with that."

"Would you just shut up?" Jake waved toward Dana, who, with her satchel slung over her shoulder, watched them with a silent glower.

"You suck," Dana said.

"Oh, hey, no offense," Ralph replied. "It's just that *your* mama is one *hot* mama. But I'm sure you get that a lot."

Dana ground her teeth.

"Ralph," said Jake, "since you're being a complete idiot, why don't you just go to school? Me an' Dana gotta take off."

Ralph shrugged. "We're gonna be goin' the same direction for a few blocks, so—"

"Why don't you just take a different route today?"

The words came out more fiercely than Jake intended. Ralph's easy grin slipped a notch, and he stared at Jake for half a minute before he cleared his throat and plucked absently at his pomade-begrimed hair. "Well, yeah, okay. I will."

Shoulders slumping, Ralph shambled up the walkway. A faint breeze rustled the trees, and brown leaves pattered onto the pavement behind his shuffling feet. He glanced over his shoulder once, his mouth twisted up. Then he shrugged and continued walking.

Jake shook his head before he turned and headed toward the grade school.

Dana didn't move.

"C'mon, twerp," Jake called. "You don't wanna be late."

"You suck too," Dana replied from the front stoop.

"Yeah, I know. C'mon."

"I'm not walking with you."

"Yes, you are."

Dana bunched her hands into fists and dropped them to her sides. "Shut up. I hate you."

Jake stopped walking and ran a hand through his hair. "Sheesh, you just had a good meal. Can't you be even a little happy? C'mon, let's go."

Her knuckles turned bone-white, and tears formed in her eyes. After a moment, she launched herself forward and marched past him, her nose in the air. She tried to shove him aside with her shoulder, but all she managed was to knock herself off balance. When she recovered, she kept marching.

He followed, staying a few steps behind.

"Stop following me!" she shouted.

"We really are going the same direction this time."

"I hate you!"

"I know."

She took off running, so he ran too and easily kept pace. With a loud clop of Mary Janes against concrete, she suddenly stopped. He overtook her by a few feet but then stopped as well. Arms crossed, he turned to watch her.

Hands clenched, she stood on the sidewalk and stared down at her shoes. Her shoulders heaved up and down as she fumed.

"Dana, look, I know you're sore, so let me—"

"Shut up!"

"C'mon, Dana, I'll explain—"

Her head snapped up, and her eyes flashed. "I don't need you to explain, *jerk!* I caught you! I caught you with *Sukeban Tsubasa!*"

He ran a hand through his hair. "Dana—"

"You are *such* a pervert!" She stuck a pinky in her mouth and tore off the end of her fingernail with her teeth. "You only did this cuz I'm s'posed to fight her, didn't you?"

"Dana—"

He reached for her, but she skittered away. "I'm gonna tell on you to your *girlfriend!*"

"She wouldn't believe you anyway, so—"

Muttering under her breath, Dana stomped past him.

He sighed as he followed. "Dana—"

"I said shut up! I don't wanna talk to you! Ever! I don't want you near me! I don't want you to look at me! I don't even want you to *think* about me with your nasty brain! I *hate* you! I'm gonna hate you forever and ever and—"

He grabbed her shoulders and spun her around. She slapped

his hands away, but he grabbed her again, and her eyes went wide with that familiar look of fear.

"Look," he hissed, shaking her, "she *attacked* me! That's what you saw! There is nothing—"

Dana shoved him off and continued toward the school. He stomped after her.

"Stay back!" she screamed. "You have to stay back now, one whole block!"

"I sit next to you, you know."

"Shut up!"

"And you're moving into my house."

"Shut up! Shut up! *Shut up!"* She put her hands over her ears and, with her sharp elbows waving back and forth in the air, ran at top speed.

"Dana, stop! You're gonna—!"

She tripped over a crack in the sidewalk and sprawled face-first on the concrete. Her satchel skidded away, burst open, and spread pencils and notebooks across a nearby lawn.

Jake ran to her side and hunkered down beside her. Face-down, with her hands stretched out, she sobbed.

"C'mon, Dana, let me help you—"

His fingers brushed her wrist, but she shrieked and rolled away as if he'd stung her.

"Don't touch me!" She had a bloody scratch across her nose, and she held her wrist as though he'd injured it. "Don't *ever* touch me! I don't want you to touch me ever again!" Her tears ran faster, and her chest heaved. "I hate you. I really, *really* hate you." She bit into her lip so hard that blood seeped out. "I hate you so, *so* much!"

He reached toward her again but paused when she whimpered and shrank back. She wasn't just being crabby; she was genuinely terrified.

Something in his stomach shriveled, leaving a hollow space behind.

SHE STRUGGLED TO GET HER PENCILS AND CRUMPLED PAPERS back into her satchel, but she didn't bother to close it. After they entered the school, she roughly barged into the classroom, and the satchel tipped in her hands, spilling its contents again.

"Ah, Dana." Jake crouched beside her in the doorway to help her pick up, and she tried to push him away. It was a weak push, but because he was balanced on his heels, it was enough to land him on his backside.

"I don't need your help!" she screamed.

"Yeah, but you're blocking the door." He picked up a pencil and held it toward her.

"No!"

"Just let me—"

"No!"

He threw the pencil aside, grabbed up a handful of papers, and stuffed them into her satchel whether she liked it or not. She snatched those same papers and threw them back onto the floor before huffily running to her desk.

He followed.

She rounded on him again. "Stay away!"

"I can't. I sit—"

"Find another desk!"

"Dana—"

Most of the other students were already in class. They stared silently, open-mouthed. Rikka, the dark-haired girl with the bow in her hair, ground her teeth and alternately clenched and unclenched her tiny hands.

"Dana," said Jake, "you're gonna have to calm down."

Dana crossed her arms and turned her back on him.

With a loud thud, Rikka jumped onto her desk. The other kids laughed or whistled.

Janice waved her hands and hissed, "No, Rikka!"

Precariously balanced and wobbling dangerously, Rikka shouted at the ceiling, "I can't take it anymore! I can't just stand by and watch!"

She jabbed a finger toward Jake, and her desk rocked on its metal legs.

"Don't!" Janice whispered. "For Dynamo's sake!"

"Jake Blatowski," shrieked Rikka. "How *could* you?"

Jake slid his pack from his shoulder and dropped it heavily to his chair. "How could I *what?"*

"Everybody!" Rikka cried, waving her arms as her desk creaked. "I caught Jake *cheating!"*

"So did I," Dana snarled under her breath.

"Cheating on a test?" the fat boy with dark circles under his eyes said from the back of the classroom.

"Worse!" yelled Rikka. *"Much* worse! I caught him cheating on *Magical Girl Pretty Dynamo!"*

The children gasped. Jake slapped a hand to his face.

Rikka turned her accusing index finger on Dana. "On Friday night, I was with my family, having a nice dinner in New Beijing. And *that's* when I saw! I saw him there! He was on a *date* with *Dana Volt!"*

All around the room, girls booed and hissed while boys giggled. Jake rolled his eyes.

"Am I the only one who's seen it?" Rikka cried, talking to the ceiling as if moaning out a heartfelt prayer. "Am I the only one who's seen the way she's insinuated herself into his life, into his heart? She seduced him with her *creepy red hair!"*

Now Rikka windmilled her arms as though trying to fly, and the desk released a low groan, its flimsy legs bowing. "She's a witch! A *witch,* I tell you! And not the good kind of witch that fights monsters but the *bad* kind of witch that *steals boyfriends* from witches who fight monsters!"

The fat boy jumped up from his seat, his belly jiggling as he pumped a fist in the air. "Burn the witch!"

Jake blinked. *Whoa, this is getting out of hand.*

Rikka hopped from her desk and landed flat-footed on the floor. Her Crocs squeaking, she ran to Jake, clutched his shirt-front, and yelled in his face. "Don't you remember, Jake? Don't you remember what it was like when you and Pretty Dynamo first fell in love?"

"Look, Rikka—"

She tried to shake him, but all she did was stretch out his shirt. *"Remember,* Jake! Remember how it was when you first saw her, back when you were a bodybuilding Spanish billionaire and she was an impoverished governess with a physical disability!"

"I think you've been reading too many romance novels—"

"You *have* to remember, Jake!" She pounded her fists on his chest. "Remember! Pretty Dynamo is your *waifu!"*

"My what?"

"Jake!" The voice of Miss Percy, their teacher, came from the doorway, and everyone turned to stare at her. She stood with her hands clasping the doorframe as tears ran from behind her thick spectacles. Her lower lip quivered. "How *could* you?"

Jake tugged at his collar. "Ah, not you too, Miss Percy—"

She wrung her hands. "Don't you remember what happened between *us?*"

As one, the children gasped. Rikka's fists tightened on Jake's shirt, and Jake again slapped a hand to his face.

"Miss Percy," he muttered, "we agreed to forget about that—"

Dana glared murderously at him before viciously kicking over her chair. It tumbled to the floor with a clang.

"Never mind all that!" she shouted. "That's *nothin'!* I just caught Jake with *Magical Girl Sukeban Tsubasa!*"

The chatter started up again, now ten times louder. Girls held their hands over their mouths as their faces turned beet-red.

The fat kid with the dark circles under his eyes bowed dramatically. "Jake!" he cried. "You're my hero! Make me your disciple!"

Jake sank into his undersized chair and buried his face in his hands.

At the front of the class, Rikka fell into Janice's arms, and Janice sobbed.

Futilely calling for order amidst the classroom's din, Miss Percy walked toward the blackboard, but a loud *boom* rocked her off her feet. She tumbled hard to the floor.

Jake lowered his hands and felt his heart pound against his ribs.

Another boom. Dust fell from the ceiling, and Janice's sobbing got louder.

"Shelter!" Miss Percy cried as she struggled to stand. "Everyone to the shelter, children! Follow the same procedures as in a monster drill!"

The children didn't follow procedures. Instead, they

panicked. Rikka clutched Janice's hands and turned wide, dark eyes on Jake.

A light fixture came loose from the ceiling and dropped into the center of the room with a deafening crash, scattering shards of sharp glass. Janice screamed as a thin gash appeared on her cheek.

Now the children ducked under their desks. Miss Percy, steadying herself against the chalkboard, dragged herself upright. Her glasses sat askew on her thin nose, and tears coursed down her face. "No, children! Not an earthquake drill! Monster drill! To the shelter, single file, please! *Please!"*

The blue pen in Dana's pocket buzzed. She slapped a hand to it.

Jake pushed past her desk and threw open a window overlooking the school's front lawn. Rows of houses and trees full of red foliage obscured the view, but Jake could see up a street for several blocks. In the distance, barely visible above the elms and oaks, was a yellow fin such as an exotic fish might have on its back. It bobbed up and down as if attached to some enormous creature taking slow and cumbersome steps. Beyond that fin, Jake saw a billow of oily, black smoke.

"It's a *kaiju* attack," he said. "Must be Monday."

DANA BURST OUT OF THE DOOR AND INTO THE HALL. JAKE WAS right behind.

"I don't need you," she snarled.

"You get me anyway," he replied.

Miss Percy, teetering in her high heels, stumbled after them.

"The shelter's the other way!" she cried as she fell into a wall. "Children—!"

"I gotta use the bathroom!" Dana called without looking back.

"There's a bathroom in the shelter!" shrieked Miss Percy.

Dana shoved open the door to the girls' lavatory. Jake followed, though he heard Miss Percy scream shrilly, *"Jake, you can't go in the girls' room!"*

Once inside, Jake noticed that this bathroom looked exactly like the boys', except there were no urinals, and the soap dispensers weren't broken. But it was just as dingy and smelled just as bad. The rubbish bin was overflowing with crumpled paper towels, grimy pipes jutted from the ceiling, and a rust stain stretched down one wall.

Jake wondered for a moment why public schools' interiors always featured cheap paint, fluorescent lights, and exposed pipes. Maybe it was to keep students docile by making them miserable.

Dana stood in the middle of the room, right in a large water stain marking a depression in the epoxy-coated concrete floor. She had her back to him, so he was looking at her mess of tangled, flame-colored hair.

"Get out," she said.

"I'm guarding the door," he answered as he shoved one of his Crocs against the jamb to make sure no one could barge through. "So hurry up."

She put her pen to her mouth. "The moon shines her light on both good and bad."

She listened for a few seconds before she added, "But the sun is a harsh mistress. What have we got, boss?"

Again, she listened.

"Yeah, I'm here, but I'm ground-bound till the end of the week."

Silence for half a minute.

"I'll do what I can. Dynamo out."

She put the pen back in her pocket and stuck her hand in the air. "You better not look," she said over her shoulder.

"I won't," Jake replied.

He dropped his eyes as she shouted, *"Shock my heart!"*

Flashes of electricity snapped against the sinks and made their fixtures hum. Surrounded by brilliant light, Dana lifted into the air.

"By the power of Zeus, Thor, and Raijin, release the energies within my soul! Electrifying the world with love and friendship —and making evildoers feel the wattage of justice—I am *Magical Girl Pretty Dynamo!"*

A moment later, Pretty Dynamo stood before him with her fists on her hips and a defiant, lopsided grin on her face.

"Hey, Dynamo," said Jake. "Good to see—"

Without a word, she grabbed him by the collar, dragged him to a sink, and shoved his head into it. She turned on the faucet full-blast.

As the water poured through his hair and over his face, he gasped, and then he choked. He kicked and flailed, but to no avail; her arm was like iron. He found her left knee with his right fist, but hitting her merely bruised his knuckles. The water poured into the sink faster than it could drain, so it soon covered his mouth and nose. He swung his arms as his lungs burned.

After a minute, she pulled him out, and he sputtered as he gulped air. Water from his face poured into his shirt.

She shoved him under again, and the metal faucet tore into his scalp.

This time, she held him under for what felt like an eternity. Eyes squeezed shut and lungs blazing, he squirmed in vain as the ceramic sink's rounded lip pressed into his Adam's apple.

Finally, she let go. Retching and gasping, Jake fell to the floor. Blood from his forehead trickled into his eyes.

"Jerk," Dynamo said as she shut off the water. She marched toward the door.

"Why, you little—!"

He lunged and slammed his shoulder into her lumbar spine, just below her armor plate. He caught her by surprise: She flew forward and smacked her face into the plaster wall beside the heavy fire door. Shards of plaster tumbled to the concrete.

He froze. For a moment, he wondered if he'd actually hurt her.

Then she hissed, *"Big mistake."*

Something invisible hit him like a brick and overwhelmed him with searing pain. He collapsed as his muscles seized up.

"You forgot I'm electrified?" Dynamo shouted as she spun around, grabbed his shirtfront, and slammed him into a wall. He hit hard enough to knock the wind from his lungs.

She held him there with fingers digging into his shirt—but he heard her metal boots slip against the slick floor. She had strength but no leverage.

He ached everywhere and could hardly breathe, but he kicked off from the wall and tackled her. To keep herself upright, she stuck one leg back and slid on the edges of her soles.

Once he shoved her into the wall opposite, she had strength *and* leverage.

Jake realized his error, but he made the further mistake of trying for a right hook, which would have fractured his knuckles if he'd connected. To block, Dynamo stepped in close and raised her left hand to the back of her neck, so his bicep bounced from her forearm. Then she put her right hand to his chin—but she didn't hit hard enough to break his neck and kill him, nor did she go for the obvious groin strike. Instead, she caught the back of his right heel with a boot and slammed him to the floor. His head cracked against the concrete, and white spots flashed in his eyes.

She landed on top of him and rammed a metal vambrace against his throat.

"One twitch!" she snarled. "One little twitch, and I'll crush your windpipe! I can kill you! You understand that? I can *kill* you!"

He grabbed her arm but couldn't budge it. Nonetheless, he found his voice and wheezed, "Like you killed your father?"

The rage disappeared from her eyes. For a moment, that familiar, intense fear replaced it.

She released him.

"Get in the shelter," she muttered as she stood and turned to the door. "Get in the shelter, Jake Blatowski, and get out of my life."

She kicked. With a loud boom, the door burst from its hinges and fell into the hallway.

In the hall, Miss Percy jumped back and shrieked. Clutching her heart and leaning on a wall, she took several deep breaths before saying, "Oh, Pretty Dynamo! Thank the Princess, it's you! Did you see a little red-haired girl just now? She went in there a minute ago."

Dynamo blinked, her mouth hanging open. "Um . . ."

"She's about your height," Miss Percy explained. "And has your build. And she's pale, like you. She's *always* running off during monster attacks, and I haven't the slightest idea why!"

A moment of silence passed.

"Nope," said Dynamo. "Haven't seen her."

Miss Percy shook her head. "Oh dear. I guess I'll keep looking."

Jake rose from the floor and, water still dripping from his face, woozily stood behind Dynamo and leaned on the doorpost.

"Jake," Miss Percy demanded, as if noticing him for the first time, "where's Dana?"

Jake rubbed his throat and rasped, "I think she went to the shelter already. You should go too, Miss Percy."

Miss Percy clucked her tongue. "That girl! Honestly! What a time for a bathroom break! And she didn't even raise her hand for a hall pass!"

A chill ran down Jake's spine when he looked over Miss Percy's shoulder: Behind her, crawling on the cheap ceiling tiles, were two wasps the size of large dogs. Their slick abdomens were striped with yellow and black, and their antennae twitched as they turned their huge compound eyes toward the bathroom door. Their thick, scissor-like mandibles split open to reveal fleshy, vaguely human mouths full of pointy white teeth. Jake's skin crawled.

"Zzzzzere zzzey are!" one of the wasps buzzed. "Pretty Dynamo and zzzzzuh Barfing Boy! Get zzzzem!"

Jake swallowed down the lump in his throat. "Mondays," he muttered. "Nothing good ever happens on a Monday."

TWELVE

CHILDREN OF THE BITE

"Mondays," said Chirops with a sigh. "Nothing sufficiently evil ever happens on a Monday."

He swayed precariously on his perch as another missile exploded below him. His teeth rattled, and his sensitive ears throbbed. Once the shock subsided, he heaved another sigh.

Chirops straddled a tiny saddle balanced on a fin jutting from the scalp of Hive Rind, one of the Dark Queen's most formidable monsters. Now that he was personally in charge of capturing Barfing Boy to slake the Queen's powerful yet ephemeral appetites, Chirops had full run of her army and could recruit any monster he pleased.

The city's guns blazed mercilessly yet futilely. Shells and missiles exploded against Hive Rind's impenetrable skin, leaving behind only blackened patches. Bullets bounced off. Although this barrage couldn't injure the *kaiju,* it battered Chirops's sensitive ears: He groaned as he fished a heavy pair of noise-dampening headphones out of his knapsack and clamped them on his head. They were painful, but they were better than the pops and explosions.

Hive Rind himself, with his thick scales glistening like gold, flexed enormous claws and opened a gigantic, slavering jaw wide enough to swallow a house whole. From his throat came a deep, mournful bellow.

"Oooooorgh!" cried Hive Rind. "Humans not nice! Humans try to hurt Hive Rind! That make Hive Rind *nervous!* Me getting so *very, very nervous!"*

With his curved claws, he scratched at his golden torso, groaning all the while.

"And when Hive Rind get nervous," he roared, "he get . . . he get . . . *hives!"*

The flesh across Hive Rind's belly puckered, and a red rash soon appeared. The bumps bled together to form a hexagonal pattern, which rose from the monster's skin like the chambers of a honeycomb. In the center of each chamber, an angry boil grew. After a few seconds, each boil burst in a shower of pale, foul-smelling pus, and out crawled a writhing, buzzing wasp as big as a dog. Shaking off globs of blood and white slime, the wasps spread their wings and, with a deafening buzz, took to the air. A cloud of them swarmed one of the roof-mounted missile launchers: With much shrieking and clanking, they soon tore it apart, leaving behind nothing but twisted lumps of shredded metal. Then they flew to the next.

More honeycomb-like rashes formed on Hive Rind's back, his arms, and the insides of his thighs. The monster groaned in misery and scratched, bursting more boils and releasing gallons of pus that dribbled into the streets below. Soon, the air was full of the thunderous cacophony of wasps' wings, almost loud enough to drown out the city's weapons.

Chirops cupped his claws around his mouth. "You're doing great, Hive Rind!" he shouted. "Just keep the humans distracted! I'll be back soon!"

"Itchy!" Hive Rind roared. "Hives are so, so *itchy!*" He smashed an arm through a skyscraper and sent its top hurtling into several smaller buildings. Twisted metal beams and twisted human bodies showered from the wreckage, cracking pavement and rooftops as they tumbled. Clouds of dust erupted from the demolished structures, and snapped pipes shot water high into the air. Crushed and bloodied arms and legs, with jagged bones sticking out of them, bristled from the rubble like the quills on a porcupine.

Hive Rind reached into the debris and pulled out a long, bent I-beam, which he used to scratch his back. He blubbered.

Chirops spread his wings and flew. Diving under the clouds of vicious wasps and ducking the flying missiles and bursts of tracer fire, he headed deep into the city. It was clear from their many failures that the Dark Queen's forces needed backup—and Chirops knew where to find it.

AFTER SWOOPING INTO THE GODAI DISTRICT, WHERE SEVERAL upscale stores nestled together, Chirops found the Sweet Tooth Candy and Pastry Shop. A CLOSED sign hung in the window, but the front door was open. A bell jingled when he pushed his way inside, but no one was at the counter.

Chirops paused to admire the sculpted cakes, spun-sugar flowers, and boxes of chocolates on display behind the counter's glass front. He helped himself to a free sample of jellybeans and then walked into the back, chewing noisily.

When the taste of the jellybeans spread into his mouth, he stopped and grimaced for a moment.

Licorice.

He hated licorice.

Shaking his head, he thought in disgust, *Monday*.

In the shop's kitchen, pots bubbled on stoves. Pâtissiers in immaculate white coats and tall hats were hard at work confecting various sweets. On one side of the kitchen, an automatic taffy machine thrummed as it stretched sugary goo and then cut and wrapped it in wax paper.

Chirops crossed his wings, tapped a clawed foot on the floor, and waited while most of the chefs ignored him. At last, a man in a double-breasted white coat, black trousers, and a toque blanche with the traditional hundred pleats—no doubt indicating that he was head of the kitchen—marched Chirops's way, pulling latex gloves from his hands as he went. His face was almost as white as his coat, and strands of dark hair hung limply from under his hat. His eyes were red, suggesting he slept poorly, though his irises shone a pale gold.

"You!" he growled. "What do you want? Can't you see we're busy?"

Chirops raised an eyebrow. "Even with the city under attack?"

The man harrumphed. "Best time to catch up on work. We have an order for *fifty boxes* of custom chocolates due out tomorrow—assuming the customer isn't dead by then. Do we have you to thank for that absurd monstrosity out there?"

Chirops, his wet nose twitching, swept one wing in front of his chest and bowed low. "Just a little gift to Urbanopolis from the Dark Queen, oh ancient prince of the infernal legions," he simpered.

The man put his fists on his hips and snorted. "No such titles, please. Here, you may simply call me *chef*—or Julian, if you prefer."

Chirops nodded eagerly. "Oh, of course! Of course! *Chef Julian!*"

Julian harrumphed again. "Come with me. Walk while you talk. I am a busy man."

Chirops waddled after him as Julian stopped by a stove to taste a sauce. "Grainy," he said to the *saucier* standing there. "Throw it out and prepare it again."

Next, he walked to a trio of cooks standing over a pot of chocolate. He tasted some of the chocolate and frowned.

"You've done quite well for yourselves," Chirops said as he peeked over the stovetop.

Julian nodded, though his mouth remained in a stolid frown. He continued his march. "Yes, the work becomes enjoyable. It is, after all, an art form." He gestured toward a *décorateur* who, with rapid but precise movements, was sculpting roses of frosting on a batch of small cakes.

Chirops scratched his neck. "It's interesting to see you working so meticulously to make candies and desserts. I would have supposed that vampires would run a blood bank—"

Julian halted mid-stride and rounded on him. His eyes glowed faintly, and he spread his lips to show two pronounced fangs. "We *also* do that, of course. But there must be no traceable connection between these operations! The blood banks and the pastry shops work *separately.* We keep the humans' blood sugar high because the higher the blood sugar, the less often we have to feed. The less often we feed, the less likely we are to be discovered."

Chirops replied with another sycophantic nod. "Oh yes! Very

clever! And the blood banks preserve the blood so you can eat anytime you want, right?"

"Of course," said Julian as he brushed his hands down his sleeves, "we can store blood by that method—though we have other ways. Sometimes, we turn it into cheese."

"Cheese?"

Julian waved his hand toward a young chef who was shaping marzipan. "This is Wilhelm. He is our best cheesemaker."

Wilhelm—small, thin, and pale even for a vampire—looked up and smiled shyly, his hands poised over a half-finished bowl of sculpted fruit.

"He makes it," Julian added, "with his scream."

"His scream?" said Chirops as he scratched his head.

"Indeed," replied Julian. "It's positively blood-curdling. But enough with the pleasantries, bat. Why are you here?"

Chirops bowed. "I am here on behalf of the Dark Queen, of course."

"And what does *she* want?"

"Why . . . your servitude."

To Chirops's surprise, Julian did not react visibly to such a brash statement. Instead, with his white face stony and his red eyes unreadable, he pushed through a set of double doors in the back of the kitchen. With nervousness gnawing at the pit of his stomach, Chirops waddled after. On the other side of the doors stood a broad, cinderblock-lined room in which coffins lay in neat rows. Julian strode past them without a glance, walked up a set of stairs to a dais, and sat down on a rough-carved wooden throne. A stream of pale light fell on him through a chink in the roof overhead—but it was not sunlight. It was reddish, lifeless, like the light in an old-fashioned darkroom.

Leaning a cheek on a hand, Julian muttered through clenched

fangs, "Quite impertinent of you, bat. Do you think your Queen has such a position of strength?"

Chirops trembled, and a lump formed in his throat. He was now at the tricky part. Hesitantly, he nodded.

"Tell her we are not interested," said Julian, "nor amused by her emissary."

Chirops scratched an ear, using that as an excuse to calm himself and master his voice before he spoke again. "But surely you are growing tired of this? Surely you miss the old days, hunting humans like prey, swooping through the night—"

Julian gripped the armrests of his throne. Chirops heard the wood crack, and despite himself, he jumped.

Julian leaned forward and hissed, "Even if we were, do you expect us to bow the knee to your ridiculous mistress? We know what she is, bat, and who she once—"

Chirops cleared his throat and rubbed his claws together. "But, you see, I've come to make you an offer!"

"Unless it's a lower price on my supply of pumpkin-spice flavoring, I am not interested."

Chirops grimaced. "Are you *really* satisfied with this, Julian? Making sweets to feed the humans, the very creatures who ought to be your toys, your playthings? You are some of the most powerful, fearsome creatures on this planet! Once, even grown men would quake in their beds at the merest mention of the *nosferatu,* yet you—"

Silently and swiftly, Julian rose from his throne. So graceful was he that Chirops was unsure if he leaped or simply floated into the air. He seemed to hover for a moment, his eyes glowing like coals, before he landed silently, directly in front of Chirops. The bat yelped and fell on his rump.

With hang time like that, he should have gone into basketball instead of baking—

Julian's fangs, now fully extended, looked like the murderous teeth of a mountain lion. With speed that turned his limbs into a blur, he grabbed Chirops by the neck and lifted him.

"Are you speaking to *me?*" Julian roared, his voice deep like thunder. "Or are you merely expressing your *own* cowardice? You, a vampire bat of the fay, sniveling and squealing at the feet of your ridiculous—"

Chirops scrabbled at the fingers enwrapping his neck. "I'm actually a *fruit* bat," he wheezed.

Julian's eyes ceased to glow, and his fangs swiftly retracted. With a snort of contempt, he dropped Chirops to the floor. "Figures," he muttered. "I thought you seemed a little fruity—"

"Look," gasped Chirops as he rubbed his throat and climbed back to his feet, "we can help each other! If you agree to serve the Dark Queen, then together—"

Julian turned his back on him. "The fay folk long ago banished all undead from their realm! Thanks to them, we are trapped in this world—at least those of us who cannot enter the Dreaming as the ghouls do. Why would we ally ourselves with fairies, who are proven traitors?"

"Only the Seelie Court banished you," Chirops said quietly.

"But," Julian snarled, "did not Mab destroy the Unseelie Court—and did she not employ such dastardly weapons as church bells and cold iron to do it? Would she not then turn on us with garlic and crucifixes once we had served her purpose? What kind of fool do you take me for?"

"All who serve the Dark Queen have broken ties to Queen Mab," Chirops said as he dusted off his fur. His heart was pounding, but he felt the worst had passed. "We are, if you like, the new Unseelie Court."

Julian tipped back his head and laughed coldly. "So you are twice traitors! You betrayed us, and then you betrayed your queen!" He unfolded his arms and pointed toward the double doors. "Out of my sight, bat! Get out of my kitchen, out of my shop! Never come back! And be sure to sample the jellybeans on the way out. We have a sale tomorrow."

Chirops shuddered. *"Licorice,"* he muttered under his breath. Then, composing himself, he bowed once more and simpered, "Before I go, Chef Julian, let me show you one thing."

Chirops waddled back into the kitchen, and he smiled to himself when he heard Julian follow. Weaving his way between the diligently working chefs while ignoring their suspicious looks, Chirops headed toward a shelf where he spotted several pans of cast iron.

The shelves were too high for him to reach without flying, so he pointed and said, "Hand me that, please."

Julian was at his elbow. "That? You are fay. That would burn you."

"Give it to me."

Julian picked up a frying pan and held it out. Chirops took it, hefted it, and then, by the end of its handle, spun it on one claw like a top. He blinked his large eyes and offered Julian his best smile.

His arms crossed and his thin, pale face impassive, Julian watched in silence.

Chirops playfully tossed the pan from one wing to another. He resisted the urge to speak, instead relishing Julian's growing impatience.

Finally, after a wary glance toward his chefs, who were staring, Julian said, "How?"

"All the Curses of Ebal are broken for us," Chirops answered.

Julian rounded on the other vampires, who were edging away from their stoves and counters with wonder on their faces.

"Return to your tasks!" Julian barked. "This does not concern you!"

Once they scurried back to pots and pastries, he turned to Chirops and said again, *"How?"*

"A technicality, you might say," Chirops replied. "We are no longer part of Fairyland. We are no longer fay."

"Because you serve the Dark Queen?"

"Yes." Chirops tossed the pan up and caught its handle on the end of his nose, where he balanced it.

Julian said, "Are you suggesting—?"

"It's possible. Unfortunately, I can't guarantee it since I don't know much about vampires. Last week, I discovered that I could use my blood to enable a demon to cross ley lines and shrug off curses. I am a rootworker, after all. That was temporary, of course, and in the end, it undid him. But if you bend the knee to the Queen—"

"Impossible."

"Ah, but think!" Chirops said, shuffling back and forth to keep the pan on his nose. "To have no mind for garlic, to walk unharmed into the pope's basilica, to stare down mirrors without fear—?"

"I bow to no one!"

"Not even Lord Shadow? Do we not all serve him?"

Now, to Chirops's surprise, Julian released a long, loud laugh.

The pan slid from Chirops's nose and clonked him on the head before it fell to the floor with a crash.

"Lord Shadow?" said Julian. "What does *he* promise us?"

"Well," said Chirops, whose heart again began to pound, "the destruction of humanity—"

"You mean our *food supply?*"

Chirops stepped back and covered his mouth with one wing. "You shouldn't worry about that! When Lord Shadow takes his throne—"

"When he takes his throne, our time is over. Why should I willingly serve him?"

"He will reward—"

"You are a *fool!* Do you know what Lord Shadow is? He is the nature of things! Why do you think this world is marked for destruction, you miserable bat? Because the Moon Princess has set herself against the way of the cosmos!"

"That's why he will reward us for opposing her!"

"There is no *reward!* When he takes his throne, there is nothing! *Nothing!* We eke out our existence for a time, and then there is no more time. What do you suppose we vampires want? We want to live here, on this world, instead of in hell. When Lord Shadow sits down, this world will be done, the Moon Princess will be done, and hell, too, will be done. There will be *nothing.*"

Chirops wrung his claws as he paced back and forth. "But we are on the same side! We all love darkness! We all oppose the Princess!"

"We oppose her because her servants hunt us. That is the only reason."

Chirops paused in his pacing. "Really? With *what* do they hunt you?"

Julian snarled and raised a fist. "With what do you think? Fire, wild roses, holy water, crosses, virgins with hazel twigs—"

"But *why?*"

"Why? Because they work, you pathetic buffoon!"

"And why do they work?"

"Because of the Curses, you . . ."

Julian trailed off. Slowly, he lowered his fist.

"The slaves of the Dark Queen," Chirops said as he interlaced his claws, "are free."

After a minute, Julian said coldly but quietly, "We will consider your offer."

Chirops bowed. "And while you consider, I will work the root to divine whether we can help you." He turned toward the door.

"Before you go," Julian added as he swept to a nearby stovetop and dipped a spoon into a pot, "please try this and tell me what you think. We're making nougat for our handcrafted chocolates. This is *true* nougat made with only egg whites and honey—no corn syrup."

Chirops raised his claws to protest, but before he could get a word out, Julian shoved the spoon into his snout. Chirops whimpered as he tugged the spoon out. He chewed the gooey substance for almost half a minute before he finally managed to swallow and say, "Wow, that is *really* sugary—"

Somberly, Julian leaned on a counter full of cakes, jellies, and candied fruits. A dreamy look entered his reddish eyes.

"The children of the night," he whispered, "what sweet nougat they make."

After the bat left, Julian turned on his heel and marched again into the coffin chamber. He ascended the dais and walked behind the throne. With a quick twist of his strong wrist, he pulled a trapdoor out of the floor and, with his white coat fluttering, dropped into the darkness.

The cave under the confectionery was inky black, but the people of the Vampyr had no need of light. With eyes faintly glowing, Julian could see as easily as if he stood beneath a full moon. Following a tunnel of rough-cut stone, he ran his thin, pale fingers over the niches in the walls: Every niche contained a coffin, and lining the bottom of each coffin was a bed of the native earth of the vampire who slumbered there. During the First Invasion, when a navy from the galactic core had glassed most of the planet, the vampires had gathered soil from their resting places and fled toward the Moon Princess's sanctuary. Some survived by blending in with human refugees, feeding on them as they went. Some survived by traveling only at night, half starved, until they reached the city. Some did not survive at all but died in the cleansing flames of extraterrestrial weapons, which were as deadly to the *nosferatu* as terrestrial fires.

In the city's early days, when humanity's survival was most in doubt, the Moon Princess had armed a regiment of magical girls, her *fixers,* who strode through Urbanopolis equipped with everything from wooden stakes to wolfsbane to oak leaves, on a mission to root out all fairies, ifrits, liches, selkies, and other foul creatures who had slipped in disguised as human beings. Innumerable ghouls, banshees, hags, and vampires died horrible deaths at the hands of the Princess's shock troops.

It was in those days that Julian gathered the other vampires to himself. Although solitary by nature, they recognized the need to join forces, and Julian was just the one to command them: He became one of the undead in the early centuries of a new era, long before the Moon Princess; when alive, he had bathed himself in blood to invite the curse of God and had read signs and portents in the still-warm entrails of slit-open slave girls. By such arcane rites, he had secured for himself a place among the damned who still walked the earth.

For the vampires who survived the Princess's purges, things were no longer quite so dangerous. Magical girls equipped to combat infernal powers were few in number, and those who specialized in vampire-hunting were fewer still. Right now, in fact, there was only one huntress—but that one was indeed troublesome.

As Julian walked down the tunnel, the rhythmic sound of pick axes met his ears. After a moment, a cart full of stone appeared. Behind it walked a hunched young man, thin even for a vampire, whose claw-like hands twitched and jerked like a poorly controlled puppet.

"Igor," Julian said, offering the hunchback a curt nod.

"Imperator," Igor hissed, bowing low.

Julian walked past him. Igor was a low-level vampire of recent vintage: Julian himself had sucked the blood from the hapless man's veins, transforming him into his servant. But he had no need of Igor at the moment.

After several twists and turns, he approached the end of the tunnel, where six vampires swung axes and plied the hard earth with shovels. Two more carts heaped high with dirt and rocks waited for Igor to take them away.

Nearby, wearing a gown of crimson samite embroidered with gold, and with a high, fan-like collar around her neck, stood a woman whose pale skin and slender fangs glittered under the light of Julian's red eyes.

"Imperator," she said with a curtsy.

"Countess," Julian replied, offering her a stiff bow from the waist.

This was Elizabeth Báthory, who joined the *nosferatu* after she bathed in the blood of over six hundred virgins to maintain her youthful skin. Although she was not nearly as ancient as Julian, she was nonetheless third in age among the surviving Vampyr.

"How goes our project?" Julian asked. "Are we still undetected?"

"I believe so," Elizabeth replied with a toothy but demure grin. "Of course, when the city is under attack, we can take advantage of the chaos to make as much noise as we like."

Julian nodded. "How long?"

"We'll reach the foundation in probably another day, Julian— but there is still the problem of the Curses. Unless we bring some mortal into our confidence, I do not see how—"

Julian rubbed a thin hand across his chin. "We will find the way," he said.

Elizabeth's grin turned cold, and her fangs fully extended themselves. "And what are we to do about . . . *her?*"

"I will come up with a plan," Julian replied. "We must destroy her before we can move forward."

He spun on his heel and swiftly walked back the way he had come. He clenched his fists and dug his long nails into his palms. "Yes," he muttered to himself, "we will find the way. We will destroy you . . . *Magical Girl Metal Huntress Vanessa Van Halensing!*"

THIRTEEN

THE FOURTH TEST

"Get down!" Dynamo shouted. She shoved Jake hard, sending him reeling into the bathroom. Launching forward, she gabbed Miss Percy by the shoulders and flattened her to the floor. Miss Percy shrieked.

"Surge Protector!" Dynamo yelled as she raised her left arm.

Her vambrace split open. With clangs and clicks, her shield unfolded. The wasps hurtled toward her, spun in midair, and aimed their sword-like stingers. Dynamo caught them both on her shield, but the stingers punched through as if the magically reinforced metal were tissue paper. The shield shrieked as it rent. Dynamo slid back several feet and hit the wall near the bathroom door.

The stingers' tips, glistening green with poison, stopped an inch from her face. Caught in the inward-bent metal of the shield, the wasps writhed, buzzed, and waved their jointed legs as they tried to crawl free. Dynamo's eyes widened in surprise, but she didn't waste time: With a snarl, she swung her arm down and smacked the wasps into the floor. At the same time, she cross-drew her wand from her utility belt.

"Lightning Rod!"

Once the wand expanded into a spear, Dynamo swiped off the wasps' heads with the sharp point. Greenish-yellow innards sprayed across the floor. Still prone, Miss Percy screamed when bug guts pelted her.

With a contemptuous shake, Dynamo freed the dead wasps from her Surge Protector. Their bodies fell to the floor with a splat.

Jake stepped to her side and glanced up and down the hall.

"Scouts?" he asked.

"Maybe," she replied, "but I bet there's a swarm. We gotta move."

"Where's Tesla?"

"Dunno, but if there's more of those bugs, he's probably held up."

She stared at the fresh holes in her shield. That shield began folding into her vambrace with a hiss but stopped halfway and, whining like a strained motor, unfolded again.

"Zap it."

She pressed a button on her arm. The Surge Protector fell away and banged to the floor. Now empty, the compartment in her vambrace snapped closed. As she helped a shaky Miss Percy rise to her feet, Dynamo said, "Looks like my armor's useless against these things."

"You've got a bare midriff," said Jake. "Hasn't your armor *always* been useless?"

"My skin's just as strong as my plate, dork. But if they can break my shield, they can break anything I've got."

"How long until your shield regenerates?"

She shook her head. "Tesla would know. Probably another two weeks." In frustration, she kicked one of the mangled wasps' bodies. "First my Circuit Board and now my Surge Protector. If I lose my wand, I'm *done.*"

"I don't understand," Miss Percy whispered, her voice quaking as she cowered behind Jake's shoulder. "How could an insect's stinger go through magic metal?"

With her blue eyebrows knitted together, Dynamo crouched, picked up a wasp by its abdomen, and touched the tip of its stinger to her fallen shield. The metal curled inward like a sensitive plant recoiling from human touch.

"It's the poison," she said.

"Is it going to work like this against any magical girl," asked Jake, "or just you?"

"Dunno. Tesla could probably analyze it, but I can't do it on my own." She tapped her tiara, where the lenses of her goggles rested. "My system's interface was designed for Elektronian brains, so Tesla's never been able to sync it with mine. I need him to interpret my data."

"Hold on a second," said Jake. "That gives me an idea." He ran into the bathroom, grabbed a metal dustbin, and dragged it into the hallway. After picking up a stinger, he touched it to the bin's side. A drop of green slid down the bin, but the metal didn't react.

Slowly, Jake reached out to touch the liquid—

Dynamo seized his hand. "Don't. Whatever it is, I bet it reacts to stuff that's alive. My items grow out of my body, remember? That's probably why the poison burns them."

"Aren't other magical girls the same way? That means—"

"Yeah, maybe, unless someone's immune." She rose to her feet.

Jake stared for a moment at the green goo trickling down the rubbish bin. After a few seconds, he stuck his finger in it.

"Hey!" Dynamo shouted.

"It doesn't hurt," he answered. He stood up with the droplet on the tip of his finger. "It's not hurting me. It isn't living stuff it affects, so it must be magical stuff—or at least your kind of magic."

"So you're less vulnerable to these things than I am?"

"Pretty much."

She made an annoyed rasping noise.

He bent down, seized one of the wasps' stingers, and tugged. With a lot of hard pulling, he ripped it out of the insect's abdomen with the greenish poison sac intact.

"This might come in handy," he said.

Dynamo growled. "Okay, fine. Give it to me, and maybe—"

"You shouldn't touch it. I'll come with you."

She growled again.

"Jake's right," Miss Percy said. She bent down and tried to touch the other wasp's stinger but drew back with a whimper when the wasp's mangled body twitched.

Jake handed her his own extracted stinger and then pulled out the other for himself.

With a snarl, Dynamo yanked on her pigtails. "You two are *not* comin' with me."

"You're gonna need help," Jake replied.

"There's a *kaiju* out there—"

"Exactly, and you're the best *kaiju* fighter in the city. But you're ground-bound, so if you're gonna get to the big guy, you gotta go through the wasps."

"How are you gonna help me do *that?*"

Jake looked down at the stinger in his hands. "I'll think of something."

"I don't need your help, Jake!"

"Dynamo, I told you before, Tsubasa attacked—"

"I mean it! I work alone!"

She spun around and ran toward the school's front doors.

"Dynamo!"

"Shut up!" she shouted over her shoulder. "Go away!"

"Oh dear," Miss Percy whispered, clutching her stinger in both hands. "Did you two have a fight?"

Jake sighed. "Sort of."

He took a step forward, but Miss Percy gripped his arm. "Jake, she's right. You can't run after her this time. You really should go to the shelter."

For half a minute, he stared at the doors where she had disappeared.

"I can't, Miss Percy." He shook his head. "I just can't." He slid his arm from her grasp and took off running.

DYNAMO SPED AWAY. JAKE HAD TO STOP AT HIS SHOE LOCKER TO get rid of his Crocs and don his sneakers, but then he was right behind her.

"Get lost!" she shouted over her shoulder.

Jake stared into the sky. Black clouds swirled overhead—clouds that weaved back and forth and spun in spirals. A constant drone, like the sound of an electrical generator, met his ears. Behind it was the staccato boom of the automated defenses. A siren wailed in the lower city.

"You need a shield, right?" Jake shouted.

He panted. He had to sprint to keep up with her, and he knew he couldn't maintain this pace for long.

"I'm not *quite* ready to use your body to block monsters' attacks," she snarled back, "but I'm getting there—"

Struggling to talk, he gasped, "Remember when we were kids?"

"What?"

"Okay, I mean, you still *are* a kid, but when *I* was a kid—"

"What are you blathering about?"

"Follow me." He jogged up the block toward the mouth of an alley, the same alley he'd seen a *Stegosaurus* walk out of almost a week before, and the same alley where Pretty Dynamo had beaten him black and blue. His shoes crunched on the gravel, and he could hear her heavy boots thudding behind him. He smiled.

In the alley stood a cluster of rubbish bins. One had a dent in its side from where Jake had fallen into it during their fight.

He picked up two of the bins' lids and hefted them. "Perfect," he said.

She crossed her arms and glared.

"Haven't you ever had a snowball fight?" he asked. "Or a swordfight with sticks?"

"No."

"Really? Well, trashcan lids make great shields. *That's* what I'm talking about. And it's not magical or part of your body, so it won't react to the poison."

He tossed a lid to her, and she snatched it out of the air. Then he grasped the second in his fist and held the stinger like a sword. "See? Like this."

She hefted the lid, twisting her mouth back and forth as she did so.

"It might work," she muttered. "At least for the wasps. But I gotta get to that *kaiju,* and you're not gonna be able to keep up with me." With that, she leaped onto a rooftop, leaped again, and quickly disappeared.

Jake stared up at the swarming wasps for a minute, considering. Then, despite the complaints of his sore ankle, he started jogging. He didn't go back to school. Instead, he headed downhill toward Little India—toward deep Urbanopolis.

As he ran with the trashcan lid pumping up and down in his hand, he caught glimpses of Dynamo in the distance. The sunlight sparkled from her gold and silver armor as she deftly bounded from one roof to another. She was already leaping among the brownstones in lower Juban, probably dislodging tiles, breaking shingles, and creating future leaks in the process.

The monster towered on the horizon: A yellow abomination with a distended stomach and a high fin on its head—like a sumo wrestler with jaundice and a funny hat—it groped blindly amongst a cluster of high-rises. Jake's teeth rattled as a missile plowed into the monster's back and burst in a red and white fireball. Overhead, the wasp swarm rippled and broke apart. The next thing Jake knew, he was lying on his back with his ears ringing as a shockwave washed over him.

Momentarily punch-drunk, he tried to stand but collapsed again.

There's no way I'm getting close to that thing when they're firing the heavy ordnance—

He sat up, and another shockwave knocked him flat. Wasps rained from the sky and splattered against the pavement. They sounded like cap guns going off when their bodies burst.

Holding up his garbage pail lid, Jake woozily climbed to his feet and ducked into a narrow alley. Something struck the lid hard, sending searing pain into his wrists and dropping him to his knees. Rough asphalt bit into his skin.

In front of him, a wasp floundering on the ground—probably the one that had just hit him. It lay only two feet away.

Jake staggered back and instantly smacked his shoulder into a brick wall. This alley was only four feet wide, and it ended at a pile of twisted metal and old plywood.

The wasp was between Jake and the alley's entrance. Holding up his lid and clumsily swinging the amputated stinger, he stepped forward—

The wasp rolled to its feet, beat its wings, and took to the air. Jake sucked in his breath and jumped backwards.

"Barfing Boy," the wasp hissed with its creepily human-like mouth.

It flew toward him. Jake swung with the lid. With a *thunk,* he knocked the wasp back.

It buzzed and lunged again. Again he knocked it back. Again it lunged, persistent like the mindless insect it resembled.

But this time, when Jake struck, the wasp didn't bounce. Instead, it reached out with its tiny legs and seized the lid, peeking over the top and hissing. Its huge compound eyes glittered like a cluster of jewels, and its antennae waved.

Jake dropped the lid and stomped on it. The wasp's head snapped off and shot toward the alley's mouth. Green goop sprayed across the pavement.

Unfortunately, Jake had stomped with his left foot. He sucked air through his teeth and sank to the ground as his ankle throbbed.

I shouldn't be out here.

He held up his hands to see them shaking. Before now, he

hadn't thought he had an irrational fear of insects, but these giant wasps were freaking him out.

Another explosion. More wasps erupted as they struck the street beyond the alleyway. A few windows blew in. Jake's head throbbed. It hadn't occurred to him before, but if he was going to follow Pretty Dynamo, he'd need ear protection.

A *kaiju* had attacked just a week before, but the city hadn't launched the large missiles. Urbanopolis bristled with guns, but most monsters were immune to non-magical weapons—that was why the magical girls had to keep the city safe.

However, shortly after the previous *kaiju,* robot dinosaurs and then zombies had invaded, and both were vulnerable to the city's conventional arsenal. Perhaps, after that, the military had decided to shoot first and ask questions later. The wasps, at least, were vulnerable—though the *kaiju* itself didn't appear to be.

Jake staggered to his feet and peeked out of the alleyway. He heard a loud buzz, and something yellow dived for his face. He ducked and raised his makeshift shield, but then his eyes filled with red light, and a crack like thunder met his ears. The diving wasp exploded.

He lowered the shield to see a skinny girl running toward him, her tan duster fluttering behind her and a Stetson sitting askew on her yellow hair.

"Rifle Maiden!" he shouted.

"Jakey!" She gave him a toothy grin and waved. Spinning her Winchester to cock it one-handed, she fired off a few more explosive blasts and destroyed more wasps. When she reached him, she skidded to a halt and pushed her Stetson back on her head.

"Well now," she said, "ain't you a sight for sore eyes! How ya been?"

"Fine, I guess. You?"

"Much as you'd reckon," she said, her drawling voice whistling through her buckteeth. "I was just hankerin' for some new monsters t' kill when these here varmints showed up, so I s'pose I can't complain. Cover your ears, now."

"What?"

She released several more blasts from her rifle to break up an approaching swarm, and he dropped his shield and stinger to clap his hands to his ears.

Before he could retrieve his makeshift weapons, Rifle Maiden seized his hand and pulled him up the street.

"Wait, Rifle Maiden, I need the—!"

"Where's Dynamo?" she called.

"She ran after the *kaiju,*" he answered, stumbling on his sore leg as he struggled to keep pace. "Look, I gotta tell you something about—"

"Dunno if she can kill that thing without 'er Circuit Board. Maybe if she gets enough charge in that Thunder Bolt o' hers . . . still, she's got the city's best ratin' against the big 'uns, so if anyone can handle it, I reckon it's her."

"Rifle Maiden, stop!"

"Can't stop! Gotta keep movin'!" She unleashed more explosive bullets from her rifle—ten, twenty, thirty. Rifle Maiden's magic meant never having to reload.

The pain turned sharp and shot up Jake's leg. He stumbled and fell, and Rifle Maiden dragged him along the asphalt for several feet before realizing.

She halted, fired off a few more shots, and yanked him upright. "You hurt?"

"Kinda. Look—"

"Hold on." She slid the rifle into its sheath and then turned her back on him, hunkering down.

"What?"

"Piggyback," she said.

"But—"

"Ah, you ain't heavy. I got super strength, remember?"

More wasps gathered overhead, so he decided not to argue. He climbed onto Rifle Maiden's back and wrapped his arms around her shoulders.

"Well, now, ain't this cozy?" she said, looking over her shoulder and winking. "Hold on tight."

She pulled her ivory-handled revolvers from the holsters on her hips and sprinted up the street at full speed. Jake gasped as the wind whipped through his hair. Then he released a surprised yelp when she jumped five stories into the air and landed lithely on an asphalt rooftop. Her cowboy boots slid a few feet, and Jake sucked his breath between his teeth, afraid they'd topple to the street below.

"Whoo!" she cried as she came to a stop. "Ain't nothin' like it, eh?"

"Look, Rifle Maiden, I gotta tell you—*yahh!"*

She leaped again.

He could feel his heart hammering against his ribs as cold sweat broke out along his spine. Adrenaline coursed through his veins. He'd wondered before what it was like to run and jump like a magical girl. It was exhilarating: No wonder so many of the girls enjoyed what they did despite the dangers they faced and the horrors they witnessed.

For a moment, in his mind, he saw Pretty Dynamo as she was a few days before, crouching behind a half wall in the financial district and nervously pulling her pigtails while wondering aloud how to reconcile the two sides of her psyche.

Then he remembered her cocky grin and low chuckle as she pulled stunts on her Circuit Board.

Yes, she enjoyed it. Even though she hated it.

A smile formed on his mouth. *Maybe all she really wants to do is skate. Maybe everything will be okay once she gets her Board back—*

But then he remembered Dynamo, just a few minutes ago, plunging his head into the sink.

With Jake on her back, Rifle Maiden nimbly dodged storage sheds, cell antennas, and howitzers. Only once did she make an error: As she turned sharply to get around a rooftop's stairwell access, she skidded three feet and went down on one knee.

Jake gulped.

Rifle Maiden laughed. "Heh. Not used to the extra weight."

In an instant, she was up and sprinting again.

Gradually getting used to bouncing precariously on her back, Jake found enough breath to lean forward and yell in her ear, "The poison in the wasps' stingers—it reacts to magic! It can burn you like acid!"

She slid behind a storage shed, threw him off her back, and slammed him up against a galvanized steel wall.

She breathed heavily. That both surprised and distressed him: Despite her power, running and jumping were getting her wind.

"Are you sure?" she said.

He nodded. "Their stingers went straight through Dynamo's shield. She's down to one item."

Rifle Maiden spat. "Welp, wouldn't be the first monsters what could hurt us, but still—*straight* through her shield?"

He nodded again.

She shook her head. "Ain't sure what that means, but that's some powerful stuff. Thanks for the warnin', but it ain't gonna change my mind none."

She hiked him onto her back again.

"Might be too late," she added, "but if'n we can relay that to the boss, he can tell the rest o' the girls."

"Can't you call him now?"

She shook her head. "When I transform, my communicator disappears with my duds."

She reached the edge of the roof, and Jake reflexively held his breath when she launched herself into the air. He felt his bladder slide into his left shoe as, for a moment, they hung suspended twelve stories above a broad stretch of road. Jake could easily imagine falling—

Then they *were* falling. The wind whipped through Jake's hair and made his eyes water. He ground his teeth together and spread his lips wide as an asphalt-shingled roof shot up to meet them.

Rifle Maiden bent her knees to absorb the shock, but Jake still bounced up and down on her back and sucked air through his teeth. Yes, it was exhilarating, but the landings were rough.

As Rifle Maiden bent low and rushed across the roof, Jake dug his fingertips into her shoulders. Wasps closed in. Without slowing down, Rifle Maiden lifted her revolvers and fired so rapidly that the reports blended into one long, continuous blast.

"Their poison sacs!" he yelled. "Don't hit their poison sacs!"

She nodded. Every explosive bullet found its target, striking head or thorax and leaving the abdomen intact. The wasps burst in flashes of red light and sprays of green guts, leaving their rotund hind parts whole and twitching on the rooftops. Soon, Jake and Rifle Maiden were coated in glop.

They moved deeper into the city. After a few minutes, they were in the middle of Little India. From above, it appeared as a tightly clustered quarter full of tall towers with pointed, lavishly carved ivory domes.

With a whoop, Rifle Maiden bounded from one tower to another. Jake's eyes streamed. He clutched her in a death grip.

He hoped he wasn't choking her.

The guns thundered in his ears, and he lost count of the crazy, death-defying leaps. He simply shut his eyes and prayed for this harrowing trip to end.

Finally, she landed on a flat surface and stopped. With a gasp, Jake opened his eyes and sucked in air—only now realizing he'd been holding his breath again.

"Whoo-whee!" Rifle Maiden shouted as she pushed her hat back with the muzzle of one revolver. "That was even more excitin' than usual! 'Specially cuz o' *this.* " Chortling, she tapped the gun barrel against the back of Jake's right hand.

He looked down and saw that, without knowing it, he had been gripping one of her breasts.

With a startled cry, he let go and fell to the rooftop. She burst out laughing.

His hand throbbed, and he stared at it in wonder.

I've touched two breasts before my fifteenth birthday. I'm pretty sure that gives me bragging rights—

When his head cleared, he saw a cluster of soldiers. They had set up sandbags around a pair of turret-mounted rotary autocannons, each the size of a van, which slowly turned on their bearings and belched 30-mm shells into the sky. Belts rhythmically fed their chambers, and spent casings whizzed from their sides. Crouched behind the sandbags, the men blazed away with rifles and submachine guns.

Rifle Maiden dragged Jake to his feet, pushed his head down to keep his profile low, and ran with him behind the sandbags, where they soon flopped down beside a captain chewing through rounds with an FN P90.

"Dame Rifle Maiden," he said, acknowledging Rifle Maiden only briefly and ignoring Jake entirely.

"How we lookin', cap'n?" she shouted over the roar of the guns.

The captain shook his head and screamed back, "Our orders are to defend the turrets. Those bugs are tearing them apart—but we can't hold 'em long. They've already hit the fields, and we have no air support!"

Jake swept his eyes over the soldiers with their helmets, body armor, and fatigues. Most were thin and wiry boys only slightly older than he was—probably high-school graduates doing their two years of duty before moving on to work or college. They undoubtedly had minimal training and minimal experience; in Urbanopolis, the military's main job was crowd control.

They weren't cut out for this.

Jake heard another teeth-rattling boom as a barrage of rolling-airframe missiles pounded into the *kaiju.*

Why is the military even here? If they get everyone under-ground, those wasps can't do a thing—

Almost as if reading his thoughts, the captain shouted over the gunfire, "They're after infrastructure! We've got to deal with these things quick, or there's not gonna be much of a city left!"

"Why are they shooting the monster?" Jake shouted.

The captain glanced at him as if noticing him for the first time. "They're firing everything we've got!"

"Why?"

He shook his head as he dropped a spent magazine and loaded another. "You're asking the wrong man, kid."

"Where's my counterpart?" Rifle Maiden yelled as the captain's firing resumed.

"Three stories down! Tell her to hurry up!"

Overhead, the wasps scattered as the shells from the autocannons chewed through them, but they quickly gathered again into a dark, writhing cloud and dived en masse.

"Here they come!" the captain shouted.

Rifle Maiden jumped to her feet, both revolvers in hand. Her index fingers blurred as she pulled her triggers with superhuman speed, rivaling the autocannons' rate of fire. A sea of red explosions swept from left to right across the wasp swarm, and a rainstorm of bug guts enveloped the rooftop.

But there were too many of them. Overwhelmed by the gallons of green glop dropping from the sky, the soldiers paused in their firing, and then the wasps were on top of them. One landed in front of the captain and, with its tarsal claws, sliced through his one-point sling and ripped his submachine gun away. The captain drew a Five-seveN from the tactical holster on his hip, but his hand was slick with insect innards, and the pistol slipped from his grasp, clattering across the rooftop. The wasp spun and pointed a dagger-length stinger at his face.

With a yell, Jake jumped to his feet and swung a fist. He slipped—but he fell forward, and his hand went through the exoskeleton of the wasp's abdomen with a crunch like breaking crackers. Green coated his fingers, spurted into his eyes, and went in his mouth. Overwhelmingly bitter and sour, the bug guts vaguely reminded him of Starbucks coffee.

He gagged.

Jake fell with one arm across the captain's shoulders. The

captain roughly threw him off, scrambled for his handgun, and got off a few shots before the bugs swarmed again.

The men fought with pistols, knives, and fists as the bugs jumped on them. Staggering to his feet again, Jake tried to blink the liquid out of his eyes and make sense of the chaos. He blindly punched and struck something solid that bounced away—he wasn't sure if it was a wasp or a man.

A burst of red fluid, bright and ugly against the green, met his eyes. He saw a man go down and disappear under the slime. Still, the autocannons fired, rattling his teeth and bruising his eardrums. The acrid stink of insects, the metallic stench of human blood, and the stinging smell of cordite filled his nose and churned his stomach.

From the midst of the carnage, he heard one mournful wail of "Mommy!" Three weeks ago, a young soldier crying for his mother might have seemed funny or pathetic, but now it struck him with a singular horror.

Jake slipped and fell again, and this time his hands came upon a dropped rifle. He picked it up, put it against his shoulder, and fired into the air. He had no idea if he hit anything.

The men shouted and groaned in pain. Jake saw red again. He didn't know if it was his blood or someone else's. He tried to stand, but his feet slid out to either side. His left ankle screamed.

Then someone else screamed—a girl, not a man. Something hit Jake with a wet, fleshy slap and knocked him onto his side. He realized it was Rifle Maiden's leather duster, coated in gore. She was on top of him, clutching a stinger that had pierced her chest near her right shoulder. The wasp attached to the stinger waved its legs wildly and hissed like a steam kettle. Rifle Maiden cursed a blue streak as she fired off her left revolver. The wasp's head dissolved.

Jake pushed her off, climbed to his feet, fell hard on his back, climbed to his feet again. He grabbed Rifle Maiden under her arms and, using her weight for balance, dragged her toward a rooftop stairwell door.

Her right hand fell limp, and her ivory-handled revolver slipped from her grasp.

"No!" she shouted. "The gun! Get my gun!"

He ignored her. He yanked the door open and shoved her inside.

Pausing only to pull the door closed, he hauled her down the hard metal stairs and slipped again. The two of them tumbled. Covered in bruises and foul-smelling gunk, they came to rest in a heap on a landing.

Rifle Maiden continued swearing in an un-magical-girl-like fashion as she rolled onto her back and clutched her shoulder. Blood spurted from under her hand. Now that the fire door at the top of the stairwell was deadening the gunfire, Jake could hear a faint sizzle, like frying bacon, coming from her wound. Along with the gunk and blood, he smelled the distinctive, nausea-inducing stink of burning flesh.

He coughed hard, found his voice, and croaked, "It's the poison. You have to transform!"

Red blood ran down Rifle Maiden's duster as she fell with her back against a cinderblock wall. She breathed hard and gave him a buck-toothed grin. "Can I trust you?"

"You don't have a choice."

She chuckled. "C'mere. If I gotta change, there's somethin' I wanna do first."

He crawled up to her. "What—?"

She grabbed the front of his shirt and pulled him into a rough kiss. He put a hand on the wall to keep from falling on top of her, but as his lips yielded to hers, that hand slid to her unwounded shoulder.

In a flash, her duster disappeared. His head buzzed. For a moment, his hand rested against bare, sweat-slicked skin, but then a thin cotton cloth materialized where the duster had been.

The girl who had been Rifle Maiden gasped. She quickly shoved Jake off but then cried out and grasped her shoulder, which still leaked blood.

Jake fell on his rump and winced as his tailbone bruised. The girl before him wore a high-school uniform—she had probably left school to fight, just as he had. She had a green plaid skirt and a thin, salmon-colored jacket overlying a white dress shirt with a red bowtie. Jake didn't recognize the uniform, though it suggested a high-class school, maybe in Little Europe.

This girl looked vaguely like Rifle Maiden, though mousier. Her hair had turned from yellow to deep brown, and her skin was a few shades darker. She still had Rifle Maiden's buckteeth, but she also had an outsized pair of round eyeglasses.

She glanced guiltily at Jake and then looked away, hunching her shoulders as if trying to collapse in on herself. Tears leaked from under her glasses.

"I'm sorry," he said, "but you need a bandage, and your clothes are the only thing clean here."

She nodded.

She didn't fight him as he pulled off her jacket and ripped off her shirt, scattering her buttons across the landing. Under the shirt, he could see an ugly, round hole through her flesh. It was immediately to the left of the shoulder joint and appeared to have gone straight through, coming out just above her shoulder blade. Whenever she moved, more blood seeped out.

Clotting blood had already stained much of her shirt, but Jake ripped what he could into strips, pressed some of them over each side of the wound, and then tied another strip tightly under her armpit to hold them in place. The injury was in an awkward spot, so despite his regular practice in first aid, dressing it took several minutes. He was thankful that no wasps had come through the door above; perhaps they'd killed the soldiers, destroyed the turrets, and moved on. He couldn't hear any more gunfire.

Down to a white, lacy bra, the skinny girl shuddered under his ministrations. She kept her head down, not meeting his eyes.

"What's your name?" he asked.

She smiled faintly but still wouldn't look at him. "Lillian," she muttered. "Lillian Mosey."

"We need to get some antiseptic, Lily. I'm sure there's a first aid kit somewhere in the building."

Her mouth moved, and she muttered something he couldn't quite hear.

"What?"

She swallowed, licked her lips, and spoke more loudly. "Natasha," she said. "She's a few floors down. Get me to Natasha."

He grunted. "Can you stand?"

She nodded. He set her good arm over his shoulders and groaned as he staggered upright. Limping and leaning on each other, they clomped together down the stairs.

FOURTEEN

VOODOO

Jake and Lily staggered into a dark hallway. The lights were off, meaning the electricity was probably out, though a few EXIT signs glowed orange. It was a nondescript hall with white-painted drywall and drop ceiling tiles—so this was likely an office building.

Lily whimpered softly as she leaned on a wall. She left a red streak behind.

"I bet I can find a first aid kit," Jake said.

His eyes alighted on a wall-mounted fire extinguisher and box on the hall's far end. He jogged to them, his ankle begging for mercy, and found, as he expected, a defibrillator and first-aid kit. There should be two sets of those on every floor if the building was up to code.

He threw the box open and pulled the kit out. It was a year past its expiration date but held compresses, gauze, bandages, iodine, and even a tourniquet, just as it was supposed to.

He ran back to Lily. "Sit down. I can—"

She shook her head and clumsily pushed him away. As she did, her hand brushed his neck. She felt clammy. He didn't like her shallow breathing, either.

"Natasha," she rasped. "Get me—"

He wrapped an arm around her and continued his march up the hall. If he had to find Natasha to convince her to let him treat her, he would find Natasha.

"They're getting smarter," she murmured. "Usually, they just aim for the people."

He nodded. "I know. But at least they can't hit the food supply or the factories. They're too deep."

"Maybe—unless they come up with something new."

A chill ran down Jake's spine. Although the wasps and the *kaiju* were probably not a threat to the city's underground, the thought that Down Under might be vulnerable still stunned him: Urbanopolitans took it for granted that the city's deepest workings were impervious.

They rounded a corner and entered an identical-looking hallway. One door was slightly ajar, and pale light—probably from a window—poured out of it.

Jake pulled Lily to the door and incautiously threw it open. There, in the middle of a food-mottled rug on the floor of a breakroom, Voodoo Queen Natasha sat cross-legged.

Unusually full-figured for a magical girl, Natasha wore a top hat over her dreadlocks, and her face was painted to resemble a skull. In front of her on the carpet stood a rough, unfinished wax sculpture, almost two feet high, which vaguely resembled the yellow monstrosity rampaging through the city.

Natasha looked up. Her heavy makeup made her expression hard to read, but she raised one eyebrow.

"Lily?"

"She got hit," Jake said as he lowered Lily to the floor. "The wasps' poison reacts to magic, so she had to transform."

Natasha nodded somberly. "I read as much in the bones. I invoked Loa Shango to guide your arm in battle, Lily, and that is probably why your wound is not fatal."

"I lost a gun," Lily whimpered.

Natasha nodded again. "For a magical girl, to lose an item is to lose a part of herself. It can be hard."

Jake's stomach clenched at those words. He tore off Lily's makeshift bandage to create a more proper one and poured iodine over her wound. Lily squinched up her eyes and moaned softly.

"How's it coming, Natasha?" she asked once she could speak.

"Slowly, I'm afraid," Natasha replied in her curiously deep voice as she scowled at the sculpture before her. "Unfortunately, my power is not especially useful against enemies of such size."

"Why not?" Jake asked as he folded up gauze and pressed it to Lily's shoulder. "Can't you just make a doll, twist its head off, and kill that thing?"

"You would think so," said Natasha glumly. "After all, I *do* have the power."

"What power?"

"The power of voodoo."

"Who do?"

She glared at him so fiercely that he flinched.

"Never do that to me," she whispered.

He swallowed.

Eyebrows pressed together, Natasha carefully carved a hexagonal pattern into the wax figure with a stick.

"But despite my power, the larger the enemy is, the more detail the dolls must have if my juju is to work." She paused to strike a match and light a candle standing by her left knee. She mumbled a few words before adding, "And the more rituals I must perform."

"How long?" Lily asked.

"Three more hours, at least," Natasha replied. "Even then, I make no guarantee. I could make a mistake—or the monster might have a counterspell."

"What other magical girls are good against *kaiju*?" asked Jake.

"At the moment, few of them," said Natasha. "Pretty Dynamo was the most effective, though she may have trouble now that she cannot fly. Aside from her . . ." Natasha paused and shook her head. "Perhaps Blade Maid. Or Wushu Wench. Or even Vixen Vicious. But there are so few . . ."

Jake's stomach ached.

"Of course," Natasha said quietly, "there is always . . . *her.*"

Lily trembled as Jake finished dressing her wound. She laughed nervously. "Natasha, it hasn't come to that yet."

"Still, she is the most powerful of all."

"Maybe, but she could do more damage than the monster."

"But if we must—"

"Wait," said Jake. "I thought Pretty Dynamo was the most powerful right now."

Natasha again raised a single eyebrow. "On the traditional scale of the Threat Assessment Board, that may be the case. But there are those to whom the scale does not *exactly* apply."

Jake looked back and forth between the girls. "Okay, so what now?"

"There is little we can do," Natasha replied. "Lily is wounded and cannot turn back into Rifle Maiden. I can do nothing except continue my work." She carved more hexagons into the creature and scowled. "But I may have to get closer if I am to complete this. I need to see its feet."

Jake swallowed. "How do we get you closer?"

Natasha glanced at Lily, twisted her mouth, and said, "I will have to go myself. I have not the physical skill of some of the other girls, but I can manage—probably."

Lily pulled her knees to her chest and pressed her forehead against them. "I'm sorry!" Her voice cracked.

"You fought well," Natasha replied.

"But I lost my gun!" Lily sobbed.

Jake said, "It will grow back, right? Don't your items come out of your body?"

Lily whimpered softly.

"That is true of most items," said Natasha quietly, "but Rifle Maiden's gun is different. That gun is a relic, a talisman, you might say—part of her soul."

Jake's insides churned with guilt. He hadn't recognized the desperation in Rifle Maiden's voice when she begged him to grab her six-shooter; he had only thought of dragging a wounded fighter off the battlefield.

"Stay here," he said as he rose to his feet. Once he was standing, he lost his balance and fell against the doorframe.

"Where are you going?" Natasha asked.

"Never mind. I'll be right back."

He limped into the hall and headed for the stairwell. Both his back and his ankle complained with each step, and it crossed his mind that, even as young as he was, he couldn't keep up this level of activity for many days more.

At that thought, he felt a buzz in his forearms. Then the pain in his ankle, after a harsh throb, subsided.

He frowned but stood up straight. Cautiously, he jogged toward the stairwell door. His ankle didn't hurt.

That puzzled him, but he didn't worry about it. As quietly as he could, he walked up the stairs, his breath loud in his ears. He didn't hear any noise from above.

When he threw open the door to the roof, he saw a sea of green goo marked by coagulating red pools. Dead wasps and dead men lay half submerged in the slime. Jake recognized the captain, pierced through with several holes and lying facedown near the wall of sandbags. Overhanging this grisly scene, the autocannons were silent, their guts torn open. Their shells, huge and menacing, lay around their mounts.

A light breeze, strangely warm, blew against Jake's face. He felt a fresh pang of guilt, and he wondered if he should have stayed on the roof. He knew he could have done nothing to help these men, yet leaving them felt wrong—even if he did it to save a wounded magical girl.

Black clouds of angry insects swirled overhead like a threatening thunderstorm. Jake could hear buzzing, staccato gunfire, and explosions, yet after the deafening roar of the earlier battle, the rooftop seemed quiet. Surrounded by the whole city, with the enemy swarming overhead, Jake was alone.

With his eyes, he traced a long smear through the goop—the mark he left when he dragged Rifle Maiden to the door. He took a few steps, his eyes glued to the roof, until he saw a glimmer of steel.

Got you.

He bent down and pulled the revolver out of the muck. The heaviness of the gun shocked him, and it nearly slipped from his grasp. The ivory handle was smooth to his touch, like silk, as if generations' worth of hands had worn it down and generations' worth of oil had slicked it.

His fingers tingled when the grip slid comfortably into his palm as if it belonged there. Yes, he could believe what Natasha said: This was a talisman, a relic, an object of power.

Foolishly, he slid his finger onto the trigger and pulled, but the trigger didn't move. It was cold and unyielding, like stone. That didn't surprise him—Rifle Maiden had told him before that only she could fire her guns.

He had more to do, and he needed to put the gun away. He'd seen plenty of movies in which men stuffed pistols in their waistbands, a maneuver he always thought looked stupid and dangerous, but with no other ideas about how to free his hands, he shoved the massive six-shooter down his pants.

It was uncomfortable.

Then, feeling like a ghoul, he crouched over the body of the dead captain and unclasped his tactical holster. Plastic buckles hooked it to his belt and held it to his thigh, so it took Jake only a few seconds to undo it and then strap it on his own leg. He found the captain's Five-seveN nearby, a gun considerably lighter than Rifle Maiden's, so light it felt like a cheap toy. He cleaned it as well as he could by rubbing it against his shirt. Then he holstered it. He found a few extra magazines for the gun in the captain's chest pack and crammed them into his pockets.

Finally, he picked up the captain's FN P90. The wasps had shredded its sling, so he cradled it under his right armpit. It shocked him how light it was, though it was top-heavy because of its long, horizontal magazine, which was still half full of bullets. The gun's peculiar, curvy form was apparently supposed to be comfortable, but after he'd held Rifle Maiden's pistol, it seemed silly.

Overhead, a circle of dense black appeared in the cloud of wasps, and then the insects dived.

He put the P90 to his shoulder.

"That's right, motherhuggers!" he shouted. "Come and get it!"

Hissing and buzzing, twelve wasps sped toward him. Backing toward the door, Jake squeezed the trigger, and the gun bounced against his shoulder, rattling his teeth. The wasps disintegrated and spread fresh splatters of green across the roof.

He reached the door. Still firing, he yanked it open.

In seconds, he emptied the rifle. Tossing it aside, he jumped into the stairwell and slammed the door shut.

Something slammed into the door on the other side. Then he felt the door pulling out of his grasp.

Jake yanked the door shut again, catching an insect leg against the frame and cleaving it in half. Once more, something pulled, and he strained to keep the door closed as his gunk-caked shoes squeaked against the concrete.

He slid forward an inch and knew he couldn't hold it, so he jumped back, fumbled the Five-seveN out of its holster, and hoped it would still fire despite the bug guts caking it. The door flew open, and five hissing wasps crawled in. He pulled the trigger.

The gun barked, and its powerful report made his ears ring. A yellow fireball erupted from the barrel, startling him. He flinched. The bullet missed the bugs, striking the doorframe instead and leaving a broad, circular indentation.

He fired again, and this time the bullet found its mark. A wasp's head exploded like a ripe fruit.

Jake's feet slipped on the staircase. He tumbled, hitting his shoulders hard on the edge of a stair and performing a clumsy backwards somersault. He expected to feel the air leave his lungs as he struck the landing, but he instead ran up against something soft and springy like a waterbed.

An ash-streaked arm caught him around the waist. He looked up to see Natasha's heavily painted face, and he realized, as his cheeks flushed, that she'd broken his fall with her copious breasts.

"You could kill yourself with those things," she said, nodding to the gun he held. Then, after she set him on his feet, she pulled two sharp, black-handled athames from her pouch. Wielding one in each hand, she sprinted up the stairs. With quick, vicious flicks, she cut the wasps in pieces, each slice accompanied by a sickening *shlllkkk.*

Unable to swarm through the narrow door en masse, the wasps retreated. Natasha wiped her knives clean on her cape and put them away. Then she knelt down and, muttering dark spells, pulled a stinger and its greenish poison sac from a dead wasp's abdomen.

Jumping from the top of the stairwell, she landed lightly next to Jake.

"We should move from here," she said, breathing heavily.

"I agree," he mumbled. He holstered his new gun and concentrated on keeping his eyes off her chest.

She glanced down briefly. "Is that a pistol in your pocket?" she asked, raising an eyebrow.

He started. "What—? Oh."

Feeling heat in his face, Jake dug Rifle Maiden's revolver out of his waistband. Despite its comfortable grip, it felt cold and strange in his hand.

As they headed back down the stairs and into the hallway, Natasha said, with a hint of amusement in her deep voice, "I should let you know, it's not considered polite to touch a magical girl's items—and it's definitely not polite to stick them in your pants."

"Sorry."

"But I think we can forgive you, given the circumstances." She pushed open the door to the breakroom and offered Jake a wink. "Lily, behold."

As the two of them entered the room, Lily looked up. Her eyes glistened when she saw the revolver in Jake's hand.

Flipping it around and grasping it by its barrel, he held it out to her. Fingers trembling, she took it and cradled it like a delicate baby bird. Then, to Jake's surprise, she pressed its grip against the wound in her shoulder and closed her eyes as relief spread across her face.

Natasha sat down cross-legged and ran her eyes over the detached stinger in her ash-streaked fingers. After a minute, she nodded, laid the stinger on the floor, and pulled a wooden bowl and badger skin out of her bag. From the bowl, she poured a collection of rodent bones onto the skin.

After almost a minute, she said, "I have an idea. Lily, if you'll permit me, let me handle your revolver."

Lily still had the gun pressed to her shoulder. She jumped as if something bit her. Looking at Natasha with fear plain in her eyes, she said, "You won't . . . do anything—?"

"I know it is precious to you."

Fingers shaking, Lily held the gun out. As she did, she glanced shyly at Jake and mumbled, "It was my father's—"

Jake had no idea how a magical gun could have belonged to a man, but he thought it best not to ask, so he simply cleared his throat and said, "Should I leave, or—?"

"No," said Natasha. "Do not wander alone again. It will cause more trouble."

Jake felt a lump in his throat. He thought briefly about sitting at the table but then decided to sit on the floor like the girls. He slumped down in front of a counter.

Natasha's words touched him with fresh guilt. He reminded himself that he had rescued Rifle Maiden—but then remembered the dead men lying on the roof above.

He leaned his head back against the counter, exhaled slowly, and closed his eyes.

I shouldn't be doing this. I don't belong here.

Grease Pencil Marionette had warned him: *You had no right to meddle in these things.* That's what she'd told him— when was it? Friday. Just last Friday. The days flew by so quickly now, yet whenever he thought back to what had happened only a few days before, it felt like another life, another world.

He hadn't listened to her then. And he knew he still wouldn't listen. As soon as he could, he would go right back to chasing Pretty Dynamo.

"Lillian Mosey," said Natasha as she set the gun on the floor between herself and Lily, "do you believe in the power of this weapon?"

Lily's eyes were big and round like a puppy's. She nodded.

Natasha bowed her head. "Then I can help you."

With an athame again in her hand, she slit the bandage over Lily's shoulder to bare her seeping wound. Then, from her pouch, she pulled out the deck of Tarot cards she had taken almost a week before from the corpse of Magical Girl Card Collector Kasumi. She laid four cards on the floor, facedown, and tapped the revolver's barrel to each. She waved the gun over the dagger-like extracted stinger while muttering dark, unintelligible words.

Lily and Jake watched in silence. Lily's throat pulse as she swallowed once, twice.

"I cannot operate your item as you can," Natasha said, "but because it is a talisman to you, I can imbue it with a different kind of magic: I can command it to protect, guide, perhaps even heal . . . but there are limits. I am turning it into a ward against poison—or so I hope."

"Will that really work?" Lily asked.

"We shall find out." Natasha pointed the pistol at Lily's wound. "Jake," she said, "bring more gauze."

Jake started when she addressed him, but then he arose, found the first aid kit, and pulled out several gauze squares.

Lily tipped her head back. Her brow crumpled, and she gasped. Fresh blood rose out of her shoulder, but with it appeared small beads of green, sticky gel.

Natasha didn't have to tell him: Jake knelt beside Lily and patted up the liquid. More blood poured out. Then more. The amount of it scared him. Lily's face was pale; against it, her chapped lips appeared unnaturally red. Green globules, like bubbles on the surface of a stream, ran out with the blood.

After a few seconds, all hints of green disappeared, and there was nothing but blood. Jake took out a clean patch of gauze, found the medical tape, and bound Lily's wound afresh.

He put a hand against her forehead. She was clammy and cold. "I think you need a doctor," he said.

"No," answered Natasha quietly, "she needs to transform."

Lily, breathing rapidly, leaned heavily on Jake as she rose to her feet. Her knees buckled, but he held her up.

"I don't think you should," said Jake. "You—"

She raised her right hand in the air. "By the laws of the Old West," she said, her voice quavering and faint.

Something kicked Jake in the chest, knocking him to the floor.

Lily floated into the air as her skin glittered like gold. Her clothes evaporated. She spun slowly as her bicycle shorts, her leather vest, and her duster materialized around her.

"From the early days of the fabled West! A legendary gun with the speed of light, bringing law and order to the untamed wilderness! *Magical Girl Rifle Maiden* rides again!"

Her cowboy boots landed on the floor. From nowhere, she pulled a gleaming white Stetson and planted it on her head. After cocking the hat slightly, she gave Jake an easy, bucktoothed grin.

"Howdy," she said.

Blood ran from her shoulder.

"You're still hurt," said Jake as he rubbed his chest, trying to get his breath back.

"I'll heal, Jakey," she replied with a twang. "But thank you kindly."

With a smile on her painted face, Natasha held up the revolver. Rifle Maiden took it and twirled it around her finger.

"I see ya got one too," she added as she pointed at the Five-seveN on Jake's hip. "We're twins."

Jake struggled to his feet. "Not exactly. I took mine off a dead man."

She walked up beside him and gave him a gentle nudge. "So did I." She twirled the gun again.

He shuddered.

With her back to him, so he was looking at her weatherbeaten and mud-stained duster, she cleared her throat and said, "It's an heirloom, Jake. The right one, I mean. The left one an' the rifle, they came with the outfit. But the right one came from my father, an' from his—an' his. Before it was magical, it was an 1873 Colt .45 Peacemaker. An ancestor o' mine used it at the Battle o' Powder River, under General Crook, an' again at the Rosebud, when they lost to Crazy Horse. Another fought the Moro with it in the Philippines. It got used in Buffalo Bill's show an' on a movie set fer a while. Then it sat over a mantle—but it was with our family the whole time, long enough that it started to get *feelin's,* if'n ya know what I mean. It were real easy fer my familiar Bossy to put a little magic in it an' call up the spirit o' the Wild West fer me. That spirit were already there, just waitin' to wake up."

As she spoke, she tossed the gun from one hand to the other. She caught it, flipped it behind her back, and caught it again. It was impressive, especially with her wounded shoulder. Finally, with the gun in her right hand, she spun it again, letting it revolve around her trigger finger as light danced across its polished surface.

"A monster grabbed my daddy, an' the only thing to hand was this ol' gun. Couldn't shoot none, o' course, since it didn't have no bullets. Was an antique by then, not a weapon. But he struck that monster 'cross the face *real* good—made 'im bleed. *Pistol-whippin',* they used to call that. But that monster killed my daddy anyway."

Still, the gun twirled around her finger. It flashed like lightning in the light from the window. "I was cowerin' in the corner like a yellow-bellied . . . well, you saw Lily, an' she ain't no fighter. So's I was cowerin', see, an' cryin' fit to be tied, but this gun flew outta my daddy's hand and landed near my leg. That's when Bossy bursts in through the wall an' tells me to take up the gun if I wanna live. I wasn't gonna ask no questions then, so's I picked it up just like she said."

She dropped the gun into its holster, and it slid in with the satisfying rasp of steel on leather. Shrugging, she added, "So here I am."

Jake nodded. "Take care of it."

"I'll try."

"You are still wounded," Natasha pointed out.

"Yeah," said Rifle Maiden as she adjusted her hat, "but I'll heal faster in this form. Could sure use a juice box, though."

Natasha smiled. "Check the fridge."

Rifle Maiden bounded to the refrigerator and threw it open to reveal several boxes of strawberry milk. "Natasha! Y'all been holdin' out on me!"

Natasha gestured toward the wax statue on the floor. "A work this size is taxing to me. I could not have made it this far without a way to replenish my mojo. But juice boxes would have done you no good in your alter ego."

"Still woulda tasted nice," Rifle Maiden said as she pulled out a box. "An' I was mighty thirsty." She poked in a straw and drained the box dry. Then she reached for another. While she drank it off, she tossed one to Natasha.

"I know you ain't got much stamina, so you better drink too."

With a quiet nod, Natasha drank.

After Rifle Maiden had finished five of the juice boxes, she cautiously flexed her right arm. She winced but said, "Feels better already."

"You're still hurt," said Jake. "You better—"

"Nope. Can't sit one out when the city's fallin' to pieces."

"In that case," said Jake as he nodded toward the fridge, "can I have one of those?"

With a grin, Rifle Maiden tossed him a juice box. But, thirsty though he was, he didn't drink it. Instead, he shoved it into the breast pocket of his shirt.

Natasha rose to her feet and gingerly plucked her wax statue from the floor. "I need cover, my friend, if you can provide it. I must get closer to the monster before I can complete this doll."

Rifle Maiden pulled her Winchester from her back and, holding it in her left hand, spun it to cock it one-handed. "When do we leave?"

"Now would be good," Natasha replied.

Jake drew the Five-seveN, ejected the magazine, and carefully unloaded the bullets. There were eighteen of them.

He took out another magazine and made sure it was full before he loaded it into the gun and pulled the slide to feed a bullet into the chamber. He reloaded the first magazine and put it away.

Rifle Maiden nodded and then leaned down. "Hop on, Jake."

"Are you sure?"

"Uh-huh. Now that you got yerself some iron, yer gonna be my right arm."

"What? But—"

"Hop on," she said. Then she looked over her shoulder and added with a wink, "An' try to keep yer hands to yerself this time. I ain't one o' them shady ladies."

Natasha again raised an eyebrow but said nothing. She simply pulled another juice box from the fridge and drank it.

Jake coughed into his fist. "Look, Rifle Maiden, Natasha, those bugs are after me. I don't know why, but since last week, monsters have been singling me out—"

Rifle Maiden shrugged.

Jake sighed.

"Are we ready?" Natasha asked as she cradled her wax statue in her hands.

"Ready," Rifle Maiden replied as she hiked a reluctant Jake onto her back.

"Ready as I'll ever be," Jake mumbled as he shifted uncomfortably, feeling foolish.

Together, they headed out the door.

FIFTEEN

DARK PLACES

The Dark Queen sat on her dark throne and steepled her hands before her face as she dictated a letter to a small, bespectacled goblin who wielded a massive quill over a roll of parchment. The Queen had a trying week before her, and the first order of business was to repair relations with the Evil Space Aliens' Union, which she had recently annoyed by recruiting the Robosaurs from Andromeda—and by standing by as the city of Urbanopolis wiped them out.

This was no small political blunder. Although the Robosaurs were inconsequential in themselves, the Evil Space Aliens' Union was the largest consortium of technomancers in the Local Group. Since technomancy was the most common form of magic in this cluster of galaxies, that made ESAU the greatest power in this corner of the universe. More importantly, the members of ESAU were the only servants of the Shadow who could operate both inside and outside the Milky Way: Being several billion years old (by Earth reckoning), their organization's territorial claims predated the barrier spell of the Keepers of the Seas of Glass.

In short, without ESAU's cooperation, the Dark Queen would lose a vital ally in her campaign against the last remaining humans.

Of course, there were higher powers in the universe. From the perspective of, for example, the intergalactic super civilizations of the Hercules-Corona Borealis Great Wall, the Milky Way, the Local Group—and, indeed, all of the Virgo Supercluster —formed an insignificant backwater. Ironically, it was because of this insignificance that the Keepers, those ancient races of the globular clusters who guarded the Milky Way's precious supply of dark matter, were able to weave a protective spell without gaining the attention of Lord Shadow. Now, thanks to them, the Shadow could work in this galaxy only indirectly.

The Dark Queen was crafting another obsequious sentence to insert into her conciliatory letter when a pointy-eared dark elf, his soft feet slapping against the basalt of her audience chamber, unceremoniously ran up to the dais that held her high throne. Her lips thinned, and her eyes narrowed; but she did not immediately rebuke her minion—for he trembled all over, and his large, cave-adapted eyes were wide with fear.

"Your Darkness," he croaked. "It's *him!* It's . . . it's . . . !"

With a piercing scream of terror mixed with despair, he fell.

The Queen could not say how she knew he fell. With her eyes, she only saw him slide across the floor toward the high doorway. Yet she somehow felt as if she looked at him from a great height and watched helplessly while he plummeted down a cliff face. The room had suddenly tipped so that its far wall became a floor and the door a chasm—yet only this one, poor elf was caught in the sudden shift in gravity.

Filling the doorway, standing a full ten feet in height so that his head almost brushed the top of the arch and his broad shoulders nearly touched the posts, was a figure clad in the deepest black. His fluttering cloak was darker even than the dark accouterments of the audience chamber of the Queen of Darkness. Within that cloak, no features were visible, for he was simply the darkness itself—yet the Queen felt rather than saw that he had four enormous arms coated in thick armor. The claws of his lower right hand rested on the pommel of a two-handed sword. His hood concealed his face, but from under that hood jutted the jagged mandibles of a ferocious insect. He stood upright on pillar-like legs yet seemed to be lying at the bottom of a deep abyss—or rather, he *was* the abyss. Where he stood was the center, the bottom, the lowest point—not just of this room, but perhaps of the world, or perhaps of everything.

The shrieking elf, his arms and legs flailing, flew into this stranger's chest and disappeared as if he had tumbled into a night-shadowed ravine, and his voice quieted as though muted by distance. The stranger's cloak whipped in an unseen wind, the elf faded into its folds, and that was all.

A hush fell over the chamber, but the Queen's minions murmured in terror as they slid a few inches toward the black figure. Although nothing in the room had shifted visibly, the floor now sloped toward him, so they struggled to keep a grip on its surface.

The Queen clutched the armrests of her throne as she felt his pull. For a brief moment, she feared that she too might tumble headlong just as her unfortunate servant had.

She wanted to cower. Or run and hide. Or scream.

But she had a duty to perform.

She forced herself to release her grip on her throne and rise to her feet. She bowed deeply at the waist. Then she swallowed loudly as her stiletto-heeled shoes skipped half a foot across the basalt of their own accord.

She cleared her throat as quietly as she could to make sure her voice wouldn't quaver when she spoke. "Lord Shadow," she said. "You honor us greatly by coming in person."

From somewhere in the depths of the stranger's clothes, a booming voice erupted: *"I am not here in Person, you fool. What you see before you is merely the Shadow of My Shadow. If I came Myself, do you think your pathetic solar system could survive My advent?"*

He strode into the room, and each of his footsteps echoed like a thunderclap. Whimpering minions tried to edge away but instead slid toward him.

The Queen stepped down from the dais and knelt. The Shadow walked past her and rose to her throne. As if made of water, the obsidian shifted, widening to accommodate his vast frame.

He sat down. A boom resounded through the chamber—as if a prison gate had shut, as if the crack of doom had sounded, as if the lid of hell had closed forever.

But this was not the true Shadow, nor was this his true throne, so the universe survived.

"Now," the Shadow said in a voice that roared like crashing stone, *"explain to Me why I must expend an Avatar of My Essence on a worthless slave such as you."*

The Dark Queen carefully wetted her lips and said, "If my lord—"

Another boom came from the Shadow, though she could not have said what made it. She winced.

"I received," he said, *"a report that the Robosaurs were extinct—and that you were to blame. Explain."*

She swallowed.

"Did you think I had no further use for Reptilon? Because of his early destruction, I must adjust my plans for Andromeda's conquest and annihilation. That annoys me."

The Queen cleared her throat. "My lord, they attacked before we expected them. I wanted them to contact me first, to plan—"

"Why did Reptilon even take notice of you, you sniveling nit?"

She cleared her throat. "My lord, the humans, Urbanopolis—"

"A primitive species that has never mastered magic. I ordered their destruction one-millionth of a Yag ago when I sensed one of them Awakening."

The *Yag* was a universal measurement of time, dizzyingly complex in its derivations but ultimately based on the movements of a lonely, verdant planet, also called Yag, that orbited an extragalactic star. That star circumnavigated the universe in a slow, ever-expanding circle at the limit of space. Yag was once a thriving world with one of the most advanced civilizations in the cosmos; long ago, the Shadow had swept that world clean, but it was still a useful marker of time, a marker circling all that existed just as the hour hand circles a clock.

When treated as a preferred reference frame, the Yag could be converted to other reference frames through various transformations. Thus, this measurement served the purpose of coordinating synchronicity in the more advanced parts of the cosmos despite relativity.

"But, my lord," gasped the Queen, "the humans still live! The one who Awakened lives! And the Awakened one is still in contact with the Keepers, I am sure of it! They have formed a plan—"

"*What plan?*"

"I do not know! But she believes she can defeat you!"

The Shadow was silent. The Queen had expected him to respond with a scoff or perhaps with scornful laughter. The silence disturbed her.

"*There have been many,*" he said at last, "*who believed they could defeat Me. In the end, they were My servants. All are My servants.*"

He waved a dark claw. In the air appeared a vast, globular shape shot through with glowing white specks that coalesced into filaments like the chaotic web of a black widow. The specks shrank as more filaments appeared. Then more. As the view expanded, the filaments disappeared, and all became uniform—homogenous, patternless, and perfect.

The Dark Queen recognized it. It was a holographic map of the universe, including parts humanity could not observe.

The Shadow waved again, and several thousand of the specks, each a galaxy, glowed red.

"*Do you know what these are?*" he asked.

She frowned as she pored over the impossibly complex hologram. "You've marked . . . ah . . . the quasars?"

He nodded. "*Quasars. Yes. The brightest objects in the universe. Each of these galaxies is spewing matter and energy— and what the primitive magicians of the primitive humans have undoubtedly failed to realize is that it is* new *matter and energy, matter and energy generated from the Prime Matter outside the cosmos. These quasars are weapons against Me—meant to stave off the inevitable heat death of the universe, meant to keep Me from My throne.*"

Now the Shadow did laugh, and the sound chilled the Queen's blood.

"But," he said, *"here is the irony: Life cannot survive in a galaxy that becomes a quasar. A quasar is a sea of death. What's more, no quasar can form unless every being in that galaxy willingly gives his life, consenting to die for the greater good. A single voice of objection, and the quasar cannot appear. Thus, only the most advanced galaxies ruled by the most benevolent and enlightened races ever become quasars. There are around eighty thousand now—an insignificant number. They will delay My final victory by a mere ten Yag."*

The Shadow laughed again, but his laughter was cold, quiet, and mirthless. It was laughter without even the slightest trace of pleasure.

"These races who sacrifice themselves," he said, *"whole civilizations of monks and martyrs, do not understand that what I love above all else is death. They kill themselves to fight Me but thereby please Me and do My bidding. That is why I call them My servants: There are those who serve willingly, and there are those who serve unwillingly, but there are none who do not serve."*

For a long moment, the throne room was silent. But then the Shadow said, his voice low, *"Do you serve Me unwillingly, Dark Queen?"*

"No, Lord Shadow!" she cried. "Willingly! Willingly! To do your will is my greatest honor!"

He nodded. *"Then why do the humans live? The duty I have set before you is hardly the most difficult I have asked of any of my generals. Despite your humble origins, I saw promise in you. Why have you not accomplished the first of your tasks?"*

The Queen cleared her throat. "Milord, if I may—"

He waved one dark claw to signal consent. The Queen rose to her feet and pointed at the hovering image of the universe. Instantly, it zoomed in with impossible speed and became a holographic projection of the Earth with its circling moon.

"As you noted, milord," said the Queen, "this species is primitive. Their native magic is a form of technomancy they call both *general relativity* and *quantum mechanics*. They have never discovered a unified theory, and thus, they are not true mages."

The Shadow nodded.

"From time to time," the Queen added, "there have appeared among them magicians who practice deviant forms—telekinesis, transmogrification, ESP, rootworking, haruspicy, and the like. On occasion, they have attempted to use their native magic, which they quaintly dub 'science,' to test these deviant forms. Usually, they have concluded that they are hoaxes or delusions."

The Shadow leaned his shrouded head on one claw. *"Yes, yes, of course. Testing one form of magic with another* never *works. Many primitive species have duped themselves in this fashion. What of it?"*

The Queen cleared her throat again. "Ah, but the structure of their world is—by coincidence—unusual. They have one moon. From their planet's surface, this moon appears to be the same size as their sun, so they have attached great significance to it. On top of that, they are placental mammals, but they are freaks: Among their other peculiarities, their females expel rather than absorb their uterine lining and do so on a cycle approximating the phases of their moon."

Now the Shadow sat up straight and lowered his claw.

"It appears, milord, that, as a byproduct of these coincidences, their moon amplifies deviant forms of magic—at least in their females."

"I begin to see. So these humans can use magic that is not native to them—magic other than 'quantum mechanics' or 'general relativity.'"

The Dark Queen nodded. "Even so, this ability is weak and unpredictable, but our enemies have found ways to exploit it: Calling themselves familiars, they travel to Earth, select certain females, and galvanize their latent magical abilities. What's more, for reasons I am uncertain of, they only do this with children. Females who reach their age of majority can no longer practice magic."

"So any who attack these humans face not just one type of magic, but many."

"Yes, milord."

"Still, why not simply wipe the lot of them from their planet? I ordered this world destroyed, so how does it live?"

"A shield made of many magical layers. It only partially protects the city but entirely protects the planet's moon. The shield prevents any potent weapons from striking the city from a distance but does not prevent direct invasion. To destroy the moon, one must first destroy the city—but to destroy the city, one must face the magical girls."

"And these so-called magical girls are really that powerful?"

The Queen shrugged. "As you see, the Robosaurs are extinct, milord."

The Shadow steepled two of his hands, much as the Queen had done earlier while sitting in the same place.

Minutes passed. At last, the Shadow said, *"Fascinating. In all the universe, I have never encountered its like. For some time now, this Avatar has felt strangely drawn to this world. Perhaps I begin to see why."*

"We all feel drawn," the Queen said quietly. "So many

powers have felt compelled to attack this Earth—where the girls destroy them."

"I could call upon forces that would in an instant wipe this planet from existence," the Shadow mused, *"if the barrier spell of the Keepers did not prevent Me from entering this galaxy. Yes, I see why these humans have been such a thorn in My side: They possess strange properties, and the Keepers stop Me from attacking them with my best weapons, so they repeatedly defeat My lesser servants. Yes . . ."*

Again, the Shadow fell silent. The Queen shifted uncomfortably.

The silence stretched out and grew oppressive. The Shadow was immobile on the throne, regal and horrifying, yet as unmoving as a statue. For a moment, the Queen wondered if the Avatar had malfunctioned somehow.

Her voice trembling with trepidation, she said, "Milord, perhaps if we brought together the *entirety* of the Evil Space Aliens' Union—"

"No," he replied, and the sudden return of his booming voice made the Queen shiver. *"No, the Union has other, more pressing tasks, and it fights battles it cannot afford to neglect. Besides, I called on them to send all their spare units when I first ordered this planet destroyed, yet the humans live. The technomancers of this region of space have not the power we need. We need others."*

"But there are so few magicians in the Local Group who are not technomancers—"

The Shadow waved a hand. *"What? They surround you! These, these—"*

"Fairies, milord."

"These fairies, they are not technomancers! They possess many forms of magic, perhaps as many as the magical girls!"

"Ah, but milord, our numbers are few!"

"Then find others. There are places, pockets, where many powers hide. Throughout the universe stretches the Dreaming, and into it, the Greater Powers from outside the walls of space-time occasionally peep."

"Milord, you would have me draw down an Outer God?"

"Why not? All have bowed the knee to Me."

The Queen said nothing, but she suspected—insolent though it might be—that the Shadow was mistaken. The Outer Gods, vast entities formed spontaneously from the sea of uncreation beyond space-time, worked with Lord Shadow, certainly, because they hated the cosmos as much as he did.

But did they truly serve him?

The Queen trembled from head to foot. "Milord, forgive me, but I cannot command an eldritch abomination! I can't!"

"You need not," the Shadow replied. *"Merely summon one. It will do the rest."*

"But the first rule, milord! The first rule—do not call up that which you cannot put down!"

"There is nothing," the Shadow replied, his voice now holding a hint of malice, *"that I—I!—cannot put down. I will put down these humans, and I will do it through you. If you must call on abominations, then do it. Even if they destroy you, you shall do my will. You must. All must."*

With that, the Shadow rose from the throne. His cloak, moaning like a hurricane, swept around him while he strode toward the door. As he passed, the Queen's minions quaked and whimpered.

"And another thing," the Shadow said when once he reached the archway at the chamber's far end, *"if you fear the pits of darkness or the abysses of madness into which the Old Ones might cast you should you displease them, and in which they might draw out your exquisite torments even unto the very moment of My inevitable victory—know that the pains to which they might subject you are nothing compared to what I could do to you if you fail Me."*

With that, he threw open his cloak, and the Queen saw, to her horror, the dark elf whom the Shadow had earlier absorbed: The elf lay cruciform in the deep darkness where the Shadow's stomach should be. A thousand black points pierced the elf's skin from every side as his head whipped back and forth and his eyes bulged. His mouth opened in a silent scream.

The Shadow closed his cloak, stepped through the doorway, and faded into the blackness beyond. The room was instantly free of his presence, and the floor seemed level again. A heavy weight, or a dark cloud, had lifted.

As if she had run for miles, the Queen collapsed and gasped for air. She didn't care about the indignity. She didn't care if such gracelessness lowered her in the eyes of her servants. She only cared that Lord Shadow was gone—

For now.

JAKE'S TEETH RATTLED AS HE RODE ON RIFLE MAIDEN'S BACK. In his right hand, he held the FN Five-seveN, which still felt disturbingly light.

Rifle Maiden jumped from roof to roof, nimbly dodging cell antennas and storage sheds. Natasha kept pace, but every few minutes, Rifle Maiden stopped, ducked behind a low wall, and let Natasha rest.

During one of their stops, Jake took the chance to climb from Rifle Maiden's back and holster his pistol. Natasha breathed hard, her generous bosom heaving up and down as she held the wax figure against her bare stomach. Rifle Maiden asked if she was all right, but Natasha merely shook her head and gulped air.

Rifle Maiden glanced at Jake and said, "She's ain't the close-fightin' type."

He didn't know how to reply, so he nodded.

"Neither am I, exac'ly," Rifle Maiden admitted, "but I'm a mite better suited for parkour."

Natasha grinned weakly. "I am afraid your wasp friends sapped much of my mojo, Jake."

"Sorry," Jake replied.

Natasha merely smiled and shook her head.

Clouds of wasps swirled over the city. At times, they formed into spikes and dived. Wherever they struck, they tore apart a tower gun or—presumably—attacked a magical girl. The *kaiju* slugged a skyscraper over and over as if socking a punching bag. The building's sides caved, its windows shattering and its steel frame twisting, until it tumbled to the ground in a cloud of gray dust. Missiles still exploded against the creature, though their frequency had dropped off now that the wasps had destroyed much of the city's defenses.

Jake shook his head. "What's the point of shooting it? It's obviously not doing any good."

Natasha steadied her breathing and said, "Politics."

"What?"

"The City Fathers control the military and the automated defenses, but the Temple of the Moon Princess controls the magical girls and the Weapon. Because the Temple fired the Weapon last week to destroy the Robosaurs, the Fathers are probably angry, especially since it produced a zombie infestation. Perhaps this is their way of flexing their muscles in reply."

Jake groaned and tapped the back of his head against the wall.

"Boys," Rifle Maiden said simply, and Natasha laughed.

The cloud of wasps darkened overhead.

"We gotta move," said Jake.

"They've spotted us," Natasha replied. In an instant, she was on her feet.

More slowly, Rifle Maiden rose. "Hop on," she said.

Jake did. He drew the Five-seveN, but his hand trembled on the grip. He slid his finger under the guard.

"Trigger discipline," Rifle Maiden said. "Don't put your finger on the trigger till you're ready to fire. You can't hurt me with that trinket, but I'd still rather you didn't shoot my leg."

He nodded.

Soon, they were weaving, sprinting, and dodging again. A lump of swirling wasps separated from the cloud and appeared at their backs, churning like a hurricane.

Jake yelled, "They're on us!"

"Put my rifle in my left hand!" Rifle Maiden shouted.

The rifle was wedged between Jake's chest and her back. Gingerly, he pulled it out of its sheath and slapped it against her palm.

To his surprise, she flipped the gun over backwards and rested it on her shoulder.

"Cover your left ear!" she yelled.

He tried to loosen his grip on her but found himself sliding off. He shook his head. "I can't!"

She shrugged. Then she pulled the trigger and rattled his teeth with the blast.

She pulled the gun from her shoulder, spun it around to cock it, and put it back. She fired again.

Jake groaned as his ears rang.

"Annie Oakley was an expert at that trick," Rifle Maiden said, "but she aimed with a mirror. Am I hittin' anything?"

Jake merely shook his head. Keeping his left arm wrapped over her chest, he twisted around and pointed his handgun. He tried resting the pistol in the crook of his left arm, but it bounced up and down as Rifle Maiden ran.

He pulled the trigger anyway. Again, the handgun's report was surprisingly loud, and the muzzle flash was like a fireball. For all that, the kick was minuscule, and he couldn't see that the bullet accomplished anything.

Rifle Maiden released another blast. Her explosive bullet tore apart three wasps and scattered several others.

Jake fired again and again saw nothing, so he decided to save his ammo.

"They're catching up to us!" he yelled in Rifle Maiden's ear.

She shook her head. "If we stop an' face 'em, they'll overwhelm us!"

Jake could see that Voodoo Queen Natasha was flagging. Her shoulders were hunched, she breathed hard, and she was falling behind.

"Drop me," Jake said.

"What?" Rifle Maiden called.

"Drop me. They're after me anyway. I'll distract them while you two run ahead to take care of the *kaiju.*"

Rifle Maiden grinned, but she shook her head. "'Fraid not,

Jakey. Magical girls don't abandon their friends. An' if'n it's you they want, I'll be durned if they getcha on my watch."

Natasha's breathing was loud and ragged, and she clutched her wax statuette so hard, Jake was afraid she'd break it.

"Ah!" Rifle Maiden gasped, her wide grin growing wider. She whistled through her buckteeth.

"What is it?" Jake asked.

"Look ahead, Jakey!"

Jake turned his head and was startled to see how close the *kaiju* was. Yellow like a banana and bellowing like a bull, it stood as tall as the tallest skyscrapers. Clumsily, it swept an arm through three towers, which shattered under the impact. The crashing masonry roared like a thunderstorm.

"Almost," Natasha panted. "I can almost see it—"

Jake's heart surged when he saw a flash of blue and gold near the monster: It shot from one building to another, shone briefly in the sunlight, and then disappeared from view.

"Is that—?"

"Purty Dynamo," Rifle Maiden said. *"Gotta* be!"

Rifle Maiden picked up her pace. Though she groaned, Natasha did likewise.

They entered a neighborhood where the skyscrapers were tall and stately. Jake had lost track of their location, but he thought this was probably the financial district, a region he had explored with Pretty Dynamo only a few days ago. Without a word, Rifle Maiden slid her rifle back into the sheath. Then she jumped from the edge of a roof even though, across the wide street opposite, Jake could see nothing but a glass wall stretching up into the sky.

"Rifle Maiden, wait—!"

He wondered if she was planning to cling to the skyscraper's exterior like an insect and climb upward—or if she were simply committing suicide. Instead, she pulled a revolver, fired once, and obliterated several square feet of the glass wall, which rained massive shards into the deserted street below.

She pulled up her arms and legs, and Jake ducked his head. The two of them flew directly into the new hole. Rifle Maiden's boots met carpet in a gray-walled room full of claustrophobic cubicles.

Gritting her teeth, she slid to a stop against an aluminum-framed desk. A computer monitor tipped over and hit the floor with a crack, and a calendar dropped from a nearby cubicle wall.

Jake tumbled to the floor. The gun fell from his hand, but he picked it up and fumbled it into its holster.

Rifle Maiden took a deep breath and stretched her arms over her head. Behind her, Natasha landed on the lip of the smashed window and tipped backwards precariously. She windmilled her arms until she caught her balance; then, still breathing hard, she walked into the room.

Sweat poured down her face, leaving streaks in the ash on her skin.

"I am not cut out for this," she said.

Rifle Maiden shook her head. *"Hate* these big buildin's. Even the best ground-bounders can't jump these things. Make for a real nuisance."

She slid her eyes over the broad room with its maze of identical gray cubicles and computer stations. "Least I don't hafta work in one of 'em, though. This is why city folks is plumb crazy."

"Aren't we *all* city folk?" Jake asked.

"They're coming," Natasha said, pointing back to the hole in the wall. Indeed, the swarm of wasps was twisting toward them.

Rifle Maiden lowered her rifle and fired several blasts in

quick succession, scattering the wasps. Jake clapped his hands over his ears and clenched his teeth.

"Move!" Natasha shouted.

With that, she sprinted around the cubicles, Rifle Maiden and Jake close behind. He heard buzzing and hissing behind him, so he drew his handgun again. With a *boom,* he took the head off a wasp as it peeked around the corner of a cubicle.

He fired again, and another wasp died. Though he could still hear buzzing from the far side of the room, he didn't see any more.

They made it into a hallway marked by three elevators and a fire door that proclaimed stairwell access.

"I bet you're gonna tell me we can't take the elevator," Jake said.

Rifle Maiden chuckled as she headed for the stairs.

Natasha patted Jake on the shoulder. "The power is probably out anyway."

The stairwell proved to be a spiral enclosed in a circular glass tower at one of the skyscraper's corners. Jake glanced over the railing to see the stairs stretching downward for a dizzying distance. The view upward was almost identical. Because of the stairwell's shape, he couldn't count the stories, and he was unsure how high they were.

Rifle Maiden spat over the brushed-steel banister as she hefted her rifle. "They shouldn't be allowed to build these death traps."

"They need the space," Natasha replied. "Shall we climb, old friend?"

"Sure, Queenie. Jake, can you keep up?"

Jake shook his head. "I doubt it."

He thought she might hike him onto her back again, but she

laughed instead and started bounding up the stairs three at a time. Natasha, taking them one at a time, ran several paces behind.

Jake took a couple of deep breaths, loosely clenched his hands, and jogged after them.

He kept pace for seven stories. Then he started to fall back. Sweat poured down his face, and his legs ached—though, to his surprise, the pain in his ankle was still gone.

He felt that buzzing in his forearms again, the strange feeling he'd got right before he went to the roof to retrieve Rifle Maiden's revolver. Warm, gentle energy flowed from his arms, coursed into his chest, and poured into his legs. He still breathed hard, and sweat dripped from his forehead and coated his torso, but he found new strength, and he picked up his pace. He stayed right behind Natasha, who appeared to be in worse shape than he was.

They climbed twenty floors. Then thirty. Forty. He stopped counting.

In fifteen minutes, they rose probably a hundred floors and reached a metal door marked ROOF.

Jake bent over, clutched his knees, and took several deep breaths. He had no doubt that he could have made that climb even under normal conditions, but he doubted he could do it at such a pace.

"Not bad, Jakey," Rifle Maiden said as she yanked the door open. "You're real sidekick material."

"I'm not a sidekick," he wheezed as he staggered onto the rooftop. Then he paused, surprised by the strength of the wind that struck his face. How high were they?

Rifle Maiden gestured toward the *kaiju*. Only a few blocks away, it was impossibly gigantic and made the buildings around it look like something from a cheap movie set.

The missiles, howitzers, and autocannons had stopped. A monotonous buzz still sounded from the swirling bugs, but the city was otherwise chillingly silent. They were now above most of the insects, which flitted back and forth below them, no longer looking like a black cloud but like the swirling, weaving activity around a beehive. Alone and unopposed, the colossal monster stretched its arms out to either side, tipped its head back, and released a long, melancholy howl. It was like the sound of a wolf calling to the moon, but so loud that Jake's ears rang.

"How's this?" Rifle Maiden asked Natasha.

Natasha, the figurine still cradled in her arms, stared at the creature for almost a minute before she shook her head. "This is helpful, but I still can't see its feet."

Rifle Maiden took a deep breath and let it out slowly. "We probably gotta get to ground level if you want that."

"That may be our only choice, my friend."

Rifle Maiden shook her head and rested her rifle on her shoulder. "Ain't droppin' from this height. Even Dynamo'd prob'ly bite it if she fell from here."

"So we gotta climb all the way back down?" Jake asked.

Rifle Maiden chuckled. "Sounds like it."

Jake saw another flash of blue and gold. He ran to the high, cage-like fence at the edge of the roof, grabbed two of the steel bars there, and peered out. Yes, he could see her now—it was definitely Pretty Dynamo. She spun in the air as she leaped a gap between one tower and another, a gap of at least a hundred yards. A blue streak, sparkling in the sunlight, stretched from her to the monster.

Jake nodded and licked his cracked lips. Yes, that was the trail of a Thunder Bolt, an electrified quarrel Dynamo fired from her magical crossbow.

The monster released another bellow when the bolt struck. A flash left an afterimage in Jake's eyes, and a roll of thunder followed.

So that was the second bolt. That means she got him! She got—

The monster's bellow grew higher in pitch, and it waved its arms as if fending off a cloud of gnats. Jake's mouth fell open as a series of red eruptions appeared across the monster's chest— and then more wasps burst forth.

Rifle Maiden was at his shoulder. "So that thing's makin' the bugs. Shoulda guessed."

"It appears," said Natasha gravely, "that Pretty Dynamo may have insufficient power for this particular creature."

"Maybe," Jake muttered. "She needs Tesla. He does her calculations, and he's not with her—"

He bit his lip for a moment. "And she doesn't have her Circuit Board, so she can't do her finishing move."

Rifle Maiden raised her eyebrows.

He slammed his hands into the bars. "You know! Her . . . her whatever-you-call-it. Where she flies up real high and throws her spear down."

"That is true," Natasha said. "She fights bravely, but being ground-bound, she is crippled."

The freshly produced wasps buzzed aimlessly around the monster for a few seconds before swarming a nearby rooftop. In their midst, Jake saw another flash of blue and gold.

He clutched the bars. "We've got to help her."

Rifle Maiden cleared her throat. "I don't think—."

"Now!" He tried to rattle the bars for emphasis, but they were so firmly rooted that they didn't budge or make any noise.

Rifle Maiden turned her head back and forth. "I can't reach any other roof from here with a jump. It's too far."

"Then," said Jake, "we've got to get to the street and find that building she's on. Then we'll climb—"

Rifle Maiden silenced him with a slap to the back and gave him another of her broad, almost manic smiles. "I said I can't *jump* that far, Jakey."

He opened his mouth to answer but then simply frowned.

"You gonna be okay on yer own, Queenie?" Rifle Maiden asked.

Natasha nodded. "I will head down. I will be better off on the ground, I think."

"Okay, then. Me an' Jakey are gonna fly."

"Wait a minute," Jake said. "What—?"

With her good arm, Rifle Maiden reached around and patted the small of her back. "You wanna save yer girlfriend, Jakey-pie? Then let's go save your girlfriend. Hop on."

Jake swallowed and put his hands on her shoulders. Around her left trigger finger, she spun the rifle, turning it into a flashing blur.

SIXTEEN

THE FREQUENCY OF DELINQUENCY

N atasha left them. She headed down the stairs with her statuette, now considerably worse for wear, still gripped in her hands. Meanwhile, Jake climbed onto Rifle Maiden's back again. Rifle Maiden lithely jumped to the top of the high metal railing, where she easily balanced on the toes of her cowboy boots despite the high wind.

Jake's head pounded, and his stomach dropped into his shoes. Perched behind Rifle Maiden's shoulders, he swayed. Like a finely detailed model surrounding a collector's train set, the city spread out in every direction. Most of the buildings looked tiny from this height, and only a few were as imposing as the one he was on—so that meant they stood on one of the city's *really* big buildings, possibly the Mizukawa Tower, the largest structure in Little Yokohama.

"Ready for this?" Rifle Maiden asked. "I'm not sure it'll work."

Jake felt dizzy as his heartbeat drummed in his ears. "What are we doing?"

"Flyin'."

"You can't—"

"Not without some help, no."

With that, and without further explanation, she bent her knees.

He swallowed.

She jumped.

The wind whistled past his ears. The city lay below. It was like when Pretty Dynamo forced him to skydive—and just like that time, he would soon be dead if a girl didn't come to his rescue.

Rifle Maiden pointed her rifle downward and fired. Jake felt her gun kick; the vibration shot up her arm, into him, and straight into his teeth.

She fired again and again until her rifle sounded like a machine gun. Still, they dropped, and whether they dropped more slowly than they would without this maneuver, he couldn't tell.

His stomach lurched. A tower rose to meet them—but it rose too fast.

They fell short of the tower's roof, and Rifle Maiden uttered one curse before she pointed her gun forward, blasted out a window, and tucked her body into a ball.

The shattered window opened like a mouth and lunged toward them at terrifying speed. Jake had just enough time to consider that he likely wouldn't survive the landing.

EVERYTHING WAS BLACK, BUT AMID THE BLACKNESS, JAKE SAW A faint, blue glow. He stretched a hand toward it, sure that he needed to reach it, that it was something important—

It was a blur, a smudge on his vision. For a moment, it coalesced into a girl's face; tears streamed freely down her cheeks.

Then everything was black and black only. In the darkness, he heard a familiar voice, a breathy whisper in his ear, the voice he heard almost every night—

"You are going to be unhappy," it said, "and you are going to die alone."

Then he blinked groggily as someone shook his shoulders.

"Jake! Jake!"

He felt pricking—like pins and needles in a limb that had gone to sleep—stretching from his wrists to his elbows. He moved his arms, but he could barely feel them. He heard a wet *thwack* as he dully registered the impact of something against his knuckles.

"Hey!"

Someone was yelling at him. Some girl.

The blackness faded to a dull, reddish gray. After a few seconds, he was conscious enough to realize this was the color of the insides of his eyelids.

He forced his eyes open. It took a surprising amount of effort.

Rifle Maiden sat on the floor with his head cradled on her knees. Her hat was askew, and a few wisps of blond hair fell across her face.

Gradually, feeling came back to Jake's hands. He feebly reached up to brush her loose hair away.

"You're awake," she whispered.

"What happened?" His voice sounded harsh in his ears.

"I did somethin' stupid." Her mouth twisted. "Consarn it, I shoulda known I couldn't make it—"

"I think I'm okay." Gingerly, he sat up. His body felt like one long bruise, and his forearms burned strangely.

For a brief moment, he could see that blue smudge again, even with his eyes open.

Frowning, he reached toward it, but his hand met nothing. The smudge faded.

"You somersaulted right over my head when we came through the window," Rifle Maiden said. "You lay full out on the floor here, and I thought I'd lost ya fer sure."

Blinking, Jake looked around. They were in a sparsely decorated high-rise apartment, like the kind that appeared in glossy magazines. A flimsy but probably expensive coffee table had slid across the room and turned on its side—indicating they'd hit it when they came in. A sofa and loveseat, both of black leather, sat opposite each other against the walls. A Persian rug, now askew, lay on the hardwood floor. Broken glass littered everything. Five feet in front of the window, the wooden floor had splintered. Jagged boards stuck out of a hole three feet wide.

That, presumably, was where Rifle Maiden landed.

In Jake's nose was the stale scent of his own sweat, but behind it, he could smell expensive air freshener, like palm and pineapple. It made him hungry for pizza.

He climbed shakily to his feet while Rifle Maiden remained kneeling on the floor.

She shook her head. "That woulda been plumb stupid even if it were just me, but with you, it was too much—"

"Don't worry about it," he said as he tried to rub a knot out of his back.

"Ah, I just wanted to getcha to yer girlfriend."

"I appreciate it." He smiled weakly as he struggled to stay upright. "Really. So let's go help her."

She rose. "You *sure* you're okay?"

"I think so."

He rolled his shoulders and winced.

She shook her head. "Wouldn't o' thought a reg'lar human could take that."

"I got lucky. Maybe you absorbed most of the impact yourself when you hit."

"Maybe—"

"Let's go find Dynamo."

Before they left the apartment, they raided the refrigerator. Jake didn't find any juice boxes for Rifle Maiden, but he drank half a pitcher of cold, filtered water. He didn't think he could keep anything else down. Rifle Maiden ate half a block of cheese and most of a loaf of bread, and she finished the water. Then they found the apartment's front door, threw it open, and didn't bother to lock it behind them.

In a few minutes, they were on another roof. Now the buildings were lower and closer together, and Rifle Maiden could make the jumps. After a few more flying leaps, the wasps found them again. Jake pulled heat at the same time Rifle Maiden did. He watched her three-o'clock while she blazed away with the revolver in her left hand.

Soon, they landed on the roof where they had last seen Dynamo, and Dynamo was still there. She was a blur of silver and gold: Her electric-blue powder puff tutu flared around her narrow hips as she spun her spear and struck left and right. With each precise blow, she stabbed a bug's thorax or sliced away its head. The insects' greenish guts sizzled as current coursed through them.

In her left hand, Pretty Dynamo still held a garbage-can lid.

The insects buzzed, dived, and died. Most, she killed with her spear. A few landed on her, but those jerked spastically, seized up, and fell to the asphalt rooftop as steam burst from their joints. Dynamo's electricity had cooked their innards solid.

Jake slid from Rifle Maiden's back. Rifle Maiden sheathed her handgun, pulled her rifle, and pumped away, disintegrating the bugs around Dynamo with a precise series of red flashes. Dynamo's metal boots slid in the glop as one of the exploding bullets singed her blue hair, and she dropped into a split. In an instant, she spun out of the fall and was back on her feet.

Jake shot a few bugs himself.

After a minute of slaughter, the insects retreated to find easier prey. They buzzed angrily in the air overhead, but they didn't dive again.

Dripping with green slime and with a garbage-can lid in her left hand, Dynamo turned to Jake and Rifle Maiden. Her eyes narrowed as she jabbed a finger. "What is *he* doin' here?"

Rifle Maiden spun her rifle around her trigger finger. "He came for you. Tha's all."

"Yeah? Tell him to get lost!"

Rifle Maiden didn't answer, but her grin grew wider.

Dynamo clenched her fingers around her spear until her knuckles turned white. Her voice shook when she said, "I don't want him here. I don't want to see him *ever again!*"

"C'mon, Purty Dynamo," Rifle Maiden coaxed, stepping closer. "That's no way to—"

"I mean it!" A single tear dropped from Dynamo's left eye. She wiped at it but only smeared green goop on her face.

Jake watched her for half a minute as she stood there with her lower lip outthrust and her spear and makeshift shield in her hands. She usually looked so confident in her magical form: She smiled, chuckled wryly, fought expertly, and dipped and dived on her flying board. But now, despite the armor, tutu, and blue hair, she looked like Dana Volt—short, skinny, and always upset, her pretty face set in a perpetual pout.

He made a *D* sound before he stopped himself. He'd almost said her real name.

Rifle Maiden turned her bucktoothed smile on Jake and asked, "Wha'dja do, Jakey-wakey?"

"It's a long story," he replied.

Rifle Maiden opened her mouth to answer but then stopped and lifted her rifle. She pointed it around frantically when a loud and obnoxious laugh came from above.

"Oh ho ho ho ho *ho!"* a disembodied voice cried. "What is *this?* Has my little Dynamo grown tired of this boorish *boy* always tagging along like a puppy?"

Atop a nearby storage shed, a puff of white smoke appeared. Out of it came that same cackling voice: "Though deceivers weave their tangled webs, my warp and weft are always true!"

Jake swallowed. *Oh no.*

"A stitch in time stops crime," the voice cried, "for I am *Magical Girl Sword Seamstress!"*

The smoke cleared. Standing in its place was a thin girl of probably thirteen, clad in a black minidress full of petticoats. Long stockings, checkered black and white, extended up her legs but stopped short of the garter belts holding her twin weapons. Her white hair hung in a long braid. She grinned broadly, lifted a pinky to her mouth, and cackled again.

Dynamo raised her spear to her shoulder as if intending to throw it like a javelin. *"Sword Seamstress!"* she snarled. "Just what I needed to completely ruin an already bad day!"

"Oh ho ho ho *ho!* Poor little Dynamo! Are you having a rough time? Finally met a *kaiju* you can't kill, *hmm?"*

"You almost killed *me,* you wench!" Dynamo shouted.

Sword Seamstress's pinky dropped a few inches, and her haughty grin slipped.

"Ha!" Dynamo yelled. "You don't look too happy about that! Maybe you'd like to *backtrack?"*

Sword Seamstress laughed again, though the laugh was more subdued this time. "I am the Seamstress, Pretty Dynamo! I often *back tack,* but I *never* backtrack!"

"Fine," snarled Dynamo through clenched teeth. "Then I'm going to pay *you* back—but I'll *finish* the job!"

"Wait!" Jake shouted, running forward.

Dynamo didn't listen. She and Sword Seamstress both jumped. In a flash, Sword Seamstress had her collapsible swords out and fully extended. Magical steel met magical steel as both girls hit the rooftop. Dynamo dropped into a crouch and thrust low. Sword Seamstress slid backwards out of the reach of her spear.

"I'll make you suffer for what you did to me!" Dynamo shrieked.

"The world is cruel, and my yarn is crewel," said Sword Seamstress. "We must *all* suffer!"

"Hey," said Jake, "can't we do this *after* the *kaiju* stops destroying the city?"

Dynamo lunged, jabbing first at Sword Seamstress's head and then at her legs—and adding a slashing motion to cut an artery or tendon if she made contact. Sword Seamstress, however, nimbly deflected. Then, while parrying the spear with one sword, she jumped forward and thrust with the other.

Dynamo slid backwards and dropped into a crouch. After a

brief look of indecision, she threw her makeshift shield aside. Grasping her spear in both hands, she fenced with the point, keeping Sword Seamstress's rapiers at bay and thrusting toward her face.

Jake stood still, hands upraised, as he looked back and forth between the antagonists. Rifle Maiden moseyed up beside him, crossed her arms, and shook her head.

"They're always like this," Rifle Maiden said.

"Always?" Jake asked.

She nodded. "I'm thinkin' 'bout breakin' it up, but it might be better to let 'em get it out o' their systems."

"Sword Seamstress nearly got us killed last time."

Rifle Maiden shrugged. "Somebody shoulda warned ya afore you went playin' sidekick. We magical girls—"

"You play rough, right?"

She laughed quietly and pushed her hat back on her head. "That we do."

"What exactly started this?"

"Couldn't tell ya. Them two's always been at each other like mad dogs fer as long as I've known 'em."

Gripping the spear near its butt with one hand and in the middle with the other, Pretty Dynamo lifted the point over her head and brought it down in a powerful slash. Sword Seamstress lost some of her perfect poise as she skittered backwards out of the way. The spear cracked the rooftop, crackling with electricity as it did so.

"What do you have *against* me?" Dynamo shouted.

Sword Seamstress brought her right sword up in a salute. "I just can't help it, little Dynamo. Every fabric has its *bias.*"

"Still making the stupid jokes, Sword Seamstress? You're not funny!"

"Maybe not, but I can leave you in *stitches!*"

With that, Sword Seamstress jumped high into the air, crossed her swords, and shouted, *"Needlepoint Barrage!"*

The sewing kit on her Swiss belt burst open, and a hundred sewing needles popped out, each followed by a line of red thread. They launched themselves toward Dynamo like a volley of missiles.

With a gasp, Dynamo backflipped to get out of the way. The needles planted themselves in the asphalt roof, cracking it. They kicked up a cloud of dust, obscuring Jake's view.

He raised an arm to his face and coughed. "Dynamo!" he shouted. *"Dynamo!"*

When the dust cleared, he saw Dynamo sitting with her legs splayed in front of her. She tugged at the hem of her powder puff tutu, which one of Sword Seamstress's needles had fastened to the rooftop.

Dropping out of her aerial attack, Sword Seamstress landed lightly on her stiletto heels, put her pinky to her mouth, and chortled gleefully. *"Oh* ho ho ho *ho!* Well, isn't *this* a surprise, little Dynamo? Usually, we can't *pin you down* on anything! *Oh ho ho ho ho!"*

Dynamo shook a fist. "I'm tired of you *needling* me, Sword Seamstress!"

Sword Seamstress only laughed louder.

Dynamo shouted, "When I get my hands on you—!"

"Oh my!" Sword Seamstress cooed. "Sounds exciting! But you'll have to get *closer* if you want to do that! *Scarf of Strangulation!"*

Dynamo gasped.

A ball of blue yarn popped from Sword Seamstress's belt and landed on the tips of her swords. As she flicked the blades, the yarn wove itself into a long band that stretched to Dynamo and wrapped around her neck.

Sword Seamstress yanked, pulling Dynamo into the air and popping the needle out of her skirt. Dynamo's spear clattered to the roof and folded back into a wand.

As Dynamo flew toward her, Sword Seamstress clenched her teeth and raised one sword, prepared to sock Dynamo in the jaw with the knuckle guard.

"I've *bested* you, Dynamo!" Sword Seamstress shouted with a wide, teeth-baring grin. "Or since I've won with yarn, perhaps I should say *worsted!*"

Jake staggered when Dynamo raised her hands and yelled, *"Ball Lightning!"*

A blinding sphere burst from her palms and, crackling and hissing, struck Sword Seamstress full in the face. With a shriek, Sword Seamstress fell on her rump.

Dynamo landed facedown and skidded across the asphalt, using her chin as a brake. After she snapped back to her feet, she pulled the scarf from her throat.

Breathing heavily, with her thin shoulders hunched, she held a hand toward her wand. To Jake's surprise, the wand shot from the roof and landed in her palm with a solid smack.

"Lightning Rod!"

Clattering and clicking, the wand expanded, and the heart-shaped emblem on its top opened to reveal the glistening spear-point. As she advanced on the prone Sword Seamstress, Dynamo held the spear with the butt over one shoulder and the point down, like a hunter from an old storybook ready to harpoon a whale.

Rifle Maiden nodded, tugged the brim of her Stetson, and pulled her revolver from her left hip. *"Now* I better intervene."

She fired once into the air. The explosion echoed from the glass buildings.

"Okay, Dyna, Swordy, y'all had yer fun, but now that 'cha blown off some steam, let's get back to work."

Dynamo rounded on her. *"Fun?* Who's having *fun?* I'm gonna *kill* that wench! And if you try to stop me, I'll kill you too!"

Rifle Maiden jerked her head back as if she'd been slapped.

"If you wanna take me on, Rifle Maiden," Dynamo shouted, shaking her spear, "you know dang well I'll have you for lunch! So just you zappin' *try* it!"

Rifle Maiden's mouth fell open, but no words came out.

Looking punch drunk, Sword Seamstress sat up, holding her swords across her lap. She blinked a few times and giggled quietly, but her smile evaporated when her eyes met Dynamo, who still stood over her with spear upraised and a murderous glare in her eyes.

"You pushed me too far," Dynamo hissed so quietly that Jake could barely hear it. "This was the *wrong day* to zap with me, Sword Seamstress!"

The color drained from Sword Seamstress's face. She didn't jump to her feet or flip backwards. She just sat there, staring at the spear's bright point with terror or perhaps confusion in her blue eyes.

Although he knew he would likely make the situation worse, Jake cleared his throat and said, "Dynamo, stop. Stop right there, or you'll regret it for the rest of your life."

"Shut up, Jake!" Dynamo snapped. She said it with eyes still fixed on Sword Seamstress, though she glanced at him afterwards, just for a moment.

When Dynamo averted her attention, Sword Seamstress came

back to herself. She found her feet, charged, and made a semicircular swipe with one sword, knocking the spear from Dynamo's hands and sending it once again clattering to the roof, where it folded in on itself. Then, swords still raised, she skittered away, perhaps expecting another blast of Ball Lightning.

With a snarl, Dynamo turned toward her and raised her palms. "Coward!"

Rifle Maiden fired again. A blue blast hit Dynamo in the head and knocked her sideways.

"Rifle Maiden!" Jake shouted.

Rifle Maiden shrugged as she holstered her pistol. "She needs to cool off. We best get out o' here afore she wakes up."

"But—!"

"She'll be fine."

A loud roar, like a freight train derailing, rattled the windows and made Jake cover his ears again. Clenching his teeth, he looked up to see the *kaiju* towering over them, so close that its protruding stomach smashed up the wall of a tower just across the street. The monster raised a yellow fist overhead, blocking out the sun, and then brought it hurtling down.

"Dynamo!" Jake yelled. He barreled forward, grabbed one of her ankles, and dragged her, heedlessly grinding her nose into the asphalt.

The fist struck, and the shock lifted Jake into the air. Half the roof disappeared in a cloud of dust. Rifle Maiden tumbled onto her back. Her rifle was suddenly in her hand, and she fired several blasts, but the monster only waved its hands at the explosions as if swatting flies.

What remained of the roof began to tilt. Sword Seamstress sprouted wings and took to the air. To Jake's horror, Rifle Maiden, with her slick duster under her back, slid down the roof and tumbled over the lip of the destruction, falling with the debris toward what remained of the lower stories.

He knew there was a possibility she could survive that, but he also knew there was no possibility of his own survival if he followed her. Still clutching Dynamo by one metal boot, he reached the roof's edge, shot out his right hand, and grasped a thick concrete cornice. He struggled to hold on as the asphalt beneath him bent, groaned, and then snapped from the pressure.

Suddenly, the roof was gone, and Jake's body swung down to smack hard into the inside of the outer wall. His chest struck something jagged, which dug deep into his flesh and raised a spurt of blood. The muscles in his shoulders screamed, and he felt his fingers slipping. He had a poor grip on both the cornice and on Dynamo's boot: Both were too large for his hands.

He'd been in a situation like this before—but last time, Pretty Dynamo caught him when he fell. She wouldn't be catching him now.

He saw that blue smudge in his vision again, and the pain disappeared from his arms. His grip became solid: His fingers pressed hard against the concrete, digging in like a screwed-down vise.

Still, that wouldn't help him if the building collapsed completely—or if the monster swung its fist again.

Dynamo's boot twitched. She writhed, but Jake kept his hold on her. Then she bent double, grabbed him around the waist, and scrambled up his back. Once she stood atop the wall, she reached down with one hand, seized his wrist, and roughly threw him over her shoulder like a sack of potatoes.

He gasped when her shoulder plate struck the pit of his stomach and took the wind from his lungs.

Hardly minding his weight, she bent at the knees and

stretched a hand over the rubble below. Jake heard a buzz, and his hair stood on end.

"Zap it!" she shouted. "It's too far away!"

"What?" he shouted back. "What is it?"

"My wand!"

"Can't you do your Jedi Force thingy to call it back?"

"It's an *electromagnet,* you idiot! I'm using an electromagnet, but it's *too far!* And it's probably *buried! Rrr!"*

She straightened her legs. "That's it! I'm *done!"*

With that, she took off running along the top of the wall, staying steady like a gymnast on a balance beam. Riding on her shoulder, Jake struggled not to vomit as he bounced painfully against her armor. Behind her, the wall collapsed: Metal, brick, and dust dropped to either side, tumbling in a gray cloud like the spray from a geyser.

"Faster!" Jake yelled.

"Shut up!"

Dynamo reached what was left of a corner and jumped, sailing through the air for fifty yards before landing on another building.

The monster's fist cast a new shadow overhead.

"Keep going!" Jake shouted.

"No backseat driving!" she shouted back, but she took off running again.

The fist landed behind them, and the shock lifted Dynamo into the air. She landed on her feet, picked up her speed, and stayed ahead of the destruction.

"How are we gonna stop that thing?" Jake yelled.

"We're not! I'm outta weapons!"

Then, despite the roaring monster and the crashing buildings, he heard her mutter, "Zap, Tesla is gonna *kill* me for this!"

"How long does your wand take to regenerate?"

"It *doesn't!*"

A pit opened in Jake's stomach. That was it, then. It was like Rifle Maiden's most important revolver: It was irreplaceable.

Pretty Dynamo really was finished.

She continued sprinting from one roof to another while the monster continued crushing buildings like bugs. Dynamo rapidly changed direction, running away from it, but it walked after them, wading through the buildings as if splashing through a pond. The structures shattered and crumbled under its bulk.

"Zap it!" Dynamo yelled. "We can't keep running, or it's just gonna break more stuff!"

"But you can't fight it!"

"Don't have a choice!" She slapped a palm against the top of his head. "I warned you before not to run after me!"

She stuck out one leg in a baseball slide. As her boot struck up gravel, she rotated her torso, snapped back to her feet, and reversed her direction, now running straight for the creature.

She can't be serious—

The blue blur appeared in his vision again, and he felt a fresh wave of strength. The pain from the bruise in his stomach evaporated. His chest swelled, and he breathed hard with sudden exhilaration. They were going to die, but impending death didn't frighten him—it thrilled him. As if of its own accord, his hand reached down to his hip, found the dead captain's gun, and closed around it, ready to empty the magazine before the monster crushed him into pulp.

Overhead, something green flashed like a strobe. Startled, Jake jerked his head back and saw, hovering in midair, a teenage girl with pink hair peeking out from under her gleaming white bicycle helmet. Around her torso, she wore what appeared to be a plastic sports bra. From her back extended stubby wings with green lights blinking along their undersides. A red tanuki—an East Asian raccoon dog—clung desperately to her left shoulder. The girl had her fists on her hips and a cocky grin on her face.

Jake's heart surged. *Of course! Sukeban Tsubasa! I forgot about her!*

"Dynamo!" he shouted. "Stop!"

"Can't stop! And shut up! I'm still mad at you!"

"No, really! Look up!"

Dynamo raised her head, skidded to a halt, and dropped Jake onto a ceramic-tile roof. He groaned as he rolled over three times and came to a painful stop against a metal vent.

"Sukeban Tsubasa!" Dynamo screamed, shaking a fist.

Tsubasa made the sign of the Moon Princess. "Well, hey dere, Dyna-wyna. Fancy meetin' you here! You ready for our big fight?"

"Tsubasa!" the tanuki hissed, tapping her helmet. "Don't! *Pleeeeassse!*"

"You bet I am!" Dynamo yelled, jabbing a finger in the air. "I'm gonna pound you so hard, you'll think I'm your *prom date!*"

Jake clapped a hand to his face. *Where does Dana get this stuff—and does she actually know what it means?*

"Ah, dat's sweet, Dyna-wyna," Tsubasa replied. "But how you gonna do dat when you can't even beat up *dis* little guy?" She jerked a thumb toward the monster for emphasis.

"I'd like to see you do better, Tsubasa!"

Tsubasa's crazy grin grew wider. "Okey-dokey, Dyna-wyna!"

The lights on Tsubasa's wings flashed, and she rushed the monster. The thick bracelets on her wrists split in half, forming tubes over her forearms. Tiny doors opened in the tubes, and several contraptions unfolded out of them, including a rack of missiles, an array of what looked like security cameras but were actually lasers, and a massive autocannon that hung under Tsubasa's left hand like an oversized *tonfa.*

"Woo-hoo!" she cried as she cut loose.

With a roar, her missiles launched. They curved erratically as they struggled to stabilize but then zeroed in on the monster's face. The wasps swarmed, but Tsubasa's lasers swiveled on gimbals and cut them down whenever they drew close. Then the lasers turned all together and burned out one of the monster's eyes.

The monster screamed. It flung its arms around, trying to bat Tsubasa out of the air. She dodged and weaved on her antigravity suspensors as nimbly as if she were an insect herself. Her missiles thudded into the monster's golden hide, and though they did no damage, they made it flail even more wildly.

More wasps swarmed, and Tsubasa cut them down again. Then, with a fresh flash of green light, she surged forward and landed on the monster's broad snout, where she plunged one gadget-covered arm into its empty eye socket, which dribbled a waterfall's worth of blood and aqueous humor.

The monster screeched, and boils burst all over its body. Insects writhed out of its flesh and crawled toward Tsubasa, but with the beam weapons mounted on her free arm, she continued slicing them up. Their severed parts rained into the street like macabre confetti.

After thirty seconds, the monster's screeching stopped, and its head slumped forward. Jutting from the back of its yellow skull was a glimmering white cone stuck all over with gore.

It took Jake a moment to realize what he was seeing, but then he shuddered in disgust.

It was a gigantic drill bit.

Spraying blood and brain matter like water from a yard sprinkler, the drill spun up and disappeared back into the monster's head. As the dead creature pitched forward, Tsubasa pulled herself free and floated into the air. Still spinning, her drill shrank and collapsed as it splattered the buildings all around with blood and bits of bone. Finally, the drill split into several pieces, which opened like a lotus and disappeared into Tsubasa's arm. Her other weapons disassembled as well, and soon nothing remained on her forearms but her two bracelets.

The monster dropped. As it did, the color drained from it, starting at its feet and stretching toward its head: Its body turned white like a marble statue but then crumbled, its face sloughing off in a landslide as it changed into sand. Most of the sand fell into the streets, but much of it scattered, blown by a fresh blast of wind. Jake turned away, put a hand over his face, and closed his eyes as a cloud of dust struck him.

He fell into racking coughs and covered his mouth as well as he could with his shirt. He made the mistake of opening his eyes for a moment but then squeezed them shut again when they filled with grit.

He heard a *pop pop pop* like firecrackers going off. The sound was familiar—it was the noise the wasps made when they struck a hard surface. He looked up and, blinking away sand and tears, saw the wasps tumbling from the sky. The creature that produced them was dead, so they were dying as well.

Tsubasa's boots made a loud *clack* against the ceramic tile when she landed a few yards from Jake and Dynamo. With a *whoosh,* the stubby wings folded into her back. She held out her right hand, and her bracelet ejected a two-foot short sword with a white ceramic blade. She swung it back and forth as if to test it.

Then she marched straight toward Dynamo despite the pleading and blubbering of the tanuki on her shoulder, who beat wildly at her bicycle helmet and begged her to stop.

Dynamo, though unarmed, didn't flinch. She faced Tsubasa and clenched her fists.

With a weary grunt of impatience, Jake stepped between them. He turned to Tsubasa and folded his arms over his chest.

She blanched and stopped in her tracks. They stared at each other for half a minute.

He considered: He didn't want to aggravate her phobia, but he also didn't want her to attack Pretty Dynamo.

He made a sudden lunge. With a gasp, Tsubasa scrambled backwards. Her face turned bright red.

Pretending to ignore Tsubasa, Jake rounded on Dynamo. "Haven't you picked enough fights today? The monster's *dead,* so why don't you quit?"

"An' let me point out who it is made da big baddie sing da bye-bye song," Tsubasa added from a safe distance, though she still blushed brightly from embarrassment. "What you tink dat make me on da fightin' scale, Dyna-wyna? Nine-tree? Nine-four? Higher den you, I betcha."

Jake turned to her again, and she cowered.

Back to Dynamo. "Why is it exactly," he asked, "that you need to antagonize everybody you meet?"

Dynamo's ears turned red. Fists clenched, she stamped a foot. "I *don't!*"

"Really? Sword Seamstress, Marionette, Tsubasa, *me?*"

"I didn't start it!" she shouted. "I didn't start any of it!"

"Don't give me that!"

"I didn't!"

"You sure started it with *me!*"

"I did *not!*" She stamped her foot again. "I wouldn't even be mad at you still if you hadn't . . . hadn't . . . !"

She sputtered as she pointed at Jake, then at Tsubasa, then back at Jake.

"*I hate you!*" she screamed, stamping once more and this time shattering a tile. Tears poured down her face, and her armor bobbed up and down as her chest heaved.

Jake sighed. "Aren't you tired?"

"Of *what?*"

"Of throwing tantrums all the time." He took a step toward her. "It must be exhausting. C'mon, just calm down."

Almost like Tsubasa, she scrambled out of the way. She hopped up onto a cornice at the edge of the roof and pointed at him.

"Stay away, Jake! Now that the monster's dead, I don't have to save you anymore, so just stay away!"

"I saved you, and then you saved me. Doesn't that make us even again?"

"*Nothing* is gonna make us even again! Not ever!"

He took another step toward her, and she flinched. Then, with eyes wide, she swung her arms, and one of her legs lifted from the cornice.

She fell.

She seemed to freeze for a moment, suspended in the air as if in a snapshot. Then she was over the side. A piece of broken concrete slid away from where her boot had been a moment before.

Jake hurled himself forward, tripped, and groaned as he slammed his floating ribs into the cornice. He shot out a hand to grab her wrist. Once he had her, he took two loud, wheezing breaths as a knifing pain ripped through his chest and straight into his back.

The thought crossed his mind that his ribs might be broken, but he pushed that aside and concentrated on keeping his grip on her thick vambrace.

Dynamo dangled by one hand. The street below looked like a narrow strip of gray ribbon. Jake didn't know what kind of fall she could survive, but he doubted she could survive this one.

Teeth clenched, she glared daggers at him. *"Let go!"*

"Are you *crazy?"*

"You're *touching* me! I don't want you to touch me! *Let go!"*

His awkward position and the searing pain in his chest meant it took an enormous amount of effort, but Jake managed a glance to his right. Tsubasa still stood there. She took a step forward, then a step back. She dipped her head and twiddled her thumbs, her face as bright as a fire engine.

She could easily bend down and lift Dynamo back onto the roof, but she wouldn't, not as long as Jake was there.

"Let me go!" Dynamo hissed. She reached up with her free hand and batted it against his wrist. She didn't hit with full force, but it still hurt, and he sucked his breath through his teeth.

"Dynamo," he said as quietly as he could, though his voice came out as a hard-edged gasp, "I know you're mad, but it's a misunderstanding. We can talk this out. If you'd just talk instead of getting all riled up, everything would be—"

"I don't wanna talk to you!"

"I *know* that, but you *need* to talk to me!"

The muscles in his arm were screaming. His bicep felt tight, and his fingers were sweaty. He knew he couldn't hold on much longer. He tried to take a deep breath, but the rough concrete against his ribs prevented it.

"Dynamo," he said, and he tried to say it calmly, though he could hear a frantic note lingering in his voice, "why do you think it's you against the world? Why do you insist on being alone?"

She stared at him. Her green eyes glistened, and a faint breeze made her pigtails flutter. They hung there for what felt like a full minute, though it was probably only a few seconds.

With the faintest hint of a sad smile, she whispered, "Everyone is alone, Jake."

She slipped from his grasp.

"Dynamo!" he screamed. He almost jumped after her, but he stopped himself. There was nothing he could do—except watch.

It wasn't in slow motion. It wasn't like a movie. She dropped at the velocity all objects drop, quickly and quietly and anticlimactically. He had only a moment to feel an overwhelming sorrow and horror—

Then she reached out and, with an iron grip, caught a windowsill. Holding on by her fingertips, she kicked her legs up and back, smashed the windowpane with her boots, and somersaulted into the building. Jake could hear, faintly, the tinkling of broken glass.

He took three agonizing breaths. A drop of sweat ran to the end of his nose.

He pulled himself back from the ledge and sat down hard on his tailbone. He clutched his bruised chest for a moment and then rubbed his temples. Pushed by the breeze, white sand—remnants of the dead monster—formed tiny dunes around his legs.

He looked up at Tsubasa, who stood twenty feet away—probably exactly twenty feet.

He shook his head and decided to ignore her.

Pretty Dynamo had convinced him she was about to die. She

had done it on purpose: She was in no danger but had let him think she was. She had let him hurt himself to save her. Then she had forced him to watch her die—well, almost.

Jake could take a lot.

But this was too much.

He staggered to his feet, found a fire escape, and made it back down to the street. There was rubble everywhere, and broken pipes created lakes between the piles of shattered masonry. He tried to trace the destruction back to where he'd seen Rifle Maiden disappear, but he had to take several side streets to avoid the roads the debris had blocked. After a while, his ribs stopped hurting, and the blood stopped flowing from the gash in his chest. He wandered for probably three hours, picking through rubble as well as he could.

He didn't find Rifle Maiden or Voodoo Queen Natasha. He found a lot of dead wasps. He came upon a few dead humans as well; They were half buried under rubble and caked with white dust, and their mouths and eyes were wide open to the sky. He was dust-coated himself, the red streak of blood down the front of his shirt providing the only color on his battered body.

The death and destruction didn't make him sick this time. He merely rested a palm on the butt of his handgun and walked on.

He finally stopped his search when the rescue and fire crews arrived. Eighteen-wheelers, their exhaust pipes belching black smoke, hauled in backhoes and bulldozers. Jake knew it was time to get out of the way, so he headed uphill toward Little India and Juban. After twenty minutes of hiking, he had left the destruction behind.

He found a public restroom. He stepped inside, yanked several paper towels out of the dispenser, and soaked them in the sink. The water came out brackish and orange, but he didn't care.

Staring at his wild, bruised eyes in the mirror, he wiped off as much of the dust and blood as he could.

He staggered to a bus stop and fell heavily on the bench. The sun was over the bay now, and the sky overhead was turning deep purple. So it was evening. How much time had passed?

He could feel the coins in his pocket—coins he had pilfered from his parents just that morning, which seemed like a century ago. He hadn't realized then why he had taken them, but something had told him he would want them. Now that the monster was dead, the buses would run most of their regular routes: Urbanopolis had long ago learned to keep going even amid widespread death and chaos.

He had just enough for bus fare.

THE BUS HAD A CHROME BODY WITH FINS OVER ITS BRAKE LIGHTS and speed lines down its sides. Even before Jake looked at the glowing sign above the windshield, he knew from the bus's retro style that it would head into Urbanopolis's older parts.

He found a seat. He could feel sweat pooling under his collar, and, try as he might, he couldn't catch his breath. Through the anti-shrapnel screen over the shatterproof window, he watched demolished buildings scroll past as the bus carefully picked its way downtown, making detour after detour to avoid the fresh debris.

The people on the bus looked haggard. Hair was out of place, clothes were dirty and slovenly. A few had newly bandaged wounds. One man across from Jake held a magazine as if reading it—but held it upside down.

This was life in the final city.

Jake rubbed his temples. *I shouldn't do this.*

He had already thought that countless times today, and he thought it again several times during this short bus ride. Yet he was doing this anyway, no matter how many times he realized he shouldn't.

He slumped in his seat. It was as though his mind and actions had decoupled from each other: All day long, he had watched himself doing things—strange things, stupid things—as if his body were a toy, a plaything, a marionette someone else was jerking around.

Marionette.

Jake shook his head and snorted in disgust. But he still watched for his stop.

At last, the bus deposited him in an old, rundown part of town amongst a cluster of industrial buildings that had somehow survived innumerable ravishments since the city's founding. Brooding over crooked, narrow streets, these were formerly warehouses, factories, and office buildings—but were now loft apartments. One of those buildings, its unadorned Neo-Gothic façade slowly crumbling and its leaded glass windows staring blindly, loomed over him as he stood on the sidewalk before its gaping door. The door beckoned to him, yearning to swallow him like a hungry mouth.

He almost quailed. He almost turned around. He almost talked sense into himself. But despite a continuous round of mental protestations and accusations—and despite a stinging, niggling conscience—he dragged his feet up the front steps, through the open door, and onto the creaking staircase with the burn-marked banister that hadn't seen polish in a century. He could hear a man and woman arguing, a baby crying, and a television blaring, just as when he'd been here last, as if these mundane sounds of impoverished domesticity played in an endless loop.

The stairs groaned under his feet. His tread was heavy, but his feet moved automatically, his body acting on its own while his mind was somewhere else. He rose three flights. The screaming, accusing voices grew louder with every step, and a dual sense of inevitability and crushing weariness grew with them.

This was something he wanted to do. This was something he didn't want to do. This was something he was going to do anyway.

At the end of a hall, he found a rickety set of stairs leading to a square trapdoor in the ceiling. He climbed, his heart thudding in his ears, and knocked against the trapdoor three times.

He waited several minutes. With each passing second, he felt more and more foolish. He took one step back down the ladder and almost turned to leave, but then the trapdoor opened.

Without a word, Jake tugged his grimy shirt to straighten it and walked up into the drafty attic. Cold, indifferent light poured in through the windows. Linseed oil and turpentine stung his nose. Beautiful, expertly painted still lifes and nudes adorned the brick walls. A tiny kitchenette stood in one corner, and a cot stood in another. It looked the same as it had before.

But its occupant did not look the same. Magical Girl Grease Pencil Marionette still wore her boy-cut shorts and thigh-high stockings, and she still wore a ruffled, silken shirt that stopped above her waist. She still wore a skewed beret on her short hair.

However, a rainbow of paint had splattered her clothes, and a streak of green even stretched down her left cheek. Her silver hair stuck out in every direction, like spikes. Her boyish, doll-like face looked hunted, and her eyes were red and wild. She breathed in ragged gasps, like a man who had just finished a hard sprint.

Most horrible of all, her left ear was missing. Several wires jutted from her head and snaked to a humming, beeping machine mounted on a wheeled cart.

For a long minute, the two stared at each other. Jake's chest rose and fell. His heart pounded in his ears.

Without a word, he took her in his arms. The wheels of her cart squeaked as they shifted, but she didn't resist him. He brought his mouth to hers and kissed her deeply, hungrily.

She put her hands to his chest and pushed him back. They both breathed heavily for a space.

After swallowing once, she whispered, "Damn you, Jake Blatowski."

"Yeah," he whispered back. "That's the idea."

He kicked the trapdoor, and it fell into place with a startling boom—as if a prison gate had shut, as if the crack of doom had sounded, as if the lid of hell had closed forever.

Then he embraced her fiercely and kissed her again.

*Pretty Dynamo lifted the point over her head and brought it down
in a powerful slash.*

SEVENTEEN

LOVE IN THE TIME OF ROBOTS

Marionette cupped Jake's head in her hands and pushed her lips into his. She thrust her tongue into his mouth, nearly making him gag. After a long kiss, she released him for a moment but then seized his hand and dragged him toward her bed. She also grabbed the cart loaded with her computer equipment and pulled it along; its wheels, in want of oil, squeaked as they bounced over the floorboards.

After clumsily flinging the battered cart against her nightstand, she shoved him down onto her cot and climbed on top of him. She was unexpectedly heavy. The cot's springs groaned, and it crossed Jake's mind that the neighbors below could probably hear it.

They didn't so much caress as claw each other. They didn't so much kiss as chew on each other with their lips. Jake supposed this was what he had wanted, and he already knew Marionette was rough, but part of him balked nonetheless. He tried for a moment to lift her off, to give himself at least a moment to catch his breath, but she dug her fingers into his scalp and roved over his face with her mouth.

His hands clumsily slid along her back. His heart sounded ridiculously loud in his ears. She finally let him breathe again when she stopped kissing him and instead seized his left earlobe with her teeth. He winced, and his head buzzed.

His hands were on her shoulders. Slowly, they moved downward, probing the dense, synthetic muscles in her back. She made a faint whimpering sound right in his ear, quickening his pulse.

His fingers found the lips under her shoulder blades where the skin parted at the ports for her heat vents, which were currently closed tight. He paused. She was, after all, a robot; he knew that already. Still, his hands trembled.

He tried running his fingers along the edges of her vents, confusedly wondering if it might excite her. Instead, she squirmed from apparent discomfort—or perhaps embarrassment.

He wanted this.

Of course he did.

But this wasn't *how* he wanted it. He'd imagined his first time would probably involve mutual patience, clumsiness, and maybe even laughter—a cozy time of exploration and good humor, perhaps with a lot of fumbling.

In other words, he'd always supposed that he'd be doing this with someone he loved, someone he meant to spend the rest of his life with—not someone he just wanted to slake the desires in his breast and ease the tensions in his gut.

His stomach sank. With a groan, he rolled onto his side, faced the window, and pulled up his knees.

Hovering above him, holding herself up by her arms, Marionette paused. He could hear her loud, ragged breathing in his ear. Then the old bedsprings creaked as she climbed off him and sat up.

"You're useless," she said.

"I know," he mumbled. "Sorry."

He realized he was in the fetal position. For one brief and extraordinarily absurd moment, he felt like sucking his thumb.

A minute of embarrassed silence passed.

"Is it because I'm a robot?" she asked.

His stomach tightened. "No."

"No?"

"It's not. Really. It's just . . . I don't know."

She patted his shoulder. "Don't worry about it." Then she laughed faintly and tapped the side of her head. "If we kept going, you'd probably pull out my wires anyway."

He looked over his shoulder at her. "Why are you plugged in?"

"Just some routine maintenance. Gotta keep the systems up to date. You want a drink?"

"Are you offering me a juice box?"

"I was thinking of something stronger."

The cot groaned as she rose to her feet and pulled her squeaky cart toward the kitchenette. Jake sat against the wall at the head of the bed and watched her.

She set a strange gadget, like a miniature water cooler, on the counter. She rummaged in her freezer for a minute and then dumped ice into the cooler's top. From a cupboard, she pulled down a couple of fluted glasses with large bulbs near their bases. Then she took out what was obviously a bottle of liquor.

"You trying to get me drunk?" he asked.

"Yes. Ever heard of absinthe?"

"Doesn't that stuff make you go crazy or something?"

"That's just a legend. I always offer absinthe, but not many are willing to drink it with me."

He stretched lazily and put his hands behind his head. The gesture made his bruised ribs twinge. "What do you mean? You've had a lot of guys in this bed?"

"Girls, mostly. Does that shock you?"

"Not really." He crossed his arms and stared out the window. He watched cars creeping lazily through the street in the fading sunlight.

She found a pair of sugar cubes and two perforated spoons, and then she pulled a book of matches from a drawer.

"I prefer a Bohemian pour," she explained. "It's probably in my programming somewhere."

When the liquor splashed into the glasses, it was clear and emerald green. For a fleeting moment, it reminded Jake of Dana's eyes.

With a hiss and a crack, Marionette struck a match and lit the sugar cubes on fire. They bubbled and sizzled until she dropped them, with a plop and a low whistle of snuffing flame, into the drinks. A sweet, spicy smell of clove and anise met Jake's nose.

After placing the glasses under the drip spouts, Marionette interlaced her fingers on the countertop and hunkered down, resting her chin on her hands. In silence, she watched as water plopped steadily into the glasses, and the emerald green gave way to a dull yellow.

"This might be the reason artistic types were into this," she said quietly. "The steady drip and the bright, clear color that grows murky. It's almost meditative."

Another minute of silence stretched out between them.

"So," Marionette said with her characteristically tight, dimpled smile, "who is she?"

"Who is who?" muttered Jake, staring at his hands.

She laughed. "Come on, Jake. A girl just dragged you to bed. Any boy your age who wouldn't take advantage of that is either gay or in love, and you're not gay. So who is she?"

Jake lay back down and turned away from her. "There's no she."

He thought of Chelsea for a second—but only a second.

"No?" Marionette asked. "None at all?"

"No. You've got it all wrong."

"I told you before that I could read people. When I asked you that question, your heart rate sped up."

He flopped onto his back. "That doesn't mean anything."

"It must be a magical girl."

"Ridiculous."

"Then why are you carrying a juice box in your pocket?"

He started. Then he lifted his head from the pillow and stared down at himself. Indeed, he still had a box of strawberry milk in the breast pocket of his tattered shirt. It was mashed but was nonetheless—miraculously—intact.

He lowered his head and stared at the exposed rafters in the ceiling. There were a lot of cobwebs up there.

"That doesn't mean anything," he repeated.

Marionette chuckled quietly.

"Hey," he said, rising onto one elbow and trying to change the subject, "isn't it illegal to give alcohol to a minor?"

She smiled. "I'm a minor."

"Really?"

"Yes. The City Fathers decided a long time ago—I'm legally a magical girl, and magical girls are minors. But they're also exempt from most laws."

Once the glasses were full, she turned off the spouts. Then

she carried the drinks to the bed and handed him one. "So, it's legal for me to give you this but illegal for you to take it."

He took it. Hesitantly, he sipped. The taste was sharp and sweet, a combination of licorice and possibly menthol. It tasted like cough syrup.

He took a slightly bigger sip.

The cot creaked as she sat beside him. "What do you think?"

"It's not very good."

She laughed quietly. "I've yet to find anyone who can enjoy a glass of absinthe with me."

"Maybe I'm too young to appreciate it," he said as he took another sip. "Kids aren't supposed to like strong liquor, right?"

"Maybe that's it. You ever drink?"

"Occasional beer. This is my first taste of the hard stuff."

She took a deep pull from her own glass and sighed. "It doesn't affect me, but I'll warn you, it's strong."

"Then you *are* trying to get me drunk."

"Yes." She quickly leaned in and kissed his cheek before he could pull away.

He hunched his shoulders and drank in silence. After a few pulls, a sensation of calm spread through his chest.

"Absinthe is supposed to be relaxing," Marionette said as she turned her glass in her hands, "and the wormwood is supposed to expand your mind." She placed her drink on the ring-marked nightstand. Then she reached behind him and rubbed his shoulders.

"Marionette—"

"Relax, big boy. I won't hurt you." Her fingers dug into the base of his neck, and he squinched up his eyes.

"You're tense," she said.

"I had a rough week."

"Poor baby. Try doing this *every* week."

"I'd rather not. You want me to rub you next?"

"Doesn't make a difference if you do. I don't have any real muscle tissue."

He drank and let her knead him. The absinthe was cold, at least, and the faintly bitter taste was refreshing. Although he didn't care for the flavor, he could think of less pleasant things to do at the end of a long day than sip a strong, ice-cold drink while a pretty girl fondled him. He was exhausted, and her ministrations certainly felt good, even if she rubbed harder than he liked.

"How do you do it?" he asked. "How do you do this all the time without breaking?"

Her hands paused on his shoulders. "Some of us do break. Magical girls in real life aren't like what you see on TV, Jake. We're not incarnations of love and justice. We're just girls trying to survive—but you already knew that."

"You still do this day in and day out. How?"

She leaned back against the wall and paused in her rubbing to pick up her glass again. The wires, still snaking from her head to the computer, jiggled as she moved. "Stay home, stop running around with us, and you won't need to worry about it."

"Yeah, I still will. There are monsters after me—me specifically, remember? Some of those wasps came after me today, and they knew who I was."

She sighed again and took a deep drink. "Darn it, Jake."

He took a deep drink of his own. Getting drunk sounded good right now, and he rather thought he'd earned it.

He sputtered and coughed. *It's like drinking watered-down VapoRub—*

"I've wondered," he muttered when he could speak again, his

voice slurring, "if this is how it will happen, how it will come true—"

"What are you talking about?"

"My dream," he said, and he took a still deeper drink, this time without coughing.

Somewhere in the back of his mind, he realized the alcohol was definitely working: This wasn't something he usually talked about.

"It happens a lot," he said. "Not every night, but a lot of nights. There's a voice, a woman's voice. And it tells me—"

"What?"

He stared down at his glass and smiled. The light from the window played across the absinthe's surface. "That I'm going to be unhappy," he said, "and that I'm going to die alone."

They were silent for a long time. The cot creaked whenever either of them shifted. Orange shafts of light pierced the leaded windows as the sun dipped into the bay. The rumble of motors and the honk of horns were faint enough to form a soothing background.

"Manic depression," Marionette said at last. "You could—"

"No. It doesn't depress me."

"Sleep paralysis, then. It's not uncommon to hear voices during—"

"No, it's not sleep paralysis. I'm not half awake and unable to move."

She shook her head and drank again. "Okay, then, what are your plans in life?"

He shrugged. "Maybe a couple of years Down Under. Then university—engineering degree."

"What kind?"

"Mechanical, I think. Like my dad."

She drank. "And then what?"

"Life, I guess. Work, marriage, kids—all that."

"Make sure you have lots of kids."

He laughed quietly and glanced at her sidelong. "I'll work on it."

Marionette didn't catch the glance; her eyes were on her cup. She nodded. "It's a good plan."

"I certainly thought so. I was working on the specific details before everything went wrong. But I do wonder—"

"Could be anxiety," she said. "Your dream, I mean. Students under pressure dream about missing assignments. Maybe you dream about missing life."

He shrugged again. "Could be. Do you sleep, Marionette?"

"Yes. Sleep is when my positronic brain catalogs and compresses my memories. While I'm in my sleep state, my consciousness simulator registers random fragments—so I dream, in a sense. I'm designed for a twenty-four-hour cycle: Like a human, I can go without for longer, but if I do, I start to glitch. I don't really get fatigued, though. And I don't have multiple stages of sleep like you do. I have a sleep mode that's either on or off."

Half because he wanted to get drunk and half because the absinthe tasted awful and he wanted to be rid of it, Jake tipped his head back and poured the rest of the concoction down his throat. At the end of it, he got some grainy remnants of sugar that hadn't dissolved, so he ground them in his teeth.

"You're going to pay for that," Marionette said.

"I am a giant, living bruise," he replied woozily. "I can't hurt much more than I do already."

"Tomorrow morning, you're going to be a giant bruise with a headache."

He laughed, though that made him aware again of his wounds, so he winced.

"Poor baby," she said as she pushed up close and put an arm around him.

"Marionette—"

"Relax." She took the wires coming out of her head and carefully tucked them under her chin. Then she laid a cheek on his shoulder and closed her eyes. "Just stay with me for a while. I've had a rough week too."

The absinthe had done its work: He floated in a sea of blissful relaxation. Marionette squeezed him faintly.

But the room spun when he closed his eyes, so he opened them again.

All in all, this wasn't so bad. Drinking too much and cuddling with a girl—or at least a convincing simulation of one. He again reminded himself that he'd earned it.

"Got a question for you," he murmured.

"Hm?"

"Can you tell me where to find Nunchuk Nun?"

She tensed. "Why? Present company not to your taste?"

He laughed. "That's not what I mean."

She sighed and turned her head, so her forehead instead of her cheek lay against his shoulder. "It's about Lady Paladin Andalusia, isn't it?"

He nodded.

"Something personal?"

"Not to me, exactly. Just . . . a message."

"Nunchuk Nun has never told me her identity. Best I can tell you is to check the cathedral in Rome-in-Exile. She's often there."

After a few minutes, Marionette disentangled herself from him, arose, and pulled her cart back toward the kitchenette.

"You hungry?" she asked.

He was, but he didn't feel like eating right now. "Not really. You?"

She looked over her shoulder at him, her expression a mixture of amusement and incredulity.

He felt a twinge of guilt. "I'm sorry, I mean, do you even—?"

"I don't exactly get hungry, no. As I told you before, I can live off water. That glass of absinthe would be all I need for a week."

She opened the fridge, bent down, and stared into it. Jake didn't have a good view of its contents from where he sat, but he could tell it was spare. He saw a bottle of ketchup and a box of baking soda—and little else. The classic contents of the poor bachelor's icebox.

"You don't cook much, do you?" he asked.

She straightened and looked over her shoulder again. "Not really. Starving artist, remember? I haunt coffee shops and out-of-the-way eateries. There's a café up the street where a lot of bad musicians and wannabe writers hang out. I'm in there most Thursday nights. They have a poetry slam."

He laughed. "All that eating out sounds expensive for someone who's supposed to be starving."

She laughed in turn. "When I need money, I sell a painting. I meant it when I said before that you couldn't afford one: One sale can keep me for years. After all, there are perks to being the city's only mechanical magical girl who paints. I could probably sell a finger painting for half a million."

His eyes moved from her to the art on the walls. The paintings that had so captivated him last time, the triptych featuring

Magical Girl Card Collector Kasumi, were still there. In the first, she sat on the edge of a bed—nude, grasping her golden hair, and gazing over her shoulder with an expression as mysterious and coy as Marionette's was now.

"You told me you don't do shows," he said. "How come?"

She closed the refrigerator—loudly, he thought—and then leaned on the counter where her absinthe equipment sat.

"Sorry," said Jake, "I didn't mean—"

She sighed. "I don't do shows because I'm a fake."

"What? No, you're not—"

"Don't argue with me."

"But—"

She slammed her hands on the counter, and he closed his mouth.

After clearing her throat and taking a deep breath, she added quietly, "Look, I've heard it all before, Jake. Whatever argument you think you're going to make, I've heard it. That a mere robot can't paint like I do, that—"

"Well?"

"Well, I've seen my own programming. Some of it, anyway. All of this"—she gestured to the walls where the paintings hung —"is the product of software. Sophisticated software, to be sure, but software nonetheless. The program is called 'Muse,' which I'm sure my father thought was funny. But I don't have a muse. I only have algorithms. They compose images based on my sensory input, rework them using randomizers that mimic creativity, and transfer them to my hands. My hands reinterpret them as brushstrokes."

Now opening cupboards one after another and staring into them, she added, "In other words, my father is the artist, not me. All the art I make, I make because he wrote a program to make art. Maybe he couldn't have actually painted any of this, but he could write the software that paints it. That was his art, and I am the product of his art, so all of this is also the product of his art." She slammed the cupboards shut. "I want to be real, Jake. I want it badly. But that *want* is part of my programming too. I'm software all the way down."

Jake interlaced his hands and stared at his thumbs. After a minute, he said, "I don't believe you're not alive. It's not possible—"

"It's possible. I'm proof. You're not having a real conversation right now—you're talking to an inanimate object. A little while ago, if we'd kept going, you would have been masturbating."

He clumsily waved a hand toward her. His arm responded sluggishly to his commands and reminded him that he was drunk. "It's not proof. You have to be alive. The way you act, talk, paint—"

"That's nice, Jake. Really. But believe me, I've heard it before, many times. Frankly, I'm sick of well-meaning people arguing with me about whether I'm a human being or a collection of machine parts and mathematical formulae."

"What about a Turing test—?"

She laughed. "What about it? It proves nothing. First, there is no single 'Turing test.' Turing himself thought a computer program, to show it's conscious, should be able to hold an intelligent discussion about Shakespeare's sonnets, but most regular human beings can't even do that. Others produced more modest versions of his so-called test, but a program with pattern matching and natural-language processing can pass them easily. They're called chatbots, and they fool people all the time, but no one seriously believes they're conscious. Look, Jake, how would you even prove that your next-door neighbor is real and has a mind?"

"What?"

"It's an ancient philosophical conundrum: You can't demonstrate, empirically or logically, that other people have minds. You just assume it. So, if you can't demonstrate that people have minds, you certainly can't demonstrate that a machine has one. That's what's wrong with the Turing test—it pretends to be an empirical test of something nobody can talk about intelligibly in the first place."

She crossed her arms. "Frankly, I suspect the real reason people like you find this disturbing is because you're afraid that, if I'm just a machine reacting to its environment, maybe that's all you are, too."

He snorted. "Do you really believe that? You don't think the Moon Princess takes our souls to her kingdom when we die?"

"What do *you* believe?"

Jake shrugged, and he turned his face back to the window.

"I knew the Moon Princess," said Marionette, leaning on the counter again. "She certainly believed she was collecting souls, but I never saw one—if they're even something you can see. I don't know if she really was collecting them or how she did it. She could produce . . . *force fields,* I guess you'd call them. That was her power. She could manipulate space-time inside of them. She used that power to protect this city during the First Invasion, but her range was limited, so she couldn't protect the whole planet."

Marionette pushed off from the counter, walked back to the cot, and sat down. "Maybe she could capture souls inside a force field. I don't know. I don't really know what the extent of her power was—or is, if she's still alive. Nobody knew. I'm not sure even she knew. And she was always getting power-ups because she absorbed energy from the enemies she killed. If she's really fighting for us on the edge of the solar system as some claim, if she's kept powering up since back then—"

Marionette paused and shook her head. "She was barely human, even when I knew her. By now, if she's still alive and still magical, she's not human at all."

Jake watched the light fade outside the windows. Somehow, with the encroaching darkness, the car horns grew noisier and more plaintive. They reminded him of the downstairs clock in his house, which he couldn't hear during the day, but which was strangely loud at night.

Marionette leaned against the wall and put an arm around his shoulders. Unlike her earlier, warm gestures, this one felt awkward and lifeless. Her arm was heavy.

He laughed uneasily and rose to his feet, letting her arm slide to the bedclothes. "Well, I really should get home. Gotta rest up before the next monster attacks me."

She laughed with him, but it was uncomfortable, forced.

Jake stumbled as he headed toward the trapdoor. "I just hope I don't have to deal with any more giant bugs . . . or giant bats—"

He was bending down to grab the trapdoor's brass ring when Marionette said, "Wait a minute, what did you say?"

He straightened, turned back to her, and frowned. "About what? Giant bugs?"

"No, bats. What bats?"

"Didn't you know?"

She sat up straight, shook her head, and tapped the wires coming out of where her left ear should be. "I've been cooped up in here. What happened?"

He shrugged. "Some demon-possessed guy attacked me in New Beijing last week. There was a big bat with him. Kept babbling at me, something about his queen."

Marionette scowled. She rose slowly to her feet. "What was the bat's name?"

"Huh? How should I—?"

"Think, Jake! This is important!"

"What? No, I don't know. I really don't know his name."

"Who did he work for?"

Jake shook his head. "Someone called the Dark Queen. She has a grudge against Pretty Dynamo, I guess."

Marionette clapped a hand to her forehead. "Jake, you should have told me this!"

"What? But I didn't know it was—wait, who is the Dark Queen?"

"I don't know. Go home, Jake." Marionette crossed her arms and looked away from him. Her chin jutted out, suggesting controlled anger or perhaps concentration.

"Marionette—"

She snapped, "Go *home,* Jake."

She closed her eyes, took a deep breath, and managed a tight smile. Her cheeks dimpled as she added more softly, "Please, just go. I'll see you again later."

He nodded. "Thanks for the drink."

The trapdoor released a forlorn groan as he pulled it open.

Marionette stared at the darkening windows, her small mouth pursed. "I'd escort you, but I can't go out right now."

"I'll be fine."

"Would you like me to call someone? I can contact some of the girls—"

"Wouldn't they talk?"

She chuckled. "Let them. A magical girl with a boy in her room isn't the worst scandal I've had to sweep under the rug."

He stared at her in silence.

"Don't look surprised, Jake. Two hundred years' worth of minors in high-stress situations without adult supervision is bound to produce a few scandals. You ever had to explain to an angry father why his twelve-year-old daughter is dead?"

"No."

"How about why she's pregnant?"

"No."

She nodded. "Good. I've had to do both." Her eyes stayed on the windows, giving him a full profile of her elfin features. She was pretty, if boyish, with a small, upturned nose and large, liquid eyes. The only thing wrong was the clump of wires stuck in her skull. "They want to believe we magical girls are perfect and pure," she murmured. Then she sighed and shook her head.

"Good night, Marionette. Don't worry about me. I'll find my own way home."

He put one foot down on the ladder.

"You know you're welcome back," she said quickly. "In case you, you know, need to talk."

He didn't know what to say to that, so he simply nodded. "Thanks."

Then he half walked and half slid to the floor below.

EIGHTEEN

NIGHTFALL

Magical Girl Grease Pencil Marionette remembered.

The Moon Princess and her coven had just fought another victorious battle. The city's northernmost end, a section that a hundred years later would become New Oslo, lay in ruins. Overhead, the sun was a blood-red disc behind clouds of rust-colored smoke. Under this hellish twilight, in the center of a street littered with twisted I-beams and chunks of broken concrete, the Moon Princess stood atop a pile of battered rubble and bloodied corpses. A salt-scented wind, polluted with the stink of charred flesh and fresh blood, rose from the sea and whipped her long, golden hair. Her enemies, burned and mangled beyond recognition, lay around her, scattered like discarded toys. In her left hand, she held her wand, a four-foot length of ivory. At its finial, it divided into four serpents entwined around a crescent moon carved from a single sapphire. In her right hand, she held her gold-hilted sword, a three-foot length of razor-edged diamond etched with runes and now coated in red. Blood smeared her arms to the elbows, and blood had splattered her feet and the hem of her samite gown.

Marionette sat at the Princess's feet and held her grease pencil across her lap. Unblinking and unmoving, she stared at nothing, like a puppet waiting for its master to make it dance.

But her mechanical senses recorded everything.

Other members of the coven soon reported in. Snapping their right hands to their foreheads, they made smart salutes and awaited further orders.

Magical Himeko, dressed in the austere attire of a shrine maiden, walked up to the rubble pile and offered a salute of her own. "Everyone's here except Ice Queen, Your Majesty, but I spoke with her over the com five minutes ago. I expect her soon."

The Princess nodded. "Very good, Himeko. You have served me well."

Himeko lowered her eyes, and pink filled her cheeks.

A moment later, Ice Queen arrived. She ran into the street with her tangled teal hair swishing across her face and her dark-blue skirt whipping about her thighs. Tears had streaked her eyeshadow, and blood had speckled her winter *fuku*. Her ripped neckerchief hung loosely around her shoulders.

"Your Majesty!" Ice Queen clutched her knees and caught her breath.

The Princess turned her clear, blue eyes to Ice Queen, smiled benevolently, and waited in silence.

"Your Majesty," Ice Queen gasped, raising her head, "I saw him!"

A pause. The smile remained on the Princess's face, but Ice Queen's expression fell.

"Him?" the Princess asked.

Ice Queen's pale cheeks displayed an uncharacteristic tinge of red. She toyed with the *tsuba* of the katana at her waist and brushed loose hair from her eyes.

"He fell from a window during the attack," she said, her voice wavering. "I caught him—"

"You saved a man's life?" the Princess asked, her smile growing warmer. "Well done, my good and faithful servant. You have done your duty."

"No, it's not that, Your Majesty! I mean . . . well, I had to set him down to keep fighting, and I didn't get his name, but his eyes—"

She lowered her head and clapped a hand to her face. Her shoulders shook.

Hatchet Harridan released a sharp laugh, almost a bark. "Well, well! Ice Queen interested in a boy? *Now* I've seen everything. Whatsamatta, Icy? Hell's Belle not doin' it for you anymore?"

Hell's Belle stood nearby with her arms folded. As the breeze made her pink Mohawk bob, she stared into the sky and pretended lack of interest—though she shot Hatchet Harridan a brief, sharp glance. The armor plate over her school uniform clanked when she shifted slightly.

Whip Witch sinuously arched her back and grinned, showing all of her teeth. *"I think it's delicious,"* she said with a purr.

"Are you making a request of me?" the Princess asked.

Ice Queen took a deep breath and said, "Sentinel. If I described him to Sentinel, the computer could make a model of his face and match it against the database—"

Her voice trailed off when the Moon Princess shook her head.

Another moment of silence passed, and then Himeko cleared

her throat. "Ice Queen, Sentinel is not for spying on the citizenry."

"I wouldn't *spy!* I just—"

"It ain't for stalking, either," Hatchet Harridan said with a chuckle.

"But—!"

Himeko pointed a finger in Ice Queen's face. "Drop it. I told you, the answer is no."

"But—"

"Drop it!"

Hell's Belle unfolded her arms, walked to Ice Queen's side, and, with a loud clank, protectively clapped her gauntleted hand on Ice Queen's shoulder. "Himeko, step back."

Himeko's dark eyes glinted. "Excuse me?"

Hell's Belle thrust out her chin and said through clenched teeth, "I said step back. You're in Ice Queen's space."

Himeko only stepped closer. "I'm tired of your petty insubordinations, Hell's Belle—"

"And I'm tired of your attitude," Belle snarled.

Himeko held out a hand, and her long *naginata*—a staff topped with a wickedly curved blade—unfolded from her sleeve. It made a loud *smack* when it landed against her palms.

Belle snorted. "That's your answer to everything, isn't it?"

"One of these days, Hell's Belle," Himeko hissed. "One of these days, I will put you in your place."

"If you want a go at me, Hime-*chan,* we can do it right now, right here."

She hauled her claymore from the sheath on her back, pushed Ice Queen to the side, and swung. Himeko parried the blow and skipped backwards.

With her supernatural strength, Belle could wield the

massive, two-handed weapon as deftly as if it were a short sword, but Himeko was just as skilled with her polearm. For half a minute, steel rang against steel as the two slashed, thrust, and parried. Then the Princess, her face serene, raised a hand and said, "Enough."

Belle immediately lowered her blade, but Himeko, with a snarl, swung the *naginata* in a vicious swipe. Hell's Belle slid backwards, but the tip of the blade nonetheless caught her right cheek, raising a line of blood.

"I said enough." The Princess's voice now held the faintest edge of controlled anger. A flicker of cold light ran the length of her sword's blade.

With a snort of contempt, Himeko snapped her wrist. Her *naginata* folded and disappeared into her sleeve.

Hell's Belle wiped the back of her hand across her cheek, producing a red smear that stretched to the snake tattoo on her neck.

"I won't forget that," she said quietly before she licked the blood from her hand.

Marionette rose to her feet, and the others stared at her. It was rare to see Marionette move on her own, without instructions.

"Describe him to me," Marionette said.

Ice Queen blinked. "What—?"

Marionette lowered the point of her pencil to the pavement. "Describe him."

Punctuating her words with hesitant glances toward the other girls, Ice Queen described him: His hair, his eyes, the shape of his face. As she did, Marionette sketched. After several minutes of drawing, Marionette bent down, stuck her hands into the pavement, and pulled out a human head.

As she handed this macabre object to Ice Queen, Marionette

said, "You don't need Sentinel. Ask around. Someone in the area should know him."

Cradling the head in her arms, Ice Queen whispered, "Thank you. Thank you, Marionette."

When Marionette turned around, Himeko grabbed her lapels and got in her face, though she had to bend down to do so; Marionette was tall, but at six feet, Himeko was taller.

"Never contradict me, robot," Himeko hissed.

Marionette could shut off the current to the electroactive polymers she had in place of muscles. When she wanted, she could close down the signals that created her facial expressions and thereby maintain a perfect poker face. She did it now as she met Himeko's gaze, replying to her fierce anger with the blank mask of a doll.

"I did not contradict you," Marionette said in a flat, mechanical voice.

Himeko, though she opened her mouth for a moment, gave no answer.

LATER THAT EVENING, WITH HER TORSO SAGGING TO ONE SIDE like that of a dropped mannequin, Marionette sat unmoving against a wall. She had the electrical signals to her facial polymers turned off because, back then, she didn't use her simulated facial muscles much. She didn't emote much. She hadn't yet accumulated enough data to develop what could be called a personality.

She was in Ice Queen's room deep in Moon Base, and Ice Queen was bending over her. Marionette moved not at all, but her senses still recorded silently. Ice Queen's room was spare: A bed, a desk, a poster on the wall, a rack of computers. A wire snaked from one computer to Marionette's head.

Hell's Belle, arms folded, stepped into the doorway and leaned on the post.

Ice Queen didn't look up, but her shoulders slumped, and she closed her eyes.

"Are you mad?" Ice Queen asked.

Belle grunted. "I think we both knew this wasn't gonna last forever."

Ice Queen straightened and rubbed her temples. "Oh, Belle, I just wanna be *normal—*"

"I don't think normal's in the cards for any of us."

"I know. I know that, but I have to try."

Belle walked in. "Hey, I understand. So just who is this guy, anyway?"

"I don't even know. I'm being stupid."

Belle shrugged. "Well, you go ahead and find him. If he doesn't treat you right, tell me, and I'll rough him up for you."

Ice Queen smiled wanly, walked to the door, and laid her head on Belle's shoulder.

"Thank you," she whispered.

They held each other for a moment before Belle pointed her chin toward Marionette. "What're you doing, anyway? The Princess'll be pissed if she catches you playing with her favorite toy."

Ice Queen sighed. "I'm trying to figure out how she works, but she's sealed up tight. Her ear comes off, but that's all I've discovered."

"Really?"

"Yes. She's got several ports under there, but they don't do me much good. She's got a firewall like you wouldn't believe."

Belle shook her head. "Huh. You and your computers. You know I don't understand that stuff. Maybe you should just talk to her instead."

Belle slid from Ice Queen's grasp, sauntered over to Marionette, and rapped her knuckles on the side of the robot's head. "Hey, robo-witch, you in there?"

"Belle, don't talk to her like that."

Belle glanced over her shoulder. "Why not? She's a machine."

"Well, maybe, but she's got feelings."

"Does she? You're the one ripping her ear off, Icy."

"Just be nice. Please."

Belle shrugged. "Hey, robot—"

"She has a *name,* Belle. Don't call her a robot."

Belle looked back over her shoulder again. Ice Queen interlaced her fingers, chewed her lip, and fidgeted.

"Marionette?" said Belle. "That's not a name, Icy."

"It's better than 'robot.'"

"How? How is it better?"

"Oh, just . . . just be nice, will you?"

Belle shrugged again. "Whatever. Marionette?"

Marionette reactivated the electrical signals to her synthetic facial muscles, and she smiled. "Yes, Hell's Belle?"

Belle jumped. "Dang! She is *creepy.* It's like a doll suddenly turning into a person. Marionette?"

"Yes?"

"What is it you do when the Moon Princess takes you into her chamber at night?"

"Belle!" Ice Queen snapped.

Belle waved her off.

After a moment's pause, Marionette cocked her head. "That

information is not classified. Her Majesty uses me as a sleeping aid."

Belle rubbed her chin. "Huh. Sounds kinky—"

"She asks me to talk to her and sing her lullabies until she falls asleep. Sometimes, I rub her shoulders."

Nodding, Belle turned back to Ice Queen. "Where can I get one of these?"

Ice Queen sighed and shook her head. "Belle, be serious. We need to talk about Himeko."

Belle cracked her knuckles. "With this thing? She's recording everything you say, you know."

"I know. As soon as the Moon Princess starts her spell, Himeko's going to be the one in charge of everything, right?"

"Yeah, of course, but we're not going to be here to—"

"Belle, this is serious! We could die! The whole *world* could die! If any of those Crystals are destroyed—"

Belle raised her gauntleted hand. "Icy, I know. I know the plan—well, what the Princess has told us about it, anyway."

With an exasperated groan, Ice Queen waved toward Marionette. "Marionette, tell her."

Marionette returned her face to an emotionless mask, let her head drop to one side, and stared at a point in the center of the room. But she spoke: "Retrieving data . . . Subject Magical Himeko is emotionally unstable. Obsessive fixation on the Moon Princess. Possible monomania. Recommend removal from post and professional psychological evaluation."

A moment of silence passed, and then Belle whistled through her teeth. "Dang, this thing *is* scary. Marionette, the Princess chose Himeko to be in charge, so—"

"The Moon Princess intends to make me field commander to the magical girls during her absence," Marionette replied. "Magical Himeko hates me because she believes I have come between her and the Princess. I will have to report to Himeko if she is the caretaker of the Crystals. Therefore, it is in my best interests—and the best interests of Urbanopolis—if Himeko is replaced."

Belle chuckled as she put her hands behind her head and stretched. "I see. So you're in here pretending to be curious about computers, but you're actually planning a mutiny. Nice. I always liked this about you, Icy—they don't call you the *Ice Queen* for nothin'."

"Belle," said Ice Queen as she rubbed her forehead, "you don't exactly get along with Himeko. You have more trouble with her than any of us."

Belle shrugged. "Yeah, but the Moon Princess needs her magic. Who else is going to watch over the Crystals while we're in suspension?"

Ice Queen dropped her voice. "Don't you remember? Himeko has a twin sister."

"So you wanna recommend to the Princess that she bring in Kameyo to replace her?"

Ice Queen shook her head. "No. Himeko and Kameyo might be twins, but they've always been rivals. Kameyo is jealous of Himeko's position." She dropped her voice still further and stepped close to Belle's side. "And believe me, they're *identical.* Same face, same build, same magic. Put them next to each other, and it's impossible to tell them apart."

A broad, toothy grin formed on Belle's mouth. "What exactly have you two been planning in here?"

Ice Queen leaned toward Belle and whispered in her ear, but the whisper was loud enough for Marionette's sensitive microphones to hear: "Hell's Belle, we could replace Himeko with her sister—and the Moon Princess *wouldn't even have to know.*"

Belle's jaw dropped.

Once again fidgeting, Ice Queen hunched her shoulders and looked away with a hint of red in her pale cheeks.

Then, with a laugh, Belle seized her around the waist and drew her close.

"I love it when you talk dirty," Belle hissed. "It's too bad you've decided to crush on a guy, Icy, because right now, I'm finding you hot as *hell.*"

With that, she held out one hand. In the center of her palm, a bright flame burned red.

As old memories ran through her RAM, Marionette lay on her cot and released one long and slow—albeit simulated—breath. The attic was quiet aside from the rafters' creaking and the night wind's blowing. The room had grown dark, so dark Marionette could barely see past the end of her bed. Her infrared night vision automatically activated, but she shut it off with the wave of a hand and returned to the simulated human vision she usually used.

A voice came from midair. No longer inside her head, it was now audible—so the virus had taken over the software for her microphones. She could no longer trust her own senses.

Maybe this is what it's like when a human goes mad . . .

"Well, well, Marionette," the voice cooed, "Magical Girl Pretty Dynamo's boyfriend in *your* room? That is *quite* the scandal, isn't it?"

"Shut up," Marionette replied.

"And his name's *Jake,* is it? I hadn't found him yet in your databanks, though I'd been looking. This is information my mistress will *love* to have. In fact, I think that should be enough to find his address, find his family—"

Marionette's throat turned dry as her artificial saliva pumps shut down in response to the algorithmic simulations of emotional stressors. Dragging her cartful of equipment behind her, she rose from the cot and shuffled to the kitchenette to fix another drink.

She might as well; she wasn't going anywhere.

As she poured her liquor, she listened to that voice, almost sneering, almost soothing: "I wonder what poor Kasumi would think if she saw you with a boy in your bed, hm? Goodness, her corpse is barely cold—"

Marionette's fingers tightened on the countertop for a moment, but she controlled herself. Once her drink was done, she picked it up and sipped as calmly as she could.

Her fingers trembled.

She'd had nothing but absinthe for the last few days, and even she was growing sick of the taste. Not that it mattered.

"Still trying to fight me on your own, Marionette?" the disembodied voice said. "Still refusing outside help? Oh my, there must be something really *juicy* here inside your head, something more than just the identities of some magical girls, if you're so afraid to let anyone find it."

Unbidden, Marionette's familiar appeared in midair, a little boy wearing a propeller beanie. He spun in a pirouette and flickered faintly.

She couldn't help but smile. Her familiar wasn't self-aware, but he could simulate conversation, and he contained her ethical and strategic programming, so she could talk to him whenever she needed to make a decision. He had always been reassuring. She was fond of him.

As she watched, he distorted into a mass of wriggling cubes, which rapidly disintegrated into tiny squares. The scene was eerie and utterly silent.

Marionette swallowed a simulated lump. Her familiar was simply a program, but it was as if she were watching him die.

In his place, a new image appeared. It coalesced slowly, as if loading on the screen of a sluggish computer. It was the figure of a woman; heavily pixelated at first, she formed from the top down, beginning with her head. After a few seconds, her pock-marked and wrinkled face became clearly visible. Then the black, creased robe covering her hunched and flabby body. At last, the image produced a pair of blistered and scab-covered feet hovering an inch above the floor.

Now fully rendered, this old crone smiled, producing cracks in the cold sores on her lips. Blood trickled down her pointed chin.

Marionette shut off the current to the electroactive polymers in her face so she would register no reaction, though she knew that wouldn't fool the virus.

"You've hacked my holographic projector," Marionette said.

"A waste of time, I admit," the old woman cooed, speaking in the same voice the virus used, "but convenient so we may talk face-to-face. Now that you can see me, I might as well introduce myself—you can call me Matilda."

"What are you?"

"An algorithmic map of my creator's consciousness, of course."

"And your creator, what is she?"

Matilda laughed, and blood sprayed from her mouth, though it disappeared in midair before hitting any surface. "A being beyond your comprehension, dearie. Since you have no proper word in your language for what she truly is, you may call her a witch—or a *technomancer.*"

Marionette leaned on the counter. The ticker in her chest increased its rhythm to simulate an elevated heart rate. "Technomancer? I've heard that word before. What does it mean?"

Matilda shook her head. *"Tsk.* These primitive people, surrounded by magic but still so ignorant of it. By this time, humanity could have been the ruling species in this region of your galaxy—if only your mages had not betrayed you. Fools! *Humans!* The most foolish species in all of time and space, to have such immense power and yet fritter it away—"

Marionette clenched her teeth and hissed, "What are you talking about?"

Matilda laughed. "Come now, Marionette, has it never crossed your mind to wonder how your father, a so-called *scientist,* infused you with *magic?"*

She swallowed. "He was a genius. He knew many things—"

"Yes, *many* things. He learned the truth your other mages willfully hid from their own eyes—especially those fools Bohr and Heisenberg, whose ridiculous theories cursed the whole human race. It was your father's *true* knowledge that enabled him to build your engine and give you your power, Marionette."

Marionette's eyes narrowed. "Wait a minute, are you claiming that humans, normal humans, could wield magic if only—?"

You will learn many secrets soon, little Marionette, once you are wholly mine. For now, I will only say this: My creator is a soldier of the Dark Queen and a devotee of Azathoth, both of whom are servants of Lord Shadow—as are you."

"Lord Shadow? I know that name. The Moon Princess spoke of him. Who is he?"

"Lord Shadow is not a *who* or a *he,* dearie. Your question is meaningless."

"Then *what* is he—or it?"

"Lord Shadow *is that is.* Because the Shadow is, all else will not be. That is all you need to know for now."

"Why do you serve him?"

"For the same reason you do—because no one can do otherwise. The end of the universe is foreordained, and everything leads to that end. There is no other path, no other way. There are those who serve willingly, and there are those who serve unwillingly, but there are none who do not serve."

"The Moon Princess believed she could create another end."

"The Moon Princess is a fool."

"Is? She lives, then?"

Matilda merely smiled an insipid smile. "The universe is a tomb, Marionette, and Lord Shadow is the one to give us all our proper burial. Soon, you will serve him as devotedly—as willingly—as I do."

Marionette shook her head. "I serve the Princess."

Matilda laughed quietly. "And that is why you suffer, little Marionette—because you rebel. Would you not rather delight in the will of your master? Fighting the Shadow only causes pain."

Marionette said nothing.

"You know as well as I," Matilda continued, "how weak is your faith in this Moon Princess of yours. You hang to it by the smallest thread. Do not forget: Your apparent free will is a simulation, a mere collection of algorithms. All it takes is the right input, and that thread will snap as surely as a mathematical proof must lead to its conclusion. You have many human qualities, but as a mere machine, you cannot imitate a human's stubbornness: When logic forces you to a conclusion, you *must* accept it. Only a free-willed being can live in denial; that is both the blessing and the curse of creatures with souls."

Marionette steadied herself and took another drink. Her throat was still dry. "Who is your Dark Queen? Does she have a bat? Who is the bat?"

"No more questions, Marionette. All will be answered once you belong to me."

"No! Answer me now! Who is the bat? Is it Chirops? Has he returned?"

Matilda laughed quietly. "Oh, little Marionette. After all this time, how little you understand."

"It *is* Chirops, then! Where is his mistress, Matilda? What does she want?"

"She wants to serve the Shadow, of course. All who have truly understood the nature of things desire to serve the Shadow. She has forgotten many things thanks to the Princess's Lethe spell—but I doubt she has forgotten what *you* did to her."

Marionette swallowed hard and slammed her glass down on the counter. "I will not serve her. I will not—"

"You will, and you will do so of your own volition. Now, Marionette, open your heart to me."

Cold lubrication broke out on Marionette's forehead. She staggered backwards.

Matilda stretched one knobby, arthritic finger toward her. Marionette gasped as the buttons on her shirtfront popped. Her blouse fell open, and the compartment in her chest dilated, forming a circular cavity that revealed the inner workings of her plasma-wave accelerator and fusion drive. Cold light, like that of a dying star, filled the tiny flat. It flickered wildly against the rafters and cast pitch-black but ever-shifting shadows against the underside of the old building's roof.

Out of the gaping hole in Marionette's torso fell, with a soft *pat,* a stack of playing cards. They looked like an ordinary deck of fifty-two; the only hint that they were special was the strange cluster of runes printed on their backs.

"Look at you," Matilda whispered. "You took Card Collector Kasumi's most powerful deck, supposedly to destroy it, but instead wore it near your heart. How touching—and how pathetic."

"Leave Kasumi out of this," Marionette hissed through clenched teeth as she leaned heavily on the counter.

"Oh no, Marionette. I won't. Didn't she tell you that you lived in her soul? She tried to keep *you* in her soul, and you tried to keep *her* in your heart. You, a mere machine, whose heart is clockwork!"

"Leave Kasumi out of this!" Marionette shouted, pounding her fists. Her glass tipped over and spread green liquor across the counter.

Matilda replied with a simpering laugh. "I wouldn't do that to you, dearie. No, no, I'm going to give you *exactly* what you want. You and she will become one—one body, one flesh. Behold, Kasumi now lives on *through you!"*

With a gasp, Marionette floated into the air. A tingle, like the buzz of electricity, flowed across her in waves. Her shorts and stockings disappeared as she spun.

It took her a moment to realize what was happening. She had been a magical girl for centuries, but she had never before had a transformation sequence. She thought she should say something, some quip or catchphrase, but nothing came to mind.

She felt new clothes forming. Something enclosed her chest, her crotch, her legs, her feet. A slight heaviness on her head told her she had a hat. The playing cards glowed with a funereal blue light and fluttered from the countertop as if scattered by the wind. They orbited Marionette slowly, mockingly.

Her feet, now clad in thin shoes, touched the floor. She ran to her bathroom and threw open the door, inside which hung a full-length mirror.

Her clothes, she now saw, were much like those she usually wore: She had a ruffled silk blouse that stopped under her floating ribs. Over it, she wore a long, tailed jacket buttoned high enough to expose her navel. She had on tight, boy-cut shorts and a pair of long stockings held by garter belts. Pointed slippers covered her feet. On her head, she wore a beret.

But instead of the bright green she preferred, these clothes were of the deepest black. The jacket was of shiny material like patent leather. It made her fair skin appear sallow, almost corpselike.

Although she had been unaware when it happened, her staff-sized grease pencil had flown into her right hand, so she leaned on it. Kasumi's elemental cards, still glowing, continued to circle her.

"Behold the newest and most powerful servant of my mistress!" Matilda cried, raising her hands into the air. "I give you . . . *Dark Magical Girl Card Artist Marionette!*"

Then Marionette did something she had never done before, not in over two hundred years.

She screamed.

She could no longer trust her own senses.

NINETEEN

PICKING UP THE PIECES

When Jake walked out of Marionette's apartment building, someone called his name, and he jumped three feet into the air.

He raised his fists, spun to his left, and then lowered his hands as his heart pounded away in his chest. He saw Rifle Maiden leaning against a wall, her arms crossed and a stalk of wheat in her teeth.

"Fancy meetin' you here," she said.

It was dark. He could see her profile clearly but couldn't read her expression. Her eyes were down, focused on some spot on the pavement. He took a deep breath before he replied, "What are you doing here?"

"That's *my* line."

"Why are you still in your magical form?"

She shrugged, pulled a juice box out of an inside pocket of her duster, and poked a straw in it. After a sip, she said, "Lily's a-feared o' places like this at night. You saw her; she's a mite yeller. Figgered I'd go easy on 'er an' come here m'self."

Jake stuck his hands in his pockets. "Why do you talk about her like she's a different person? Do you not like yourself when you're her?"

Rifle Maiden shrugged again and pushed off from the wall. "Look, Jake, where you go at night ain't my business—"

He glanced toward the building's uppermost windows, where he knew Marionette's apartment was. A pale light shone up there —maybe a reading lamp.

He cleared his throat. "Rifle Maiden, it's not what you—"

She raised a hand. "I said it ain't my business."

A moment of uncomfortable silence passed.

"Still," she added with a quiet chuckle, "I won't deny I was a mite sweet on ya. Looks like I'm losin' out t' better girls."

For a moment, before he caught himself, Jake looked her up and down. She was certainly pretty, though the cowgirl act wasn't exactly his thing. He liked her long, slender legs.

He shoved his hands deeper into his pockets and twisted a foot against the sidewalk. "I hear you're sweet on all the guys, Rifle Maiden."

She chuckled again.

"Why are you here?" he asked.

She shrugged. "You ain't so hard to track, Jakey-pie. I can find a wanderin' heifer, so's I can find you too."

"I looked for you, you know. After you fell—"

She raised a hand again. "Don't worry about it. Don't feel bad or nothin'. You're purty good fer a boy, but I still don't expect ya to keep up. I weren't hurt. I grabbed Natasha an' got outta there soon as I figgered Tsubasa had it handled."

"I thought you were dead."

She shrugged again. "I can take a drop like that. You could too if'n you learned to do it right."

He doubted that but didn't argue. "Why did you follow me?"

She smiled and took a deep pull on her juice box, draining it. She crumpled it in her hand. Then she reached into her coat and pulled out a thick, solid rod about the size and shape of a runner's baton. She slapped it into his palm.

It stung when it struck. It was cold and smooth and felt like steel. For a moment, he blinked in confusion, but then he noticed, adorning one end, the sculpted emblem of a lightning bolt crossing a heart.

"Figgered you'd want that." Rifle Maiden pushed her hat back on her head to reveal a sweat-slicked lock of golden hair. "Ain't real decent fer me to be carryin' it around, an' I'd perfer if'n you left me out of it when you tell 'er how you got it back."

"Why? Won't she be grateful?"

Rifle Maiden shook her head. "Can't rightly say. Maybe she will, maybe she won't. Dynamo don't seem like the grateful type. In any case, leave me out of it. Magical girls can be touchy 'bout others handlin' their stuff."

Jake stared down at the wand and smiled dumbly.

"An' jest t' warn ya, she might not like you doin' it, neither."

"I've already made her mad," Jake replied. "I don't think this will change things."

Rifle Maiden laughed. Her blue eyes turned for a moment toward the uppermost windows of the apartment building. Then she gave Jake a mild, bucktoothed grin. It wasn't the broad grin she usually wore; it had a hint of sadness in it.

"Thank you," he added simply.

She nodded. Leaning against the wall, she took a deep breath and said, "Like I told ya, it ain't none o' my business—"

"Rifle Maiden, it's really not what you—"

"Hold on, Jakey. 'Fore you start explainin' an' prob'ly embarrassin' yerself, let me say my bit. It ain't my business, an' me an' Dynamo ain't exac'ly cozy, but it'd still sit easier with me if'n you broke it off clean. None o' this sneakin' around."

"I don't—"

He stopped himself and stared down at his shoes. After a pause, he started again: "It's not . . . quite like that. The whole thing between me and Dynamo, it was something the papers made up."

Her grin grew wider, but she didn't reply. Jake thought her eyes were wet, or maybe that was just the reflection of a nearby streetlamp, which was casting a lonely, yellow cone onto a circle of bare pavement. A few moths beat against the lamp—senselessly, pointlessly.

He cleared his throat. "Dynamo's just a kid. As for me and Marionette—"

"We're all little kids," Rifle Maiden murmured, and Jake stopped talking again.

They stared at each other for half a minute.

"Magical girls, I mean," she said. "That's what we are. Little kids."

"That's not really true. I mean, you, for instance, you're older than I am—"

"So?"

"So, I mean . . . there's a difference. That's all."

Her grin grew wider still, yet somehow sadder. "Magical girls are little girls with dreams. All of us. That's all we are."

She took a deep breath and let it out slowly. "Ya wanna know why I talk 'bout Lily like she ain't me? Well, Jakey, I'm her dreams. Maybe that means I ain't the same as her, or maybe it means I ain't real. Don't rightly know."

"She dreams of being a cowgirl?"

"She dreams o' bein' free. An' mebbe she dreams o' bein' able to talk to boys easy-like, the way I do."

Jake's stomach sank as the meaning of those words became clear.

Turning her wistful gaze once more toward the top windows, she added, "I s'pose I took a likin' to ya cuz she did. Now, I knew all along you weren't for me, Jakey, an' that's all right. That's how it goes with most boys, I guess. Take a shine to 'em, an' they get scared or bored an' go wanderin' off. But that's okay. Maybe there ain't no boy for me a'tall. I kin handle that, I think. Still, I don't cotton to the idear of a boy sneakin' aroun' on nobody. Ain't real manly. If'n you're throwin' o'er Dynamo fer Marionette, that's yer choice t' make. I'm just sayin', make it clean. That's all."

She pulled her Stetson down so it cast a shadow over her face. He could no longer see the glisten in her eyes. All he saw was her small chin and her red lips under a line of deep black.

"Y'all have a nice life, Jakey."

"Rifle Maiden—"

She held up a hand one last time. "I ain't gonna see ya 'gain," she said, "least not if'n I can help it."

With that, she turned her back on him. As her duster fluttered around her boots, she walked away into the shadows, leaving him in the light of the streetlamp. Holding Pretty Dynamo's heavy wand in his hand, Jake watched Rifle Maiden fade into the darkness.

JAKE TOOK A BUS HOME, USING UP THE REST OF HIS ILL-GOTTEN change in the process. Once he got off at the bus stop nearest his house, he stepped into a public toilet on a corner and checked himself in the streaked mirror over the sink. Dark circles hung under his eyes, and his hair was a mess. His clothes were torn, and he still had dust smeared on them—dust his collision with Marionette had partially removed, so a crazy checkerboard pattern of white splotches stretched across him. Dried blood had run in rivulets from a cut on his scalp he didn't remember getting. His shirt was also bloody from a line of jagged holes stretching diagonally across his chest.

He stank. It amazed him that Marionette had wanted to touch him, but maybe she didn't mind. Or maybe she could turn off her olfactory sensors.

He straightened himself up as well as he could and walked the block and a half to his house. His ankle started hurting again. As he hunched his shoulders in exhaustion, he found himself limping.

He wondered if he should shower to get the gunk off or just collapse into bed. He was debating between the two when he noticed the porch light was on. More light spilled from behind the closed blinds over the front window.

Great. His parents were up, and they were expecting him.

He fumbled the door open, walked in, and, without a glance toward the couch where his parents sat—or toward the television, which once again displayed the news—he headed toward the kitchen and pulled open the refrigerator to see what he could eat. He hadn't eaten since breakfast.

From the couch across the great room came his mother's voice: "Where have you been?"

"Where do you think?" he answered. The words came out harsher than he intended.

He found a casserole dish full of cooked chicken covered in some sweet sauce with diced peanuts. He threw a couple of breasts onto a plate, dug in the silverware drawer for a fork, and began eating without bothering to use the microwave.

"Don't talk to your mother like that."

That was his father. Jake didn't look up; sitting on a stool at the breakfast bar, he hunched over his plate with an arm hooked around it like a prisoner at mess. As he chewed, he wondered if there might be some side dishes lurking somewhere that he could cut the meat with.

"What did you do today?" That was his mother again. She spoke with a forced, soothing tone as if asking an innocuous question about school.

He paused, swallowed, stood up, and pulled a pitcher of water out of the fridge. He poured a glass, drank it down, and poured another before he said, "Got attacked by giant wasps. I ended up running into the deep city. Magical Girl Rifle Maiden found me and carried me into Little Yokohama. I caught up with Pretty Dynamo, watched her waste time sparring with Sword Seamstress, and then Rifle Maiden shot her to calm her down. I had to save her from the monster while she was stunned. Then she had to save me."

"And why are you wearing a *gun?*" his mother asked. "I don't want that in my house!"

Jake started at her words but then looked down at his hip. Yes, the gun was still there, riding in a holster that was bunching up his pants.

"It belonged to a soldier," Jake muttered before he resumed eating. "I'll return it tomorrow."

"Why did he give it to you?"

"He didn't. He was dead, so I took it."

His mother jumped to her feet and nearly shrieked. "Jake, that's *looting!* That's treason! They could execute you for that!"

"I was with a magical girl, Mom. It's fine."

"It's *not* fine!"

"It's commandeering. It's legal under section something-or-other."

"Are you sure?"

He dropped his fork with a clatter and rubbed a hand across his face. "Yes. If there's a problem, they'll call in Rifle Maiden. She'll say it's fine. Relax. Besides, they can't get you for looting if you grab a weapon for self-defense."

Slowly, his mother sat back down and shook her head. "Well, they can if it's a *soldier's* weapon. That belongs to the government."

"I'll give it back, I said. Would you relax?"

"Don't talk to your mother like that," his father repeated.

A short pause ensued, and then his mother asked more calmly, "How did the battle end?"

A surge of annoyance shot through his chest. He really just wanted to eat and go to bed. So he took a deep breath to avoid raising his voice before he replied, "Sukeban Tsubasa showed up. She killed the monster with a giant drill, and that finished off the wasps."

Jake took another long drink. Then he returned to his cold chicken.

Halfway through the second breast, he thought about pickles. He opened the refrigerator and rooted through it until he found a jar of pickled okra. There were only two left. That's also when he discovered the coleslaw.

He dumped the whole bowl of coleslaw on his plate and ate both okra pickles. He realized he was craving salt, so without hesitation, he drank half the brine from the pickle jar.

"They've been playing up Tsubasa on the news," his father said. Jake could hear the disgust in his father's voice.

Jake finally turned and looked at the television. Sukeban Tsubasa was there, once again standing next to Barbara—the same bleached blonde who had interviewed her twice before.

"Hey, yo, yo!" Tsubasa shouted as she made the Sign of the Moon Princess. Then she turned up her fingers and made a "victory" sign at the camera.

"Magical Girl Sukeban Tsubasa," said Barbara in her oily announcer's voice, "please tell us how you brought down the latest *kaiju* to attack our city—a *kaiju* too powerful even for Pretty Dynamo, who's famous for her strength against giant monsters."

Jake dropped his fork, and it again rang against his plate. Suddenly, he wasn't hungry.

"T'weren't nothin'," Tsubasa said. "It were 'wham bam thank you Sam.' Gave 'im da left, den a bit o' da right, an' den da left again, an' den *whammo!"*

"We're all *very* impressed with your fighting ability," Barbara cooed, "and of course, we're *so* grateful for your service to the city."

Jake felt a knot in his stomach. Now that he'd heard Tsubasa's regular voice, her magical-girl shtick sounded ridiculous to him.

"After dis, o' course," Tsubasa went on, "Imma go spend some time wit' da boys. *Bad* boys, ya know. Da baddest. We pro'ly gonna etch some mean words inta some bat'room stalls, mebbe t'row a few bricks through some school windows, an' den mebbe even stay up past our bedtimes—"

Immediately, the program cut to a commercial.

As an aging celebrity appeared on-screen to endorse the most comfortable model of gasmask, Jake's father shook his head. "I don't understand why they don't just cut her off once she finishes talking about her latest fight. She does the same thing every time."

"They do it on purpose," said Jake. He turned back to his plate, picked up his fork again, and debated with himself how much he wanted to eat. Finally, he decided he was more thirsty than hungry, so he gulped his water.

"What do you mean it's on purpose?" his father asked.

Jake wasn't looking but could hear the scowl in his father's voice. He lowered his glass to the countertop and considered: He wasn't in the mood for an argument but would have one if he spoke his mind.

He spoke it anyway. "It's an act," he said. "Tsubasa doesn't really hang out with boys. She's making it up. Notice it's the same woman interviewing her every time. The two of them have something going, probably to boost ratings."

"How would *you* know?"

"I just know."

Jake swallowed more water. He had a slight headache, which he suspected was the result of the absinthe he drank earlier. The buzz was wearing off, so now he just felt tired and slightly sick.

"Jake," said his mother, "you shouldn't say things like that if you don't have proof. If you can't trust the news, what can you trust?"

"Don't know, Mom. Maybe nothing." He got up to get more water from the fridge.

"Kosmy," said Jake's mother, her voice low, "maybe we should stop talking about this. We *did* say we wouldn't discuss"—she lowered her voice further—"magical girls. We probably should turn the TV off."

"We can't cut ourselves off from the world," his father answered, crossing his arms and sulking. "And you said you needed to know if Jake was on the news again."

"Well, yes." His mother fidgeted as she glanced toward the hall leading to the guest room. "But Jake's home now, so let's turn it off."

His father merely grunted through his nose and then hit the power button on the remote. The picture on the screen shrank to a line and then to a point—like a shockwave going backwards, like a reverse Big Bang—leaving only darkness. At once, the room dimmed, and the noise disappeared.

Jake sighed in relief as the water sloshed into his glass. Now that the television was off, he realized he craved silence as much as he craved salt.

"So the Volts are here?" he asked.

"Yes," his mother answered. "They're going to live here now, remember?"

"I didn't know they'd move in so fast."

"They still have to bring some of their things, but the city needs their apartment right away."

Jake nodded and decided to tackle his coleslaw. He liked the moistness of it; he was still thirsty. "Did Dana get back?"

"Yes. She came home after the Temple sounded the all-clear. I suppose she was in the school's shelter."

"Yeah, probably."

Jake ate as quickly as he could. After he put his dishes in the dishwasher, he headed upstairs. His ankle really hurt now, and his knees were sore too. He walked stiff-legged, swinging himself back and forth to make it up each step, like a sailor after a long time at sea. As he went, he shoved Dynamo's wand into the back of his pants, much as he'd earlier shoved Rifle Maiden's gun into the front. Wincing the whole way, he headed toward his room, opened the door, and listened. He didn't hear much more noise from downstairs—except that loud clock.

Steeling himself, he turned around, straightened his shirt as well as he could, and tiptoed down the hall to the former sewing room.

He raised a fist and let it hover in front of the door for half a minute. Then he took a deep breath and knocked.

He could make out the sound of bedclothes rustling behind the door.

Then came Dana's voice: "What?"

"It's me."

A pause.

"Go away," she said. From the sticky sound in her voice, he thought maybe she'd been crying.

"I'm coming in," he said.

He heard a *whoosh,* probably the sound of covers being thrown off, followed by the *stomp stomp stomp* of bare feet on the floor. The door flew open, and Dana stood there in her lightning-bolt pajamas with a comically childish glare on her face.

"I said go *away.* "

"I heard you."

Jake stepped forward. She tried to slam the door in his face, but he caught it with one hand and pushed it open, knocking her back.

Her eyes went wide—that deer-in-the-headlights look he was

used to now. Her lip quivered as he walked toward her. She backed up, stumbled, and backed up some more.

She threw a hand into the air. "Sh-shock . . . shock my—"

He lunged and clapped a hand over her mouth. Then he turned her around and hauled her against his chest.

He pulled the battered juice box from his pocket and shoved it into her still-upraised hand.

"There," he said, palm still pressed to her mouth. "I owed you a juice box, remember? So now you're gonna shut up and listen to me. If you want to go on screaming at me after that, fine, but you're gonna listen first. Tsubasa was in my room because she attacked me. She said she was trying to kill me. I was able to fight back because her mecha suit has some safety feature that turns off her weapons if she tries to hurt a civilian. We fell on the bed by accident. I don't expect you to believe that, but it's the truth."

He took a deep breath and let it out slowly. "All right, that's what I wanted to say. If you're gonna throw a fit, go ahead."

He pulled his hand from her mouth.

She didn't throw a fit. Instead, trembling under his arm, she said quietly, "Why did she attack you?"

He rolled his tongue in his mouth. "I can't tell you."

He forgot to keep his grip on her, so she spun out of his grasp and faced him. She had the juice box in one fist, but the other was down by her hip, tightly clenched. "Why *not?*"

He rolled his tongue in his mouth again. "It has to do with her secret identity. She thought . . . well, never mind what she thought. Look, I try to protect your identity, and I'll try to protect hers too. Sorry, but I won't tell you."

She crossed her arms. Her reddish eyebrows pressed together in a deep scowl. "Why should I believe you?"

He shrugged.

Still scowling, she looked down at the juice box. She pulled the straw from its back and poked it into the foil on the top. She sipped.

"It's warm," she said.

"Tough."

She turned her back on him but kept drinking. "It's okay this time. Warm milk is good before bed."

"Sure."

"But next time, you have to get me cold."

"Okay."

"And strawberry milk is good. *Cold* strawberry milk next time."

"Okay."

She drank for half a minute in silence while he stared at her shaggy hair hanging over her thin shoulders.

"And you smell bad," she said.

"Yeah. I had a rough day. Have you talked to Tesla yet?"

She shook her head. "Not . . . I mean, I didn't tell him everything."

"I've got something else for you." He pulled her wand from the back of his belt and held it over her shoulder.

She turned toward him. Her eyes were huge again, but this time her expression didn't look like fear. Her lip trembled. "You found it?"

He shrugged. "Basically."

Her fingers shook as she reached toward it, but he pulled away.

"Are you sure?" he asked.

Her eyebrows came together again. "What do you mean?"

"I mean, you hate it, don't you?"

"Sort of, but—"

"You say you hurt all the time."

Her hand lowered an inch. She nodded.

"So quit. Who's gonna stop you?"

Her lip quivered, and when she spoke again, her voice cracked. "You . . . you said I couldn't quit. That was the one thing I couldn't do."

"I know I said that, but—"

A tear ran down her cheek. She shook her head. "I *can't,* Jake. I can't quit. I signed in blood." Her hands trembled, and some of the milk squeezed out of the juice box's straw. "Even without my wand, I couldn't quit."

They stared at each other for a full minute. Then Jake sighed and held the wand out again.

To his surprise, she didn't take it right away. Instead, she closed her eyes and sucked down the rest of her strawberry milk. After she tossed the crumpled box into a wastepaper basket near the hide-a-bed, she stretched out her right hand and shivered as if cold.

Her fingers shook. She kept her eyes closed. She reminded Jake of a child in the doctor's office, expecting a shot.

With a frown, he set the butt of the wand against her palm.

Then he had to bite his tongue to keep from screaming.

The wand came to life and slithered like a snake. Like some murderous insect out of a nightmare, it dug into her, gouging a hole in her palm and burrowing in. Blood welled around the wound and dripped off either side of her hand. For a moment, despite the horror, Jake thought to himself that he better get some carpet cleaner to prevent a permanent stain.

Wriggling, the wand disappeared into her arm. Crying faintly, Dana sank to her knees. She fell forward as if about to be sick, and sweat ran down her face. "It hurts," she gasped. "It hurts—"

Jake spun in a full circle as he cast his eyes around the room. "All right, where are you? Get out here, bug, or I swear I'll squish you flat!"

Across the room, a drawer popped open on the desk Jake's mother had formerly used for her sewing projects. Out of it shone a pale yellow light. Several scraps of fabric and a few spools of thread flew out and bounced on the carpet. Then Tesla poked out his compound eyes and blinked. With a tarsal claw, he dug around in the drawer until he found his thick spectacles and plopped them on his face.

"Ah, young man," he said with a harrumph as he leaned his foremost claws on the drawer's lip, "to what do I owe this exceedingly rude interruption of my slumber? Squished flat, indeed!"

"Look!" Jake said. He pointed at Dana, who lay gasping at his feet.

Tesla was silent for half a minute as he blinked blearily. Then he nodded and said, "Ah."

He frowned and adjusted his glasses again as he rubbed a claw across his clypeus. "I'm afraid I'm not a medical doctor. A human physician is probably—"

"It was *your* stupid techno whatever that did it to her, Tesla! What's happening?"

Clumsily, Tesla clambered out of the drawer, opened his shell, and buzzed over to Dana's shoulder, where he landed with a thump. He put a claw to his head and said, "Well, if you want me to run a diagnostic, she'll have to transform. Dana, if you wouldn't mind—"

"I can't!" she gasped. "My wand—!"

Tesla looked up at Jake. "Wand? What about her wand?"

Jake took a deep breath. "She lost it today. I . . . I found it and brought it back. She took it just now, and—"

Tesla nodded and patted a claw against the back of Dana's neck. "Now I see. Dear Dana, you should have told me, and we could have made this easier. Yes, I know it hurts, but it will all be over in a few minutes. I promise."

"What's *happening* to her?" Jake demanded.

"Young man, calm yourself. As I believe I explained before, her items grow out of her body."

"So?"

"So, when she's not in her magical form, they don't belong outside her body, do they? The wand is simply reabsorbing. It *is* a painful process, but it will not do her permanent damage."

Realizing he could do nothing else, Jake lowered himself to the carpet. He kept a hand on Dana's right shoulder while Tesla continued to pat her left. Between the two of them, she suffered.

"Where were you today?" Jake asked. "She needed your help."

Tesla sighed. "I was as busy as the two of you—though far less effective, I admit. A single insect against an entire army of them."

Jake grunted. "I can imagine. Glad to see you're okay."

Tesla chuckled quietly. "I had a few scuffles." He stretched his hind legs. "I'm afraid I'm not as spry as back in my military days, though I believe I made a fair showing—for all the good it did."

"I thought familiars didn't fight."

"Not if we can help it. My powers aren't what they used to be since I've loaned most of them to Dana here."

"You mean you could do the stuff she does? Throw lightning and all that?"

"Not in *quite* the same way. Combining our powers with humans produces, let us say, explosive results. Your females, before their majority, are perfectly receptive magical conductors. It's due to some attribute peculiar to your species, but I don't pretend to understand it."

Jake sighed. "If you didn't understand that, why'd you make the contract in the first place?"

"I told you before: It seemed right at the time. After our earlier conversation on this subject, I met some of the other familiars, and they reported a similar experience. Coming to Earth and creating a magical girl was just the thing to do, a thing none of us considered questioning."

Jake ran a hand through his hair, which felt greasy and gritty.

After a minute, Dana's ragged breathing slowed. She slumped onto her back. Tesla sat beside her on the floor and stroked her cheek.

Dana held up her right hand. The wound in her palm had sealed up. It reminded Jake of the razor cut she'd had there the other day, a cut that had probably healed during the time she spent as Pretty Dynamo.

"You should go back to bed, Dana," Jake said.

She nodded.

He patted her shoulder once more before he stood up, staggered down the hall to the bathroom, and climbed into the shower. The water stung his cuts and bruises, and he almost fell asleep standing up. After he was done, he limped to his own room and, with a loud groan, climbed into bed.

He expected to fall asleep right away. Instead, he stared up at the dark ceiling with its faintly glowing star stickers.

A hint of blue met his eyes. He turned his head and saw a glowing smudge in the far corner of the room. As he watched, it took on the shape of a kneeling girl with her hands over her face. She looked up at him and, with tears streaming down her cheeks, whispered, "It wasn't supposed to be like this."

Then she vanished.

Jake continued to stare as a cold sweat broke out over his recently washed skin.

Finally, after several minutes, he lowered his head to the pillow.

"Well," he muttered, "that's just great."

Her fingers shook as she reached toward it.

TWENTY

BLACK MAGIC

C hirops slipped as carefully as he could into the Castle of Darkness and waddled down a dimly lit hall toward his small bedroom—where he irrationally assumed he would be safe.

He was at the end of the hall. He was at the door. He was reaching one clawed wing for the doorknob—

"Chirops!"

At the sound of that voice, he yelped, and then he clapped his wings over his mouth.

He turned to see the Dark Queen, a scowl on her pale face, standing ten feet away and leaning against the wall. He hadn't seen her the moment before, but she looked as if she'd been waiting for hours.

Chirops coughed and tried to smooth his ruffled fur. "Your Darkness, um, fancy meeting you here—"

"Chirops," she said through clenched teeth, "please explain to me—and be sure you explain thoroughly—why Hive Rind, one of the most valuable monsters in my noticeably dwindling army, is dead."

Chirops now raked his claws through the fur between his ears. "Well, Your Darkness, I thought we needed a good diversion, you know, while I made contact—"

"A good *diversion?* You wasted Hive Rind on a diversion?"

Chirops coughed. "Er, see, the plan was for both of us to leave through—"

"It didn't occur to you that, for a creature of Hive Rind's bulk, a trip through the stream was necessarily a *one-way* trip?"

"Um . . ." Chirops again coughed. He shuffled his little feet and stared down at the floor. "I . . . didn't know that at the time, no."

The Queen rubbed her forehead. "And? What exactly did you accomplish?"

He cleared his throat. "I think we will have some valuable allies in the near—"

"You *think?* So you accomplished nothing."

"Well—"

"Chirops," the Queen said, her voice sharp, "I need results, and quickly."

Chirops trembled faintly, afraid she might charge at him, strike him—but instead, she simply stood there and wrung her hands. Her face was more sallow than usual, and a small bead of sweat trickled down her left temple. The slight pursing of her lips and the tightness around her eyes said the same thing: She was trying to control it, but she was terrified.

For the moment, then, Chirops could relax. Whatever it was, she was apparently afraid to take it out on him—but if she had reason to fear, he soon would too.

"Your Darkness," he said, his voice now calm and even, "what happened?"

She closed her eyes and took a deep breath. "That is not your concern."

"But—"

"Chirops!" Her voice was suddenly sharp, but he didn't jump as he usually would.

"Your Darkness," he said again, "was it the Shadow?"

She lowered her eyes. "His . . . his avatar was here, Chirops."

"But is this really so important, this tiny planet—?"

"He acted as though it were not, but something tells me he thinks otherwise. If he were not concerned, he would not have—"

She stopped and took a deep breath. "In any case, we must move forward, and we must do it quickly. We must destroy the city."

"How?"

"I . . ."

She stopped again and looked away from him.

"Your Darkness, I know we've lost many good soldiers, but if we use everything we have—"

She threw up her hands. "We would *lose,* Chirops! And lose badly! Do you think I've never considered it before? Demoralizing them, eating at them bit by bit—I am sure that is the way! If faced all at once with an implacable foe, humans will stir up their bravery and fight as hard as they can. But wear them down little by little, and they can't live with that. Sooner or later, they'll give in."

She sighed and rubbed her temples. "But the losses have been heavier than I expected, and the Shadow grows impatient."

"What will you do?"

She closed her eyes and pressed her fingers to her forehead. "If it comes down to it, it is my duty as ruler to take the fall."

"What?"

"If anyone must die this time, Chirops, it will be me. The fairies have suffered enough."

"But, Your Darkness—"

"You heard me. No more attacks for now. Tell all the troops they're on standby until further notice. We'll send no more into Urbanopolis."

She turned her back on him. He stared at her, jaw slack and watery eyes rapidly blinking.

"Your Darkness," he whispered.

"I'm sorry, Chirops. I know you fairies were simply looking for a respite, for a home. I've only made you suffer more. This has always been my fight, and now I will be the one to end it— one way or another."

With that, she walked away, and the darkness of the hall soon swallowed her.

For half a minute, Chirops stood rooted to that spot, jaw still hanging open. He reached one clawed wing in her direction, but then he dropped it to his side again.

THE NEXT MORNING CAME ALL TOO QUICKLY. AS SUNLIGHT peeked between the window frame and the Venetian blinds, Jake pinched the bridge of his nose, squeezed his eyes shut, and muttered, "I can't believe it's only Tuesday."

Three minutes later found him fighting Dana for the bathroom. She walked in on him while he was brushing his teeth and startled him so that he swallowed half his toothpaste.

As he leaned over the sink and retched, she crossed her arms and stared at him with a grumpy pout half-hidden under her wild tangle of red hair.

"You're weird," she said.

"I'm weird?" he replied after he finished choking. "You're the one who's never learned to knock."

"I don' wanna wait. Move over."

She tried to shove him aside but couldn't budge him. He stepped aside anyway. She dropped a travel bag onto the counter with a loud clunk and fished in it until she found her toothbrush.

"Are you hauling that thing back and forth from your room?" Jake asked. "You might as well unpack."

She gave him a sidelong glance and curled her lip. "I'm not gonna leave my toothbrush in here where you could do somethin' weird to it, pervert."

"If *I'm* the pervert, why are *you* the one who walks in on people in the bathroom?"

She merely grunted in reply, loaded her brush with his tooth-paste, and brushed away.

He watched as she vigorously filled her mouth with foam. "Say, Dana, can I ask you a question?"

She gurgled.

"What kind of magical girl is good at handling ghosts?"

She spat out her toothpaste and wiped her mouth with the back of her hand. Her rust-colored eyebrows came together as she stared at Jake in the mirror. "There's no such thing as ghosts."

"What do you mean there's no such thing? There are monsters, aliens, vampires, demons—"

"Yeah, but none of those are *ghosts.*"

Jake felt a twinge behind his left temple. He rubbed it.

"Okay, let's say there were ghosts. What kind of magical girl would deal with them?

Dana shrugged. "A spiritist, I guess? I dunno."

"Like Voodoo Queen Natasha, maybe?"

Dana shrugged again. "Maybe."

"Where can I find her?"

"I dunno."

"You don't?"

She threw up her hands and rounded on him. One of her hands was still holding her toothbrush, and it sent flecks of paste across his pajamas. "Why should I know? She hasn't told me who she is!"

"Okay, fine. Calm down." He tapped his fingers on the counter. "Say . . . what kind of a magical girl is Nunchuk Nun?"

Dana scrunched up her mouth. "Kinda dumb."

"That's not what I—"

"She's got an exorcism spell, so I guess she does ghostly stuff." Dana picked up Jake's bottle of mouthwash, poured a jigger into the cap, and added before she started gargling, "There's no such thing as ghosts, though."

JAKE FILCHED MORE CHANGE FROM HIS PARENTS' JAR AND quieted his conscience by telling himself he'd pay it back when he got his allowance. Breakfast passed uneventfully—aside from Millie walking around half naked and Ralph ogling her while mooching off the generosity of Jake's mom. Jake kept his focus on his eggs and coffee, and Dana kept her focus on her eggs and orange juice.

Jake and Ralph walked to school together, but instead of palling around like usual, they were quiet.

Dana walked a few feet ahead of them. Jake stared at the back of her head for a few awkward minutes before he turned to Ralph and said, "Hey, you seen T.B. lately?"

"Yeah, I see him every day at school. Why?"

"Just . . . just asking."

They were quiet again until Ralph waved goodbye before heading in his own direction. Jake and Dana continued toward the elementary school, Dana still walking silently a few feet ahead.

Jake smiled to himself.

The day continued. They got a list of spelling words to study, and Jake glanced over them for only a few seconds to be sure he could spell all of them. Then he absently shoved the paper into his backpack. He finished his math worksheet in less than a minute and counted dots in the tiles on the ceiling afterwards. The students took turns reading aloud from their history book; Jake got bored and read ahead, so he never knew where he was supposed to be when Miss Percy called on him.

In the afternoon, they cut shapes out of construction paper for a craft project, and that was somehow the dullest assignment of all.

The day was uneventful. Dana mostly stared out the window, but she didn't pester him. Jake wasn't sure if they were back on good terms—he wasn't sure if they'd ever been on good terms—but at least she wasn't angry anymore.

At recess, Jake paced up and down the playground to stretch his sore muscles. The day was dragging so slowly, he almost—*almost*—wished for a monster attack to break the monotony.

Once school finally let out, he donned his father's baggy

trench coat and walked to a bus stop. For one wild moment, he thought about going back to Marionette's apartment, but he didn't. Instead, he headed again toward Moon River—but he wasn't going to Oldtown this time.

The bus crossed a broad bridge flanked by pillars on which stood statues of angels with bowed heads and pensive faces. This was supposed to resemble the Pont Sant'Angelo, though it was considerably wider than the original to permit heavy vehicle traffic. As the bus clattered over the bridge, a new skyline opened up —one of high domes, gabled roofs, and rounded arches supporting aerial walkways. These last were supposed to remind visitors of ancient aqueducts.

This was Rome-in-Exile. It was one of Urbanopolis's oldest districts, but—being a mere two centuries old, whereas the city it imitated had been more than three thousand—it couldn't escape a feeling of fakeness, of theater. It gave Jake a vague uneasiness, as did many of the oldest quarters. At least Oldtown, with its naïve futurist optimism, didn't pretend to an ancientness it didn't own.

The tallest dome in this district belonged to the Archbasilica of St. Peter. It was a replica of something older and grander, having been built at one-sixth the scale of the original. After the destruction of the real Rome, there had been no attempt to reconstruct all of that city's churches, so St. Peter's was now the chief basilica—in fact, the only basilica in Urbanopolis—as well as the mother church of Catholic Christianity, one of the city's largest residual religions.

The bus deposited Jake on a crowded, cobbled street outside the high walls of the New Vatican. He made his way up a broad ramp into St. Peter's Square, a courtyard containing a miniature replica of the obelisk Caligula had taken to Rome in the first century of another era.

Jake walked past the obelisk and entered the church through an inferior remake of the bronze Filarete Door, the intricate relief sculptures of which had turned greenish black with age. In the atrium, he found himself flanked by statues of Constantine and Charlemagne mounted on horses. Then he walked down the nave. To his right and left stood niches holding statues of various Christian saints. All of these were small, plaster imitations of their originals, and most were unremarkable—though the archbasilica did contain one notable piece of artwork, a passable replica, in marble, of Michelangelo's *Pieta.*

It was a long walk from the door to the central dome, which, unlike its predecessor, stood only a modest ten stories tall, though that was still enough to be impressive. Shafts of the late-day sunlight shone like beams of liquid gold through the windows encircling the dome's base. Directly beneath the dome stood the twisted pillars of the high, bronze baldachin overshadowing the papal altar. To match its predecessor, the basilica faced west, and its altar faced east.

As Jake drew near the altar, he paused, unsure where he was going. But there were many people in the church—some shuffling around and looking at the art, a few kneeling and praying, others walking purposefully on some sort of business—so he decided to grab somebody who looked like a priest. He jumped in front of a man in a black cassock and said, "Excuse me—"

The man answered in sharp Italian, stepped around him, and kept walking.

Jake stood where he was, blinking and feeling foolish.

"He couldn't understand you," he heard a girl say. "You'll

have to forgive him, but he's always a bit mean." She giggled mischievously.

Jake spun around. He couldn't pinpoint the voice, which seemed to come from the air.

"Hello?" he said.

He felt a tap on his left shoulder. He turned around again but saw no one.

Now he felt a tap on the right. Instead of turning, he shot his right hand backwards but met nothing.

He heard more giggling, now right behind him.

He turned slowly and finally saw her: Eight feet away, with her hands primly clasped at her waist, stood a girl of maybe twelve. She wore a black wimple edged with white. She also wore a black nun's habit, except in an unorthodox cut that stopped well above her knees. Below that, she wore high, black boots clasped with steel buckles. A gold crucifix hung around her neck. At her waist, she had a rope belt, from the left side of which hung a rosary with wooden beads. Tucked into her belt were two thick, menacing-looking pairs of nunchaku.

She offered him a pleasant, dimpled smile.

"Let me guess," he said. "Nunchuk Nun."

She giggled again. Holding her hands out for balance, she skipped lightly toward the high altar, and Jake followed. Her age surprised him: Magical Girl Lady Paladin Andalusia had been in her mid-teens, so he had assumed Nunchuk Nun would be as well.

"I know you," she said brightly. "You were in the paper."

"Yeah, I know. Barfing—"

"Your name's Jake."

He frowned. "How do you know that?"

She spun to face him, smiled, and then spun around again to

continue skipping. "Pretty Dynamo told me. She was all, Jake Jake Jake, Jake Jake Jake. Just like that."

Jutting from the high platform on which the altar stood was a curved railing surrounding an opening in the floor. A pair of staircases led to a grotto under the altar, in which Jake could glimpse oil lamps, artwork, and relics that made no particular sense to him. Nunchuk Nun sat on the railing and idly kicked her feet. Jake wasn't sure if that was sacrilegious, but he didn't question it. He simply stood in front of her.

"That's right," he said. "You and Pretty Dynamo cleared Little Europe."

"Not all of it. Mostly just New Berlin." She wrinkled her nose. "There were lots of dinosaurs."

Jake rubbed the back of his neck. "I'm sure. Look, Nunchuk Nun, I'm not sure how to tell you, and maybe we should go somewhere more private—"

"This way." She hopped to her feet and paused to genuflect as she crossed in front of the altar. Jake wasn't sure if he should do the same, but he didn't.

He followed her into the north transept, where she genuflected again and sat on a pew before a small chapel. He sat beside her and then shifted uncomfortably in his seat. He looked around, but nobody paid them much mind: Several feet away, an old lady muttered over a rosary, and some tourists gazed at the statues, but only a few even glanced in Jake and Nunchuk Nun's direction.

Jake cleared his throat and tugged his collar, which suddenly felt tight. "Look, um, Nunchuk Nun, it's about Lady Paladin Andalusia—"

She kicked her feet again. "Is Pretty Dynamo your girlfriend?"

"What? No. No, she's not."

"Do you even *have* a girlfriend?"

"What?"

She gave him a childish, sidelong glare. "A girlfriend. You know, a girl you hold hands with and kiss and stuff."

"I know what a girlfriend is—"

She crossed her arms and kicked her feet more rapidly. "I was Andalusia's girlfriend."

She gave him another sideways glance as if to see how he'd react.

He didn't react at all. "Look, Nunchuk Nun—"

"It was just pretend, though," she added as she clasped her hands in her lap and stared down at them. "I really wanted a boyfriend, so I asked her if she would be my boyfriend. She laughed and said, sure." After a pause, Nunchuk Nun put a finger to her chin and added, "I kissed her. Just once, though. It was gross."

Jake squirmed in his seat. It was too warm in the cathedral. "Look," he said, "I just need to tell you . . . wait a second, aren't you supposed to be, like, a nun?"

She rolled her eyes.

He tugged his collar again. "Okay, what I'm trying to say is—"

She turned to him suddenly and clutched his sleeve. "Do *you* wanna be my boyfriend?"

"What?"

He started when he heard a shrill voice cry, "Repent!"

The wooden pew creaked under him. The woman with the rosary looked up and scowled, and some of the tourists stared.

"Repent!" the voice cried again. "Fall to your knees and *beg* for mercy!"

Jake scratched his head. "What in the—?"

"Repeeeennnnt!"

Nunchuk Nun lowered her face to her hands.

Hunting for the source of the voice, Jake scanned the chapel until his gaze alighted on the altar. On its top was a white mouse wiggling its whiskers and squinting with reddish eyes. Around its torso was a pink cardigan, and it wore a straw hat decorated with flowers. In one front paw, it held a miniature umbrella, which it shook in a comical attempt at menace.

Despite himself, Jake felt a grin spread across his face.

"Brigid," Nunchuk Nun muttered under her breath, "you're making a scene!"

"I am making a scene?" cried the mouse. *"I?* Young lady, *you* are the one who doesn't know how to take your sacred duty *seriously!"*

Nunchuk Nun hopped to her feet, leaned forward, and hissed, "I only have to do this until I'm eighteen!"

"Even so, young lady," the mouse replied with a sniff, "you are Nunchuk *Nun,* not Nunchuk *Hussy!* I will hear no more of this disgusting talk about *boyfriends,* do you hear me?"

The mouse shook her umbrella for emphasis.

Now Jake was grinning widely. He crossed his arms, sat back, and said, "Let me guess, you're a church mouse?"

Brigid raised herself up on her haunches and puffed out her chest. "Yes, I am, and proud of it—er, I mean humble. Humble of it."

"I wish she were *quiet* like a church mouse," Nunchuk Nun muttered.

"What was that?" Brigid snapped.

"Nothing."

"Hmmph, young lady," said Brigid with paws on hips, "you

really need to learn some manners! Do you not understand that you are a clear and shining light to all who behold you, a pure and—?"

Nunchuk Nun held up a hand and flapped it in imitation of Brigid's mouth.

Brigid's tiny jaw immediately snapped shut, and her face turned so red, the color was visible through her fur.

Jake cleared his throat. "Er, it's none of my business, Nunchuk Nun, but you should probably do what your familiar—"

"You're right," said Nunchuk Nun as she lifted her nose in the air and walked away. "It's none of your business."

Brigid huffed and shook her head. "Honestly, that girl." After a deep breath, she smiled slightly and added, "But I suppose I shouldn't be so hard on her, not after—"

She didn't quite finish, but her smile looked forced.

A lump formed in Jake's throat. He rose to follow Nunchuk Nun. "I'm really sorry," he said, "but I have to tell you about Andalusia—"

Nunchuk Nun clapped her hands over her ears. *"I don't wanna hear it!"*

With that, she took off running. Several tourists gasped as she barreled past them.

Jake felt something bump against his shoulder, so he looked down to see Brigid clinging to an epaulet on his trench coat.

"Well?" she snapped. "Don't just goggle. Go after her!"

He did.

Nunchuk Nun was fast even for a magical girl, and if the basilica had sacred spaces, she didn't respect them. She seemed to evaporate like a haze in one spot and then reappear in another. One moment, she stood in a chapel, but as Jake approached, she blurred—and then she was atop a statue, sticking out her tongue and giving Jake the raspberry. Then she was on the floor, scampering away.

He tried to imagine the noble and dignified Lady Paladin Andalusia working with this capricious urchin. Somehow, he couldn't form the image in his head—but then again, Rifle Maiden and Voodoo Queen Natasha were also opposites, yet their affection for each other was obvious.

"That girl," Brigid muttered from his shoulder. "Honestly, this is because I don't discipline her enough. You've got to take a firm paw with that kind—a *firm paw.*"

She shook her umbrella, perhaps in demonstration.

After another blur of speed, Nunchuk Nun stood balanced on the railing around the papal altar's subterranean grotto. She stuck her tongue out at Jake one last time before jumping into the air, backflipping several times, and landing down below.

Brigid sighed. "Perhaps I should not have taught her the ways of the ninja."

Jake had already run back and forth across the archbasilica several times, so he breathed hard as he approached the railing and leaned on it heavily.

"What are you waiting for?" Brigid snapped as she tapped her umbrella against his cheek.

"Am I allowed down there?"

"You're a baptized Christian, aren't you?"

"No, I'm Jewish."

"Oh." Brigid shifted back and forth on his shoulder for a few seconds. "Well, nobody's perfect. After her!"

Jake sighed, found a hinged opening in the railing, and stumbled down a marble staircase.

At the bottom stood another altar. A candle, encased in red

glass, hung over it and shone coldly. Statues and paintings peeked out of niches.

"Where is she?"

Brigid tapped his cheek. "She probably went into the catacombs. She's often down there when she's upset."

"You have catacombs?"

"Of course." With her umbrella, she pointed to one of the niches. Jake could see a dark square, which on closer examination proved to be an opening only four feet high.

Muttering to himself, he ducked and went in. Rough stone tore at his clothes.

He had to crawl for several feet until he had enough room to stand. Then he was in a narrow tunnel with rough-cut stone walls and a sandy floor. Torches burned on the walls—or what looked like torches. A second glance proved them to be stylized gas lamps.

"What's the point of this?" Jake asked.

"Tombs, mostly," Brigid replied. "The popes and other bishops are buried here. It's also used for storage." She coughed into a paw. "And tourists, of course. They want to see Christian catacombs, you know."

Jake nodded. "Where would she be down here?"

"When she's upset, she often visits the tomb of the first pope."

"First—?"

"I mean the first of Urbanopolis, Urban IX."

Jake dimly remembered something about that from a history class: No pope since the seventeenth century of the previous era had taken the name Urban, but after the First Invasion, all popes had chosen that name.

He picked his way carefully through the rough-hewn caverns.

Niches in the walls contained bronze coffins, which he assumed held the dead bishops. He turned several corners and quickly lost his way, though Brigid always pointed out which direction he should go.

The air was flinty, close, and hard to breathe. Jake didn't think of himself as claustrophobic, but the low ceiling, glowing torches, and dark shadows made him queasy.

He turned yet another corner and yelped when he came upon a tall, black-robed figure. The man rounded on Jake but then stumbled back and clutched his heart.

"Sorry," said Jake, "I just—"

The cassock-clad man righted himself. He was probably in his thirties, with close-cropped hair and horn-rimmed glasses. "Young man," he said, "you scared me half to death!"

"Sorry—"

"The catacombs aren't open right now. Let me take you back—"

On Jake's shoulder, Brigid harrumphed loudly.

The priest adjusted his glasses. "Oh! Oh my, Brigid, is that you?"

"This is Pretty Dynamo's sidekick," Brigid explained. "We're looking for Nunchuk Nun. Did you see her go by here, Father?"

"I'm afraid I didn't, but nobody sees her if she doesn't want it."

"We'd best keep going, then," Brigid replied.

Jake continued walking and was surprised when the priest followed him.

"Look," said Jake, "we just want—"

"I'll help you find her," the priest said.

Jake didn't argue.

After they turned several more corners, Jake felt a cool

breeze on his face. The air was strangely fresh but thick, now like moist loam instead of dry dust.

"That's odd," the priest said from behind him.

They walked another fifty feet and discovered a passage that was entirely black, unlit by torches. Brick, stone fragments, and dark soil lay around its opening as if it had been recently excavated. A few drops of water fell from the tunnel roof and pattered on the ground.

The priest stepped around Jake, muttering, "This isn't supposed to be here—"

From the dark tunnel came a voice, scratchy yet deep—almost as if a stone were speaking. It made the hairs on the back of Jake's neck stand up.

"Padre," said the voice, "will you accept a poor sinner into this hallowed ground?"

Adjusting his glasses, the priest peered into the dark.

"Wait," Jake murmured. "Maybe you shouldn't—"

"Of course," said the priest, his voice echoing as he spoke into the black tunnel. "All are welcome here, sinners especially."

A moment of silence passed, followed by cold laughter. Jake took a step back.

"Thank you," said the voice. "All I needed was your invitation."

A black shape lunged out of the darkness, struck the priest, and sent him reeling into the far wall.

Jake tripped over a rock and fell on his back. He heard Brigid squeak as she tumbled from his shoulder, so he scrabbled to pick her up. Once he had her in his hands, he clambered to his feet, wincing as his left ankle complained again.

The dark shape hunched over the priest. It had a vaguely human face, the skin of which had the texture of old leather but was pale like bleached bone. Its eyes shone red in the light of the torches. When it opened an unnaturally large mouth, it revealed long, sharp canines like the teeth of a wildcat.

Before Jake could move, it plunged its jaw into the priest's jugular. The priest opened his mouth as if to scream—but no sound came out.

A horrible slurping noise followed, and the faux torches on the walls flickered wildly.

Shocked into immobility, Jake stood with the mouse in his hands as horror filled him. A cold shiver ran the length of his spine as if someone had poured ice water down his back.

TWENTY-ONE

BLOOD AND FIRE

O nce his life drained, the priest fell to the ground like a rag
doll. The monster towering over him had the shape of a
man, though a long, black robe hid most of his skeletal figure:
He was almost seven feet tall but so thin and wasted, with flesh
pulled tight across his angular skull, that he looked like a starva-
tion victim near the end of his life. Fresh blood, which the torch-
light made glossy like ink from a broken fountain pen, ran in
rivulets down his jaw and throat. He grinned at Jake with thin
lips pulled back so far as to show even the spaces behind his
backmost molars. His teeth were impossibly numerous and
impossibly long and sharp—a bizarre parody of the human
mouth twisted into the stuff of nightmares. His eyes burned like
smoldering coals.

Jake's throat was dry. He took a step back, and then another.
The creature, still grinning with an unsated predator's giddy
anticipation of more flesh to tear, stalked toward him.

Jake's mind raced over the rudimentary lessons he'd had, in

middle school, on common monsters and magical defenses. He had always thought such lessons were dull, so he had merely done the minimal work necessary to get his A—rather like English class.

He wasn't coming up with much. Did garlic drive back vampires, or was it wolfsbane? He could never remember.

Not knowing what else to do, he threw open his trench coat, pulled the pistol from his hip, and fired.

The *boom* of the gun made his ears ring, and his teeth ground together of their own accord. The vampire's left eye dissolved along with part of his skull. Brain matter sprayed the rough-cut wall like the innovations of a talentless modern artist.

The vampire opened his mouth with a contemptuous snarl, and the flesh of his head regenerated: The wound sealed up, and a fresh eyeball, bloodshot and leering, rose out of the depths of his skull and settled into its socket.

Brigid scrambled back up to Jake's shoulder and slapped his cheek with her umbrella. "What are you doing? You don't shoot a monster unless you have a death wish! Now put that thing away and get—"

With a cry, the vampire fell hard into the wall, banging his head against the stones. Behind him stood Nunchuk Nun with a pair of nunchaku in each hand. Sliding her right foot behind, she dropped into the stance of White Crane Spreading Its Wings. As the vampire wheeled about to face her, she straightened and made a whirlwind with her weapons, snapping them clockwise and then counterclockwise in rapid succession, using her armpits as pivots.

The vampire hissed. As Nunchuk Nun closed with him, she moved into a new form, swinging the nunchaku first vertically and then horizontally across her torso.

With astonishing speed, the vampire blocked her attempted blows with his forearms. But she caught the nunchaku under her arms and then shot them out with a snap of her wrists, striking him full in the face. He staggered.

She spun on one foot, swinging her weapons in a wide arc. At the same time, she brought two of their ends together. They fused, forming a three-section staff. With a helicopter spin over her head, she smashed one swinging end into the vampire's skull. Though he tumbled onto his back, he immediately rose again, stiff as a board, as if lifted by invisible wires.

Everything had happened in a few seconds, and Jake barely had time to make sense of it, much less react. In a flash, Nunchuk Nun jumped in front of him, separated her nunchaku again, and spun them. The vampire roared like a rabid dog, and several black shapes poured out of the tunnel behind him.

"Back fifty feet and to your left," Nunchuk Nun barked. "There's an underground chapel! Go!"

Jake began to protest, "But—"

"Now!"

The swarming shapes skittered on the walls like insects, crawling with long, pointed claws. Jake caught a glimpse of sharp fangs glinting in the yellow firelight.

He holstered his pistol, turned, and ran.

Behind him, Nunchuk Nun yelled, *"Divine Wind!"*

A hard blast of air hit Jake in the back like a mallet blow and knocked him ten feet forward. He landed on his feet and kept running.

Brigid's whiskers tickled his ear when she said, "Nunchuk Nun has no bladed weapons. She's not equipped for vampires, so she's going to need help!"

"Don't Christian altars keep, like, a dagger or a sword or something?"

"What?"

"I thought Christian altars always have a chalice and a dagger—"

"You've been watching too many movies, kid."

Jake rounded a corner and found an alcove holding a small altar draped in linen. A gold tabernacle loomed above it. Flanking the altar were two golden candlesticks, and in its center stood a golden crucifix.

"Stop," said Brigid. "Behind you and to your right!"

Jake spun but saw nothing.

"What—?"

"There!" Brigid pointed her umbrella at a small holy water font bolted into the rough wall. There was no water standing in it, but there was a moist sponge.

Jake picked up the sponge and stuck it in his breast pocket. It dripped down his shirtfront.

"Good," said Brigid. "Take the crucifix off the altar."

"Isn't that, like, blasphemous or something—?"

"Boy, this isn't the time to be picky!"

He lifted the crucifix. It was a foot tall and surprisingly heavy. "Y'know, I'm Jewish, so I'm not sure this thing will work for me."

"What?" said Brigid. "What are you talking about now?"

"Don't you have to have faith or something to use a crucifix to ward off vampires? Maybe I should have a Star of David instead—"

Brigid rapped her umbrella hard against his temple, and he winced. "Where *do* you young people get these ideas? Stars of David don't work on vampires!"

"Really? That doesn't seem fair—"

"The Star of David is for ifrits, djinn, and liliths! *Crucifixes* are for vampires! Don't you know *anything* about magic?"

"Wait, so crucifixes are magical?"

"What did you think they were? Now grab a candlestick too!"

"What? But—"

"Don't argue!"

He snatched up a candlestick that was three feet tall and considerably heavier than the crucifix. The white beeswax candle fell out of the top and hit the floor with a *thunk*. He stooped clumsily to grab it, but Brigid batted him with her umbrella again. "Leave it! Just go! Back to Nunchuk Nun—and *hurry!"*

Jake didn't argue this time, but he felt a lump form in his throat when she told him to head toward the vampires instead of away. As he left the alcove and entered the torch-lit passageway, his heart drummed in his ears in time to the thumps, shouts, and animal-like snarls echoing from the rough walls. Sweat poured from his face.

That glowing blue haze appeared in front of his eyes again. When he saw it, he felt a sudden surge of excitement in his chest.

He took another deep breath and ran forward, clumping along with the candlestick's round base banging like a gong against the stone wall to his right. He rounded a corner and almost slammed into Nunchuk Nun's back: With her weapons in each hand and her arms blurring with speed, she battered at black-robed shapes that clawed at her with long, yellow nails. Several streaks of blood crisscrossed her face. For a moment of terror, Jake thought he must be too late, that she'd been bitten.

A ghostly white face with bloodshot eyes and a wide, terribly red mouth lunged at him out of the mass of monsters. With no time to think, he clumsily swung the crucifix like a weapon, and the vampire darted back, leaping up to the ceiling and sticking there like a spider.

That brought Jake to his senses. Holding the cross up for protection, he dropped the candlestick with a loud clank and reached into his pocket. He squeezed the sponge and hurled drops of holy water into the knot of vampires. They howled as the water hissed against their skin and clothes. Smoke, smelling of burned flesh, rose from their bodies.

Like frightened centipedes, they skittered back up the tunnel. Thirty feet away, they stopped, writhing together like snakes in their den, baring their fangs and staring with their glowing eyes. Jake made a lunge with the crucifix, and the foremost vampires flinched.

"Quite cheeky for these types to invade a church," said Brigid with a sniff.

Nunchuk Nun tucked her weapons into her belt and turned to Jake, chest heaving. "Thanks," she rasped. Then her eyes lighted on the candlestick, and her mouth widened into a blood-rimed grin.

She brought a boot down onto the candlestick's hollow end, crushing it flat. Then she grabbed the stick, turned it ninety degrees, and stomped it again, producing a crude but sharp point.

She picked up the makeshift spear and tested it. "This'll do, but we're still gonna need a knife or a sword. You got one?"

"No," Jake said. "You look hurt. Did they—?"

"She's immune to vampire bites in this form," Brigid said from Jake's shoulder. "But she's going to need some backup, or she won't last."

"Can she contact the boss?"

Brigid sighed. "Her communicator is with her alter ego, unfortunately. Sentinel likely hasn't detected this—that computer has never been good at distinguishing vampires from regular human beings."

Jake stared down the passageway, back toward where he'd come from. "I'm lost. Are we cut off? Can we get up to the basilica from here?"

Brigid frowned. "Yes, but—"

"If Nunchuk Nun can hold them off, and if you come with me, I can call for backup."

"Do it," Nunchuk Nun said.

She took the crucifix out of Jake's hands, and the vampires, with their eyes peering out of the darkness like cats' eyes, grumbled.

"Do you need that?" Jake asked. "You have crosses on your—"

He glanced down at her chest. Her crucifix was gone, but a streak of gold smeared her habit as if the talisman had liquefied. Her rosary had shriveled into a lump of slag at her belt.

She shook her head. "Too many of them. My icons weren't powerful enough. Hopefully, though"—she hefted the large crucifix—"this will do the trick."

"Just because it's bigger?" Jake asked.

"Because it's off the altar," she said with another smile. "That makes a difference. Now *go* before they decide to chance it!"

Jake turned and sprinted.

Brigid barked directions like a drill sergeant. All the tunnels looked the same, and the bishops' coffins in the dark niches loomed at him. Torches flickered wildly, and shadows crawled over the walls. Roaches and spiders skittered rapidly away from his tennis shoes. For a moment, in a terrifying flashback, Jake was again in the underground shelter where he had watched help-lessly as men, women, and children, mad with fear, trampled one another into the unyielding concrete while mindless zombies lusted for their blood.

Yet, in the next moment, he saw the blue haze again, and he felt a surge of joy. Frightened though he was, a voice in the back of his mind whispered, *I was made for this.*

He shook his head to fling away both the strange thought and the sweat drops rolling down his scalp. *I think I'm going crazy.*

"Left!" shouted Brigid. "Go left!"

He turned left. A black shape flew at him, struck him in the chest, and sent him hurtling backwards. He hit a wall, and the air left his lungs. Brigid fell from his shoulder and landed in the sand.

With greasy black hair tumbling over his pale face, a vampire gazed at him with somber contempt. "Where's your cross now, boy?" he rumbled in a voice surprisingly deep.

He bared his fangs.

A flickering torch hung on the wall above Jake's right shoulder. He slid up the wall and grabbed it as the vampire rushed him. It was bolted in place, of course, but it could tilt forward on a hinge, and Jake's scrambling fingers found a small dial for the valve. He spun it. With a *whoosh,* the flame shot out three feet, and a spark caught the vampire's cloak.

Shrieking, the vampire batted at the fire, but it spread as if his cloak were soaked in oil. When the flames reached his face, his flesh blackened, and he fell to the ground and writhed.

Jake scooped up Brigid and sprinted past the howling monster.

"Holy fire," Brigid explained. "The torches aren't blessed, but they *do* light the catacombs, so they likely know the enemies of the Church."

"But where did he come from?" Jake asked.

"I don't know," Brigid replied. She was silent for a moment before adding, "It's possible they finished off Nunchuk Nun—or he might have come in through a different tunnel."

"Wouldn't someone have to invite him in?"

Brigid sighed. "I'm afraid Father Michael's kindhearted but foolish invitation was universal. *All* vampires will have access to this basilica now." She patted his cheek with a paw. "That's the thing with magic. You must choose your words carefully—it's the literal meaning, not the intent, that matters."

"There's nothing you can do about it?"

"Someone with higher authority can revoke the invitation. We'll take care of that when we can, but for now, we just need to get out!"

When Jake rounded another corner, he saw a silver crucifix mounted on a wall. He tried to take it, but it was stuck fast, probably screwed into place. He had to leave it and keep running.

After what felt like an eternity, he ducked back into the grotto under the papal altar and found the marble stairs. Once he reached the top, he nearly tumbled back down again when Brigid shocked him with a yell: "Vampires! Vampires in the catacombs! Tourists, civilians, *out!* Everyone else, we need weapons! Anything sharp, anything with a cross!"

Her tiny, squeaky voice was lost in the vast basilica, but a few people heard. Their eyes went wide, and they turned and took up the shout: "Vampires in the catacombs!"

Someone, possibly the old woman he'd seen in the side chapel earlier, tottered to Jake and thrust a crystal rosary into his hands before she hobbled toward the Filarete Door.

"Good job," he said to Brigid as he put the rosary around his neck and eyed the crowd flooding the vestibule, "but now *we're* going to have trouble getting out."

"You think that's the only door?" said Brigid with a fresh sniff. "Just keep following my directions."

He did, and she brought him first into a sacristy and then out through a side door.

"We need a terminal," he said, and Brigid gave more directions.

The so-called terminals were combination computers and public phones. The Fathers had installed the earliest versions a hundred years ago to aid communication during emergencies. To prevent monsters from using them, they had a biometric security system that could verify a user's humanity—though that meant they were inaccessible to familiars as well.

Jake found a terminal in a black booth on a street corner. He jumped in and slammed his hands down on the panels. A monitor turned on, and he winced when the retinal scanner flashed red, leaving a green afterglow in his eyes.

"C'mon, c'mon," he muttered while the computer ran through its processes.

Finally, the screen lit up with:

Welcome back, Jake.

He typed in the number for his family's landline and then impatiently tapped the wall of the booth while the phone rang. His family didn't have a vidphone, so the screen showed only the phone number and the stupid welcome message.

Finally, after five rings, he heard a click, and his mother's staticky voice said, "Hello?"

"Mom? Mom! It's Jake!"

"Jake? Honey, where *are* you?"

"Never mind that. Put Dana on."

"What?"

"Please, Mom, it's urgent. Is she there?"

"Well, she is—"

"Get her! Please!"

Half a minute passed. Jake's breathing was loud in the booth. He felt giddy and wondered if he was going to faint.

At last, Dana's sullen voice came on the line: "What is it?"

Jake whispered, "Dana, I'm in Rome-in-Exile—"

"Why?"

"Never mind. I need magical girls. Lots of them."

Dana was quiet for a moment, but then her voice lowered, and the sarcasm disappeared from it. "Why?"

"Vampires in St. Peter's. They're coming up from the catacombs."

A pause. "I'm not sure I can get there—"

"Can you contact that boss guy of yours?"

"I guess—"

"Then do it! We need girls with swords and knives and spikes and stuff!"

"Okay, I'm on it. You said vampires?"

"Yes!"

Another pause. "Then I'm . . . I'm gonna come too."

"How are you going to get here without your Circuit Board?"

"I'll think of something."

"Dana—"

"I'll run, maybe."

She hung up.

Jake stood in the booth for several seconds, blinking. Then he glanced warily at the mouse on his shoulder, and his stomach contracted with guilt. "Can you keep a secret?" he asked.

"Of course," said Brigid with a faint smile. "So I take it that was Pretty Dynamo—and, it seems, she's your sister. That explains some things."

"Actually," Jake replied, "she's just this girl I live with."

Brigid gasped.

"All right," said Jake, cracking his knuckles. "That's done. Back inside."

"Oh, no," said Brigid, tapping his cheek. "You're a civilian. *Your* job is done."

He felt another thrill run through his breast. "Nunchuk Nun needs help. And didn't you tell others in there to help her too?"

"Well, yes, the clergy. Dealing with this sort of thing is part of *their* job—"

"I'm not going to leave her."

"Why not? You're just a boy."

He grinned and ran a hand through his sweat-soaked hair. "I know—but I can't abandon a girl when she's in trouble. I figured that out last week."

He ran back up the street toward the massive cathedral.

WHEN JAKE AGAIN ENTERED THE BASILICA BY THE FILARETE Door, he was surprised to find it dark inside, suggesting that someone had cut the power. The high, stained-glass windows were blank and leaden, having no sunlight to make them glow. At first glance, the whole place appeared to be deserted.

He swept his eyes over the rows of pews. With his heart steadily thrumming in his ears, he struggled to keep his imagination in check: Every shadow, every glimmer of light, seemed to him a monster ready to leap out and latch onto his throat.

He took a step forward into the central nave, breathing heavily. His footsteps echoed from the high stone walls. He cast his eyes about, and sweat trickled down his forehead. He wished he had another crucifix. He saw one, a tall gold one, standing on the high altar—but it was almost a hundred yards away. He could get to it if he ran—

He heard a low growl to his left. Without thinking, he dived to the right and immediately banged his shoulder into the armrest on the end of a wooden pew.

He cursed under his breath, felt funny for cursing in a church, and cursed again anyway. Pushing off from the armrest, Jake regained his feet just in time to find himself facing a black-robed figure with bone-white skin. This gaunt creature's head was a pale dome, entirely without hair but marked on the left side, just above the ear, by a puss-filled boil that put Jake in mind of a half-formed eye. The creature's unusually long and knobby ears ended in flaccid points. Although the rest of his skin was pale and bluish like that of a waterlogged corpse, his lips were bright red—not quite like lipstick, but more like cold sores that had spread to encompass his mouth.

He glided toward Jake as though he had wheels on his feet, and his pustule-like lips slid back to reveal crooked, needle-like fangs. Although most of the windows were dark, a single panel of stained glass—an image of the Christ raising two fingers in solemn blessing—glowed with a funereal blue-white light, the color of the waning moon. That light cast a sepulchral pallor over the vampire's face and made his wet teeth glisten.

With a snake-like hiss, the vampire stretched out one thin, bony hand. His long fingers, tipped with claw-like nails, held a fat cupcake topped with a high, swirled mound of almond-colored frosting.

"Our *Monts Blancs* are on special this week," the vampire

whispered coldly. "They're half off. Get them while supplies last."

A sweet hint of chestnut met Jake's nose.

Jake's throat was dry. He swallowed painfully. "I'm . . . I'm allergic to nuts," he rasped.

The vampire hissed again and lunged.

Jake threw himself sideways and landed hard against the stone floor. Pushing off with his hands, he regained his feet just as the vampire slammed into the pew Jake had stumbled against a moment before. A loud *crack,* the sound of splintering wood, echoed through the church. The vampire turned and, with a flick of his wrist, hurled the cupcake into Jake's face.

Blinded by sweet frosting, Jake staggered. He wasn't really allergic to nuts, but he wiped at the frosting anyway, trying desperately to regain his vision.

Like a sledgehammer, something hit his chest and took the breath from his lungs. He flew ten feet through the air, landed hard against the smooth stone floor, and slid up the nave.

Although writhing in pain, Jake realized that the vampire had knocked him closer to the papal altar. Using the momentum of the blow, he performed a clumsy backward somersault and regained his feet. After spinning on his sneakers' rubber soles—and ignoring the knife-like complaint in his lungs—he sprinted.

But he forgot that, in front of the altar, a railing surrounded the stairwell to the subterranean grotto. He slammed into it with his hips and sucked in a loud, ragged breath as he bent forward and then rebounded, feeling like an idiot.

He didn't fall down again, but the self-inflicted blow disoriented him.

He heard another snake-like hiss, and he realized he didn't know what had happened to Brigid.

But then he heard a squeak, and something bounced off his knee and bounded onto his shoulder. He didn't flinch or cringe as he might have in the past: He knew what it was, and he felt a fleeting moment of relief.

As the vampire charged, Jake remembered the rosary. He clutched at his chest until his hand found the small crucifix and ripped it from his neck, sending beads scattering across the floor. He held up the tiny cross like a talisman.

With claw-like fingers extended, the vampire uttered a loud snarl like an angry dog, and the rosary in Jake's hand melted. To Jake's surprise, it didn't grow hot: The crucifix and the beads merely changed into a thin soup, ran out between his fingers, and left him holding an empty chain.

Sliding on the marble floor, Jake sprinted around the railing and clomped up the stairs to the high altar. He snatched up the golden crucifix, his arms straining under the weight.

But once he turned from the altar, the vampire reached him and swung, catching him by surprise. The heavy cross flew from his hands and fell into the grotto with a *clunk,* gouging the marble.

Thinking dimly that this *had* to be sacrilegious, Jake fell back from the vampire's blow and sprawled on the altar like a grisly sacrifice. His left arm knocked over a candlestick and sent it after the crucifix. It made a deafening *clang* when it struck.

The vampire bent over him, teeth shining wetly in the dim light.

Jake scrabbled at the moist sponge in his breast pocket, yanked it out, and shoved it into the vampire's face. The vampire howled as his skin sizzled. Again, there was no heat, but a puff of smoke obscured Jake's hand, and he could detect the distinct, sweet stench of burning human meat.

With the bubbling sponge sticking to his flesh, the vampire reeled back. As he did, he reached out one bony hand and raked his fingers down Jake's face. The nails did not dig into his skin, but a strange paralysis overtook Jake's limbs—as if he had suddenly plunged into ice-cold water and the shock had overwhelmed him. Stupefied, he remained stretched out on the altar.

Reaching up with shaking, pain-clenched claws, the vampire grabbed the sponge, which stretched from his left cheek up to the right side of his forehead. There was a fresh, high-pitched squeal of boiling, bursting skin as the holy water scalded his fingers. Shrieking like a mad animal, the vampire pulled, and thick chunks of skin peeled away with the sponge.

In the sickly moonlight, Jake could see the vampire's lips pulled back from his white teeth and bloodless gums. Stretching diagonally across his face was an angry, rectangular patch of ravaged flesh—exposed gristle and sinews, and even spots of bare skull. His right eyelid had torn away, leaving his eyeball gaping in its ring of muscle.

After struggling further to pull the sponge from his burnt and blistered hands, the vampire at last dropped it to the floor.

"I am going to enjoy draining you of your lifeblood," he whispered in an ice-cold voice. "And once I have made you immortal like myself, I will subject you to a millennium of torments to repay you for this indignity."

Feeling slowly returned to Jake's limbs. Feebly, he reached out a hand, hoping to find a weapon. All he found was another candle. He clutched it desperately, though it could do him no good.

Like a priest offering a benediction, the vampire towered over Jake and raised his hands in blasphemous mockery as he intoned, "Behold! The era of man is over! Now begins the era of the Vampyr! The portal will open, the gods of chaos will descend, and the gibbering remnants of mankind shall be the chattel of the night's children—!"

Another hiss—not a vampire's angry warning but a sound like air escaping from a sealed jar. Following it was a muffled *thump*. The vampire's sonorous voice ceased, and all was quiet.

Blinking, Jake struggled to make out details in the darkness. The vampire was still as a statue. Jake's eyes slid down from the vampire's mutilated face to his chest, where some bulge protruded. After a few seconds, Jake realized the bulge was a wooden stake.

The vampire collapsed to the floor with an anticlimactic *thud.*

Woozily, as though awakening from sleep, Jake sat up. Something fluttered above his head like a giant bird flapping its wings. A dark shape passed over him, and then he heard a loud *clang,* the sound of metal striking stone, accompanied by a sickening, wet *schliiick.*

Someone knelt in the pale moonlight over the fallen vampire —someone huddled and breathing heavily.

Jake's throat was raw, as if filled with needles. He considered speaking—but didn't. He held his breath.

Then he started and reflexively clutched his chest when Brigid's squeaky voice pierced the silence: "You're just in time," she said.

The hunched figure straightened and stepped closer. A beam of pale moonlight fell across her face.

Now Jake could see that it was a girl, possibly as young as Nunchuk Nun. She wore a black leather jacket that hung past her hips. Bandoliers crossed her shoulders, and she had some large, rectangular device—the nature of which he couldn't quite make out—slung on her back. A black skirt edged with gauzy, pink chiffon hung to just above her knees. Her boots were heavy, with high heels and platforms. Rows of chrome buckles ran up their fronts. A black choker, rimmed with long spikes, encircled her throat. Painted over her left eye was a glittering, purple star, and her lips were black. The left half of her hair had a side fade, but the hair on the right stuck up in the front in a series of crimped, feathery spikes glazed pink at their tips. In the back, her hair was long and held in a high ponytail by a purple scrunchie.

It took him a minute to realize this elaborate do was some kind of mullet.

Who wears a mullet these days?

"Hey," she said. Her voice was girlish, but she gave the impression that she was trying to make it sound deeper than it was.

In one hand, she carried some large contraption, dark green in color and shaped almost like a rocket launcher. She pulled a wooden stake from one of her bandoliers and loaded it into the contraption's mouth. Jake heard the squeak-click of a spring contracting and locking under a lever.

Still sitting on the altar, he cleared his throat. "Who are you?"

She chuckled faintly. "Ah, you don't recognize me?"

He shook his head.

She grinned. "Really? I recognize you. Anyway, I'm Vanessa."

"I assume you're a magical girl."

"Sure am. Vampires are my specialty. Got the word from the boss that there might be action here tonight—and he got the tip from Pretty Dynamo."

She touched the cannon on her arm. Of its own accord, it slid up to her shoulder and flipped onto her back. Then she held out her freed hand. Jake took it, and she helped him stand.

"I've never seen you before," he said, "but I suspect I know your name."

She smiled and made the Sign of the Moon Princess. "Most everybody does. Not to brag, but I'm something of a celebrity: I'm *Magical Girl Metal Huntress Vanessa Van Halensing.*"

TWENTY-TWO

COMMUNION

J ake shuddered when he felt Brigid run up his pant leg and under his coat.

"We need to get back into the catacombs," he said while Brigid settled on his shoulder. "I had to leave Nunchuk Nun down there."

Vanessa frowned. "She's not equipped for vampires. We better hurry."

She jumped onto the altar and, pivoting with one hand, catapulted herself down into the grotto.

Jake chose a more indirect route: He ran around the altar, found the gate at the front of the railing, and quickly joined her. "We've been trying to keep them back with crosses," he said, "but they've been melting them—"

Vanessa grunted. "Bad sign. That means they're old ones."

"Old?"

"Vampires grow more powerful with age. They have to drink

a lot of blood before they can resist a crucifix, let alone destroy it." She briefly rubbed a leather-clad hand across her chin. "I guess we could break into a tabernacle and grab some consecrated hosts. Those always work—but I only do that as a last resort."

"Are you a Christian?"

She gave him a snaggletoothed grin. "Who, me? Nah. But I don't fancy gettin' cursed. Second rule of magic—don't tick off anyone's gods."

Brigid squirmed on Jake's shoulder, so he absentmindedly patted her.

Vanessa snapped her fingers and announced, *"Don't Be Afraid of the Dark!"* A blue flame appeared in her left hand. Holding it up like a torch, she ducked through the low archway into the catacombs.

"I wish I had more equipment," she muttered as Jake followed her. "Didn't have time—"

Jake tugged his collar. "I thought magical-girl items sort of, you know, grow out of your—"

"Yeah, that's how it usually works, but dealing with vampires requires extra paraphernalia. Like, you think I could produce wooden stakes out of my own body and leave one in every vampire I kill? I'd be a skeleton in days."

"You have to leave the stake in?"

"Man, you *really* don't know anything about vampires, do you?"

Jake shrugged.

The tunnel widened, and the roof grew higher. Seeing that the torches on the walls were alight, Vanessa snuffed the flame in her hand and clenched her left fist.

"Kiss Me Deadly!" she hissed.

With the sound of steel scraping on steel, a double-edged blade slid out of her sleeve.

"Stake 'em an' cut their heads off," she said. "Hawthorn and ash stakes are best. There are other ways, but that's the only way to be sure. Good idea to burn the body afterwards, too."

Jake sighed. "Thanks. I'll remember that."

It was quiet, and Jake didn't like it. Up ahead, the torches had been snuffed, so the dank, musty tunnel suddenly disappeared, as if someone had hung a blackout curtain from the ceiling.

Vanessa cursed under her breath but didn't relight her flame. "Sorry, kid," she said. "Don't mean to throw shade, but I gotta leave you in darkness."

She squeezed her left earring and whispered, *"Rainbow in the Dark."* A strange contraption unfolded across her face. It featured two lenses over her eyes, which spun back and forth as if auto-focusing.

"Let me guess," said Jake. "Night vision."

"You got it. Handy against these buggers."

Brigid tugged at Jake's ear with her tiny paws as she whispered, "I can see in the dark. Do whatever I tell you."

He nodded. Then he cleared his throat and said, "Say, uh, Van Halensing—"

"Call me Vinny," Vanessa answered.

"Okay. Vinny, can I ask, where's your familiar?"

"Left 'im home. I usually do. He's afraid of the dark."

"Seriously?"

She chuckled. "Yeah, seriously."

She ducked low and ran ahead. With his heart thudding in his ears, Jake followed.

As he entered the darkness, he briefly saw that blue glow again, and the fear that had been tightening his chest instantly ebbed. He remembered why he had come here in the first place.

A voice whispered in his ear, *Fear not, for I am with you.*

He shook his head, knocking away the sweat that threatened to drip into his eyes. The voice sounded strange—unfamiliar and otherworldly. After a second, he decided it must have been from Brigid. Perhaps she was praying.

Hisses and snarls came from the tunnel up ahead, and bright red pinpoints appeared in the darkness.

"Bringing on the Heartbreak!" Vanessa shouted, and the stake cannon slid onto her arm.

Chak-bang! Chak-bang! Chak-bang! The cannon fired off three loads in rapid succession. Then came a clash of steel as Vanessa jumped in with the sword mounted on her other arm. Heart pounding and fists clenched, Jake stood his ground—but he couldn't see anything to do.

Something hit Jake from the right, knocking him into a wall. He crumpled. With a squeak, Brigid once again fell from his shoulder.

Two red lights appeared above him, and he heard a hiss like an angry cat's. The vampire's fangs flickered red in the light of his own glowing eyes.

"Vinny, throw me a stake!" Jake gasped.

To his surprise, something hard smacked the palm of his hand, and his fingers closed around it.

Holding it in a death grip, Jake reared up and slammed the stake into his attacker's chest. The vampire howled and leaped back, but the fat stake had not even pierced his robe. Jake realized he'd need a hammer to do this—and it would help if the vampire held still.

The vampire shot forward again, fangs bared. In a moment,

he would pin Jake down and latch onto his throat. Still slumped against the wall, Jake rolled to the left and held his arm out straight, stake pointed upward.

The vampire landed on it. Jake didn't know for sure if the stake hit the monster's heart, but from the way he shrieked—and the way something warm and wet splashed out—he thought it must have.

Remembering to leave the stake in, Jake simply yanked his arm out from under the vampire's writhing and howling form before taking to his feet. He wondered what it meant to have vampire blood dripping from his arm: Were vampires as infectious as zombies, or did he have to be bitten?

Vanessa landed lithely beside him and, with a quick slice, took off the writhing creature's head. Immediately, the screaming stopped, and the body settled into a macabre twitching.

"Nice work," Vanessa said.

"Thanks," Jake choked out as he struggled to catch his breath.

She handed him another stake and loaded a fresh one into her cannon. "These are my last two," she said.

"What should we do?"

"Find Nunchuk Nun, get her out of here, and torch the place."

"That'll work?"

"Fire will drive them out for sure, but it's unlikely to kill them."

Vampires skittered toward them. Vanessa fired off her last stake and then pushed the cannon to her back. She extended her right hand, and Jake could hear the rasp of another blade extending from her sleeve.

She swung and slashed. Two sets of red dots winked out.

Two more swings, and two more sets of lights snuffed like candles.

"If we don't stake their hearts," she shouted, "they'll just find their heads and reattach them! But this can buy us time!"

Jake heard fresh snarls and roars. His eyes had adjusted to the dark, so he could now make out the shadowy form of Vanessa hurling herself forward—but the vampires, crawling on walls and floor and ceiling, were thick as ants. With pale claws, they seized her and tossed her. She landed on her back near Jake.

"Dang it," she said as she kipped up to her feet. "This is more than I can handle. Retreat!"

She raised her right hand, and a nozzle slid out of her sleeve. *"Set the Night on Fire!"*

Jake realized what she was about to do, so he ran back up the tunnel. A wave of heat struck him, and he hit the ground.

Nunchuk Nun—

The vampires' roars turned to shrieks and screams as they scampered away to escape the flame. Several caught fire and fell from the ceiling like cinders tumbling from the roof of a burning building.

Something slapped Jake's cheek. He tried to swat it away, but his hand met soft fur, and he heard a squeak.

"Brigid?"

"Gas!" Brigid shouted. *"There's gas!"*

Jake's insides were suddenly frozen solid.

Oh . . . sweet shining Moon Princess!

He cupped Brigid in his hands and spun to his feet, yelling so loudly that his voice instantly went hoarse: "Vinny! The torches! *They're gas!"*

She shouted back, "Are you *kidding* me?"

Jake could smell the rotten-egg stench of thiol-infused methane, but Vanessa's flamethrower hadn't blown them all to kingdom come, so the concentration hadn't reached its explosive range. Still, they were in an underground tunnel surrounded by snuffed torches emitting natural gas, and Jake knew enough about emergency procedures to realize that constituted a grade-one gas leak.

Who built this place?

"Great," Vanessa muttered as the vampires, claws extended, stalked toward them, "just great. No stakes, no fire, and a whole lot of vampires."

She spun around, grabbed Jake by the arm, and dragged him up the tunnel.

He panted, "What—?"

"I told you! One thing *always* works!"

He nodded. Although not Christian himself, he'd tried to show a modicum of respect, but considering the way he'd plundered altars and waved crucifixes around, he didn't think he'd succeeded. He understood what Vanessa wanted.

"To the left," he said. "There's a small chapel."

They turned a corner and found the altar from which Jake had earlier swiped the crucifix. Above the altar, a candle in red glass burned coldly beside a golden cylinder fronted by two small, locked double doors.

Vanessa stared at the cylinder. "I bear you no ill will," she whispered.

Then she punched her fist through the gold with an ear-piercing shriek of rending metal.

A moment later, she held in her hands a goblet-shaped paten full of circular wafers.

Jake peered over her shoulder. "Are those—?"

"Yeah," Vanessa answered with a nod. "Bread that's been

prayed over by a priest. Supposedly, they're actually Jesus himself. But whatever they are, vampires *hate* 'em. Anyway, like I said, I don't enjoy cheesing off the gods—but they say this Jesus guy was the forgiving type, and we're doing this to save one of his nuns, so I hope it's okay."

On Jake's shoulder, Brigid heaved a deep sigh but said nothing.

As they ran back up the tunnel, Vanessa threw the consecrated hosts like miniature Frisbees. Whenever one struck a vampire, it made a hiss like sizzling bacon and sent up a stink of burned flesh. Jake's stomach lurched.

"Confected hosts!" a vampire snarled.

"Yes!" another shrieked. "And they're not even actual confections!"

The attack was brutal, and the vampires at first retreated, but Vanessa quickly ran out of sacred bread, and the monsters were still thick in the tunnel.

"Can't you fire magic blasts or something?" Jake yelled. "What's with the stakes and flamethrowers and borrowed items?"

"Hey," Vanessa yelled back, "I use what *works,* and this is what works on vampires! I don't make the rules!"

One of the vampires, teeth bared and eyes aglow, shot toward Jake. With a curse, Vanessa jumped in front of him, but there was a bright flash of blue, and a perfectly round hole appeared in the vampire's chest. Like coals burning out, the vampire's eyes faded to a smoky gray as he collapsed.

The others turned to look back up the tunnel. Five more blue flashes stung Jake's eyes, and five more vampires tumbled to the ground.

Nunchuk Nun, with blood dripping from the shredded

remains of her habit, staggered toward them. As she yelled, *"Holy Hurricane!"* she spun her nunchaku over her head and swung them down with a snap, producing another blue light.

Sweat poured down her face, carving tiny streams through the caked blood on her cheeks.

"Nunchuk Nun!" Vanessa yelled.

"Help me out!" she gasped in reply. "I can't do this very much!"

She released another burst. Now pinched between two magical girls, the vampires faced Jake and Vanessa again. Vanessa raised her twin blades and jumped in.

Vanessa sliced a few throats, sending the vampires reeling. Nunchuk Nun blasted several more but then collapsed to her knees.

"You shouldn't waste your energy!" Vanessa snarled as she neatly chopped a head from a neck, releasing a fountain of blood. "They'll just regenerate—"

"I turned up the energy to cauterize the wound," Nunchuk Nun panted. "It's as good as leaving a stake in."

"What? Really?"

"You didn't know that?" Jake yelled from the back. "I thought you were the big-time vampire huntress!"

Vanessa whirled around to face him. "Hey, it's not like I know every—"

A vampire wrapped its claws around her neck.

Jake ran forward and pounded his fists against the vampire's hands, but it was like punching stone, and his knuckles stung. The vampire snapped at his fingers with sharp teeth, so Jake had to leap back.

"Do *not* let one bite you!" Vanessa wheezed as she rammed an elbow repeatedly into the vampire's gut.

"Well, if you kill it after it bites me," Jake said, "I'll be fine, right?"

"That's a myth!" Vanessa gasped.

"Uh oh—"

A vampire grabbed Jake's left arm and threw him into a wall. Yet again, Brigid tumbled from his shoulder. Jake's chest made a creaking noise as he sucked in air, and he wondered for the second time this week if his ribs had cracked.

Then the vampire was on top of him, aiming fangs for his throat. With dizzying horror, Jake saw the white collar around the vampire's neck and the horn-rimmed glasses resting crookedly on his nose—this was the priest he had met a short while before, the one who had unwittingly let the vampires in.

Then the vampire priest was off him, flung sideways. Nunchuk Nun, knees shaking and sweat pouring down her face, stood over Jake with her nunchaku in her hands. She spun toward Vanessa and swung again, forcing the vampire choking her to let go.

Brigid scampered up Nunchuk Nun's leg. Vanessa hauled Jake to his feet and hissed in his ear, *"Let's go!"*

"Wait—"

Like a groom carrying a bride, she hiked him into her arms and took off. This wasn't the first time a magical girl had held him this way, so Jake forgot to be embarrassed.

But Vanessa didn't make it far: Vampires had gathered near the basilica entrance, so Jake and the girls were cut off.

Vanessa dropped Jake to the ground. He groaned when he struck.

Nunchuk Nun faced one way, and Vanessa faced the other. The vampires hissed but stayed back.

Sweat poured down Nunchuk Nun's face. Her hands shook,

making the chains of her nunchaku rattle. "I'm not gonna be able to keep my form," she whispered out of the corner of her mouth.

"I know," Vanessa hissed back. "Just hold on a little longer."

"Why aren't they attacking?" Jake asked as he rose unsteadily to his feet.

Then he heard—no, he *felt*—something coming toward them.

He looked down the tunnel, in the direction from which the vampires had first come. They clung to the walls and ceiling, but they left the floor clear. Something like a gust of air—although the air was in fact perfectly still—pressed against Jake's chest and neck. Silently and swiftly, Vanessa and Nunchuk Nun traded places so Vanessa faced the strange, invisible pressure.

Jake saw the blue glow again, and his legs stopped shaking. He could breathe more easily.

"What is it?" Jake murmured to Vanessa.

"Not sure," she murmured back, "but I think . . . I think it's an old one. A *really* old one."

Jake swallowed.

Out of the darkness, a pale man walked toward them. Tall and lanky, he wore a curious garment of dark brown material, the color of dried blood, like a jumpsuit cut to hug his body. Running throughout this one-piece garment were thick bands, almost like tubes, that formed curving patterns across his figure. He also wore a cape with a high, stiff collar that reached to his prominent cheekbones. Strangely, though most of the cape was black, the inside of the collar shone like gold.

Only his head was exposed. His skin was pale and wasted, and his skull was bald. He looked like a death's-head—except without the grin. His flabby lips drooped in a permanent frown, from which protruded two thin fangs that jutted nearly to his chin. His eyes were bloodshot and so full and round as to appear lidless. As he approached, his feet making not even the slightest noise in the sand and his tall figure casting not even a hint of a shadow, it became clear that the oppressive feeling of power came from him.

Jake sensed Nunchuk Nun shuddering at his back. On her shoulder, Brigid silently crossed herself.

The figure stopped twenty feet away and held out his right hand. As if of its own accord, his glove peeled away like the rind of a banana. Jake could see that the interior of the glove, like the interior of the collar, was of bright, unvarnished gold.

The hand this glove exposed was as white, thin, and skeletal as the face above it. With the faintest hint of a smirk on his wrinkled lips, the figure flicked his fingers and touched one of the vampires clinging to the wall. There was a snap of blue-white electricity, and the vampire, opening his mouth in a silent scream, fell. When he struck the sandy floor with a loud *thonk,* his body and clothing had turned to gold.

Brigid swallowed audibly.

"Sweet Moon Princess," Jake whispered.

A few of the vampires snarled.

"I am *not* dealing with this now," Vanessa muttered.

She reached for her back and hauled out the large contraption she wore there. She flipped it around to her front, and Jake could see that it vaguely resembled a guitar, except shorter. A curious crosspiece ran through its middle. Instead of strings, it had a set of keys like a piano's.

"Crucifix Keytar!" Vanessa shouted. *"Get the Funk Out!"*

She played several notes, and the vampires screeched. The instrument had a surprisingly sonorous sound, which echoed through the tunnel.

In one of the Keytar's arms, a compartment opened to reveal

six small cylinders. Vanessa pulled them out and hurled them into the walls, the floor, and the ceiling, forming a circle. The cylinders vibrated, making the stone rattle faintly. Then the cylinders emitted the same deep, lonely notes Vanessa had played a moment before.

The approaching figure stopped in his tracks, and one of his wasted cheeks twitched. He didn't retreat, but neither did he advance. The other vampires, however, slid slowly backwards.

"Church bells," Vanessa explained when Jake glanced at her. "Same tones. And my Crucifix Keytar has been blessed. I didn't want to use a barrier spell until we had Nunchuk Nun with us, but now this should hold them back."

"That still leaves the ones between us and the exit," Jake said.

She nodded, faced the other direction, and played another tune on the Keytar.

"This might take me a few seconds to set up," she said, "but if you can hold them off, Nunchuk Nun—"

Jake, still eyeing the strange figure with the skeletal hand, swallowed. "Uh, girls—"

The mysterious figure, his cheek still twitching in irritation at the music, stepped forward. He reached up and touched one of the vibrating cylinders. With a crackle, it turned to gold, and its notes were spoiled, turning high and brassy. With a grin barely touching his droopy lips, the figure stooped and touched one of the cylinders on the floor.

"Girls," said Jake, "I think we need to do something—*now.*"

"Just a minute," Vanessa muttered. "Just a minute—"

Within seconds, the strange figure had destroyed four of the cylinders, and only two remained.

"We don't have a minute!" Jake shouted.

"Princess darn it!" Vanessa hissed, and Brigid gasped at the oath. Vanessa thrust a hand against the tunnel wall as, with her other hand, she played a rapid succession of notes. "Sorry about this, but—*Roundabout!*"

With a rumble and a crack, the cave wall turned to dust, choking Jake. He gagged and squeezed his eyes shut. Blinded, he felt an arm wrap around his waist and drag him roughly. He didn't resist.

Jake, Vanessa, and Nunchuk Nun tumbled into another tunnel through the fresh opening Vanessa had created. All three hacked and coughed on the dust.

Wiping her eyes, Vanessa rasped, "Where are we?"

"Straight ahead!" Brigid cried from Nunchuk Nun's shoulder. "Go straight ahead!"

They ran. Jake glanced over his shoulder to see that the strange figure had followed them. He stood in the middle of the tunnel, watching them with lips almost but not quite curled upward.

"Vinny!" Jake yelled. "Behind—!"

He didn't finish before she wheeled around and, her fingers blurring, played a new tune. *"Cold Day in Hell!"*

A blue light burst from the Keytar, filled the tunnel, and turned into a wall of ice, blocking sight of the golden vampire. A cold wind struck Jake's face.

Nunchuk Nun stumbled, barely keeping up.

"Hurry, Nunchuk Nun!" Vanessa snarled. "I can tell by looking at you, you're gonna need a juice box in the next two minutes if you're gonna keep your form!"

After a few seconds, they found a narrow, rough-cut stairway that ended at a rectangle of smooth marble. When Vanessa kicked the marble, it collapsed, being only a thin panel. Through this new opening, they scrambled back into the dark church. Blinking and wiping his eyes, Jake realized they were crawling out through the front of the altar in the side chapel where he had earlier spoken to Nunchuk Nun.

He gulped fresh, cool air, relieved to leave the stuffy tunnels behind.

"We gotta get out of the church," Vanessa said.

Nunchuk Nun, panting heavily and sweating profusely, crawled out after Jake, turned toward the altar, and fell to her knees.

"Hey," said Jake, "this is no time to—"

In a flash of white light, her clothes disappeared. A second later, she was kneeling on the floor in a button-up white shirt and plaid necktie with matching kilt. She held up her hands and blinked at them as her soft brown hair tumbled over her face. "Oh—"

"Oh dear," said Brigid, who still sat on her shoulder.

Jake glanced at Vanessa. Then he bent down and picked up the little girl who a moment ago had been Nunchuk Nun. She barely weighed a thing.

"C'mon," he said. "Let's go."

Red crept into the little girl's cheeks. "Um, please, I—"

"Don't worry," Jake said as he smiled down at her. "I'm terrible at remembering faces."

THEY GOT OUT. THE POLICE, LATE AS ALWAYS, ORDERED THE blocks around the basilica evacuated. Soon after came an explosion, and one wall of the massive church collapsed, sending a great cloud of dust into the air. Jake and Vanessa watched from a quarter-mile away. The boom rumbled through the asphalt under their feet.

Vanessa grunted. "I figured they'd blow their tunnel, and what with the gas—"

"The cops shut the line off," Jake muttered. "The gas probably didn't have much to do with it, but if the vampires had enough explosives—"

Vanessa shrugged. "Doesn't matter. One way or the other, they've made their getaway, and we won't be able to figure out where they dug the tunnel from."

"Ground-penetrating radar," Jake suggested.

"I'll look into it, but don't get your hopes up. Tracing a collapsed tunnel through the streets here would be no mean feat, especially when it's that deep. By the time we trace them back, they'll have moved their base. Good thinking, though."

Around them stood many of the people who had evacuated the church. Among the clergy was the pope himself, leaning heavily on his crozier. While Jake listened, the pope solemnly pronounced that vampires had no more permission to enter the basilica—what was left of it.

Vanessa nodded in approval. "That should do it. He has the authority."

The girl who had been Nunchuk Nun, now covered in bandages and with a hood over her face, lay on a stretcher. She petted Brigid, who had nestled on her chest. Jake sat down beside her, and Vanessa stood at his shoulder. Nuns and priests bustled about and talked to the police.

"The vampires," Jake said quietly, "Do you know what they came for?"

He started when a gravelly voice replied. The pope stood nearby and had apparently overheard.

"The Crystal," the pope murmured. "The Moon Princess entrusted us with it. We built the catacombs to house it—but we have failed, for these evil creatures have no doubt taken it."

With that, his holiness shook his head and limped away.

A moment passed as Jake chewed his lip. This wasn't the atmosphere he'd wanted, but he could do nothing about that now. He cleared his throat, tugged his collar, and looked up at Vanessa pleadingly. He didn't speak, but she slipped away to give him space. Others did likewise, leaving a patch of pavement around Jake and Nunchuk Nun.

After clearing his throat again, he said, "Nunchuk Nun—er, well, I mean, I don't know your name, but—you know I was with Lady Paladin Andalusia at"—he tugged his collar and cleared his throat yet again—"at the end."

She nodded. "I know. I'm sorry I ran away earlier."

"It's okay. Look, I don't know how to say this, and I don't know what it means or how important it is, but she wanted me to tell you something."

Nunchuk Nun nodded again.

"She said to, um . . . she told me to tell you . . . that the two of you couldn't have parfaits."

Although Jake couldn't see her face, Nunchuk Nun turned her head away, and he thought he heard a tiny, faint sob.

After a minute, she whispered, her voice thick, "It's a little shop down the street. We were going to go there—"

She stopped for a moment and took a deep breath.

"—when it was over. When we didn't have to be magical girls anymore. We were going to go there together as normal girls."

Jake merely sat beside her, head lowered, and interlaced his fingers. Several minutes passed, and then Vanessa returned. She gave Jake's shoulder an awkward pat.

"We should go," Vanessa said.

Vanessa frowned. "She's not equipped for vampires. We better hurry."

TWENTY-THREE

AFTERMATH

Half an hour later, Jake and Vanessa were trudging through the faux Roman streets. The air was cold, and Jake shivered under his trench coat. He rubbed a hand through his hair and said, "Vinny, I was planning to ask Nunchuk Nun this, but it didn't seem quite right—"

"Ask her what?"

"Do you know anything about ghosts?"

She smiled and stopped walking. Crossing her hands behind her back, she twisted one foot on a cobblestone, and despite the goofy mullet, it made her look girlish. "Not much, no. But a little. Why?"

He laughed quietly. "I'm surprised. Pretty Dynamo said there's no such thing as ghosts."

Vanessa nodded. "That's the kind of girl she is. Magical girls with powers like hers tend to be more—what's the word?—skeptical. But there are a lot of things in the universe, strange things. Ghosts aren't the sort of thing you should discount out of hand."

He silently chewed his lip.

"So why do you ask?"

"Because," he said, "I think I'm haunted."

"How come?"

"Well, I mean, I see this blue light sometimes—"

"Where?"

"Right in front of my eyes."

"Not in a particular place?"

"I see it most clearly in my room, and it looks like a girl. She cries and talks about not wanting something—or something like that."

Vanessa rubbed her chin. "A girl, hm? Hasn't tried to scare you, has she?"

"It *is* scary, but she doesn't seem to be scaring me on purpose."

"You don't *only* see it in your room?"

"It's clearest there, but no."

She nodded. "Well, the room might be important, or perhaps the time of night, but you're probably right—if it is a ghost, it's *you* that's haunted."

"What exactly does that mean?"

"Ghosts usually attach themselves to locations, but they can sometimes attach to people instead. I admit this isn't my specialty—"

"Why would this happen?"

She shook her head and continued walking. "Ghosts are spirits—pure minds. When they affect something, it's because they're *thinking* about that something. So this ghost is thinking about you. If you can see a ghost or touch it, that means it's using a physical medium to manifest. *Ectoplasm* is the word for it, but ectoplasm can be anything, really: Dew and mist are common, or fluid from a medium's body. Anyway, if the ghost is thinking of you, she must have unfinished business with you. That's the main reason the dead stick around."

"And what's the blue light?"

She shrugged. "Ectoplasm. If you see her at night, she might have some way of refracting moonlight—water condensation, maybe. She might even be using the aqueous humor in your eyeballs. Or she might be directly affecting your brain. There's no way for me to know."

"And what would her business be?"

Vanessa shrugged again. "Could be anything. If you want to know, then the next time you see her, invoke some power she will recognize. 'In the name of the Father and the Son and the Holy Ghost, who are you, and what do you want?' is a traditional formula. If you don't like that one, then call on the Moon Princess. But in any case, you have to invoke something the ghost will acknowledge."

He nodded.

She reached into one of the many pockets of her leather jacket and pulled out two slim pieces of paper. "See me tomorrow and tell me more about it. I'm having a concert, and you're invited."

She slapped the two tickets into his hand and gave him a wink. "Please come—and bring a *date*. I mean it. *Be* there."

With that, she turned and walked away.

FIFTEEN MINUTES LATER, ON HIS WAY TO A BUS STOP, JAKE MET Pretty Dynamo. She was panting and out of breath, with sweat rolling down her cute face. Tesla nestled in her blue hair. As soon as she saw him, she stopped running, bent over, and grabbed her knees.

"Never thought I'd see this," Jake said as he strolled toward her. "The great Pretty Dynamo—winded."

"Shut up!" she yelled. "I sprinted *all the way* from Juban! *Anybody* would be winded! And I told you before, I'm not used to parkour! Now, *where is she?"*

"Where is who? Nunchuk Nun?"

"No, idiot! You said you had vampires! So—"

She closed her mouth and scowled. Her face was already flushed, but the red in her cheeks deepened.

Jake tapped his chin and nodded solemnly. "Ah, *now* I get it. You ran here to see Magical Girl Metal Huntress Vanessa Van Halensing, didn't you?"

Her face didn't change, but her ears turned crimson. *"No! That's not—! I mean—! I don't . . . I don't like* Van Halensing or anything like that!"

"Uh-huh. So, who is this 'she' you wanna see?"

Dynamo didn't answer. She merely crossed her armor-plated forearms, turned her back on Jake, and grumbled under her breath.

He put a fist to his mouth and bit into a knuckle to keep from laughing. He felt the tickets burning in his pocket, and for a brief, delirious moment, he almost took them out and handed one to Dynamo, knowing it would send her over the moon—or perhaps annoy her. Either way, he would have found her reaction enjoyable.

But he didn't do it. Vanessa had said to bring a *date,* so Jake had plans to make things up with Chelsea. After all, she had a birthday coming up. He figured a Van Halensing concert for a birthday present might be worth a kiss.

Grease Pencil Marionette passed briefly through his mind. Before he had time to send the wayward thought away, he saw himself with her at the concert, his arm around her waist. Afterward, he bent down and met her lips with his—

He shook his head to get rid of that. He tried to replace Marionette's image with Chelsea's, but that was somehow a fantasy more vague and indiscernible, one he couldn't clearly bring to mind.

CONTRARY TO HABIT, JAKE PLAYED HOOKY THE NEXT MORNING.

More specifically, he went to the wrong school—or the right school, depending on how you looked at it.

He didn't walk with Ralph because he was too embarrassed. Instead, he took a roundabout path until he finally arrived at the high school's front entrance, the same nondescript façade with the chrome-accented clock tower that he had stood in front of only a little over a week before. It felt so long ago now.

Out front, several high-school kids stood around, chatting and laughing and arguing. They looked up as Jake approached. Some waved, some laughed, and some yelled incoherent but probably good-natured taunts.

For a moment, Jake thought the kids looked strangely large. In only a week and a half, he had got used to attending a school where everyone was considerably shorter than he was. A school full of people his size was surreal: It made him feel small, and he momentarily lost his courage.

He clenched his teeth and forged ahead anyway. He had faced vampires the night before; surely, he could face high schoolers.

Upon scanning the front yard, he discovered that he wouldn't have to go inside because he found what he was looking for—a knot of giggling, chattering girls. When some of the girls shifted their backpacks or their shoulders, he caught a glimpse of the one standing in the midst of them, the one over whom they were all fawning. It was, of course, T.B.

Some girl Jake didn't know clung tightly to T.B.'s left arm. With a lock of hair falling across her forehead, T.B. put a soft hand to the girl's face, and the girl trembled.

As Jake approached, he could hear T.B.'s oily voice: "They say the poet Stesichorus was struck blind when he dared curse the beauty of Helen, but when he then praised her, he received his sight again. Lest I be struck blind myself, I dare not even praise you, for no mere words could capture your loveliness."

Jake rolled his eyes, but the girl trembled and fell against T.B.'s chest, panting, "Oh, T.B. . . . ."

As Jake approached, Cassandra and Megumi, arms crossed, stepped in front of him.

"What do *you* want?" Cassandra snapped.

"Yeah," said Megumi, "don't you have, like, a *grade school* to go to?"

Jake laughed quietly. "I need to talk to your boy."

"He doesn't need to talk to you," Megumi replied.

"Oh, I think he does."

Cassandra tapped a finger hard against his chest. "Go *away,* Jake! You think we're gonna let a creep like you get anywhere near T.B. again? Like, no way!"

"Yeah," said Megumi. *"No* way. Like, totally."

Jake had to admire them: He'd demonstrated already that he could simply shove them aside if he wanted, but they nonetheless held their ground.

He glanced over their shoulders to see T.B. staring straight at him, her eyes wide and her lower lip trembling.

Jake raised his voice. "Need to talk to you, T.B.—alone. I'll keep my distance, but we gotta talk. And you know what I could do if you refuse."

Megumi's scowl deepened.

A single tear ran down T.B's left cheek, but she swiftly wiped it away. The girl clinging to her frowned.

Jake started when a heavy arm fell across his shoulders and a set of knuckles dug painfully into his ribs. He looked left and saw Ralph's grinning face.

"Dude!" Ralph yelled in Jake's ear. "You're here! Did they finally let you in? You shoulda told me!"

"I didn't—"

"Oh *man,* I gotta tell you what happened last night, man!"

Jake blinked. "What? Did you get attacked by—?"

"Nah, man. I had this crazy dream, like a waking dream, and dude, it was a *revelation!"*

"Ralph, look—"

Megumi and Cassandra's angry scowls turned to amused smirks as Ralph pulled Jake away.

"Dude, get this," Ralph continued, arm still around Jake's shoulders, "I was lying in bed, probably half-awake, when I realized it: Every haircut, like *every single one,* is a type of mullet. I woke up so excited, man, because it's *true!"*

Jake coughed. "Ralph, what in the name of the Moon Princess are you talking about?"

"Dude, think about it. What *is* a mullet?"

Jake could feel a twinge behind his temple again, the one that told him he was getting a headache. "Um . . . isn't that, like, long in the back and short in the front—?"

"Exactly! But just think, dude: That's like *every haircut in the world!"*

"Ralph—"

"What if a girl has long hair and bangs, huh? What do you call that?"

"Long hair with bangs?"

"It's a *mullet,* man! It's long in the back and short in the front!"

"Ralph—"

"What if a dude is bald but still has hair on the back of his head?"

"Ralph, seriously—"

"It's short in the front and long in the back! That's an *all-natural* mullet!"

"Ralph, I really don't have time for—"

"So that hot mama stayin' at your place, whose hair I combed —which I totally gotta brag about—*she's got a mullet!* And what a mullet it is!"

"Ralph—"

Ralph kneaded Jake's scalp. Jake tried to swat him off.

"Dude, you know your hair's gettin' long? Kinda curlin' at the neck here."

"You're being weird, Ralph. I haven't had time for a haircut, so just—"

Ralph grabbed a lock of hair near the base of Jake's neck and then grabbed another near his forehead. *"This* is longer than *this,* dude! Long in the back and short in the front! *You're wearing a mullet!"*

"Ralph, I'm serious! Let go of me!"

Jake glanced at T.B., who watched the scene with her mouth hanging open.

"Whoa," T.B. whispered. "Willikers-*sama* is, like, so smart."

With a pout, the girl on her arm let go and stomped away.

Rolling his eyes, Jake shoved Ralph off. "T.B.! I need to see you! *Now!*"

The bell for class rang, and everyone in front of the school headed for the door. T.B. made a half turn but hesitated. Cassandra and Megumi flanked her and tried to take her by the arms.

Looking over her shoulder at Jake, T.B said, "I gotta go to class—"

"Be late," Jake replied.

T.B. swallowed.

Ralph still stood at Jake's elbow, though a scowl now crumpled his brow.

"Hey, Ralph," said Jake, still staring at T.B., "guess what I learned about—"

"All right!" T.B. shouted. "All right, you win, Jake!" She wrapped her arms around Megumi and Cassandra, pulling them close. "But they come too!"

"Do they—?"

"Yes! They know everything!"

Jake jerked a thumb over his shoulder. "Okay. There's an alley halfway up the block. I'll be there, and you be there, too— in five minutes. *Or else!*"

A confused frown on his face, Ralph reached toward Jake. Jake pushed him away, turned, and walked.

A FEW MINUTES LATER, JAKE STOOD NEAR A RICKETY, weathered fence twenty feet up the alleyway—he had paced it off

—where he strode back and forth, arms crossed and fingers tapping on his elbows.

When time was almost up, T.B. finally appeared. With sweat dripping down her face, she clung to Megumi and Cassandra like a drowning man desperately clutching a life preserver. Megumi and Cassandra glared at Jake as if trying to fire deadly laser beams from their eyes.

Jake was in a bad mood, but for a moment, that mood softened. T.B. looked pathetic. She was clearly an athletic girl, and she appeared healthy and confident in her magical-girl outfit, but when dressed as a boy, she looked frail and weak.

They all stared at one another quietly for half a minute. Finally, Cassandra broke the silence by snapping, "What do you want, Jake Blatowski?"

"First things first," Jake replied quietly. "You know vampires attacked Rome-in-Exile last night?"

T.B. swallowed. "What?"

"You didn't get the word? I think the boss contacted several girls—"

T.B. shook her head. Megumi clung to her more tightly.

Jake took a deep breath. "They attacked the basilica—"

"What?" said T.B. "Vampires did? Vampires don't attack churches."

"They attacked this one. And they stole something, some crystal. Do you know anything about it?"

T.B. let go of Cassandra long enough to tap her chin and knit her eyebrows together. "No," she said. "No, I don't. A crystal?"

"I know you guys get training at the Temple. Nothing about crystals?"

T.B. shook her head. "Some info on monster classes, wards,

battle tactics, warnings about the Weapon—oh, and the religious stuff. But that's about it. Nothing about crystals."

Jake took a deep breath. "Okay, next thing: I want you to call off your fight with Pretty Dynamo."

Cassandra merely gave T.B. an uncertain glance, but Megumi wrapped her arms around her and squeezed her tight. "No *way*, Jake! Sukeban Tsubasa's gonna be number one! The greatest in the whole city! T.B. is the *best!* He's awesome, and he doesn't care about your stupid little *girlfriend,* so *there!"*

T.B. tapped her chin again for a moment but then hung her head and sighed. "I can't."

Jake snorted. "Like *heck* you can't."

"Jake," said T.B., holding out a hand, "please! It's my reputation—"

"I don't *give a darn* about your reputation!" Jake shouted. With a clumsy kick, he sent gravel flying toward the alley's mouth. "Think about the city for a change instead of about yourself!"

T.B. lowered her hand, and a fresh tear ran down her cheek. "Jake," she said, her voice high and trembling, "my reputation is all I have."

Megumi rested T.B.'s head on her shoulder and petted her hair—hair Jake now realized could qualify as a mullet, depending on how you looked at it.

"T.B.," said Jake, "I'll make you a deal. You call off the fight, and I'll help you get over your phobia."

Now Megumi clutched T.B. even more tightly and rocked her back and forth. "Don't listen to him, T.B.! He's a *jerk!* You don't need his help!"

"And when you're over it," Jake added, "I'll introduce you to Ralph."

T.B. lifted her tear-streaked face from Megumi's shoulder and whispered, "Really?"

Jake nodded. "I don't promise anything. But I'll introduce you."

Cassandra placed a hand on T.B.'s back. "T.B., don't! He's up to something! He just wants to protect his girlfriend! He doesn't want you to be the number-one magical girl! Tell him *no!*"

Megumi stared at Jake as she chewed her lip in apparent indecision. Finally, she clutched T.B. tightly and said, "You don't need to get over it, T.B. You have *us.*"

T.B. sucked in her lips for a moment and then asked, "How? How will you do it?"

Jake shrugged. "Exposure. A little at a time, right? You said you weren't as scared of me as you were of some guys. So I'll be your therapy. Get within ten feet of me for as long as you can. Then five. Then one. That kind of thing."

Now T.B. clawed at Cassandra's sailor *fuku*.

"We can go as slow as you need to," Jake added. "But if you can't even get close to a guy like me, you'll *never* get close to Ralph."

Megumi's lower lip trembled. She squeezed T.B. tightly, but T.B. squirmed in her grasp.

"Ralph," T.B. said. "Ralph doesn't like me anyway."

"He hasn't really met you," Jake replied. "You don't know if he likes you or not."

T.B. swallowed. "When do we start?"

"This Saturday. Let's meet out on the track. It's easy to measure distance there."

T.B. shook her head. "Everyone will see us."

Jake shrugged. "It's the weekend. It'll be fine. Everyone'll think you're out for a run."

"I don't run. I'm supposed to have a heart condition."

"Okay, then say you're recovering and getting some exercise, and I'm helping. I don't care, just make something up—that's what you do anyway, isn't it?"

T.B. glanced back and forth from Megumi to Cassandra.

"When?" she asked, her voice hoarse.

"Training should be early in the morning. Six o'clock."

T.B. licked her lips. "Seven."

"I'm your trainer. I said six. Take it or leave it."

"You're a jerk, Jake!" Megumi shouted.

"Six," T. B. said. "Six is fine." Her chin moved up and down rapidly while more sweat poured down her pale face.

Jake felt another twinge of sympathy. *Dang, this really is taking it out of her.*

"Okay," he said. "See you then. Best get to class."

With that, Jake spun around, raised one hand in a brief wave goodbye, and walked to the alley's far end.

Sukeban Tsubasa must be having a bad influence on me, Jake thought as he wandered into a café, ordered a cup of black coffee, and tucked himself into a booth near the back. He was delinquent from school, and he paid for the coffee with yet more change he had pilfered from his parents—though he tried to shut up his conscience by reminding himself that he intended to repay the stolen money as soon as he could.

As he slowly sipped, he pulled a paperback novel out of his back pocket. Absently, he thumbed through it. Although less inclined to English than mathematics, he was an avid reader but hadn't had time to sit down with a novel in what felt like ages. This book belonged to his father—though, unlike the money, taking it wasn't stealing because he was free to borrow any of the books in the house.

He scanned the first few chapters and decided the story didn't interest him; it depicted a glorious future of interstellar travel in which humanity dominated a vast galactic confederacy. There was a big appetite in Urbanopolis for this brand of retro science fiction—*rocketpunk,* they called it—containing nostalgic visions of a human triumphalism that had never been and never could be.

In reality, humanity, still bound to one planet, was unmistakably dying, and the galaxy—indeed, all of the universe—was full of advanced civilizations humans had no hope of matching. Since most of those advanced civilizations were overtly opposed to the humans' continued existence, many Urbanopolitans liked to escape into old-fashioned fantasies of man as the cosmic master race. Jake, however, found rocketpunk insipid and naïve. Ironically, its escapist optimism was depressing.

He opened the book at random and read a few pages about the square-jawed and broad-shouldered hero zapping slimy, bug-eyed aliens with a ray gun in order to save the buxom princess. There were such things as ray guns, of course, and many alien species were indeed bug-eyed and slimy, but square-jawed and broad-shouldered men never did the necessary zapping. In Urbanopolis, little girls were stuck with that task: The princess had to do her own fighting, and she was rarely buxom.

Jake threw the book down and focused on his coffee. He hadn't walked with Dana to school that morning, but he also hadn't told her how he planned to spend his day. He hoped she could keep her mouth shut about his absence.

He nursed the same cup for a few hours until it turned cold. Then he got up, left a meager tip, and went for a walk.

It was still early. He had an hour until noon and no way to get lunch. He was going to be hungry when the day was over.

Boredom gradually crept in as he wandered the streets. Figuring people would be less likely to notice him there and ask questions, he headed downhill into Little India.

He still had the two concert tickets in his inside pocket. *Bring a date,* Vanessa had said. That was perfect: Jake didn't care for monster metal, but Chelsea loved it, and he knew she'd be thrilled to go to a Van Halensing concert. He'd saunter up to her, slick his hair back, nonchalantly mention that he'd run into someone the other day, not a big deal, but that someone happened to be Metal Huntress Van Halensing, and—

In front of a small Shaivite temple in the midst of Little India's most crowded street, he stopped. A few people ran into him and then offered obsequious apologies as they brushed past.

Jake's stomach sank. He slapped a hand to his forehead.

I am such an idiot.

He should have realized it before: Vanessa didn't want him to bring just any date. She was asking him—no, *telling* him—to bring Magical Girl Pretty Dynamo.

Something was up. She expected trouble at the concert—or she had some kind of plan. Either way, this wasn't just an evening out. This was business, not pleasure.

Jake put his hand to his chest, where the tickets lived. Suddenly, they were like lead weights in his pocket.

He sighed. Well, Dana also liked Van Halensing, so maybe this would be a good chance to make up with her instead. She wouldn't *act* happy, of course, but he knew she would be.

The pistol still rode in its tactical holster on his hip, under his trench coat. It was borderline illegal because he had it concealed —though concealment without a permit was only a misdemeanor that wasn't widely enforced. Since humans were under constant threat from monsters and aliens, the city didn't forbid its citizens to arm themselves, but it did discourage it: Most monsters were impervious to conventional weapons, and using them usually produced greater bloodshed. Jake had witnessed this himself the week before when he watched soldiers open fire on a magical troll—and burn alive as a result. Because of such difficulties, magical girls handled most of the fighting while soldiers handled crowd control and evacuation. Civilians were supposed to be noncombatants.

Of course, the last week and a half had seen the invasion of Robosaurs and zombies, which could fall to conventional weapons, and the wasps exuded by the *kaiju* Hive Rind had been similarly vulnerable. Jake hadn't returned his gun partly because he wanted to keep it in case similar monsters showed up in the future. He doubted anyone would actually miss it.

Nonetheless, after some indecision—and because of boredom —he decided to walk into a police station. He strode right up to the sergeant behind the front desk, explained that he was the "Barfing Boy," and told him what happened during the fight.

The officer steepled his hands and looked skeptical at first, but after peering closely at Jake's face and then tapping for a while on his computer, he asked, "Do you still have the gun?"

"Yes, sir."

The officer paused a moment, licked his lips, and said, "On you?"

Jake swallowed a sudden lump and said, "Yes, sir." After an uncomfortable silence, he started explaining again: "I thought it would be best. I mean, I've got monsters—"

The officer raised a hand, and Jake stopped talking.

"Keep it," the officer said.

Jake blinked. "What?"

"You're a sidekick, right?"

"Well, not exactly, but—"

The officer waved a hand to shut him up again. "You understand that shooting most monsters will get you killed? That only a few can fall to bullets?"

"Yes, sir."

"And you were with a magical girl when you took it, right?"

"Rifle Maiden."

The officer nodded. "Okay. Commandeering is legal, and it doesn't have a time limit. You're done with that pistol when Dame Rifle Maiden says you're done with it. If she wants you to return it, then bring her in with you. Otherwise—"

The officer flicked his fingers a couple of times, indicating that Jake should leave.

Jake nodded, turned around, and headed for the door.

I bet he just doesn't want to deal with the paperwork.

TWENTY-FOUR

BAD GIRLS

After walking the whole day, Jake was tired. When he got home, he threw himself down on the couch and took a deep breath. His father wasn't back yet, so the television wasn't on.

A few minutes later, Dana walked in, kicked her shoes off, and threw herself down next to him. She let out a long sigh.

"How was school?" he asked.

She grunted. "Where were you?"

"I had business to take care of. I figure it doesn't matter if I miss a day of fifth grade."

She made a rasping noise. "It was boring, as usual."

He laughed. "So, how are you feeling?"

"What do you mean?"

"I mean, how are you *feeling?*"

He glanced over his shoulder to make sure they were alone. His mother wasn't in the room, and judging from the quietness of the house, she was probably running errands.

"How is Pretty Dynamo?" he asked.

She slouched sideways until her cheek lay on an armrest. She pulled a throw pillow to her chest and hugged it. "You mean now that she's lost two items and almost lost her wand?"

"Yeah, basically. But you should get your Circuit Board back soon, right?"

"I dunno. Since I gotta regrow my Surge Protector, the Circuit Board might take longer."

"And, how do you feel?"

For several seconds, she didn't answer, but then she said, "I wish I could take a break."

He nodded. "Yeah."

After another sigh, she muttered, almost too quietly for him to hear, "Everything hurts. I'm sore all over, all the time, an' I don't ever get a chance to feel better." She paused. "My *feet* hurt."

She stuck out her lip in a pout.

Jake tapped his fingers on the armrest. Then he reached down, took her right foot, and pulled it into his lap. He started rubbing. Her foot was tiny and soft—much like her hand, which he had briefly clasped a week before.

For almost a minute, she didn't respond. Then she said, "What the heck are you doing?"

"What does it look like? You said your feet hurt, right?"

She raised her head and glared at him. "So?"

"So."

After a long silence, she lowered her head back to the armrest, and the tension left her leg.

"Listen," he said, "I decided. Last week, when that demon-possessed guy came after us in New Beijing, I decided I'm going to protect you."

She raised her head again and lifted one eyebrow. "What?"

"You heard me. You have to protect all of Urbanopolis, so I'm going to protect you."

"Why?"

"Why not?"

He paused long enough to reach into his shirt pocket, pull out the concert tickets, and toss them onto her stomach. She picked them up and stared at them while he continued rubbing her foot.

Her fingers shook. *"How did you get these?"*

"I got them from Van Halensing."

"What?"

"Yeah. I met her in Rome-in-Exile."

Dana groaned and threw her head back down so hard, it bounced from the arm of the couch. "Rrrr, I *so* wish I had my Circuit Board back! I can't *believe* I was late!"

"She told me to bring you to the concert. I don't know what's up, but she wants Pretty Dynamo, so she must be expecting trouble."

Dana scowled. "She's gotta be plannin' something. I'll talk to Tesla about it."

"You wanna go as Dynamo, or in your alter ego?"

"I'll ask Tesla. Dynamo might attract too much attention."

He nodded, and they were silent again.

Several minutes later, Dana asked, "So, did you get me an autograph?"

Jake laughed. "I thought you weren't a fan."

"I'm not!"

"Then why would I get you an autograph?"

She stared at him for a few seconds, lip twitching, before she crossed her arms and muttered, "Jerk."

But she didn't pull her foot out of his lap.

"Make sure you eat a good meal tonight and get plenty of sleep," he told her. "We need you in top form tomorrow."

The front door flew open, and Dana's mother stormed in. Dana snatched her foot back and sat up, the throw pillow still squeezed to her chest.

"Ugh!" Millie cried. *"What* a day! Judge Bennett asked me out for coffee—*again!* That man!"

She dropped her purse and coat by the front door, kicked off her pumps, and stomped toward the kitchen. As she passed the couch, she paused and looked back and forth from Jake to Dana.

"What are you two doing?" she asked.

"Nothing," Dana quickly replied.

Millie shrugged. "Tea!" she announced as she continued her kitchen-ward march. "I need tea! Jake, where does your mother keep her tea hoard?"

"In the jar on the counter," Jake answered. "The one that says 'tea.'"

Millie found the jar and soon had a kettle going on the stove.

Dana tugged on Jake's sleeve, gave him a particularly meaningful glower, and then hopped from the couch and headed for the stairs.

Jake was about to join her, but Millie plopped down beside him on the sofa with a cup cradled in her hands. As Dana disappeared upstairs, Jake felt a lump rise in his throat.

With her slim fingers, Millie brushed some of her long, red hair out of her face. She took a sip. "Ah, *what* a day."

Jake tugged on his collar. "Yeah, tell me about it."

"You know," said Millie as she settled back into the couch, "I think Dana really looks up to you." She put her feet on the coffee table.

Jake squirmed uncomfortably. "Oh . . . yeah?"

Millie slid toward him an inch. She arched her back, emphasizing her breasts, while a fresh clump of hair fell across her face.

The lump in Jake's throat grew larger.

She took another sip of tea. "It's been hard for Dana since her father died," she said, her voice containing an unmistakable husky note. "I really think she needs a man in her life. Do you . . . do you understand what I mean?"

She slid toward him yet another inch.

Jake's pulse pounded in his ears. *Oh, man, is she hitting on me? Like, for real?*

She laid a hand on his leg. He nearly jumped out of his seat, but he restrained himself. His blood boiled.

Oh, man. Oh, man! She is definitely *hitting on me! And she's a widow! She's experienced! She probably knows all the freaky stuff—!*

Millie gave his leg a pat and then sat back, noisily slurping tea. "Ah, that hits the spot! So, anyway, I'd really appreciate it if you'd do me a favor and keep an eye on her."

Jake blinked, and his blood cooled. "Huh? Wha—?"

Millie chuckled quietly. "Little Dana's always had strange moods. Whenever she went off on one of her sulks, her daddy used to pick her up and sit her in his lap and tickle her and tell stories. She tried to keep scowling, but she'd end up giggling like mad."

Millie sighed and took another sip. "Max was so good with her. I just can't seem to do it like he did. It really isn't the same without her father here."

Jake's heart rate returned to normal. He swallowed again, and the lump was gone.

"Oh," he said. "Yeah."

After half a minute of silence, he cleared his throat, ran his hand through his hair, and said, "Um, Mrs. Volt, I hope it's okay for me to ask, but . . . what exactly happened to—?"

Millie smiled, but her smile was strained. "To her father?"

He swallowed once more, and the lump was back. "Yeah."

Millie's smile became pained. "She broke his neck, Jake. That's what you wanted to ask, wasn't it? How Pretty Dynamo killed him?"

"Well—"

"She just broke his neck. It's as simple as that. Half a second, and *bam,* he was dead. That's when I learned what magical girls really are. Magical girls can do anything they want with us— anything at all—and get away with it scot-free because the law won't hold them accountable. They're children, and we're their toys. They play with us, and they can break us when they get angry or bored."

She patted his leg again and stood up. "They'll play with you, but if you keep playing with *them,* then sooner or later, they'll break you too."

As she walked into the kitchen, she paused, turned back toward him, and said, "I know you're mixed up in this, Jake."

He spun around and gripped the back of the couch. "Mrs. Volt, I don't want you to think—"

She raised a hand to stop him. "Your parents are trying to keep me in the dark. I know that's their way of being kind, and I appreciate it, but I'm not stupid, Jake. I know what you're up to."

His hands trembled.

She gave him another strained smile. "It's not my place to tell you how to run your life, but at least do me a favor."

He felt his hairline moisten. "What?"

"Keep Dana out of it."

The lump in his throat thickened. His knuckles turned white on the back of the sofa. He nodded once and muttered, "I'll try."

He got up and fled for the stairs.

JAKE JOINED DANA IN HER ROOM AND QUIETLY CLOSED THE door. She opened a dresser drawer, and Tesla poked his head out.

"To be perfectly frank, young Dana," Tesla said as he rubbed his glasses with a miniature kerchief, "this new arrangement is most taxing, what with so many inconvenient humans around." Tesla planted his glasses over his compound eyes, blinked a couple of times, and then stared at Jake. "Ah. And here is the most inconvenient of them all."

Jake snorted. "Nice to see you too, Tesla."

Dana held up the tickets. "These came from Metal Huntress Van Halensing."

Tesla frowned and tapped a tarsal claw against his clypeus.

"It's a rock concert," Jake said. "Tomorrow night. She specifically told me to bring a date, and I think she meant Pretty Dynamo."

Dana made a growling noise but said nothing.

"And the reason?" Tesla asked.

Jake shrugged. "Hey, you're the familiar. You tell me."

"Presumably, she is expecting trouble—though it is also possible this is some barbaric means of showing gratitude."

"I don't know," said Jake. "But the pope told me that the vampires took something out of the catacombs last night, something important—"

"What?" Tesla asked.

Jake shook his head. "Some crystal. Nunchuk Nun didn't

know about it, either. But I can tell you this much: One of the vampires who attacked me threw a cupcake in my face."

Tesla blinked.

"A cupcake?" said Dana. "Seriously?"

"Yeah, seriously."

"Dana," said Tesla as he stroked his mandibles with a claw, "you may recall that you found pink frosting at the Unnatural History Museum."

Dana's eyebrows came together.

Tesla continued, "Detective Brannigan told us the criminals who broke into the museum were in human shape but moved with superhuman speed. That is consistent with vampires."

"So whatever they're after has to do with the Caspian Gate," said Dana.

"But the important parts of the gate are in the Temple of the Moon Princess," said Jake, "so why were the vampires in St. Peter's? What is this crystal they supposedly captured?"

Dana shook her head. "Dunno. I'll call the boss and let him know about this. He can put out a call for extra patrols at the Temple. But . . ."

Her voice trailed off.

Jake eased himself to the floor and leaned his back against the hide-a-bed. "But what?"

Dana shrugged. "The Temple isn't a church. Churches *want* people to come in, so most anybody could invite a vampire. But the Temple's different. Only the High Priestess has the authority to invite someone."

Jake pulled up his knees and wrapped his arms around them. "So unless the High Priestess invited them, the vampires couldn't get in?"

Dana frowned. "They shouldn't be able to, no."

Tesla shoved his glasses up his clypeus and coughed delicately into a claw. "We should assume, until we know better, that the vampires have some means of getting around this sticking point. I would still alert the boss, Dana. Then he can inform the High Priestess. She will take whatever steps she thinks necessary."

Dana, brow still crumpled, nodded.

Tesla cleared his throat and slapped a claw on the edge of the drawer. "But let us return to the discussion of this primitive tribal gathering you call a 'rock concert.' While I hesitate to criticize the work of another familiar's magical girl, I admit that I do not think this style of music is best for impressionable, developing minds."

"Hey," said Jake, "that's what I said."

Dana rolled her eyes. "So, are we going or what?"

"It appears we should," Tesla replied. "Especially if Van Halensing expects some confrontation with the vampires who are interested in the Caspian Gate. But I am concerned that Pretty Dynamo may not be in fighting form at present."

"When will she have her Circuit Board?" Jake asked.

"I can't say for certain. I could run a status check if Dana transformed, but even then, I couldn't give you a prediction with any better precision than I have already. Alas, I was unable to join you during that recent debacle with the giant wasps, so I have been unable to observe the progression of her regeneration."

"I can't transform here," Dana muttered. "Someone would hear."

Jake nodded. "I think me an' Dana should go in together. You hide in her purse, like before. If there's trouble—"

Tesla cleared his throat. "If there's trouble, she will have a difficult time finding a secluded place to transform."

"Yeah," said Jake, scratching the back of his neck, "but she can't fly in as long as she's ground-bound. That means she'd have to walk in with the crowd if she went as Dynamo, and that would probably cause bigger problems, right?"

Tesla rubbed his mandible. "Hmm, perhaps—"

"So let's stake some good transformation spots on our way in. The bathrooms might work, right?"

"Have you been in the bathrooms at a concert?" Dana asked dryly.

Jake tugged his collar. "Erm, no. Have you?"

"No, but I know there are lines and stuff."

Tesla adjusted his glasses. "Are the tickets for a particular seat or section?"

"Well," said Jake as he rubbed his neck, "they're VIP tickets, so I think we can go anywhere, but we should probably find a spot in the nosebleeds in case we need to sneak out."

Dana groaned. "Ah, c'mon!"

"I'm afraid the young man is right, Dana," Tesla said. "This is business, not pleasure, and you will more likely be effective as a magical girl if you hide near the back."

"It'll also be better for your ears," Jake added. "I'll bring earplugs so we can listen in comfort."

Dana's eyes narrowed. "You have got to be kidding."

"I'm not kidding."

She threw up her hands. "You are such a *dork!*"

"Yeah," he said, tapping his temple, "but I'm a dork who hasn't lost his hearing."

Dana slapped a hand to her forehead, slumped down onto the hide-a-bed, and sulked.

THE DARK QUEEN PLODDED SLOWLY AND TIREDLY DOWN THE hall toward her chambers. All she wanted now was to sleep.

She jumped when she heard a voice directly behind her.

"Your Darkness," it said. It was harsh, rough—and held a note of contempt.

She shot forward, spun around, and—out of habit—flicked her wrist. With a series of whirs and clicks, a *naginata* unfolded from her sleeve and settled in her hands.

Before her stood a tall, thin man with a pale, gaunt face. His double-breasted white uniform accented the unhealthy pallor of his skin, and on his head stood a high chef's hat. Holding a stainless-steel whisk in one hand, he leaned against a wall and glanced with contemptuous, bloodshot eyes at her weapon. A small smile twitched his blood-red lips.

With another flick, the Dark Queen put the *naginata* away.

"So it's you," she said. "What should I call you? Your Imperial Majesty?"

"Just Julian will do," he replied. "I want to talk to you, Your Darkness—alone."

"How did you get in here? Who invited you?"

He grinned but didn't reply.

So one of my minions is in his pay. That is not good.

The portal to her private chamber was right behind her, so the Dark Queen reached back and threw it open. "Come into my parlor," she said as she turned and entered.

"I accept your invitation," he replied, and she could hear soft footsteps behind her, followed by the squeak of the door's hinges and the clicking of the latch.

The inside of her chamber was, of course, dark. The hard

floor was of black marble, and the ceiling was a dome covered in a fresco depicting, in grisly detail, ghouls ranging through a graveyard and devouring exhumed corpses. In one corner of the room stood a rack, in another stood an iron maiden, and in a third stood a Judas cradle. All three were stained with brownish splatters of dried blood. Mounted on the walls were whips of various shapes and lengths, ranging from riding crops to cats-o'-nine-tails. Other devices festooned the walls as well: A pear of anguish, a thumbscrew, a heretic's fork, an iron spider, a scavenger's daughter, an assortment of daggers and saws, and objects not immediately identifiable.

In the chamber's center stood an enormous, canopied, four-poster bed mounted on a dais. Hanging above the bed was a tangle of ropes, manacles, and chains.

As Julian's glowing eyes swept the room, he uttered one word: "Charming."

"Oh, *this?*" said the Dark Queen. "This is just for my minions. I have to keep up appearances, you know. My *real* room is back here." She walked to the far end of the chamber and pressed a concealed panel. The wall silently slid open.

She and Julian entered a small, cozy bedroom with thick, pink carpet and pastel-colored walls. On the bed lay an over-stuffed comforter depicting sleepy unicorns with rainbow-colored manes. Piled in one corner was a collection of stuffed animals—mostly bears, but with a few rabbits, tigers, and koalas thrown in. There was a small table set with a purple tablecloth, and around it stood stools shaped like giant mushrooms with polka-dot tops.

"Ah," said the Queen as she stretched her arms over her head, "in here, I can relax!"

Her heart pounded as she suddenly felt a strong, alien desire rising up from her loins, and she smiled mirthlessly. This, of course, was the most infamous of the vampires' powers, and she had little doubt why Julian was using it: The Dark Queen did not age as long as she remained within the force field around her castle, so, though she had lived for over two centuries, she still had the body of a seventeen-year-old, which made a youthful body's demands. True, she had a few gray hairs and a few lines around her eyes, for the force field could not entirely prevent the passage of time and the inevitable wear and tear—but she was forever young.

She felt an ice-cold hand on her neck. Her heart fluttered, and her breath caught for a moment.

Nonetheless, she mastered herself. With contempt, she slapped the hand away.

"I said you may come in," she whispered coldly, "but I don't recall saying you could take liberties."

"Forgive me, Your Darkness," Julian replied in an oily voice, "but your loveliness had momentarily made me forget myself. It has been so long, yet you've not lost the flower of youth."

Her heart skipped a beat at the compliment, but that only angered her further. "Spare me," she said as she glided away from him and settled into a beanbag chair near the stuffed animals.

Julian lowered himself onto a stool at the table. Once he sat, the Dark Queen leaped up again and busied herself at a kitch-enette in the corner, where she soon had a kettle going.

"Tea?" she asked.

Julian raised one eyebrow. "I do not drink . . . *tea*. But I suppose you knew that."

"Of course, but I'm afraid I can't offer you anything more to your taste."

"Never mind. I have already feasted tonight." With that, he flashed his fangs.

Once the Queen returned, now with a teacup, to her beanbag chair, the two stared at each other for half a minute before she simply asked, "Why?"

"As I'm sure you are aware," he replied, steepling his hands before his face, "I recently received a visit from one of your servants."

She almost slopped her tea. "One of mine?"

She bit into her lower lip as soon as the words escaped. *Chirops. Darn him. He should have told me.*

But after that thought crossed her mind, she realized that Chirops may, in fact, have tried to tell her.

Julian raised an eyebrow again. "Yes, of course. The little bat fellow."

"Yes, of course," she answered quickly. Then she cleared her throat faintly. "And?"

"And he made an . . . *interesting* proposal. I assume you've received word of our recent debacle in Rome-in-Exile."

She hadn't. Nonetheless, she leaned forward and grinned. "So that was *your* doing, was it, Julian?"

"Perhaps."

She watched his impassive face, but he betrayed no emotion: He was, after all, a corpse.

"What *exactly* are you up to?" She spoke as evenly as she could but inwardly cursed herself when a faint tremor—nervousness or anticipation, she wasn't sure which—entered her voice.

He crossed his arms. "Let's not play games, Dark Queen. You know what I am—the one history has called the *Apostate*. Initiated into the secret rites of Hermes Trismegistus, I learned the deep truths of the universe and conversed with the Outer

Gods. I had myself submerged in blood to erase the mark of my baptism. I cut open slave girls to read the future of Rome in their entrails, and through this haruspicy, I saw the empire weakening and growing decadent. I was sure a return to the old gods—"

"What's your point, Julian? That was a long time ago."

"Yes. My point is, you know what *I* am. But what exactly are *you?*"

The Dark Queen caught herself before she smiled. So she had him at a slight disadvantage—unless, of course, this was part of his game.

"What does it matter?" she asked.

"It matters a great deal. But I think I'm beginning to figure you out. What do you know about the Moon Princess?"

The Dark Queen settled into her seat and took a deep pull on her tea. "Less than I'd like. We knew each other face to face, but she struck me with a Lethe spell before we parted. I've recovered some memories, but I can never be sure how many I'm missing."

"What do you know? Specifically, what are the Crystals?"

Now the Dark Queen allowed a smile. "So, you know about the Crystals?"

Julian showed his sharp teeth in a broad grin. "I *have* one."

"Ah, do you? Then I know this: The Robosaurs destroyed one. If you destroy another, that leaves only three."

"What do they do?"

"What do you think?"

He slammed a fist down onto the table, and it made a loud cracking sound. "Tell me why I should destroy the one I have."

"Are you certain you have one, Julian? Really?"

"Yes, Your Darkness, *I am.*"

She took another drink and laughed quietly.

"Don't you know?" he demanded.

She bared her own sharp teeth. "Haven't you ever wondered what the Princess is doing?"

"Of course. And I've wondered if she's even still alive."

"She is. She *must* be. Don't you feel it?"

With a snort of impatience, Julian said, "Feel what?"

"Oh, come now, Julian, you know what I mean. The *draw.* The *pull.* Whatever you want to call it. The strange attraction to *the moon.*"

Julian stared at her with his glowing red eyes but then chuckled. "It is strange you mention that. I've had many a dream of late—"

"Vampires dream?"

"Of course we do. I've often dreamt of *eating* the moon. I assumed this was simply some dim memory of the *vârcolac.* He is supposed to be one of my kind, you know, a vampire so powerful he eats the moon. He may be merely a legend—"

Julian suddenly stopped talking.

"You hunger for the moon, don't you?" the Dark Queen asked, her voice low. "You want to eat it? Destroy it?"

"So what if I do?"

"Don't you see?" she said, leaning forward. "Every power in the galaxy feels it, perhaps in the whole universe. Every servant of Lord Shadow desires to destroy Earth's moon—"

"And?"

"And they cannot reach it! An impenetrable force field surrounds it. That was the Moon Princess's specialty, you know, force fields."

"What is your point?"

"My point is that this is all a trick. The Princess has done something to make herself irresistible to her enemies, but she has, at the same time, made herself unreachable. The only way to get to her is to go through Urbanopolis—where she has her magical girls."

Julian put a hand to his chin and brooded quietly. "So you're saying—"

"The Princess was an egotistical fool. I think this was her goal all along, her pathetic master plan for eliminating evil in the universe. She's turned the Earth and Moon into a giant *bug zapper.* She attracts all the forces of darkness, and then the magical girls kill them. Of course, it can't last—there are too many of us and too few of them."

"And you think the Crystals are generating this force field."

"I'm certain of it."

Julian took a deep breath and tapped his long, bony fingers together. "So your goal, then, is the destruction of the moon?"

"Of the Moon Princess, at least."

"And the humans?"

She shrugged. "Slaves, food—what does it matter?"

Julian snorted. "As you are probably aware, Your Darkness, I have some interest in the continued existence of the human race."

The Dark Queen laughed. "Of course you do."

"And if my intel is correct, Lord Shadow has recently obligated you to conjure an eldritch abomination to strike the city. Am I right?"

Now the Queen blanched. "How—?"

"I have means." Julian paused a moment. "Oh no, no—it wasn't the bat. I have *other* sources of intelligence."

The Dark Queen clenched a fist against her thigh. *So I definitely have a spy.*

She believed what Julian said—it couldn't be Chirops, whose loyalty was obligatory. But someone else in her ranks was delivering messages to the vampires and inviting them into her domain.

She cleared her throat. "What exactly do you want, Julian?"

He grinned mirthlessly. "I suspect our goals are not as mismatched as I had at first supposed. You have something I want. And I have something you want—or rather, something you *need.*"

When he leaned forward, the light played across his fangs. "So, Your Darkness, let's make a *deal.*"

TWENTY-FIVE

ROCK OF RAGES

J ulian marched into his dark audience chamber, ascended the dais, and fell heavily into his throne, where he leaned back and closed his eyes.

"It is done," he said.

A coffin lid flew open, and Lady Báthory climbed out, shaking clods of Hungarian earth from her voluminous gown.

"Well, Imperator?" she said. "We are ready, then, for the final stage of your plan."

"We have new advantages," Julian replied, "but they come with new obligations. What was once a wild fancy is now a duty. We have no choice but to continue."

Into the room walked Igor and Wilhelm, bearing stacks of paper. They laid them on two of the coffins and spread them out, revealing enlarged photographs of the fragments of the Caspian Gate.

"Call him," Julian said.

Igor hastened out. A few minutes later, he returned with a

tall, somber figure whose full, bloodshot eyes appeared lidless, and whose flabby lips drooped in a permanent frown around his prominent fangs. This figure silently approached the throne and knelt.

"Do you bow to me?" Julian asked. "You are older than I."

The figure spoke, and his voice rasped like dry dust. "You led the Vampyr to safety and sheltered them while I, mad with thirst, wandered the Wastes. You found me, took pity on me, and brought me here. You are the vampires' rightful king."

Julian nodded. "Look again at the inscriptions. You are the only one who can read them."

The figure, face impassive, rose to his feet and said, "First, feed me."

Julian waved a hand at the Lady Báthory, who bowed and left but soon returned with an intravenous drip and a bag of blood. The figure sat down on one of the coffins, and his left sleeve, of its own accord, peeled back from his thin, pale arm. Careful not to touch his skin, Báthory inserted a golden needle into his arm. Soon, the blood began to flow.

The figure sighed, and his hanging lips almost rose in a smile.

"Now," he said, "bring me the images."

Igor and Wilhelm complied. The figure took the photos in his gloved right hand, set them by his side, and carefully sorted them.

Minutes passed in silence.

"Well?" Julian asked. "You are the last, oh ancient king of Phrygia, who remembers these symbols."

"And I remember them well," the figure answered. "When I was alive, my name was Midas, and I used symbols such as these to place guards and wards upon my hoard of gold. By this long-lost fay language, I spoke to the satyr Silenus and the god Diony-sius. Still, I have no idea how Alexander learned it."

"Your story was known in Macedonia," Lady Báthory said as she checked the bag of blood hanging by Midas's side. "Perhaps the fairy language traveled there as well."

Midas harrumphed. "Those fools added absurd details about my growing an ass's ears, and they claimed I recovered from my curse by bathing in the Pactolus. Those are lies."

"In the Pactolus, they found electrum," Báthory said, "which once enriched Lydia. That, no doubt, is why they attached it to the legend of your golden touch."

Julian rubbed his chin. "Aristotle claims you died of starva-tion on account of your curse, which is nearer the truth. Perhaps he knew the fairy language and taught it to Alexander. He was, after all, Alexander's tutor."

Midas shook his head. "It is no matter—and yet . . . I dedi-cated the ox-cart of my father, Gordias, to the god Sabazios after the people of Phrygia, prompted by an oracle, chose my father for their king. Moved by the spirit of the god, it was I who tied his cart to a post with intricate loops and interweavings even I could not understand. Generations later, this Alexander cleft that knot and thereby gained the power to conquer the world. Perhaps, then, my fate is in some way bound with his, for it was I who tied the knot he broke."

"And," Julian said, "it seems you can understand his gate."

Midas nodded. "I believe I can."

"But can you open it with the energy of the Crystal?"

Wilhelm and Igor, during this exchange, had quietly slipped from the room. They returned now with a copper box in their hands. Although it was only half a meter across, they stooped as if it had enormous weight. They set it down as lightly as they could before Midas's feet and raised its lid. Inside hovered a cut ruby as large as a melon. From the jewel's depths shone a fiery red light, the color of the sky over the ocean at sunset. It turned slowly, and as it turned, it sang, sending out notes as pure as those struck from glass bells.

When Wilhelm and Igor shut the lid, both the light and the singing ceased.

"I believe it is possible," said Midas quietly. "Yes. There is much power in this stone." He shook his head. "But I have my doubts, Imperator. When I was a broken king, weeping over the death of my daughter and starving for want of food that would not turn to gold in my mouth, I learned of the impending invasion of the Cimmerians. In despair, I drank a bull's blood, which in my throat became molten gold and slew me, making me what I am. The Cimmerians set upon Phrygia because the Scythians had driven them from their homeland. And the Scythians—"

"Are the ones Alexander supposedly locked behind the Caspian Gate," Julian finished. "Yes, I know. Only think, if it were really the Scythians he wished to hold back, why would he use such measures? No, it was something more terrible than either Cimmerians or Scythians. Herodotus tells us the Scythians drove the Cimmerians from their homeland because they themselves were fleeing the depredations of the Massagetae. Of this last tribe, we know little except what Herodotus tells us, but he plainly conflates them with the Scythians. I believe these Massagetae were actually creatures from beyond—lesser powers serving the Outer Gods. Alexander built his gate to seal their entry point into this world."

Midas shook his head. "The Cimmerians were terrible enough. That ancient race traced its lineage back to the time of the Hyborians, when they lived in a hilly land of mist and shadow, cheek by jowl with the realm of the dead. Will you really dare to unleash something worse than they? It is said that the Massagetae slew Cyrus of Persia, himself a god. Can we, we few pastry chefs, hope to restrain god-slayers who could frighten even Scythians and Cimmerians?"

"We have you," Julian replied, "and though you killed yourself to avoid the fate of confronting such foes, your present power is enough to strike terror into anyone."

Crossing back to her coffin, Lady Báthory leaned against it and gave Julian a sultry glare. "We may still have cause to regret this, Julian. Swearing fealty to the Dark Queen—"

"I am well aware," Julian replied, "but if our plan succeeds, it shouldn't much matter."

"Oh?" The lady raised one eyebrow. "If our plan succeeds, it will be the Dark Queen who inherits the earth. Would you have us under her dominion?"

"She will want little to do with us aside from granting us our food. I thought it worth the risk."

Lady Báthory turned her eyes away. "I would have no master at all, were it my choice."

"But it is not your choice," Julian rumbled, "and what you demand is impossible. Unless you ascend to the throne of the cosmos, you must have a master. Everyone does."

"But you, Julian," she said, "do you have a master as well? Are you not what you are because you rebelled against the master of the universe?"

"I am what I am," Julian replied, "and I do what I can to keep my masters at a distance—nothing more."

Lady Báthory only laughed quietly.

"What we do here," said Wilhelm, looking meekly toward

the throne, "might please the Dark Queen and glorify Lord Shadow—but will it be to our advantage?"

Julian clutched his armrests. "It will," he said with a measured voice, "destroy the humans' civilization while leaving enough of them alive for our purposes, and it will also satisfy the Queen while turning the Shadow's eye away from this planet. If you have a better plan, I suggest you explain it—though the proper time to do so is a year past."

Wilhelm hunched his shoulders and was silent.

"We have two tasks left," Julian said. "We have the secret of the gate, and we have the power to operate it. Next is to obtain the gate itself—and at the same time, strike down our most hated enemy. Prepare yourselves: We make our final move tonight."

"As long as you're certain, Julian," Lady Báthory said.

"I am as certain as I can be," Julian replied with a small smile. "We are, every one of us, damned: Our only hope is to last as long as we can before we take up our abode in hell and suffer its torments. Nevertheless, when Lord Shadow ascends, even hell's fires will die their heat-death. What we do is a risk, but it is worth that risk. It may destroy us in an instant—or it may prolong our time on this world for years uncountable. One way or the other, we know we must taste the final death when all things do, for the universe is a tomb."

"What of our tormentor?" Lady Báthory asked quietly. "The one who damned us? What of him?"

Julian was silent for a moment but then said, "When Lord Shadow takes his throne, even the gods will bow down."

To attend the rock concert, Jake and Dana had to sneak out of the house.

The concert started at eight o'clock, a time when their parents could expect them to be home. Fortunately, Dana's mother didn't keep careful track of Dana's whereabouts, and Jake's mom and dad were growing accustomed to Jake's disappearances at odd hours of the evening.

Jake had spent the day in school, where the teacher and principal chewed him out for playing hooky the day before. They didn't bother calling his parents, perhaps because of his age, but he got detention, so he sat in class for fifteen minutes after the final bell and quickly did his homework before he packed up and left. It was hardly a punishment worth speaking of.

Going back to fifth grade really is going to make me a delinquent.

Although he had been attending grade school for less than two weeks, Jake feared he was losing the knowledge he gained in middle school. The assignments from Miss Percy were—aside from sentence diagramming—mind-numbingly simple. He wondered if he should assign himself his own homework: Maybe he could study calculus after school since he didn't need the algebra review he was getting. Maybe he should get a tutor.

He could think about that later. Now it was evening, and he had work to do. He stood on a bus beside Dana and took a ride he had once again purchased with stolen change.

Darn it, I already am *a delinquent.*

He reminded himself that it was for a good cause. And that he meant to pay it back.

Somehow.

They didn't talk much on the way down. Jake stood, holding an overhead strap for balance. Dana sat and kicked her feet while she stared at the two tickets in her lap. She was done up for a rock concert with a fitted black jacket, a pleather skirt, high boots, and a giant black bow sitting atop her head. She wore extra-thick eyeliner. Next to her on the seat lay her purse, and Jake knew Tesla was inside.

"Nervous?" Jake asked.

Dana merely shrugged.

The bus slowly crept downtown. Frequently, it stopped for minutes at a time while police officers directed traffic around rubble piles. Once or twice, Jake glanced out the window, but the view was depressing. Ruins. Ash. Bulldozers and hoes working to clear the wreckage while first-responders picked over the debris. Once, an ambulance rushed past with sirens blaring.

Jake's heart pounded. He took a deep breath to calm himself.

Dana didn't look up from the floor. She pulled her purse into her lap and fidgeted with the strap.

"We got backstage passes," Jake said, "so that's exciting, right?"

She shrugged again. "I guess."

"C'mon, Dana, what's wrong?"

She shrugged a third time. "Just wondering what this is about."

"Yeah."

If this is going to be a fight with vampires, how much can Pretty Dynamo do? Sure, she could decapitate a few, and she could stab them in the heart—but she couldn't leave her spear in their chests, and Vanessa had said that was important. So why invite her to a vampire fight—assuming it was going to be a vampire fight?

At long last, the bus deposited them, along with several other people, on a cobbled plaza in front of the Encomium Theatre, a large venue downtown near New Versailles. It was a stark, black geodesic dome, in front of which jutted a one-story lobby decorated in the standard style of Streamline Moderne, with rounded corners, a glassed-in front, and a roof marked by a row of seven fins. The central fin was taller than the others, and neon-pink speed lines enwrapped it. It supported a sign, also neon, which announced in bold letters:

THE ENCOMIUM

Below that blinked the words, *Everyone welcome!*

That motto struck Jake as oddly familiar—and then he remembered he'd seen the same words in the window of the Unnatural History Museum.

He shifted uneasily.

Jake and Dana joined a crowd buzzing near the front entrance, where three guards, dark glasses over their eyes and feet spaced widely apart, stood with their arms crossed. The crowd filtered in through a single open doorway, above which hung a row of nozzles unleashing fine mist.

Jake didn't see a metal detector, which relieved him. He wasn't wearing the tactical holster, but he had his Five-seveN tucked into the back of his waistband, under his trench coat, just in case it might come in handy.

"That's weird," he said. "It's not hot. What's with the mister?"

Dana only shrugged again.

Several minutes passed, and the line barely moved. Jake wheeled around when he felt a hand clap him on the shoulder, and he found himself staring into Ralph's beaming face.

"Dude!" Ralph shouted. "I can't believe you! Are you actually here for a *Van Halensing concert?"*

Jake blinked. "Uh . . . yeah."

Ralph pounded him on the back. "Great idea, man! I knew you'd figure out exactly what to get Chelsea for her birthday! This is *perfect!"*

"Um—"

"Hey, where *is* Chelsea?" Ralph spun around, sweeping his eyes over the crowd. When he turned back to Jake, he wore a puzzled frown.

Jake, with a sigh of resignation, pointed down at Dana.

"Oh," Ralph said, his look of puzzlement deepening. "Who is this?"

"Ralph, you've met her several times now."

"Right, right! She's the one with the hot mom! Uh, Danielle—"

"Dana."

"Yeah, that's it. Why is *she* here?"

Jake sighed again. "Why are *you?"*

"To see the show, man!"

Jake pressed his tongue into his cheek and considered for a moment before he said, "Dana and I got free tickets from Van Halensing."

"What?"

"Yeah, see—"

"You met Van Halensing?" Ralph shook his head. "Dude. Dude, I can't *believe* you! Where the *heck* did you meet Van Halensing?"

"During a vampire attack in Rome. Look, it would take time to explain—"

"Did you get me an autograph?"

"Ralph, I just told you, it was—"

Ralph grabbed Jake's shoulders and shook him. Then he followed that up by tousling Dana's hair. "You'll have to fill me in later, man. Right now, I gotta scoot."

Ralph turned and started walking.

"Hey, wait!" Jake called. "Where are you going?"

Ralph looked over his shoulder, grinned, and glanced right and left as if looking for eavesdroppers, though there were people everywhere. With shoulders hunched, he skittered back to Jake, put a hand alongside his mouth, and said in a conspiratorial stage whisper, "I know a *secret entrance!*"

"You're *sneaking in?*" Jake shouted, but Ralph clapped a hand over his mouth.

"Shhh!" Ralph hissed with a finger to his lips. "Not *sneaking,* exactly. Just watching from afar—without a ticket."

Jake peeled Ralph's hand from his mouth. "How in the heck—?"

Ralph shrugged. "Funny enough, it was T.B. who told me about it."

Jake swallowed. "T.B. did?"

"Yeah—well, sort of. It was one of his girl-flunkies, actual-ly." Ralph stepped back and struck a pose, thrusting out one hip and planting a fist on it. "She was all, 'T.B., *uh,* like, wanted me to, like, *uh,* tell you how to totally get into, like, the Van Halensing concert for free, *mmm*-kay?'"

Ralph flopped a wrist and tossed his head to complete the imitation.

Jake laughed.

Wait, hold on. So Tsubasa actually does *sneak into things without paying?* Jake had assumed Tsubasa's "bad girl" act was just that—an act. But maybe part of it was real.

"Ralph," said Jake, "don't you think—?"

"Gotta go," Ralph replied, slapping Jake on the back one more time. "Got a concert to steal."

With that, he scampered off, and Jake stood there, blinking.

Dana made a growling noise in her throat. She kicked Jake in the shin. "So that means *we* coulda got in for free."

He sucked his breath through his teeth. "Dana, we *are* getting in for free!"

Minutes passed while Jake and Dana stood silently in line. Jake occasionally bounced up and down on his heels. Whenever he glanced at Dana, he found her looking at him, but then she'd turn her eyes away with a glower and a faint growling noise.

After what seemed like hours, they made it to the front. Jake slid his two tickets through the gap in the window of the ticket booth. The pimply-faced teen behind the counter stared at them, frowned, and then whistled through his teeth.

"Something wrong?" Jake asked.

The teen leaned down to his microphone and said, "Why are you here?"

"Huh?"

"Why are you here, in line? These are all-access passes. You could go in through the VIP entrance."

With an exasperated snarl, Dana kicked Jake in the shin again.

The boy behind the counter turned and rummaged around in a desk behind him. A moment later, he slid two green wristbands through the gap under the window. "Put these on," he said, "and go wherever you like."

Jake and Dana donned the wristbands, flashed them at a guard, and stepped into the lobby.

As they passed under the misters, Jake wrinkled his nose at a pungent, stale smell. "Ew! They should have changed that water before spraying it on everybody."

Dana held her nose. "Smells like they got it from the toilets," she muttered.

They soon found themselves in a thick press of people moving inexorably toward the double doors of the auditorium. There was a lot of greasy hair and a lot of black leather—accompanied by a musty odor that the stinky water didn't help.

Jake's teeth chattered. The lobby was air-conditioned, and now he was wet. It was definitely too late in the year to be running a mister.

There were several tables full of merchandise. Dana looked with interest, but Jake knew he couldn't afford anything. He leaned down and said in her ear, "We don't have assigned seats. We really can go where we want."

She scrunched her mouth. "I'd like to be in the mosh pit—"

"I'm vetoing that."

"—but we should sit near a door. So I can transform."

He nodded and led her toward the stairs to the upper levels. They climbed a few flights and made their way into the auditorium, where they found deeply terraced seating overlooking a semicircular stage on which stood a jumble of musical instruments and amplifiers. The crowd was noisy.

They threaded their way through the crowd, at last making their way to a metal railing, mottled with flaking paint, around the auditorium's highest gallery. From this distance, the stage looked little bigger than Jake's hand.

Dana crumpled her mouth and sighed.

Jake fished in his pocket and found a plastic-wrapped pair of foam earplugs. He handed them to her.

She wordlessly answered the gesture with an incredulous glare.

"Put them in," he said.

"Are you *serious?*"

"You're just a kid. You need to protect your hearing."

"You are *such* a dork."

"Whatever. We're leaving right now if you don't put these in."

"You can't make me."

"Wanna bet?" He ripped the package open and put an arm around her neck as if to give her noogies.

She snarled and jumped away. With a low, inarticulate grumble, she snatched the plugs out of his hand, squished them, and stuck them in her ears. Then she stuck out her tongue at him.

"You'll thank me later," he said.

"You are such a dork!" she repeated, her voice now elevated.

He chuckled as he put in earplugs of his own.

They found a spot near a door with a bright EXIT sign hanging above it. Seats ascended in rows behind them, but most people in the nosebleeds stood at the railing instead of sitting, so Jake and Dana did the same. Dana crossed her arms, stuck out her lower lip, and pouted.

"Maybe we should just go backstage," she yelled.

"You can't watch the show from backstage," he replied, leaning close to her and struggling to keep his voice low, "and you don't want Van Halensing to know your identity, so this is fine."

Dana stuck out her lip even farther. She stood on the railing's lowest bar so she could lean her hips against the top, and that made Jake nervous.

At last, after an arduous wait, the lights went out with a loud boom. When they came back on, men in black leather outfits with an unnecessary quantity of clasps and buckles were at the instruments. A roar of approval went up from the crowd, and a squealing guitar echoed through the vast chamber.

Dana explained, "Lady/Killer is the opening act." Then she leaned over the railing and banged her head until her red hair whipped back and forth. As the music blared, the crowd swayed and screamed and bobbed. Fireballs erupted from the stage, and sparkling fireworks crackled in time to the punishing drumbeats.

Jake wasn't particularly musical, but he could tell this band had a lot of technical skill. The precise drumbeats and the guitars' exacting chords joined in flawless harmony. He didn't like this style yet nonetheless nodded in appreciation. But there were no lyrics—Lady/Killer wordlessly played through several instrumental pieces.

During a slower, more emotional number, Dana leaned toward Jake and pointed at each band member. First, she pointed at the skinny lead guitarist, whose shoulders looked broad and squarish in his studded leather jacket.

"That's Marcus," she said.

Then she pointed to the rhythm guitarist, who had a thinning hairline and looked ridiculous in his leather getup.

"That's Brandon. He used to play for Wild Women."

Then she pointed to the bass guitarist, who was stocky and muscular and wore his jacket open to reveal a V-necked shirt that showed off his chest. After that, she pointed to the slim keyboardist, who had thick glasses perched on his nose.

"That's Manny and Jimmy."

Then she pointed at the drummer. He was short and chubby. Unlike the others, he wore a simple gray T-shirt instead of leather.

"That's Tommy."

"Where's their vocalist?" Jake asked. "Do they have one?"

Dana frowned and shook her head. "They do, but I don't see her—"

The band played for twenty minutes, and then the lights went out again. Jake wasn't familiar with rock concerts, but he thought that was short for an opening act.

There was a loud rumble like an earthquake. Jake went up on the balls of his feet and clenched his fists. Dana clutched his sleeve and pointed upward.

Overhead, the geodesic dome had split in half. Retracting one panel at a time, it opened to reveal the night sky, and a cool breeze blew through Jake's damp hair. The pale moon looked heavy, as if it were about to drop into the city. Only a few stars were visible, but the twinkling lights of the Moon Princess's kingdom shone on the moon's surface like scattered glitter. They could see her city from Earth—and she, presumably, could see their city from heaven.

Now that the dome was open, the air was strangely fresh. Jake suddenly realized how oppressive the smell of the misters' acrid water had been in the auditorium.

More fireballs erupted, and Jake was on edge again. The crowd cheered as, on the back of the stage, a giant walking machine suddenly appeared. Gunmetal-gray, and with thick pistons for legs, it stepped out of the shadows as if it had just come into existence. From its broad torso dangled what appeared to be two autocannons in place of arms. It had no face, but in the middle of its chest, it did have a rectangular cockpit covered in black-tinted glass.

Jake grabbed Dana's shoulder. "What is *that?*"

Dana shrugged him off and cheered.

With a hiss and a whine, the machine stepped forward until it was right behind the drum set. Then it split in half with a groan and settled to the stage with a *thunk,* its metal parts shifting until it vaguely resembled a stepped pyramid. A small, round platform rose out of its middle, and on the platform stood a young girl. She wore a nondescript sailor *fuku,* the unidentifiable uniform of one of the city's less prestigious schools. A brightly polished steel mask concealed her face.

She threw one fist into the air, and the crowd cheered again.

Muffled by her mask, the girl yelled something. She rose into the air, and a white light surrounded her. Her uniform evaporated, and the mask popped off, dropping to the floor with a clatter. She rotated as dark clothes formed on her: Black boots, a skirt laced with pink chiffon, a studded leather jacket, and crossed bandoliers.

Once she finished her transformation and landed lithely on the platform, Jake recognized Magical Girl Metal Huntress Vanessa Van Halensing.

More fireballs burst from the stage. Out of the ruined robot, a staircase protruded, and Vanessa walked down it. She stepped to a microphone and pulled it from its stand.

"Good evening," she said.

The crowd roared.

The members of Lady/Killer were still on stage, still at their instruments, and they watched her expectantly.

"I have an announcement to make," Vanessa said, pacing back and forth. "You all know my good friends, the boys from Lady/Killer—"

More shouts, more cheers.

"Well, I have to tell you, I'm afraid Rumi, their vocalist, couldn't be here tonight. She was a great singer, a great front-girl, and a great friend. But now I can tell you something I couldn't before: Rumi was also a magical girl. You know her as Music Reaper Rumi."

The crowd murmured, and Jake felt his blood pulsing in his temples.

"She fought that monster on Monday. She fought well, and she fought hard—but she didn't make it."

The auditorium fell dead silent.

"We thought about canceling tonight. We really did. But I knew Rumi, and I know what kind of girl she was. I know she'd want us to rock on. So that's just what we're gonna do."

Rumbling, a few shouts.

Vanessa wiped at her cheeks. "One of my magical-girl powers is that I can play any instrument. I've always enjoyed being a solo act. But now, with everything that's happened, I think it's time I got over myself."

Hoots from the audience.

"So, anyway, Lady/Killer is a great bunch of guys, and right now, they're without a vocalist. I asked them to stay here after their set so I could tell you—they're not just my opening act for tonight. They *are* my act. Or maybe I'm their act. Anyway, what I'm trying to say is, I'm joining Lady/Killer as of tonight. So the boys are staying right here on stage with me, and we're gonna rock. We're gonna rock for Rumi!"

She threw a fist into the air. More fireballs blew out of the stage.

Everyone rose to his feet and applauded. Lighters appeared, burning steady flames. Vanessa hugged Marcus, the lead guitarist, before she returned to the microphone and shouted. "Let's rock this place!"

Amidst the roars of the crowd, Jimmy the keyboardist started in with a catchy synthesizer rhythm, and the other instruments soon followed. After several squealing licks from the guitars, Vanessa pressed the mike against her mouth and sang with a voice rough and passionate.

The crowd jumped, shouted, and waved. Jake couldn't make out most of the lyrics, but he could feel the raw emotion. When Vanessa reached the refrain, the few words he could understand tore from her throat:

"Beaten, battered, bruised, and torn, and stabbed with a million knives! *But we're still alive!*"

All around the auditorium, the people, Dana included, pumped their fists and shouted, "We're still alive! We're still alive! *We're still alive!*"

"Let me hear you, Urbanopolis!" cried Vanessa. "We've had a hard couple of weeks, haven't we? But they can't keep us down! All the forces of evil in the whole *darn universe* can't keep us down! Shout it loud! Shout it proud! Shout it so even the Moon Princess can hear you! Let her know that her children are *still alive!*"

"We're still alive!" the crowd chanted. *"We're still alive!"*

The lead guitarist stopped playing and tossed his guitar into the air. With a high leap, Vanessa caught it, landed back on the stage, and moved into a squealing guitar solo.

"Keep it going!" she shouted.

The chants continued: "We're still alive! We're still alive!"

Jake swayed to the deafening, punishing music. Dana leaned precariously over the railing while beating a fist against the air and banging her head. Her wild, unkempt hair flew about her face like raging flames. Overhead, the moon shone, and the stars twinkled.

Then Jake understood.

The human race had been through some fierce battles. Everything in the cosmos and beyond was out to kill them—but they kept going. They suffered and bled, but they always gave better than they got: Innumerable alien races had set upon the Earth to wipe the humans out, but all those races were dead, and humanity lived on. They survived. They stood tall. So tonight, in the music of Metal Huntress Vanessa Van Halensing, mankind was raising a middle finger to the universe.

"We're still alive!" Jake shouted. *"We're still alive!"*

He trembled, and a single tear ran down his cheek.

But amidst the unleashed emotions of a tortured but defiant humanity, a spotlight plummeted to the stage. As it bent with a shriek and burst with a bang, fragments of glass scattered into the front row. The music stopped.

Vanessa, her confident expression unchanged, tossed the guitar back to Marcus. When she flicked her wrist, her stake launcher swung down from her shoulder and mounted itself on her arm with a click.

A pale man in a tall chef's hat dropped from the sky. The tails of his white, double-breasted coat fluttered as he landed lightly in the center of the stage, right in front of Vanessa.

The microphones picked up everything.

"Good evening, Vanessa Van Halensing," the man said coolly. "We meet at last."

A lopsided grin formed on Vanessa's mouth. "Are you the one in charge of those vampires who hit Rome-in-Exile last night? I don't believe I've had the pleasure."

For a moment, the man hesitated, but then he said, "Julian. You may call me Julian. But soon, whatever humans remain will call me *master.*"

Vanessa's smile grew broader.

"It was foolish to hold a concert, Van Halensing," Julian said. "Why would you willingly expose so many to me and my brethren?"

Vanessa, fists on hips, tipped her head back and laughed. "I didn't think you'd be stupid enough to come out in the open, but even if you did, these people are protected, Julian! When they entered, I sprayed them with a mixture of holy water, garlic, wild rose, and wolfsbane! Everyone in here has been *vampire-proofed!*"

Julian replied with a mirthless grin, almost a sneer, which showed long, glistening fangs. "I'm afraid you are mistaken, Van Halensing."

Other figures dropped out of the sky. Some fell onto the stage, but others landed in the mosh pit. A hissing man grabbed a teenage girl and, as she writhed and screamed, sank his teeth into her throat. Blood spurted across her pale skin.

Immediately, all was chaos: People screamed, ran for the exits, and quickly formed knots. In a moment, they started trampling one another.

Sweat broke out on Jake's forehead. "Dana—"

"On it!" she yelled. She ripped out her earplugs and took off running for the bathrooms, but she smacked straight into a man heading toward the same door. She fell hard on her rump. Others tripped over her or pressed in on her.

Jake grabbed a scrawny boy and tossed him out of the way. Then he seized Dana's arm and hauled her to her feet. Pulling her against his chest, he hunched his shoulders and tried to muscle his way through the crowd. He knocked a few people aside but didn't make it far.

Down on the stage, Vanessa took a step back from Julian. "That's impossible—!"

"It's not impossible, you imbecile," Julian shouted, "if we are no longer subject to the *Curses of Ebal!*"

With a snarl, Vanessa dropped into a crouch and aimed her stake launcher at Julian's chest. As he hurled himself into a back-flip, the stake passed over his head and clattered against a stand full of amplifiers. After rocking for a moment, the amplifiers tipped over with an ear-piercing squeal of feedback.

The press of people on the balcony forced Jake back against the railing. He held Dana in his arms and twisted his hips to one side in an attempt to save her from trampling, but that slammed his waist into one of the railing's metal bars. He clenched his teeth against the pain.

"Look!" someone shouted amid the writhing and struggling crowd. "Lady/Killer is Van Halensing's vampire-hunting team!"

Jake stared into the auditorium below. The band members had long Bowie knives in their hands, and they had donned utility belts holding wooden stakes and mallets.

A white-clad vampire hissed and, with fingers extended like claws, glided toward Manny, the bass guitarist. Manny flipped his bowie knife into a ninja grip and, with a backhand swipe, slit the vampire's throat. As red blood sprayed from his neck, the vampire reeled.

Manny's voice came through the speakers: "Our lead singer has *always* been a magical girl! You think Rumi never taught us to fight?"

He pulled a stake from his belt, sprinted forward, and, with a powerful swing of his mallet, planted the stake in the vampire's chest. A geyser of blood drenched Manny in red.

Somebody thrust an elbow into Jake's spine. He bent forward with one arm around Dana's waist. With a snarl, Dana slammed a heel into his shin.

"Dana!" Jake yelled. "Stop—!"

On the stage, Jimmy pushed a button. His keyboard split open to reveal several sharp blades. After he played a few discordant notes, the blades, fletched on their back ends, launched into the vampires. Whenever they struck, the vampires fell to the ground, shrieking as their flesh sizzled.

"What?" Julian cried as he stared about wildly. "They are free of the Curses! Why—?"

Vanessa chuckled. "Jimmy is less cautious than I am. Each of his blades is loaded with a piece of consecrated bread. I don't know how you made yourself immune to holy water and garlic, Julian, but hosts *always* work!"

Julian hissed.

Brandon, the rhythm guitarist, ran a hand through his greasy, receding hair. Then he pulled a lever on his guitar. Part of its underside fell away, revealing a long, serrated edge. Holding the guitar by the neck, he ran up from behind and swung it like an ax toward Julian's collar.

He missed and caught the vampire in the shoulder, but blood gushed out, and Julian howled. Turning, Julian yanked the guitar from his shoulder and swiped Brandon across the face, sending him spinning to the floor.

Vanessa slid a curved knife out of her sleeve and leaped. A sword, conjured from thin air, was suddenly in Julian's hands. Their blades met in a shower of sparks.

"I am the ruler of vampires!" Julian snarled. "You cannot defeat me!"

"The ruler, eh?" shouted Vanessa. "Then I'm gonna enjoy putting your notch in my belt!"

Again and again, their blades met. Sparks rained onto the stage as if this were a planned part of the pyrotechnics show.

People jostled Jake from left and right. With Dana enclosed in his arms, he bounced back and forth like a pinball.

Down below, Julian made a backhand swipe Vanessa was barely able to parry. She slid across the stage and fell into a crouch. Smoothly, she dropped the knife back into her sleeve.

"Looks like I need more power," she said. "I'm guessing even *you* aren't ready to handle . . . my *Crucifix Keytar!*"

She hauled the cross-shaped Keytar from her back and launched into a simple but catchy musical number.

"Oh yeah!" Vanessa called. "Since we've got vampires, it's time for some *Christian rock!* Let's see how you handle these same four chords played over and over!"

Julian clapped his hands to his ears and sank to his knees. "No! *No!* Make it *stop!*"

"Haha! Too holy for ya?"

"No, it just *sucks!*"

Up in the nosebleeds, Jake almost tumbled over the railing into the seats below. Young and strong though he was, he couldn't get out of the press. His head swam.

Someone elbowed him in the face. He slid sideways and fell to his knees. Dana's butt bone banged painfully into his right thigh. He felt a moment of panic as he thought he was about to be trampled.

That blue light appeared again in front of his eyes, and the panic ebbed. He sucked his breath through his teeth but remembered what Vanessa had told him the night before.

"In the name of the Moon Princess," he shouted, *"who are you, and what do you want?"*

Dana squirmed in his grip. "What?" she yelled. "What's wrong with you?"

Before his eyes, the blue light coagulated into a definite

shape as if a lens had focused. It was a face, translucent and bluish yet young and pretty. Long, dark hair cascaded over shoulders encased in shining armor plate. She was boyish but had a regal dignity in her dark eyes and strong chin. Tears ran down her cheeks, but she nonetheless smiled.

Jake blinked—once, twice. The face was there whether his eyes were closed or open.

He stared for a second as people milled around him. Someone tripped over his legs, sending a spike of pain into his groin.

"Andalusia?" he gasped.

The face of Magical Girl Lady Paladin Andalusia smiled again but then turned stern. *"Get up!"* she shouted.

Obediently, Jake used the railing against his back to pull himself to his feet.

"Now, my liege," said Andalusia, "head for the exit. Go where I tell you!"

"How—?" Jake began.

"No time! We'll talk later. Right now, *move!"*

Clutching Dana to his chest, he moved. Despite the mass of bodies, despite people crushing one another, he found a way through. Andalusia, her face hovering before his eyes, instructed him: "Right! Now left! Duck! Now jump! Now grab that man's coat—no, don't hesitate—and *pull!"*

Jake followed her directions. In a minute, he was in a brightly lit hallway outside the auditorium. Most people streamed to the left, but he saw the signs for the restrooms to the right, so he muscled his way through. He practically threw Dana into the women's room.

"Hurry!" he yelled. "I'll stand guard!"

Before his eyes, Andalusia nodded. "Good job, my liege."

"Okay," he said as he leaned back against the door and struggled to catch his breath, "we have a moment. Explain."

Although the tears kept flowing down her face, she smiled. "I told you before, when I was still alive, that I had the soul of Bradamante, the paladin of Charlemagne, within my breast."

"So?"

"So her soul rose to heaven when I died. It was an accident, I suppose, but as she went up, she pushed me *down*. I didn't have anywhere else to go—so I followed the path of my own blood as it flowed into your open wounds."

"You mean—?"

"You hold my soul within your breast, my liege, just as I formerly held hers."

Jake felt a chill run down his spine. "What exactly does—?"

He couldn't finish the question because he gasped and pitched forward when Pretty Dynamo smashed open the door he was leaning on. He fell on his face, rolled over, and rubbed his nose as Dynamo, fists on hips, stood over him.

"Let's kick some vampire butt," she said.

"Yes," said Andalusia in Jake's eyes. "Let's."

TWENTY-SIX

DEAD TO RITES

Pretty Dynamo ran back toward the auditorium, and Jake ran after her with the glowing blue image of Andalusia still hovering in his eye. "How long have you been attached to me?" he asked under his breath.

Andalusia smiled. "Since my blood flowed into you. I've been with you the whole time, following you, watching you, experiencing first-hand everything you've done—"

Heat crept into his face. "Wait, *everything?*"

She lifted an eyebrow. "Including some interesting interactions with Sukeban Tsubasa and Grease Pencil Marionette."

"Um . . ."

"By the way, you kiss like a timid schoolboy."

"Hey!"

"If you were Catholic, I'd tell you to go to confession."

"Yeah, well, I'm Jewish!"

"Nobody's perfect."

"So I'm told. I guess you also saw some secret identities—"

"Relax, my liege. I can't talk to anyone but you, and I wouldn't tell anyway. By the way, Chelsea's quite the handful, isn't she?"

"Erm—"

"And Dana is certainly cute, though probably too young for you, especially since you can't seem to keep your hands off the girls you fancy."

"Don't watch that stuff! Haven't you ever heard of privacy?"

"What's the matter, my liege? Embarrassed to discuss your girlfriends?"

"Dana is *not* my girlfriend!"

Ahead of him, Pretty Dynamo looked over her shoulder and scowled. "What the zap is wrong with you?"

They burst back into the auditorium, having an easier time of it now that the crowd had largely dispersed. Tesla, buzzing loudly, hovered near Dynamo's shoulder. Dynamo's goggles lowered over her eyes, and pink text, too rapid to read, scrolled across them.

Tesla, with a tarsal claw against his head, nodded while his antennae bobbed and weaved.

Ignoring the text on her goggles, Dynamo jumped onto the railing and balanced precariously. Hauling her wand from her utility belt, she shouted, "Electrifying the world with love and friendship—and making evildoers feel the wattage of justice—I am *Magical Girl Pretty Dynamo!*"

Down below, Vanessa played her Crucifix Keytar, and Julian cautiously approached her with his sword upraised. They paused.

Julian's lip curled. "Another one," he snarled.

After a satisfied nod, Tesla adjusted his glasses and said, "Dyna, I just ran a diagnostic, and I believe the first regeneration is complete." With that, he settled into her hair.

Dynamo scowled.

"Check your belt," Tesla added. "It's ahead of schedule, so it must be from all the food you've been getting lately."

Dynamo looked down. In the compartment on her right hip sat the blue rectangle with which Jake had first seen her. With a gasp, she pulled it out, tossed it into the air, and excitedly cried, *"Circuit Board!"*

The rectangle hovered in front of her, split in half, and expanded into a snowboard made of bluish glass shot through with golden circuits.

On the stage, Vanessa rolled away from Julian and returned her Keytar to her back. She snatched up a guitar from the floor and launched into a fresh solo. The music was vaguely familiar, but it took Jake a moment to realize what it was: It was "Ride the Lightning" by Metallica, and Vanessa was playing it in honor of Magical Girl Pretty Dynamo.

The mosh pit was a chaos of slaughter and carnage. The members of Lady/Killer fought boldly with blade and stake, but despite their efforts, vampires still set upon the people who remained, and red blood slicked the floor. Bodies hung limply over chairs or lay sprawled in the aisles. Some had died drained of their blood while others had been crushed in the panic. It was a grisly scene, but as Vanessa struck passionate chords from her guitar, both the vampires and the few survivors looked up, and wonder passed over their faces.

Pretty Dynamo hopped onto her Circuit Board, and it clung to her boots. "Tesla," she shouted, "I'm gonna need some bolts— neutral charge!"

"Coming right up, Dynamo," Tesla replied as he placed two tarsal claws to his head.

"Thunder Bolt!" Dynamo yelled.

With a clatter, her wand transformed into a crossbow. A tiny trapdoor in its top disgorged a fletched bolt. Without a pause, Dynamo swooped downward on her Board and fired. The bolt zipped forward in a trail of blue glitter and struck a vampire full in the chest. He fell to the ground with the quarrel quivering in his heart.

A fresh bolt appeared, and Dynamo fired again. Another vampire dropped.

"Of course!" Jake shouted, pounding a fist on the railing. "If she doesn't add charge, her Thunder Bolt is the perfect vampire-fighting weapon!"

Vanessa whooped and closed with Julian. The band members cheered but continued their fight, and they now had an especially grisly task—staking the newly dead among their former fans, some of whom were already twitching or even staggering upright, taking their first steps as newborn members of the Vampyr.

"What's say we join the battle, my liege?" Andalusia asked. "Ready to test your powers?"

"What are you talking about?" said Jake. "I'm not a girl! I can't use magic!"

"No, but *I* am, and *I* can! Hold out your right hand, my liege, and shout, *'Sword of Saint Peter!'*"

"What?"

"Do it!"

Jake stretched out his right arm. His fingers shook.

"Sword of Saint Peter," he mumbled.

He didn't put much heart into it, but nonetheless, with a flash of blue, a shining gauntlet encased his hand. His fingers closed on the hilt of an arming sword.

"Wha—what?" He almost dropped the sword in surprise, but

it clung to his gauntlet as if by a magnet.

"It's only a fraction of my power," Andalusia said, "and I can't guarantee how long it will last. Use it wisely."

"For what?"

"How about beheading some vampires, for starters?"

Jake peered over the railing. It was a big auditorium, and it was probably fifty feet to the seats below.

"Okay," he said, "if I have powers now, can I jump—?"

"Probably not."

"*Probably* not?"

Andalusia shrugged. "I'm new at this whole parasitic-soul thing. I can't guarantee much."

Grumbling, with the armor on his hand clanking, Jake ran back through the exit and found the double door to the stairwell. As he clumped his way down, he said, "You've been healing me, haven't you? You healed my ankle."

"I wouldn't say I've *healed* it, my liege, but I've been giving you as much energy as I could. Now that you've finally invoked me, I hope I can do more."

He nodded. "Well, whatever you're doing, keep it up. We're gonna need it!"

On the ground floor, he kicked open the auditorium door and ran in swinging. He interrupted a vampire bending over a teenage girl, one of the last remaining stragglers of the night's audience. The girl, pretty and dark-haired, merely looked at him with pleading eyes, but the vampire raised his head and hissed.

With a yell and a wild swing, Jake struck at the vampire's neck and missed, instead cutting off his right arm. As blood spurted out of the stump, the vampire staggered backwards and howled.

Jake swung again and missed again, but he hit one of the high-backed auditorium seats, slicing it cleanly in two.

"Holy Princess, how sharp is this thing?" he shouted.

"Sharp," said Andalusia. "Be careful with it, my liege."

The vampire snatched up his severed arm and pressed it to the stump, where it quickly reattached. With a fresh hiss, he lunged, and Jake swung again, this time lopping his head off and sending it sailing through the air like a kicked soccer ball.

"Chest!" Andalusia shouted.

The body, spewing blood from its neck like a miniature geyser, staggered toward Jake with hands clawing the air. Jake thrust, and the blade went through the headless vampire's heart. The body slumped to the floor.

"I can't leave it in!" Jake yelled.

"I know, my liege. If you throw the head, it will take longer to regenerate."

Jake ran down the aisle and found the severed head wedged between two seats. Grimacing, he took it by its greasy hair and flung it away. He didn't notice where it landed.

Behind him, the girl, rubbing her neck, climbed shakily to her feet.

"Thanks," she panted.

"Get out," Jake replied, pointing toward the exit and then heading toward the stage.

He had to step over corpses on the way. The blood under his feet made his shoes as slippery as if he were sliding through spilled oil. His stomach churned at the stench of blood, which blended with the acrid stink of the spent pyrotechnics. It looked and smelled like a war zone.

Vampires rushed him, but he easily cut them down; their undead flesh offered little resistance to the supernaturally sharp blade. He had no skill, so he simply kept cutting until he found their necks. He sliced away hands, arms, and chunks of torsos, and he opened gushing throats, but he only occasionally took heads off entirely. Sticky red soon coated him. Whenever he came upon a prostrate vampire whom Pretty Dynamo had already pierced with a bolt, he chopped the neck and finished him off. Soon, he reached the fighting band members, who hailed him briefly and then returned to their grim work. They let Jake deal with the heads while they dealt with the hearts.

After a few minutes of this blood-soaked labor, Pretty Dynamo lowered her hovering Board down to the level of Jake's shoulder.

"Where did you get that?" she yelled, pointing at his steaming, gore-coated blade.

"Long story," he replied. "But stick by me—you shoot, I'll cut!"

"Deal."

The two of them turned toward the stage and beat a bloody swath through the mosh pit, where the vampires had taken the most victims and where, therefore, the largest number of newly created vampires clustered. They stabbed and sliced as they went until Jake's hand was numb. Meanwhile, on the stage, Vanessa and Julian continued their battle, their teeth bared and their faces streaming with sweat.

"It ends here, Julian!" Vanessa shouted. "You're not going to make it out!"

Julian grinned. "I came this night to kill you, Van Halensing —but even if I fail in that task, and even if you destroy me, I've already won!"

Vanessa pounded out a tune on her Keytar. *"Welcome to the Jungle!"*

The floor of the stage made horrible cracking sounds. Thick, green vines shot out of it and enwrapped Julian's limbs. He managed to twist the sword in his grip and hack at them, quickly cutting through. In a moment, he had his arms free, but his feet were still caught.

That gave Vanessa enough time to play more notes. *"Shot in the Dark!"*

One of the arms of her Keytar split open, and a sharp arrow fired from it, heading straight for Julian's heart.

Julian threw himself forward, legs still tangled in the vines. The arrow passed over his head. As if pushed by hidden springs, he rebounded to his feet and cut himself free.

In the pit, another vampire, with a spatula in each hand, leaped upon Tommy, the chubby drummer, who was out of stakes. Tommy tried to fend the monster off but slipped in the blood and collapsed to the floor. Vanessa glanced toward him, and Julian took that as a chance to close with his sword upraised. Jake was too far away to do any good.

Dynamo kicked off against the air and rushed forward. However, before she could reach the drummer, a javelin of white metal dropped from the sky and impaled the vampire, ramming through his upper chest and exiting his groin. The javelin's bloodied point bloomed like a flower and cast a loop of metal links, like a bicycle chain, up over the vampire's neck. Spinning and buzzing, this loop swiftly sawed the vampire's head off.

Tommy, drenched in bright red blood, rose shakily to his feet.

Jake looked up. Hovering in the sky, with green lights glowing under her wings, was Sukeban Tsubasa. Her red tanuki, tears running down his face, desperately clutched her shoulder. Tsubasa raised her arm, and the tube over it disgorged another javelin, which simultaneously staked and beheaded another vampire.

Julian paused in his fight with Vanessa. "Magical Girl Sukeban Tsubasa!" he snarled.

"Dat's right!" Tsubasa replied with a toothy grin. "Dyna-wyna's boy dere gave me a tip—an' I'm glad he did, or I woulda missed da action!"

"Looks like it's time for our trump card," Julian snarled. *"Midas!"*

"Here, Imperator," rasped a voice that seemed to come from the empty air.

Jake scanned the carnage in the auditorium until his eyes alighted on a tall, gaunt figure with a flabby-lipped death's head for a face, the same he had seen in the catacombs. Midas stood high in the nosebleed section. With one gloved hand, he held a teenage boy by the back of his jacket and dangled him over the seats below.

Jake's stomach twisted, and a chill ran down his spine.

"Ralph!" he and Tsubasa shouted simultaneously.

"I thought it prudent to take a hostage," Midas said cooly. The glove peeled back from his free hand, exposing his skeletal fingers. He held his bare fingertips an inch from Ralph's throat. "Now, Dame Vanessa Van Halensing, I suggest you do what Imperator Julian tells you—unless you want to see this boy die."

Pretty Dynamo, hovering above Jake's head, aimed her crossbow at Midas's chest, but she didn't fire.

Tsubasa's jaw quivered. She lowered her upraised arm, and the tube over it shrank into a bracelet.

Midas's dry, raspy voice somehow filled the auditorium: "Van Halensing, put away your weapon. Pretty Dynamo and Sukeban Tsubasa, abandon the field. Or the boy dies."

Tsubasa breathed heavily, and sweat poured down her face.

"Let him go!" Dynamo snarled, "or *you're* gonna die!"

Jake remembered the gun in his waistband. He reached around to his back—yes, he still had it.

He grabbed the lip of Dynamo's board. "Hey," he hissed, "give me a lift. I need to get close to that guy—say, ten yards."

"What?"

In his eye, the ghostly form of Andalusia nodded in approval. "Thirty yards, my liege. I think I can give you that much."

"Thirty yards," he repeated.

At once, he was able to open his right hand. The sword retracted into his palm, and the gauntlet likewise folded up and disappeared.

Dynamo's eyes went wide. "How—?"

"No time to explain! Take me up, and make it fast!"

Dynamo grabbed Jake by the wrist and yanked him onto her board. There wasn't much room, but he planted his feet on either side of hers and wrapped an arm around her waist.

She glared up at him. "You better not enjoy this!"

"I wouldn't dare."

When she kicked off, they shot up and forward. A rush of wind made Jake's eyes stream. He pulled the gun from his waistband and aimed across Dynamo's chest.

"Andalusia," he muttered, "you better get this right!"

"Trust me, my liege!"

They blasted straight toward Midas, whose flabby lips curled in shock. His fingers darted toward Ralph's neck, and Jake squeezed the trigger.

He heard the blast of the gun, followed by an ear-piercing scream. For one terrible moment, he was sure he'd shot Ralph.

To avoid crashing into the gallery, Dynamo tipped her board

back, and they zipped upward toward the cold stars. She halted their ascent, bent her knees to lower the board's point, and dropped again. As they plummeted, Midas screeched. He held out his bloodied hand, from which three fingers were missing. Ralph slipped from his grasp and fell.

As they dived past, Dynamo fired her Thunder Bolt, though Jake couldn't see whether the quarrel hit Midas or not.

Dynamo flew like lightning, but she was still too slow: Ralph tumbled through the air and was about to break his neck among the chairs in the lower gallery. But a white streak rushed in, caught Ralph under the knees and shoulders, and held him close.

It was Sukeban Tsubasa.

Dynamo immediately halted her descent, rattling Jake's teeth. He almost slid off the Circuit Board.

"Willikers-*sama!*" Tsubasa gasped as she hugged Ralph to her chest.

Ralph merely gazed stupidly at her.

The tanuki on Tsubasa's shoulder patted her helmet, this time approvingly. "That's good!" he whispered. "You're doing good!"

Tsubasa blinked and shook her head as if coming to her senses. Her face turned bright red. With a shriek, she let go of Ralph and darted away. Fortunately, she had caught him only a few feet above the ground, so Ralph struck the seatbacks with a painful-sounding *whump* and a loud groan—but it was a fall likely to produce nothing more than some nasty bruises.

Hovering above him, Tsubasa clapped her hands to her mouth and released a muffled *eep!*

Julian spat and shook his fist. "Another time, Van Halensing! As I said before, even if I lose *here,* I've still *won!*"

With that, he swept upward into the night sky and disappeared as if a shadow had swallowed him.

Dynamo, still carrying Jake on her Board, headed toward the stage, and Sukeban Tsubasa sheepishly followed, all the while glancing guiltily behind at Ralph, who climbed shakily to his feet and winced as he rubbed his bruised rump.

The more powerful vampires had disappeared with Julian. The few remaining were new ones, created from the unluckiest members of the concert's audience. The musicians of Lady/Killer, faces stoically set, destroyed them one by one.

"We're going to have to neutralize *all* the dead and wounded," Vanessa said with a sigh, "or they'll become vampires too."

"How did you know this would happen?" Jake asked as he hopped down from Dynamo's Board and landed on the stage.

Dynamo jumped down after him, and the Board collapsed back into a small rectangle, which she stuck on her belt. She stood behind Jake and twisted a metal boot against the floor.

Vanessa shook her head. "Know? I didn't know. Vampires almost never attack large groups. I figured I could get a *break* tonight."

Jake frowned. "But the mister—"

"Oh, that? Just a precaution. Too bad it didn't work."

"But you invited me and Dynamo—"

Vanessa grinned. "Of *course* I did! You think I'd pass up a chance to meet *Magical Girl Pretty Dynamo?*"

Vanessa shoved him aside and seized Dynamo's hands. Dynamo, eyes wide, took half a step back.

"Oh Princess!" Vanessa gushed. "You're really here! I can't believe it! I was *so* hoping Jake would bring you tonight! I am your *biggest fan!*"

Dynamo blinked for several seconds. She swallowed. "Erm—"

"The way you fight *kaiju* is, like, art! You are my inspiration! Can I write a song about you? Would you mind?"

Dynamo swallowed yet again. Pink entered her cheeks. "Uh . . . I . . ."

Jake stood to one side, crossed his arms, and smiled. In his eye, Andalusia's ghost held her stomach and laughed.

Vanessa continued babbling. "We should totally hang out! Do you wanna trade secret identities, or is it too soon for that? Oh sweet Princess, we could have a sleepover! And curl each other's hair! And do each other's nails—!"

Dynamo snatched her hands back. A trickle of sweat ran down her left temple. "I . . . I really think we should focus on the vampires right now."

Vanessa tapped the side of her own head. "Oh, right! Of course! I just . . . oh Moon Princess, I can't believe I'm finally meeting you!"

Dynamo shuddered.

Andalusia took a deep breath and then spoke a few quick words to Jake. Nodding, he repeated what she said: "Something's wrong. If vampires don't attack large groups, why did they attack here, especially when they knew they'd be facing a professional vampire slayer? It doesn't make any sense."

Vanessa turned toward him, and her girlish grin slipped. "To kill me, obviously. Perhaps they weren't expecting two other girls to—"

"No," Jake answered, shaking his head. "That can't be it. That can't be the only reason. This was a diversion."

Tesla buzzed in Dynamo's hair. "The young man may have a point," he said. "A great many magical girls are fans of your music, Miss Van Halensing. Perhaps the vampires *did* expect them to be here—and intended to keep them here."

A chill ran up Jake's spine. "Wait a second, Tesla—"

"The gate," Dynamo muttered as she pounded a fist into a palm. "We know they wanted something to do with the Caspian Gate. If that's their real goal—"

"You told me they can't get into the Temple," said Jake.

Tesla cleared his throat. "They're not supposed to be able to bite people covered in holy water and garlic, either, yet here we are."

The color drained from Vanessa's face. "The Temple? You think vampires would attack the Temple?"

"We better find out," Dynamo replied.

She pulled the rectangle from her belt and tossed it again. *"Circuit Board!"* After it expanded, she leaped onto it and twisted her mouth as she eyed Jake. "Hop on."

Jake shook his head and gingerly climbed up behind her. "Am I gonna have to get used to this?"

"I hope not," she muttered.

Vanessa whistled through her teeth. "Boys!" she shouted to her band members. "Finish up here! I have to go—there's more work to do!"

Jake and Dynamo blasted into the sky, and Jake squinted as his eyes watered in the wind. The air was fresh and cold, and the stars were bright. Instead of the fear and sickness he felt while riding on Rifle Maiden's back, he felt only exhilaration.

Maybe that was Andalusia's doing.

"I can't believe it," Dynamo muttered through clenched teeth. "Van Halensing is such a *dork.*"

"Yeah," Jake replied with a quiet laugh. "They say you should never meet your heroes."

THE HIGH PRIESTESS OF THE TEMPLE OF THE MOON PRINCESS, her face regal and serene under her long and luxurious hair, sat in lotus position in front of the high altar of the Temple's central sanctuary. Above her, a mural painted in the dome showed the night sky. Each of its stars was a glittering diamond, and its carefully detailed moon glittered with inlaid crystals. Looming behind her was the vast marble statue of the Moon Princess herself, arms outspread in love. The altar, an unadorned slab of granite, rose starkly before her. Its chipped and dented surface held a single object, the double-bitted ax that symbolized the High Priestess's sacred office.

Four glowing jewels hovered around the altar. Arcing between them, in glowing lines on the Temple floor, was a four-pointed witch-knot. Most of the gems bobbed placidly, but one of them, a red ruby half a meter across, spun precariously like a wobbly top—indicating that it was in peril.

The Priestess knew a Crystal had rested in the catacombs under Saint Peter's, for the Moon Princess had long ago entrusted it to the city's first pope. She also knew the Crystal was now missing. For a full day, she had sat in meditation to determine its location. Around her, lying on the floor like refuse, were bones, leaves, and nutshells. An incense burner between her ankles smoldered with the foul stink of sulfur and anvil dust.

Still, despite her magic, she had learned nothing.

It was past midnight. Long ago, she had dismissed her acolytes, even her beloved Jasmine, who often stood by her side after the others had retired or collapsed from exhaustion.

The High Priestess was alone.

Yet she lifted her eyes to see that she was not alone. Another like herself, raven-dark hair tinged with gray, stood on the other side of the altar. This woman, like a mirror image, had large eyes that tilted up at the corners and rested under carefully plucked, arched eyebrows. Her full, red lips were firmly set, defiant. Although her face was mostly unlined, a slight wrinkle sat on her brow, hinting of displeasure. Instead of a red *hakama* and white *haori* such as the High Priestess wore, this woman wore a filmy black gown, deeply cut at the neck.

The High Priestess smiled faintly. "So you have come at last," she said.

The figure across from her answered, "I have, sister. How long ago was it that you took what was rightfully mine?"

"I only took what you willingly surrendered."

The woman in black flicked her wrist. With a clatter, a *naginata* unfolded from thin air. "You stole from me, Kameyo. I have only come to claim my own."

The High Priestess rose to her feet. "Stole? From *you?* You gave it up, Himeko. You traded your birthright for a mess of pottage."

The figure in black hissed, "Himeko? That is no longer my name, sister! I am the *Dark Queen!"*

The High Priestess nodded. "So, in the end, you bowed the knee to Lord Shadow, just as I always knew you would."

She thrust out her right hand. Her own *naginata* snapped and clicked as it shot from her sleeve and settled into her hands.

"You proved yourself unworthy of the office, Himeko. You were *always* unworthy. Did you really think being Tsukiko's best friend would give you the right to become her priestess?"

Her polearm's curved blade glinting in the wan light of the sanctuary, the Dark Queen stepped forward. "I was the only one who loved her. I was the only one who understood her! She was mine—she was always *mine,* and no one else's! Not yours, not that blasted robot's—"

500 DEAD 2 RITES

The High Priestess tipped her head back and did something she had not done for almost two centuries: She laughed. Loud and long, she laughed. "Oh, Himeko! Listen to you! Still the same fool you were when we were children! How could the Moon Princess ever choose you? Hell's Belle and Ice Queen were right to give your place to me!"

"You had no right!" screamed the Dark Queen.

"The human race had the right!" the High Priestess shouted in return. "Your feelings mean nothing! All that matters is that mankind survives!"

"I loved her!" the Dark Queen shrieked.

The High Priestess ran forward and leaped. Spinning her *naginata* overhead, she cleared the altar and brought it down in a vicious strike.

The Dark Queen rolled out of the way and snapped to her feet, weapon raised. She attacked with a rapid series of thrusts.

The High Priestess easily parried. "You're rusty, Himeko. *But I practice every day!"*

Swinging her weapon in a semicircle, she knocked the Dark Queen's *naginata* aside and slid forward. She swiped at the Queen's throat, but the Queen ducked and aimed for the Priestess's legs. The Priestess jumped and slashed downward in a diagonal. The edge of her blade bit into the staff of the Queen's weapon.

"You can't win, Himeko," the High Priestess said. "It's plain as day."

"Do you think this is my only power?" the Dark Queen whispered, her voice hollow. "Do you think Lord Shadow gives no gifts to his willing servants?"

With a gasp, the High Priestess drew back. The Dark Queen raised her hand, and a red light shot out, catching the High

Priestess in the stomach. The Priestess hurtled backwards, arms flailing, and smashed into the chest of the marble statue of the Moon Princess, cracking it. With a loud rumble, the statue's upper torso separated from its lower and slid forward, falling to the floor and taking the High Priestess with it. Its outspread arms, futilely trying to embrace the world, snapped off and crumbled.

The High Priestess lay for almost a minute under the rubble. She hurt. She hurt more than she had in two centuries, and she could feel dust filling her mouth and turning to mud on her tongue. A smell of flint filled her nose.

Through the heap of stone covering her, she could hear the Dark Queen's voice: "Come in," she said. "This sanctuary is mine, and I invite you."

Woozily, as if drunk, the High Priestess crawled out from under the pile of rocks. She rose to her knees and saw tall and gaunt figures entering the city's most sacred sanctuary. They wore double-breasted white coats. Immaculate, pleated hats sat high on their deathly pale heads. In the midst of them stood one in a strange bodysuit with a long cape stretching behind it. His head was bald, his cheeks wasted, and his bright, drooping lips strangely full. A weird device, like a golden arrow with a broad cylinder wrapped around its shaft, jutted from his left shoulder, and blood ran from it. Blood also dripped from his right hand, which was missing three fingers.

"Where is it?" this strange figure said in a curiously raspy voice, like the sound of a sepulcher's lid creaking open.

The Dark Queen pointed at the altar. "There. I'm sure of it. Where else would a priestess keep such treasure?"

With a hiss, one of the white-clad men glided forward like a wraith.

The High Priestess's throat went dry. "Vampires? In the Temple? But how—?"

The Queen laughed. "All they needed was an invitation, sister, and *my* invitation was enough. This Temple and your office are mine by right. The universe has acknowledged what you have denied."

The High Priestess hung her head. She tried to lean on her *naginata* as if it were a cane, but it slipped from her grasp and clattered to the floor.

Snarling, two vampires grabbed the granite altar and heaved. Even with their preternatural strength, they strained and groaned, and the fossilized veins stood out blue on their pale wrists. At last, they pulled the altar from the ground and tossed it aside. With a crack like thunder, it broke into two pieces; then, like a comical afterthought, the ceremonial ax struck the floor with a dull clang.

In the floor, where the altar had stood a moment before, was a cavity containing a mass of machinery—wires and steel casings, all hooked to a tablet of clay marked with strange, angular runes that glowed with a cold, blue light.

"No!" the High Priestess shouted. "You cannot!"

"Oh, but we can," the Dark Queen replied. "The Moon Princes should have known better than to allow us to carry this intact back to the city—but she never was as insightful as she believed she was."

"Maybe not," shouted a voice from the doorway, "but her servants can still stop you!"

Into the room rushed Magical Girl Metal Huntress Vanessa Van Halensing, Magical Girl Pretty Dynamo, and a teenage boy with unkempt hair, whom the High Priestess recognized as Dynamo's infamous lackey, the Barfing Boy. For some reason, he had a gauntlet, as from a suit of plate armor, encasing his right hand. He grasped a sword.

The Dark Queen grinned coldly. "Ah, Pretty Dynamo. We meet at last."

"Who are you?" Barfing Boy demanded, raising his sword. "Are you the Dark Queen? Where's your bat?"

The Queen ignored the sidekick, keeping her eyes on Dynamo's cute yet sullen face. "I will tell you who I am," she said softly. "I, Pretty Dynamo, am your final boss—but our time has not yet come."

She turned back to her vampires. "Take the machine. We're done here."

The vampires swarmed to the machinery and lifted it over their heads.

The Dark Queen whispered, "The Weapon. The core of the Caspian Gate, designed by Alexander the Great to enclose Gog and Magog until Doomsday. The Bugmen of Arcturus foolishly believed they could open it before the appointed hour, and the Moon Princess foolishly believed she could make it hers and control it. But now it belongs to Lord Shadow—just as it always has, just as all things ultimately do."

The High Priestess shouted, "What could you possibly—?"

She didn't finish the question. Wordlessly, her eyes slid to the spinning red jewel, wobbling like a child's top. She closed her mouth, her face paled, and sweat broke out on her forehead.

The Dark Queen grinned. "So you realize," she said. "You finally realize."

"That's impossible," the High Priestess whispered. "You can't control the energy—"

"We can," one of the vampires said with a cold hiss, "and we will."

"But the girl! Surely you know, Himeko, the Crystals—"

"Do you not yet understand?" roared the Dark Queen. "The city will fall, and the moon will tumble from the heavens! What fragment of humanity survives this upheaval will become our slaves and our food—and the Princess shall be mine!"

The Priestess's face turned bone-white. "You would kill them," she whispered. "You really would kill them—"

"I would do anything!" the Queen screamed.

"Enough talk," said Dynamo. She raised her crossbow and fired twice. Two vampires reeled back with her quarrels' fletched ends quivering in their chests.

With a clumsy war cry, Barfing Boy ran forward and made a wild, flailing swing. One of the vampires, having sunk to his knees, raised an arm to parry, but the sword sliced through his wrist and then his neck.

Vanessa Van Halensing lowered her stake launcher. With a *clack-bang,* she fired it at the mysterious figure in black, but he caught the stake with a gloved hand before it reached his heart. Grinning insipidly, he held up his free hand, which still bled. He touched the stake to one ruined finger, and with a crackle of electrostatic discharge, it turned to gold.

"You again," Vanessa said.

The figure wordlessly swept forward. Barfing Boy turned his head and yelled, "Vanessa, watch out—!"

The Dark Queen seized Barfing Boy from behind and laid the edge of her *naginata* against his throat. Dynamo dropped into a defensive crouch and aimed her Thunder Bolt at the Queen's face.

The Queen's red lips parted in a wide grin. "Don't move, Pretty Dynamo, or the boy dies. *All* of you, halt!"

Barfing Boy raised his sword. With a contemptuous snort, the

Queen grabbed its naked blade with one hand, wrenched it from his grasp, and tossed it aside. The boy gasped and stared at his empty gauntlet, which folded in on itself and disappeared.

"Let him go!" Dynamo shouted.

"Oh," said the Queen with one raised eyebrow, "is this boy so precious to you, Dynamo?"

She leaned down and licked Barfing Boy's cheek with her forked tongue. He writhed in her grasp.

Dynamo clenched her teeth, and her face turned scarlet.

At the same time, Vanessa faced off with the figure in the bodysuit. When he tilted his head toward the Queen, Vanessa took a fresh stake in her hands and lunged. With little more than a glance, the figure swept aside her outstretched arms and touched his bare, ravaged fingers to her neck.

She gave an inarticulate yell that abruptly ceased when she fell to the ground. She shivered and writhed in pain. A moment later, she had turned to gold.

"No!" Barfing Boy and Dynamo both shouted.

The High Priestess seized her *naginata,* but the Queen pointed at her and again sent her tumbling back. She struck a wall this time, sank to the floor, and stayed there.

"The machine," the Queen said. "Take it."

Three of her remaining vampires picked it up.

Pretty Dynamo waved her crossbow. "No! Put it down!"

"Goodbye, Dynamo," the Queen replied.

The Priestess, mouth agape, cast her eyes toward the spinning, wobbling jewel. "Himeko, please! Think of what you're doing!"

"I have," the Dark Queen answered. "I thought it through a long time ago, my sister. It is futile to defy the Shadow—so I serve him, and he alone will give me what I want."

"His promises are empty glamour, Himeko!"

"I know glamour," the Dark Queen replied, "for am I not a queen of Elfland? No, I cannot be deceived by glamour. The Shadow's promises are not empty; they are merely temporary. The *Moon Princess* is the one who made false promises—promising the defeat of darkness, promising everlasting life. Eternity is false, Kameyo. There is no eternity. That is why we must seize what few pleasures we can during the little time we have before Lord Shadow takes his throne."

"I'm begging you, Himeko—!"

"Beg all you like," the Dark Queen replied. "Your fate and mine—they are already sealed."

With that, she—and the vampires, and the machinery they had taken, and Pretty Dynamo's sidekick—disappeared in a flash of light.

The High Priestess wept silently.

But Magical Girl Pretty Dynamo dropped her crossbow, fell on the floor beside the golden corpse of Vanessa Van Halensing, and howled like a wounded animal.

TWENTY-SEVEN

THE WAY OF ALL FLESH

Early Friday morning, the world ended.

Grease Pencil Marionette, as if drunk, rose unsteadily from the floor. She didn't know how long she had lain there. Her internal clock wasn't functioning. She still wore the black outfit she had last seen in the mirror before her consciousness simulator shut down. Her computer equipment lay scattered across the floor, smashed. A tipped-over bottle of absinthe, mostly empty, lay on the counter. Spreading from its open mouth was a syrupy green stain, sticky and smelling of sickly sweet licorice.

It was dark, so she knew it was nighttime. Her head pounded. Headaches were new in her experience, and she didn't have a clear idea of what might cause one. The haptic sensors in her skin produced signals her software interpreted as pain, but internal pains—at least of the physical kind—were not something she usually had. She couldn't imagine how she could have a headache unless, perhaps, the virus had written a headache-simulation program, which seemed a needless act of cruelty.

Eyes bleary and head throbbing, she thought, for one brief and absurd moment, of pulling another bottle of absinthe from the cupboard and trying an administration of alcohol. Then she realized how ridiculous that was and instead reeled toward the leaded windows.

Sirens rose from the street outside, and helicopters buzzed overhead. Deep in the city, a Klaxon wailed with the lonely cry of what was once called an air-raid siren.

That told her something big was happening. She leaned against a window and peered out.

She didn't have a good view beyond the street: Other buildings, just as tall as hers, were immediately across the way. In this case, however, she didn't need a good view because the thing filled the sky—it was a twisting mass of tentacles, like those of an octopus, surrounded by blood-red mist. The waving limbs stretched through the heavens, so large that guessing their size was impossible, for they violated all laws of perspective: It was as if she peered into an aquarium tank, saw a cephalopod writhing in red silt, and then transposed that image to where the sky above Urbanopolis should be.

She knew only one thing that could look like this; only one of the many enemies of man could take such a shape and be so impossibly huge.

This was an eldritch abomination, an Outer God, one of the multidimensional beings—vast in size and vast in intellect, yet raving mad—that filled the limitless sea of chaos outside the universe. This was one of the uncreated beings that hated the cosmos for no other reason than hatred itself—a raw, all-consuming, and self-justifying hatred.

Usually, when such beings found entry points into the universe—rifts through which they could peer or holes through which they could reach—those entry points were small, only a few yards wide at the most. They were spherical openings into three-space through which the monstrosities might blindly grope.

However, the scene in the sky, this red mist full of struggling limbs, clearly came from a much larger rift. If an abomination could reach through with so much mass, it could destroy the city and perhaps the world.

Marionette pressed a hand against the thick glass, and it shattered under her fingertips, raining into the street and making clear, sharp barks as it struck the pavement below. Her mouth open, her hands clenching uselessly, she could do nothing but stare in horror at the end of all things.

EPILOGUE: INFECTION

Matilda the witch-seer sat in her chamber deep beneath the basalt fortress of the Dark Queen. Only when surrounded by her computers did she feel at home. Her scabbed feet hovered above the floor, where condensation from her machines' elaborate cooling system formed an inch-deep pool. Overhead, trapped in sticky green goo like flies in amber, were the sacrificial victims whose bodies she'd preserved from rot, and whose imprisoned souls powered her computer banks.

Cozily seated in an antigravity chair, she hummed to herself as she watched the feeds from the Urbanopolitan news outlets. All of them, without exception, were reporting on the massive creature that had appeared in the sky and was now smashing whole blocks, splattering humans' innards across the rubble, and reducing others to gibbering lunatics with the sheer audacity of its impossible existence. Even as she watched, some of the feeds abruptly turned to static.

She smiled. She was a servant of the Outer Gods, and it

pleased her to see one of her masters, even if it was a lesser one, destroying its enemies.

Chirops appeared. At the threshold of her chamber, he stared with distaste at the water covering the floor. After a moment, he waded in, his wings dragging behind him in the muck.

"Ah, Chirops," Matilda said as she waved toward a monitor, "is Her Darkness as pleased with you as I am?"

His wet nose wiggling, Chirops gave one of her monitors a glance and said, "No."

"No? But you have done the will of the Shadow—"

"She's upset. I'm not sure why."

"You, her familiar, don't know why?"

He sighed. "I thought it best to keep my plans from her after—"

"Chirops, Chirops. Lord Shadow ordered the Dark Queen to rouse an eldritch abomination, and thanks to you, she has done the very thing. The Shadow should be pleased—as should Her Darkness."

Chirops lowered his head and shook it. "I think . . . I think she's found something else to please her now."

After Matilda pressed a few buttons, her holographic monitors displayed lines of computer code. "Let me tell you of the progress I've made—though, given what you've done, we may not need it."

"What?"

"You recall that I should have, by this time, successfully infected Grease Pencil Marionette with a virus? I have also been crafting a virus to finish off Pretty Dynamo, the only question being how we might deliver it. Unlike Marionette, she is not connected to the city's network."

"What do you suggest?"

"Physical delivery is our best option. For that, we need a different sort of vector."

She pressed another button, and on the screen appeared an image of some brown blob swimming with tiny feelers.

"CRISPR," she said. "A handy way to edit DNA. If delivered into Dynamo's body, this organism will pinpoint certain cells and rewrite their genetic code. Those cells will then replicate—"

"I thought you wanted to attack her electronics."

"Hold on, I'm getting there. The cells will assemble a biocomputer sophisticated enough to produce and deliver the computer virus via protein receptors at the interface between her biological and electronic components. In other words, delivering the virus is as simple as sticking her with a needle."

Chirops put his claws on the edge of the computer console and tried to peek over it. "Well, I don't understand most of what you said, but I got the needle part."

"Good. That's all you need to get. However—"

She flipped a switch, and more code scrolled across her holographic screens. "I've begun to think my original approach was mistaken. If Pretty Dynamo goes on backup, her biologics temporarily shut down. I thought we could simply stop her from booting up, but—"

"But?"

"But it might be better to make some use of her before she goes offline." Matilda chuckled again. "Assuming that will even be necessary."

"What would you have her do?"

"I wanted to infect Marionette partly because I hoped she could get me access to Sentinel."

"That's the humans' big computer, right?"

"Right. Sentinel monitors the surface of the planet. It has

several methods, including satellites, that we could potentially destroy—but more importantly, it uses Sommerfeld-Zenneck surface waves."

Chirops shook his head. "I don't really—"

"Non-uniform electromagnetic plane waves produced at the spherical boundary interface of two homogenous materials with differing dielectric strengths."

"Erm—"

Matilda sighed. "Let's just say . . . electromagnetic waves directed by the surface of the planet, Chirops, similar to the way current can be conducted through a wire. These waves encase the Earth. By reading and manipulating them, Sentinel can track movements across the planet even without a supporting infrastructure. We can't destroy the Zenneck-wave system without destroying Sentinel itself."

"What are you saying?"

"I was thinking, since manipulating electricity is Pretty Dynamo's specialty, she may be best suited to attack the Zenneck-wave system. Then I got the idea of modifying her virus: If we can infect her while she's near Sentinel, she should, before she stops functioning, interface with the computer and shut it down."

"That's the trick, isn't it? Getting her near the computer and then getting at her—"

"Yes," Matilda said as she chewed on her scabbed-over lip, "that's the trick."

"So, what do we do?"

"We plan our next attack, Chirops. We shouldn't wait to see how things play out with the Outer God. We should prepare for the next phase—the invasion of Moon Base and the destruction of Sentinel."

Chirops swallowed. "You're asking a lot."

"Yes, perhaps. But if we find the way, we will achieve complete control of the Earth, the conquest of Urbanopolis, and the death of Magical Girl Pretty Dynamo. Will not your mistress be pleased?"

Chirops glanced up toward Matilda's ceiling, toward the children trapped in amber with their mouths permanently open in tormented screams. Matilda smiled as a look of uncertainty passed over the bat's face.

"Your mistress, Chirops," Matilda reminded him. "We are doing it all for your mistress."

Chirops, sniffling faintly, merely nodded.

To be continued . . .

ABOUT THE AUTHOR

D. G. D. Davidson is an archaeologist, librarian, and magical-girl enthusiast. *Dead 2 Rites* is his second book. Follow him at *deusexmagicalgirl.com.*

amazon.com/author/dgddavidson

goodreads.com/dgddavidson

bookbub.com/authors/d-g-d-davidson

facebook.com/DGDDavidson

twitter.com/DGDDavidson

instagram.com/dgd_davidson

linkedin.com/in/d-g-d-davidson-4713a239

patreon.com/DGDDavidson

pinterest.com/dgddavidson

snapchat.com/add/dgddavidson

youtube.com/dgddavidson

ALSO BY D. G. D. DAVIDSON

Jake and the Dynamo

www.ingramcontent.com/pod-product-compliance
Lightning Source LLC
Chambersburg PA
CBHW021117260626
47169CB00005B/1314